"An engaging, romantically infused SF tale of an alternative-Earth empire."
–*Kirkus Reviews*

"Readers looking for elaborately detailed world-building, intriguing futuristic tech, and sci-fi universes with a more upbeat tone will be quickly drawn into this creative work of speculative fiction."
–*SPR*, ★★★★½

"Fans of team- and world-building will enjoy accompanying this ancient Earth SF epic's inviting cast through the rainforest."
–*Publishers Weekly*

"An imaginative and immersive plunge into a futuristic landscape set 6500 years in the past. The most impressive aspect of the novel is the depth of detail in everything from the visceral environment, savage wildlife, and odd culinary options to global history, societal organization, and the dynamic relationships between the main characters. This intensely creative future world is well thought out and undeniably unique, particularly when it comes to technological advancements. *A Buzz* is a striking vision of a futuristic alternate history."
–*Self-Publishing Review*

"A high-stakes sci-fi adventure set in a technologically advanced South America."
–*Independent Book Review*

A BUZZ

Volume 1

JACOB LIGHTMAN

First Edition: November 2021

Cover Artwork & Design by Jeff Brown Graphics

ISBN 979-8-9851476-0-5 *(paperback)*
ISBN 979-8-9851476-1-2 *(hardcover)*

To Grandpa

4479 B.C.E.
THE LAND
MOUNTAIN NORTH PREFECTURE
WILD TERRITORY
BINGDOLE
RAINFOREST REGION
HIGHLANDS REG
PRAGODOL
ALBRONDER
KRITZIDDLE
CRAWLDSAY
GRINZOL
MOUNTAIN REGION
WRATSHIDE
ZANDER
SUN CITY
MOUNTAIN CENTRAL PREFECTURE
INABLAY
MOUNTAIN SOUTH PREFECTURE
NODGEDROWDE
NAJEERAM
OWANTAY
MOON CITY
PLAINS REGION
FOWDLEK

CHAPTER ONE

A little over 6,500 years ago, a team of military members in a control room regained their composure while operating the vehicle that floated toward their main destination, high above the thick and wild rainforest canopy. A bomb had just detonated, sending an expanse of the forest floor—complete with soaring trees, boulders, and wildlife—straight into the foggy air, aimed at any foreign passersby. Projectiles shook the vehicle, and the culinary experts on the bottom floor surfed to maintain balance as the glider absorbed the impacts. The alert team quickly accelerated to avoid most of the flying debris, but everyone knew that Jaway's quick reflexes had saved the day. A few scoops of mud splattered onto one of the outer windows of the upper control room, dripping down before the automatic cleaners cleared them away.

"Another tough one, guys, but we made it!" Jaway said, catching his breath.

A bead of sweat seemed to fall in slow motion from the tip of his narrow nose onto his shoe. He lifted his foot to wipe the sweat onto the calf of the other leg. After clearing his face swiftly with a forearm, he turned his head to watch the remaining forest fall through the cloudy canopy and back into the open crater within the sea of green.

"Make sure to note that exact location for Central Command," Jaway said.

"Affirmative, Commander!" said T. A. Curtis, one of Jaway's dedicated terrain analysts, before a preprogrammed air video popped up from a small pyramid fixed to the control panel.

A stunning woman dressed in a fashionable, form-fitting version of infantry gear spoke with motivational undertones: "Congratulations, Commander Barbour and the team, for your continued service to our people. By gathering information, you are leading us toward the goal of completely uniting The Land, from the west coast mountain range through the vast central rainforest, to the highlands in the east and the plains in the south. Remember that you are a catalyst for peace, and in order to gain political rest, any group rebelling against these ideals must either integrate or be subdued. Your families back home are incredibly proud of everything you do! Because of your valor, you will all receive special rewards tonight after you dock."

The adrenaline-filled team slowly looked around, and then the fifteen crew members transformed from shock to celebration within a second. They jumped and hooted and hollered about the upcoming rewards. Morale was a huge priority, and a tool used to keep military members inspired to continue. Back in Jaway's hometown of Zander, he'd never imagined he would lead a troop through the most dangerous and remote regions of civilization in search of information about tribes that were not yet loyal to The Land. Different regions had merged over time to create the country that now stretched from coast to coast, but the Wild Territory in the north was still in revolt.

After Jaway had finalized his first round of training at age sixteen along with his neighborhood friends, he was identified as a leader with high ability scores and moved on to a special academy for his last year of studies. In The Land, military service was compulsory, and after finishing school requirements, each resident was assigned to a branch for three years. This period was usually from the ages of either eighteen to twenty-one or nineteen to twenty-two, unless it was deferred for a major reason. Because citizens received full adult rights by age sixteen and usually moved away from home a few years later, by the time most people reached age twenty, they were quite sophisticated.

"Can you find out what the reward is, Commander?" whispered A. P. Krizzles. She winked and elbowed Jaway playfully, then flashed her eyes from corner to corner, pretending nobody else could hear. He smiled— she always treated him like a big brother.

After he checked the information briefing, Jaway's voice rang throughout all three levels of the vehicle, which was known as a glider. "Tonight, ingredients for home-cooked meals will be delivered, we will be granted extra free time, and we will all receive double compensation for the day!"

The crew's celebration grew even more raucous for a few minutes, and then they returned to their essential duties.

Many years before this moment, the Royal Academy of Technology had uncovered components of the human mind that changed the trajectory of technology for the entirety of civilization. This began when the emperor commanded the Royal Academy to investigate ways to improve production in factories, with a focus on an assembly line that manufactured coins for The Land. He wanted to know how the operators could increase focus and reduce mistakes, and then to apply that knowledge to similar operations.

With a focus on brain function, the academic team made it clear to the mint workers that they were not being reprimanded—the researchers simply wanted to study the way the brain worked. The staff recorded data each time an error occurred, then shared freely about what had happened. During a survey, many coiners described feeling as though they were on autopilot, because each of them performed one task, then passed their materials to a neighbor to accomplish the next one. This was repeated until the product was complete and ready for inspection.

During one logged instance, an employee said that when they heard five beeps, they would walk across the large room where they worked to press a button that introduced a new design for the next material. In this case, silver metal sheets rolled on an assembly line to where they were placed under a stamp machine that would engrave the coin design. Gold sheets automatically replaced the previous metal; however, the insignia needed to be changed by hand.

One day, there was no notification, and the worker was not prompted to press the button. Because the operator assumed they'd already completed the task, the gold coins received the wrong design, which was only spotted during inspection toward the end of the process. When the worker tried to access memories from that day, they assumed they had finished the routine, but did not remember clearly.

The analysts agreed that the coiner was performing duties through the subconscious mind, and this was why they described the shift as foggy, occurring in a trancelike state. Upon looking at other studies, the researchers concluded that this was a common experience for all humans. This other part of the mind was responsible for any brain functions that had become automatic, like walking, breathing, eye movements, or learned skills. While the subconscious mind could control multiple thoughts simultaneously, the researchers believed the conscious mind was only accountable for a small percentage of thoughts. The study also concluded that this was the reason why people were not generally successful at multitasking. Completing many operations at the same time resulted in mistakes.

With this in mind, the Academy advised employees to focus on one project at a time, and move to another job only when the previous one was fully executed.

From this study, a creative analyst designed a piece of technology that could monitor subconscious cognitive functions. After training with it, the brain could control external devices in the same way it controlled things like running or moving a finger. With this advancement, people could easily send thoughts to a gadget to look up information or compile words for a report. The problem up until this point was that inventions could process information at high speeds, yet citizens could only input small amounts of data, and this was incredibly slow. The innovation of sending information directly to a mechanism removed the glacial practice of entering characters of written language and resulted in rapid input and output. After many years of trial and error, innovators developed a small chip called a kleck. Implanted into ear cartilage, the kleck exported information at rapid speeds from the brain to devices.

Jaway was highly proficient at operating his kleck, and he used it to control the glider and interact with many different tools. During Jaway's lifetime, all babies were issued a kleck at birth so that each person developed motor movements and kleck skills at the same time. Baby toys and toddler gadgets transitioned with all stages of growth, morphing into more complex items. As children developed the ability to read and write, they also studied how to utilize the kleck with a myriad of mechanisms. Surprisingly, people could learn to control innovations with the same instant subconscious control that was used routinely in daily life. It was just as easy as standing up.

One of the instruments projected text into the air and allowed the user to write as fast as they could think. When Jaway was growing up, he could write a short composition in a matter of minutes because the kleck allowed massive amounts of information to transfer at the blink of an eye. As he began taking academics more seriously throughout school, he quickly stood out as highly skilled at controlling external devices. Not only was he proficient in transferring information, he also picked up new concepts quickly and effortlessly, to the point that he was at the top of his class in ability to manipulate machinery.

Military academy training occurred alongside regular classes around age seventeen or eighteen, and lasted one full year. All citizens knew they would serve in the military, but they did not know in which capacity until they were granted an assignment after graduation. Because of Jaway's advanced ability and high interpersonal relatability test scores, he received training for operating machinery and effectively leading groups of people. Jaway was enamored with the way he might be able to apply the many years of serious studies in practical situations. During indoctrination classes, he dreamed of increasing peace among The Land and making the world a better place. If only he'd known how his service would play out.

Jaway and his team often spent free time comparing what it was like to grow up with different backgrounds and regional influences. They were fascinated that although many facets of life were markedly different, they'd all grown up with deep connections to family and friends. This was because all localities of The Land shared a common culture that deeply prioritized close interpersonal relationships. Households from each territory of The Land spent countless hours together; helping one another and enjoying rich company over meals or group activities. It was not uncommon for families to hug or hold hands while out for a walk. Close friends showed different physical forms of affection but bonded just as intensely.

A. P. Krizzles was the most attractive member of Jaway's team. She had been granted sincerity and humility in equal amounts to her beauty. Her long, flowing, wavy hair was usually pulled back to reveal a sharp jawline, high-edged cheekbones, and light-gray eyes that sparkled and reflected surrounding colors. Long, dark eyelashes framed her uniquely colored eyes. People often stared directly into her pupils and felt like everything in the world stopped. Babies and toddlers were drawn to her perfectly proportioned face and could not break their gaze, no matter how hard they tried. While waiting in supermarket lines, crying babies would become silent and lock in on what they saw as a twinkly, gorgeous, mysterious being.

Although it was hard to believe, A. P. Krizzles was mostly unaware of her own beauty and usually was embarrassed by extra attention. As a girl who grew up humbly, raising animals and tending flax crops with her extended family, she always wondered why people stared directly into her eyes like they were hypnotized. A young, fit body and clear, glowing skin were the natural byproducts of enjoying sports while growing up and staying active on the family farm in the Eastern Highlands.

Every generation on record from A. P. Krizzles's bloodline were farmers, so each person who contributed to her DNA had honed skills that were necessary on the land to successfully grow crops or raise livestock. These highly sensitive agrarians could smell impending rain or feel that a storm was on the way. It was their job to be keenly aware of any change in the surroundings in order to keep their livelihoods safe by protecting animals or strategically harvesting fields. Research from the Royal Academy of Knowledge concluded that heightened senses were passed down through DNA, as was the case with A. P. Krizzles. Military teams had incredible respect for any agricultural personnel, because this unique ability allowed them to sense danger or signals from nature. In the past, many agricultural personnel had provided invaluable information about animal activity and warned troops of hazards like tsunamis, tornados, and uncontrolled fires. This allowed their teams to take more advantageous positions and remain safe from destruction.

Jaway and his comrades were sent to high-risk zones because of their expertise and courage, in contrast to other teams that lacked the skills to succeed in comparable environments. Although Jaway's troop was elite and functioned at a high level, they did not take each other too seriously. It was their job to gather information about outlying groups or tribes, and they avoided any combat. Traveling through uncharted, wild, and remote territories came with many unique challenges. Weaving through the skies above the lush rainforest could be risky and unforgiving.

In addition to natural factors, manmade obstacles included rebel groups, which frequently planted bombs that detected vehicles. These foes kept them on their toes. There were also no light beams outlining road paths in these skies, so the operators had to create their own routes while avoiding any possible dangers along the way. In developed areas of The Land, an intricate web of lights created driving lanes, around the height of three standard homes above the ground. These lanes were parallel to the ground, with one direction on the top in purple, and the opposite direction just below in orange. This design prevented crashes and kept drivers safe, but occasionally something would still fall from the sky. Architects installed roofs of heavy marble or stone in some regions for added safety. Looking through crafted windows on the vehicles revealed the sky roads, which were not visible to the naked eye. Avoiding light pollution was a priority so that people could still watch the stars at night, as this was a standard hobby. While drivers retained overall control, transportation automatically sensed the beams and remained within the lanes.

The crew members commonly referred to each other by using the first letters of the colleague's job title followed by their last name. For example, Agricultural Personnel Krizzles was shortened to A. P. Krizzles. More informally, others would call her by only her last name, Krizzles. The main exceptions to the standard abbreviations were for the commander, lieutenant commander, and captain out of respect for the three highest-ranking members of the crew. So Lieutenant Commander Pama would not be shortened to L. C., though she could still informally be addressed as Pama.

In contrast to smaller passenger gliders, Jaway's military glider had eight walls with clear windows from floor to ceiling, along with three inner levels. The bottom of the octagonal prism housed many rooms, including the kitchen, living quarters, gym, and engine room. The level above this contained the lower control room, and the next story was the upper control room, which provided views in every direction. An elevator ran in the center up to the rooftop. Thankfully, the bomb planted by the rebel group only damaged the outer front side of the glider. These and many other technological advancements empowered The Land to unite most regions from coast to coast.

CHAPTER TWO

"Psst. Psst, Jaway! Check the message I sent to you." Gozee whispered to his cousin from two rows behind.

Thirteen-year-old Jaway pretended he was continuing to work, acting conflicted about finishing the assignment. He could not control the urge to inspect his humorous cousin's message, though, which was certain to be entertaining. When he finished up a section, he read the information that Gozee had sent and chuckled once, his shoulders bouncing. He fought a huge grin by clenching his lips together after remembering he was in a quiet classroom surrounded by silent students working on assignments. The two were best friends and the same age, so they were frequently placed in similar classes.

The white room was mostly empty, with four very long marble tables and simplistic chairs. Pyramids perched on the tables in front of each pupil, as though surrounded by vast, empty, miniature deserts. Documents with moving text hung in the air above most of the triangular-sided boxes. Their history teacher sat at the front of the classroom at a simple table that faced the students, with four polyhedrons placed haphazardly on the granite slab. A much larger pyramid, on a stand in the front of the room, projected the requirements for a research essay based on the origin and history of current technology in The Land.

Gozee always managed to finish assignments early, and would then research humorous topics with the extra time. That day, he'd found a surprising article written about the early stages of kleck trials, and how the klecks had emitted an array of unexpected and, in some cases, embarrassing sounds. Class ended and the boys walked out together, both noticeably taller than all of the others, and spoke in the hallway.

"Man, that is so funny! I can't believe the test klecks were making those crazy noises, and even right in the ears of the wearers. You always find a way to uncover gut-busting info about anything." Jaway laughed with his best friend and cousin, and they slapped hands in a secret handshake.

"Well, my dad told me a little about it, so I knew it was there somewhere!" Gozee said as they continued the intricate gripping and fist-tapping routine.

During school, Jaway's generation had created documents with an elitser. Elitsers looked like simple pyramids. A user spoke words in their mind, and then the kleck sent them to the elitser and phrases appeared as text in the air. An infogrammer was often used in conjunction with an elitser, and allowed operators to research different topics. The infogrammer, pronounced *in-faw-gruh-mer*, with an emphasis on the *faw* and a fast *gruh-mer*, contained all past information, current facts, and events according to the Royal Academy of Knowledge. Citizens imagined saying the words silently to themselves, and then the kleck sent these to the infogrammer. When the pyramid projected the text into the air, the user could navigate through the information.

With any new invention, experts at the Royal Academy of Technology tested, executed trials, and retested in order to develop the most effective merchandise. Most deficiencies were fixed before any creation was fully released. Many concepts commonly made it to the trial phase but were not successfully launched. Because of this, people were accustomed to witnessing experimental products in use near Zander, where Jaway and Gozee grew up. The large city was the capital of The Land, and it housed the Royal Academy of Technology. As different innovations became readily available to the masses over time, klecks and kleck-related items revolutionized everyday life, as well as the entire educational experience.

Five years earlier, the eight-year-old boys had spent a rainy day inside Gozee's house, which was crafted in the typical style of the Mountain Region. These homes were usually three stories high with a basement and a back yard. Jaway loved spending time with his male cousins because he had two younger sisters at home.

"These games have been fun, but I'm getting bored," said Gozee's older brother Rick, who was twelve, with malaise pasted all over his face.

The boys collected the playing cards and placed them back in the case next to the board games and craft projects that were strewn about the floor of the living room. Gozee and Rick's father, Harold, wanted the boys to grow up without relying completely on the many recent innovations available for entertainment. As a result, Jaway's Uncle Harold limited access to a lot of technology-based activities at home. He valued the skills that the boys would gain while learning to come up with their own ideas for amusement. It would force the boys to be imaginative and gain the ability to creatively solve problems.

"What do you guys want to do? It's raining, so we can't go outside," Jaway said with equal amounts of boredom and bursting energy.

"I have an idea. What if you asked our dad to tell stories from when he and Aunt Helena grew up? He's working, so if *you* ask, he might say yes." Gozee looked at Jaway, and a glimmer of hope sparkled in his eyes.

"Just make sure you milk it as much as you can," Rick coached Jaway with anticipation of hearing thrilling exploits from long ago. Because their dad was busy with an important project, they knew that if Jaway asked, there was a higher chance of tearing him away and hearing fascinating descriptions of days gone by.

"Yeah, I can give it a shot. I think I can schmooze him."

The boys provided more guidance about approaching Uncle Harold so they could gorge on tasty morsels of adventure. Jaway walked up to the next floor, while the other boys huddled halfway up the staircase in order to spy on the interaction, ready to run and pretend they'd been playing cards all along. Uncle Harold was at a desk with an elitser when Jaway approached him. Harold was tall and had a trimmed silver beard with thick curly hair that bounced in every direction around his head.

Jaway walked over with his chin down and looked up with puppy eyes. "How's your work going, Uncle Harold?" the boy said, then waited for a response and for an opening to go in for the kill.

Uncle Harold took a few seconds to get to a stopping point, then looked up over his glasses, which clung to the tip of his nose.

"I've been quite productive today, Jaway. How is your day going?"

"We've been having a lot of fun playing cards, and we made up a bunch of games. We can't play outside because of the rain, so I was hoping you would have a few minutes to tell us one of your cool stories from when you and my mom grew up." Jaway smiled.

Uncle Harold contemplated if he had the time to spare. "You know what? I can find some way to finish this later." He shared just as much fervor for the tales as Jaway did.

Rick and Gozee ran back downstairs and set up a card game to pretend they'd been playing all along and had no hand in orchestrating a set-up.

Uncle Harold and Jaway walked down the stairs to the living room, where Harold sat on the couch.

"Alright boys, gather around. Jaway is our guest, so welcome to story time with Uncle Harold." He laughed to himself, thinking about how much had changed over the years. "I heard that the bad weather should be finished by tomorrow, so that is good news for you boys."

He appreciated that the kids still valued his memories from a much simpler time, before a lot of the current technology had been introduced to the masses. Old devices, or the lack thereof, seemed foreign and intriguing because of the advancements that surrounded the children. In The Land, it was common for extended families to be very close, and Jaway spent a lot of time with his uncle's family—they lived nearby, and his cousins were in his age group. Uncle Harold was especially close to Jaway's mom, Helena, as they'd grown up only three years apart.

Gozee and Rick put away the cards and grabbed the coziest pillows, then took a seat on the family room floor with crossed legs. Falling to the rug, they simultaneously fell under their dad's storytelling spell.

Uncle Harold began by gently emoting while peering over his spectacles with the same amber-colored irises that were shared among all the relatives. "As you know, Jaway, your mother and I grew up on farmland between Crawldsay, which was the capital city about one hundred fifty years ago, and the rainforest line. We did not have all of these doodads and fancy contraptions like we do today. Because life was more basic, the few gadgets we did have seemed like magic to us. Typically, everyone where we grew up only had exactly what we needed, with no extra frills and just a few sets of clothes. We spent a lot of time working the land for what we had, but we were happy and enjoyed life."

The fact that Harold had been raised on a farm made it even more exciting for the boys. They loved hearing about the animals, dirt, and adventures from the mysterious era.

Looking at Jaway, Uncle Harold continued, "One warm sunny summer day, your mother and I started our normal routine. I must have been twelve, and that would have made Helena nine years old. We got up, and after Grandma Barbara made us breakfast, we fed the animals. Then we filled a wheelbarrow with fence posts and wire and rolled out to create a new stretch of pasture next to the passion fruit vines. The sweet fruits grew on trellises in straight rows so they looked like green walls, spotted with dark purple spheres. We laboriously dug and pounded stakes into the ground for a few hours, joking and chatting all the while to make it fun. It was an exciting time, because we would have new space for the livestock. We decided to complete the fence to the end of the plot of land and then we were going to take an afternoon break.

"Right when we'd nearly reached our goal, your mom was about to reveal a punch line, and all of a sudden, I looked up and couldn't see the sun. It was completely dark, and we could only hear a loud, high-pitched rumble. I shouted to Helena, 'Where are you? Can you hear me?' When I realized we couldn't see or hear each other, I dropped to the ground and covered my head."

The boys looked up, all with wide amber eyes and concerned faces, imagining their caretakers in danger.

"By that time, it was pitch-black. All I could feel was a creepy fluttering against my exposed skin, and I simply hoped for the best. It smelled sweet, like when we cut the grass. I kept shouting loudly after covering my mouth to take a breath, but the roar around us drowned me out. I finally managed to find your mother's leg after sweeping around with my arms. We held each other close, and it was like we were in a pitch-black room. Then all the lights came on. We could see the sun again, so we slowly stood up and then jumped up and down. We were relieved to be safe. Then we looked over at your grandpa's passion fruit vines, and there was not one iota of green left. We had never seen anything like it. When we got back to the house, we learned that it was a tornado of passion cicadas. Have you ever seen cicadas?" Uncle Harold looked directly at each of them.

They shook their heads, intrigued about what kind of creature could execute this experience.

"Cicadas usually live hidden under the ground as nymphs that look like big juicy caterpillars, and then come out every fifteen years. When they emerge, they have big red eyes, bodies the size of my hand, and wings, and they make a high-pitched clicking sound." The boys' eyes became humongous as they imagined these monster bugs that they would probably see in the future.

"These were passion cicadas, so they targeted passion fruit. That year, everyone was surprised, because they came out five years early. The colossal cloud of clicking cicadas emerged without warning, so there was no way we could have prepared."

"Were you guys okay?" Jaway's face looked terrified yet fascinated as he imagined his nine-year-old mom surrounded by the frightening bugs.

"Yes, we were fine. Thankfully for us, the creatures only wanted the plant life."

"Phew," said Jaway.

"But our fruit crops were not as safe. The cicadas could strip an entire field in the time it took me to dig one fence post. So when the swarm stumbled upon our passion fruit vines, they did not hold back." He continued with a furrowed brow. "There was nothing we could do but wait and then see months of hard work eaten in a matter of minutes. It was just a few days before passion fruit harvest, and Grandpa Paul was relying on that crop. He projected it to be worth four gold coins. Do you know how many citrines that is?" Uncle Harold asked this last question with the lilt he used for trivia, hoping that one of them would know the answer.

"Four hundred, Dad!" Rick was equally proud of his advanced math and swift reply.

"Yes, you are correct. Imagine what we could do with four hundred citrines if three citrines could buy a shirt. It was a huge blow to our livelihood. The family managed to survive, but we only had enough for the bare minimum, even after selling most of the livestock and other produce." Uncle Harold looked visibly, and uncharacteristically, shaken while remembering the difficulties they'd faced. "So when time came for Harvestium, we did not have much left to make up for the loss." He shrugged his shoulders, nodded, and curled one side of his mouth up with a look of concern.

Harvestium was an annual holiday where families came together, enjoyed the company of one another, and celebrated the harvest.

"The day before Harvestium, Grandma Barbara tried to cover up her disappointment that she would not be able to make the special dishes that everyone loved. By this time in years past, she would have already baked many sweet dishes and prepared for the next day. With a heart full of sadness, she wished that she could make a turkey, but resigned herself to the inevitable outcome of limited ingredients. As far back as she could remember, they had always baked a Harvestium turkey.

"The next day was the famed gathering, and that morning your Grandpa Paul, me, and your mom set out in our metal, horse-drawn buggy to sell the remaining produce as a last-ditch effort to save the holiday. After an unsuccessful attempt in the city, we headed back home. While we were driving in awkward silence, a transport vehicle came out of nowhere, passed us recklessly, and lost control while swerving on the remote road. Grandpa navigated the carriage from side to side as we braced ourselves. Only his strong black horse kept the carriage from flipping over. By the time we came to a complete stop, we were blocking the road, and the transport vehicle was long gone. We all got out to check the horse and buggy for damage. Grandpa comforted the panting, shining, dark beauty, and thankfully everything was fine."

Uncle Harold continued softly, "We saw something fall onto the road, but the mysterious projectile was gone by then. As we walked around the vehicle, your mom spotted something moving behind a nearby tree."

"Bwoahah!" the kids shrieked.

Uncle Harold paused for dramatic effect as he looked into the distance. This pulled the kids even deeper into the story. They glanced over their shoulders, wondering if something was really there.

"Helena immediately spread all of her fingers open and, with her hands next to each other, moved them toward the ground. This was code to stay quiet. Then she pointed at the tree with a nod and wide eyes to indicate that we should look in that direction. So we immediately froze and inspected it, but still couldn't see anything there. Even though Helena was only nine, she was skilled at formations. So she motioned for Grandpa and I to head around the back of the tree.

"By the time we got there, we both finally saw the disguised, puzzled, plump poultry in a lush bush. We closed in on him, and in no time we were on our way home with the biggest turkey ever. Grandma was so happy she cried when we got back. Through the tears, she asked us, 'How in the world did you ever pull this off?' Your mom explained the whole story excitedly, and Grandpa and I filled in here and there.

"That day we feasted with the family like no Harvestium before. The bird was so large that we ate leftover turkey recipes for four days. And we knew it was a sign that the world would always provide. Either that, or your Grandma was a magician!"

They all laughed hysterically because of the way he told the story.

CHAPTER THREE

"It must have been a few months after the hallowed Harvestium holiday. The greenery returned quickly, as did some of the wild produce that disintegrated into thin air. We always took advantage of the land, and foraging gave us kids something fun to do. In order to gain the most profit, it was imperative to know the plants and their uses. Fruits and vegetables grew randomly in the wilderness, while different flora were integral ingredients in healing creams and elixirs. Don't you know we were always the ones to come in and swoop up whatever was there?" He beamed with pride.

"Each summer, chokecherries grew wild around the farm among the trees, and thankfully they were spared. Once the berries turned a dark reddish-black, we would pick them all day long and store them in the cool basement. When we gathered enough, your grandfather would take us kids into town, where we would exchange them for coins. Like I said earlier, I was the oldest and must have been twelve years old. Your mom," he said, looking at Jaway again, "was nine, as I said, I think. Uncle Travis was eight and Auntie Rose was really young. She must have been six. Well, we would get one citrine coin for five handfuls of chokecherries, and that was a lot back then. This was just when they started the trials for klecks."

"Woah, how did you even *live* without klecks?" Jaway tried to visualize life without the daily conveniences the devices brought.

Uncle Harold responded while pressing down his thumb and pointer finger over his silver mustache, which grew like a carefully clipped canopy. "It was fine because long ago, most people did not have them. We had a lot of fun and always manifested a way to stay occupied. The klecks were part of a wide variety of experimental electronic gadgets. So around this time, only hip, trendy rich folks had them. We wouldn't even have known where to begin to be part of a trial like that. We looked at many Zander citizens as hoity-toity city dwellers. They would take trips to the countryside to buy naturally sourced foods because the deep, black soil made them rich in taste and nutrients. There was even a woman who came every single year to fill a bucket with fresh manure to bring back to her house plants. Can you imagine? I don't think she knew that it needed to decompose first, but she swore by it." As he chuckled and leaned forward and back, the children looked at each other in disgust, pinching their noses and laughing, proclaiming different versions of revulsion. They always loved Uncle Harold's stinky-sided stories.

"As it was, the wealthy teenagers would come with their families and look down on us country folk who lived much simpler lives. Their fancy clothes and luxury items made them seem like huge red flowers growing alone among the blackest lava rocks and gray ash. That's not to say we didn't keep our pride. Don't forget that your Grandma Barbara was so charismatic that she won a national competition for beauty and poise in her youth." He added a wink while leaning toward the kids, and they laughed and smiled with pride.

"But I digress. Their futuristic vehicles, clothes, and excess money were a bit overwhelming for us. At that time, the Royal Academy of Technology was still testing family gliders, which are now known as vrodilops. Back then, they were nothing more than an idea of something that might become a functional invention."

Jaway said in his naturally childish voice, "Woah, can you picture a time without any vrodilops? I can't even dream of a life without my entire glider toy collection! The antiques are my favorite."

"You are correct. There were no glider toys yet either." Uncle Harold took a break to let the boys process, then continued with the story.

"Well, that summer was perfect for chokecherries. Some of the other trees that were stripped of their foliage let in extra light, and it rained the exact amount so that the trees had deep-colored clusters from bottom to top. And we spent days and days picking them until the morning came for us to exchange our chokecherries for citrine coins. We woke up early and put on our best outfits. Grandpa always reminded us to put on our 'spiffy duds' before heading into town. Jaway, your mom Helena was so excited to see how many coins we could get that she didn't sleep a wink the night before. She came out to breakfast with her shirt on backwards, so Grandma Barbara sent her back to get herself together before we ate.

"Your grandma always greeted us when we got up and asked, 'How's my dolly? Did you sleep well?' while pinching our behinds. 'What do you want for breakfast, sweetie?' she would ask, and we would choose between cold foods or a cooked meal. While enjoying our food together, we talked about what we could get with the coins we would earn that day. And we estimated how many we could get with the spoils of our crop. Back then, three citrine coins could pay for a new shirt, a bar of chocolate, or a live theatrical performance with root beer candies! That was what we did for fun, and we were happy." He nodded his head and smiled while he paused, breathing in deeply and remembering the past with fondness.

"When we arrived to the shop to turn in our chokecherries, we stood quietly while Dad lifted the heavy containers over the counter. We waited in anticipation to see what they were worth. When we found out they yielded twenty-eight citrine coins, we jumped in the air. It was almost as though time slowed down.

"While in midair, we noticed the Klinkhammer family, with all five temperamental teenagers, enter the naturally sourced market. It felt like there was a dark quietness covering our entire bodies from head to toe. By the time my siblings and I returned to the ground, we erased any joy from our faces. We stood still, knowing that if the kids had been alone, they would have reminded us that our measly citrines were nothing compared to their wealth. This was a rich family from Zander, which was the capital city of The Land, just like today. The elaborately dressed crew loved visiting their summer house in the countryside and finding goods to bring home. This clan knew their social circle would be impressed with any latest finds, and envisioned offering atypical delicacies at parties while pretending to eat them daily. 'Oh, these old things, we eat like this all the time,' they probably imagined saying, while surrounded by fashion victims and the socially elite."

The kids looked captivated.

"Before coming to the countryside, the Klinkhammers had klecks inserted in their ear cartilage at the Royal Academy. You could see the bandages, and they were very proud to have them noticed. We were sure they anticipated concerned questions about a possible injury and most certainly had practiced bragging in the mirror about the exclusive chance to try a cutting-edge invention. The klecks were status symbols, and the family was trying to display that they were open to new advancements and had the necessary resources and contacts to be part of the study. That day, Mrs. Klinkhammer's crew casually walked through rows of shelves and gathered many seasonal, nutrient-rich items foraged from nature. She found chokecherry jams, artisanal wines, and gorgeous crafts made from local resources. As they were shopping, she discussed which acquaintances in their social circle would be impressed with the items. She would say things like, 'You know Sharon? No, not that Sharon . . . Sharon from the club. Yeah, that Sharon, she is going to be so jealous!'"

The boys laughed at his attempt at a female voice with a unique accent.

"All of a sudden it was like the earth delivered the most fantastic gift of all to us kids. We had been waiting off to the side while our wages were being confirmed. Watching the Klinkhammers was always difficult, because we felt inferior in the shadow of their blinding opulence. All of us kids wanted nothing more than to get our coins and leave. But in that moment, we began to hear a faint noise. As we looked around the market, we realized it was coming from each of the Klinkhammers. They appeared confused, searching for the same sound. Then a loud buzzing came out of each newly bandaged ear, where the klecks were inserted.

"We later found out through the town gossip that a tingle had started at Mrs. Klinkhammer's ear and traveled down the entire side of her body, like she was being tickled by a fear-inducing feather. Mrs. Klinkhammer was terrified of mosquitoes and allergic to bee stings, so she swatted the air around her head, and her offspring started to do the same. Mayhem erupted among the household as they dropped items and threw products into the air. They began swerving to avoid the insects they thought were swarming. 'They're diving at my head!' Mrs. Klinkhammer shouted as she ran toward the exit with her children behind her. The store owner watched with wide eyes and a dropped jaw. 'We'll come back later!' she exclaimed before leaving the shop.

"Mrs. Klinkhammer's face showed an uncontrolled and confused reaction. She was so distracted by facing her fears, she had a difficult time processing that the ear chips were creating the sound. Her immense pride in them also prevented her from admitting that the advanced technology had caused such a display. When they stormed into their mysterious transportation, we were so shocked we just stood and stared out the window at the chaos. Retractable stairs dropped to reveal a door in the back of the sensor-covered, half-oval contraption."

Jaway listened even more intently, his interest piqued by anything related to gliders.

"And after they had gotten into the experimental vrodilop, we stood watching as another customer quietly tried explaining with raised eyebrows, 'There's a fancy chip inside their skin under the ear bandages. They are supposed to send your thoughts into a new kind of gadget.' Grandpa tried to seem concerned for their wellbeing, because he wanted to teach us to be kind, but we just stood staring out the window in shock. The prototype vehicle hovered, and then a huge explosion from the rear thrust it down the road, away from the shop. All of the storage shelves shook, and the artwork on the wall even shivered in fear, or giggled in laughter, whichever you prefer. We each ducked as a reflex from the immense blast.

"After we slowly stood up to assess the damage, a local customer named Mary turned her head to the side, put her fists on her hips, raised her eyebrows, then said with a straight face and adorable accent, 'Oh I need all that like I need a hole in my head!'"

The boys roared with glee.

Uncle Harold continued with a subdued smile, committed to the integrity of the story, "As you can imagine, after that comment we could not hold back either. We laughed so hard that our tummies hurt and your mom fell on the floor. We literally had to lift her from the tiles because she couldn't stop cackling. Thankfully, the shop owner came back in time to shift our focus to the citrines."

He switched to a different voice. "'Here are your twenty-eight citrines, and thanks for bringing in these high-quality chokecherries. They will make some mighty-fine wine, jams, and sauces.' We looked at each other with pride as we dreamed of what we could get for seven citrines each. Because of what we witnessed that day, we never felt ashamed of being poor. No matter how much others looked down on us, we knew that we had enough, and we could be creative with the little that we had. The Klinkhammers escaped unscathed with only some wounded pride and possibly light whiplash."

"What did you buy with the citrines, Dad?" Gozee asked, still catching his breath from laughing so hard.

"I got my very first bicycle and a jar of blue sparkle paint. I fixed it up, good as new, and gave it a full custom exterior! And I think your mom bought a few dolls and a new dress. We were all happy and proud of what we had earned with hard work and ingenuity. And there you have it, the 'hole in my head' story!"

The kids clapped joyfully and discussed their favorite part of the tales.

It went unsaid that the klecks and pre-glider glitches were ironed out over time. Uncle Harold was one of the best storytellers around. He fabricated elaborate scenes, embellishing with captivating facial expressions and hand movements. He created images in his listeners' minds and had an uncanny way of drawing them into a story. The children particularly enjoyed his humorous impressions of the characters.

While the boys were still speaking furiously, Helena walked in the door, dripping from the downpour.

"Whew, I forgot my andoofers, so I'm drenched." She wiped her long, flowing hair with a towel before hugging and kissing each of the boys and Uncle Harold.

Andoofers were sets of glasses that cast an invisible shield over the wearer to repel the rain.

"Ah, what do we have here? Story time, kids?"

"Yeah Mom, Uncle Harold told us all about the Harvestium turkey and the 'hole in my head' story!"

"Do you remember how Mom broke out in tears when we walked up with a huge turkey? She was one of the kindest people I ever met." Helena sat down as if she were in her own home.

"Yeah, I include it in the story every time!" The corners of his mouth rose, and he breathed in and out slowly, remembering their mother fondly.

"Remember the blue metal flake bike you had? That was sure an amazing paint job!" Helena made an effort to lift the mood.

GLIDER
CROSS-SECTION
Control Room 1
Control Room 2
Office
Top Hatch
Elevator
Control Panels
Quarters
Kitchen
Communal Area
Fydon Storage
Engine Room
Bathrooms

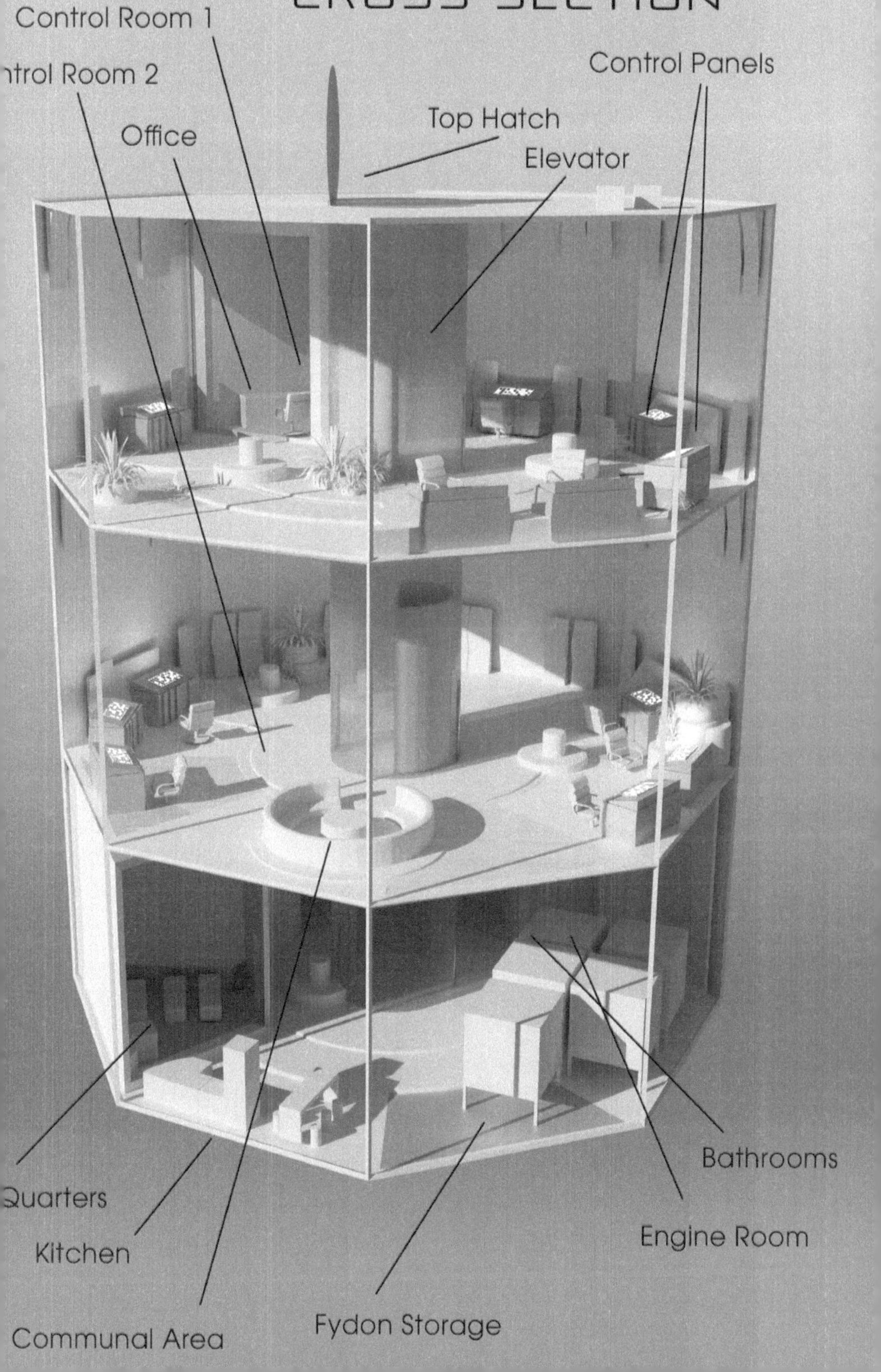

CHAPTER FOUR

"Technology Officer Jeffers, can I get a full report on the status of that blast, where it came from, and who is hiding in the rainforests around that area? Central Command will love this information." Jaway fought to maintain a calm demeanor.

"No problem, Barbour. I'll get right on that," T. O. Jeffers said as she controlled multiple devices on a desk in front of her seat. She faced a floor-to-ceiling transparent panel that overlooked the endless rainforest. "Can you check what I've already got in the pictogrammer, Commander?" She casually moved a small pyramid to a corner on her workspace.

"Yeah, sure. I am interested to see what we have compiled so far." Jaway was intrigued, and walked over to her station in the upper control room.

"Let me pull it up." T. O. Jeffers was proud and excited to share the work, which had been quickly compiled.

A reenactment of the entire explosion popped up out of a pyramid, complete with tree trunks hurling through the air near the glider.

"This blobe looks extremely accurate, T. O. Jeffers. Nice kleck work," Jaway said with his hand on his chin and a pensive look on his face. A blobe was a moving image projected from the pictogrammer.

Jaway's radiant skin appeared to glow, just like the rare golden-yellow eyes that ran in the family. These days, he preferred a low buzz cut. The sides and back were shaved lower to the scalp in alternating rectangles for a trendy checkered pattern. His deep-brown hair color was the perfect canvas to create a strong contrast.

"What do you think of the sound effects?" T. O. Jeffers asked.

"They are superb. It reverberates exactly like the bang we heard."

Jaway's team was not the only crew that executed surveillance missions for The Land, although they were clearly the best. Some of the other troops lacked professionalism and ability. For example, one troop often processed inaccurate reports out of spite and laziness. This subpar unit had once declared that a small tribe rejected any chance of integrating into The Land, without evidence and before even communicating with them. It was later revealed that a few members of the crew wanted revenge on all Wild Territory people because of an explosion that had damaged their glider and, more importantly, their egos. They also did not want to take the time and energy to research the tribe and coordinate a contact mission.

If a group of residents in the Wild Territory wanted to join The Land, they were to be welcomed with open arms and provided the means to build a typical city. On the other hand, if a tribe was unwilling, then Central Command would pass the mission along to a combat party and devise a plan to force integration.

Jaway's team never took anything personally. They could never have even imagined inflicting unnecessary harm on a tribe by providing misinformation. Each member was serious about their job; they worked as professionals who sought the truth above any pettiness. They were renowned for being compassionate, kind, hardworking, and capable.

"Alright, continue with the report, and we can send it soon with the other data." Jaway nodded and turned to the control panel at his station.

On the outside, he remained composed and handled the circumstances, but on the inside he was panicking and felt like he should fight fiercely or sprint a mile.

His inner child uncontrollably screamed at the top of its lungs, *What in the world is going on? Why have you taken me to this unsafe place where tragedy could happen any second of the day? This is not safe. Run. Run. Run!*

In situations like these, Jaway hid all of his feelings, dealt with the crisis, and decided how to recover after the adrenaline rush. In that moment, he remembered what his mother taught him about shifting focus. So he appeared to upload information through his kleck to one of the many devices at his desk, but in reality he imagined going inside himself. He acknowledged his emotions and then visualized tapping his temples. Internally, he spoke the phrase, *Allow it to leave.* Then he took in a substantial breath and began creating a euphoric scenario.

Which happy place should I choose? Jaway thought to himself. *Ah, I've got it!*

He went back to sitting on Uncle Harold's family room floor, listening to stories. He felt protected and still, just like when he was eight years old. Jaway filled his heart with joy and serenity while he took deep, slow breaths, in and out. His body relaxed, and he became aware that he was in a new state of mind. He quickly checked for different sensations all over his body and repeated to himself, *Know how you know, release and let go.* Next, he noticed the tension in his lower left abdomen disintegrate after repeating the mantra again. Then he simply repeated in his mind, *I am safe*, each time he looked at different objects around the space. He felt secure as his cortisol levels dropped. At that point, he knew he was ready to continue with the workday for his team, calmly and full of clarity and peace. His mom had always reminded him that others would perceive him as a confident leader if he was cool and collected.

A brightly colored sunset beamed over the edge of the rainforest as the sun completed another day's work. It blazed orange, mixed with reds, purples, whites, and blues. The scenery from the upper control room was breathtaking, as there was a 360-degree view. When they arrived at the target docking location, the glider floated downward above the canopy, where cloudy dew wafted like gentle smoke above the trees.

Jaway left his station in the upper control room and took the elevator to the bottom level. There, the central common area was a spacious, open ring with seating areas around the elevator, which contained two half-circle shafts in the same cylinder. Entrance doors off of the area opened to many triangular-shaped rooms. Each had an outer wall that was clear and ran from the floor to the ceiling, revealing the outside. Sections, or the entire wall, could be made opaque for privacy, security, or comfort. Three of these rooms were living quarters with six open single beds, and hefty storage underneath. This level also contained the engine room, the gymnasium, a kitchen with dining space, two large bathrooms with showers, and the fydon room.

Fydons were smaller vehicles that fit four people each and lowered personnel to the ground while the glider parked, hovering high above the terrain. The bottom and sides of the glider were camouflaged to look like the exact current version the sky, remaining invisible to anyone on the ground.

Jaway walked past the common-area couches and into his shared living quarters to prepare for the night. Above the lush rainforest, he opened the window in his room to breathe in fresh, moist air from the thick canopy below. A soft white blanket of soupy mist vented from the trees and lingered up to the sky, only to eventually drop again over the vegetation. Suddenly, it smelled like the freshest scent he had ever experienced.

As he took a deep inhale of the crisp, clean air, Jaway noticed the rushing water below. The team had planned to set up camp near waterfalls, because the natural gushing sound helped mask their presence and provided other practical uses. Jaway stopped everything he was doing and closed his eyes to enjoy the moment. After a few low breaths, he closed the window with his kleck. The cover slid down for a seamless view of the canopy tops, and he thought about how excited he was to share the night with the team.

He truly liked spending time with them, in opposition to the expectations outlined during exclusive leadership training. Jaway had grown up believing that all people were equally important and worthy of respect. A genius intellect had catapulted him into senior leadership, but he followed his heart while interacting with lower-ranking colleagues. Thankfully, his team was so successful that his leadership style was never questioned. Jaway fostered mutual respect among his team instead of threatening them with replacement or declaring that they were expendable. After a brush with death, crew members often experienced shock in many different forms. Some had hypnotic trances or remained jumpy for prolonged periods afterward.

His living quarters bell rang. Jaway opened the door with his kleck.

"Would you like something for the aftershock, sir?" Medical Attendant Sickles asked after entering his room.

Jaway continued packing his bag. "None for me, but thanks, M. A. Sickles. How about we grab some of the black orchid elixir for the entire crew for later tonight, though?"

Black orchid elixir was produced by removing the glowing, blue-and-green center areas of black orchids. These were boiled down with water until a thick soup emerged. The result was a thick, forever-glowing liquid that could be used for many different medical issues; however, it was quite expensive, because it took a large amount of labor, flowers, and time. Lengthy studies had concluded that it not only cleared the lymphatic system, but was also highly effective for increasing morale, and treating shock in the brain.

"Okay, I'll grab two doses for each member then. See you soon!"

"Sounds good. Thanks for being on top of this," Jaway said.

A base camp was meant to be a location where glider teams had access to physical activity, academic studies, relaxation, and other basic necessities. The crew had been to this location twice before, and they all loved the gorgeous waterfall that flowed into a turquoise pool of fresh water. They were excited for extra time and resources to explore and enjoy the area more than before. The round, glittering, jewel-colored pool created an absence of foliage, which let the sunlight through to the surrounding forest floor. Normally, the thick canopy absorbed the light before it could reach the ground at full intensity. Many shelves made of boulders acted as perfect diving boards at the summit on each side of the crest. Water vigorously flowed down many other boulders along the journey, covering each with a veil of fine lace. Small rapids and fine mist emanated from the final wide, flat rock at the base. A naturally worn path and tunnel wove behind the crashing, crisp comfort. Lush green vegetation grew up to the edges, which helped keep the soil intact and generated a safe, winding, climbing path along the left side.

Waterfalls helped cover human noise so as to not disrupt local wildlife and to prevent tribes from easily detecting the crew.

Excursion Manager Price had planned the logistics for the entire stay, and now it was time for him to give the crew a brief presentation just before they were to head down to camp.

The entire team assembled in the lower control room for E. M. Price's announcement.

"Alright, I'm going to keep this short and sweet, because we've already been here a few times before. The glider is docked and in place for the night. Your fydons are equipped with everything they need, but remember to fill the tanks with water when you land. If you forget, you may have to wait for a shower. Your culinary experts, Crumpler and Didier, have everything prepared for an extra-special dinner tonight." E. M. Price carefully pronounced Didier as "did-ee-yay," to show that he knew the crew well and cared about them.

"Immediately after docking, ingredients arrived from every region, with an emphasis on Zander, and we all know that is Barbour's home city. I hope you enjoy these cozy reminders of home, or experiences from another culture." He looked over to the cooks, who wore hair nets, and gave them a nod as the crew members clapped and lightly hooted.

"Remember, these extras are from your tight work during the most recent explosion, from which we slipped away mostly unscathed!" Price clapped with a smile in Jaway's direction, because everyone knew that they'd escaped, and ultimately received the rewards, because of him.

"Our original plans were to stay only one night, but now we will stay an extra day as part of your incentive from Central Command." The crew broke out into cheers, thankful for any extra time in paradise.

Price continued after it was silent. "Tomorrow, you can participate in many different activities such as swimming or climbing the waterfall or catching up on old work. If you sign up tonight, I can plan an adventure and have it ready by tomorrow at noon. Just keep us posted on what you decide, and we will plan in more detail based on interest. Any questions?"

"Yeah when can I get my party on?" M. O. Kandova sang, drawing out the last word while bobbing her head from side to side with a dropped jaw.

Earlier, she'd overheard about the black orchid elixir, and she wanted to lighten the mood and help the team recover from the brush with death. Everyone laughed—they expected this from her, because she always had a fun spirit outside of work.

"Any *real* questions?" E. M. Price chuckled, and then waited a few seconds with no response. "Okay, if we don't have any other questions, then I'll hand it over to Barbour. Take it away."

Jaway stood. "First, I want to say thank you to a wonderful crew for being responsible, working hard, and keeping your colleagues safe. If you've never tried it, please taste the cuisine from my home city of Zander. I'm available to explain anything you're curious about. Be sure to take advantage of this extra time as you see fit. Don't forget that you are also receiving extra compensation for a job well done. P. G. Churchill will be around to check in with each of you soon. So let's enjoy!"

Personnel Guide Churchill had many duties, including counseling the troops about future aspirations, setting up new trainings, offering advice, and monitoring psychological health.

The Rainforest Region was located in between the Mountain Region to the west and the Highlands Region to the east. Except for the Wild Territory in the north, where the crew had docked, the Rainforest Region ran between those borders down to the center of The Land. In the Wild Territory, tribes roamed freely, yet under constant defense against the powerful forces of The Land. In contrast, the Rainforest Region was mostly peaceful—it had merged with The Land ninety years earlier.

Many in The Land desperately wanted people in the Wild Territory to become citizens of the modern empire. For thousands of years, the Wild Territory and Rainforest Region had remained one resistive group and shared similar genes. Striking, silver hair was said to have developed due to countless years of stress caused by continually defending their land. Some had mesmerizing strips, while others had completely silver hair almost from birth. They were known for being tall and thin, with chiseled muscles. Light-tan skin was the perfect canvas for traditional tattoos in many different shades of vivid purple. Those living in the Wild Territory adorned their entire bodies, including their faces, with tattoos. People from the Rainforest Region followed suit, to stay in touch with their roots, but theirs were more subtle.

P. G. Churchill resembled the population. He had grown up in Albronder, a peaceful, modern city on the eastern side of the Rainforest Region. He was tall and had thick, platinum-silver hair that was very short on the sides, but had more length on top, where it was slicked back. Even though Churchill shared the genetics of these people, his hair was not lighter because of stress. It had transformed with age. At forty-one years old, he was the eldest of the crew, and offered a fatherly understanding of the world to the younger members. He only had a few whimsical, yet tough-themed, bright-purple tattoos that almost disappeared against a deep suntan when he spent extended time outside. He was known to sneak snacks occasionally, so he was much more beefy than the other younger members, who strictly followed individualized meal and fitness plans. P. G. Churchill lifted a pyramid-shaped device with both hands, and his large biceps flexed. They pressed huge pectoral muscles together, which hung noticeably over the pronounced abdominals that were slightly visible through his shirt.

"For sure, Barbour! If I haven't already, I'll check in with you all soon after the tents are set up." P. G. Churchill grinned, exposing deep dimples.

And with that cue, the crew walked toward the elevator in the center, to gather items and prepare for the next day off of the glider. While Jaway took the elevator back down to his living quarters, he remembered the components of formal decompression protocol for his team, and made a plan to check in with Churchill to see that they were applied.

Five fydons were stored in one of the rooms on the bottom level of the glider. They fit four passengers each; however, one space was always left free. This was in case one fydon malfunctioned—in that scenario, the three members could relocate to different vehicles. These rectangular boxes were fitted with a bathroom and shower in the back. Retractable legs in each corner kept them off of the ground and changed sizes to make the fydon level, so they could park on even the steepest terrain. The front door was a panel that slid down to become stairs.

Jaway was first in the line of command. Lieutenant Commander Pama was next, and then Captain Serra. Each was assigned to a different fydon, so in case something happened to one of them, another leader could take over. Jaway and his fydonmates, T. A. Roberts and I. P. Hilton, gathered their belongings and placed them inside the vehicle. After they were ready, the stairs slid up to seal the door opening. Their fydon levitated and traveled through the opening in the outer glider wall. It lowered between an opening in the treetops and descended to the rainforest floor. After hovering for a few seconds, the legs retracted and leveled the vehicle. Then the team released their bicktrudes and gathered their things.

A bicktrude was a safety bracelet worn by passengers in vehicles. The thin yet wide wristbands were produced in many different colors. After they connected to the wearer's kleck, a transparent, mostly impenetrable suit surrounded them. The Royal Academy of Technology had once filled a test body with boiled eggs and glass ornaments, then dropped marble slabs on it from high in the sky, and it had remained intact. So, although bicktrudes did not promise invincibility, everyone trusted that they would be generally safe during a collision while wearing one.

The door slid down and created stairs for Jaway to exit on with his bag, which contained a personal tent. He and his fydonmates set them up on the sides and back of the fydon. The tents were small tubes that expanded through the use of a kleck, and created large, hovering cylinders. A dresser and lamp provided storage on one end, above a bed with blankets and a pillow. Jaway opened the door on the side of his individual sleeping chamber. Located in the very center, it hinged up and could act as a shield for rain to keep the inside dry. A small box below each tent housed shoes safely and securely. Jaway crawled inside to place items in the cubicle above his pillow.

"Do you guys have any extra toothpaste? I forgot mine on the glider," Jaway said.

"Yeah, I have some you can use," T. A. Roberts replied, handing it over.

"Perfect. Thanks! I'm going to get some water into the fydon, and then we should be set." Jaway was looking forward to a day of enjoyment on the rainforest floor.

As he unloaded the hose from the fydon, he looked up. Jaway always liked watching the other fydons emerging out of what seemed to be nowhere. He uncoiled a hose and laid it on the ground until it reached the turquoise pool and began pumping the pure liquid into their fydon. While waiting, he became lost in thought, and noticed the last portion of dusk light illuminating a white reflection of the waterfall rapids over the flickering surface. He felt his entire body relax as his mind filled with a sense of peace from the sound of rolling waves with a hint of nature. As he inhaled deeply, he smelled the scents of a home-cooked meal lingering from the camp kitchen, where C. E. Crumpler and C. E. Didier had begun preparing a meal for the team.

It was almost as if he'd been transported in that moment back to his parents' home, surrounded by love and freedom. Soon, Churchill appeared from the shadows and gave him a quick and quiet report on the emotional wellbeing of the crew.

"It looks like everyone is in high spirits tonight. The elixir will be beneficial this evening, to clear anything away before tomorrow so the team can focus on being here."

"Perfect! Be on the lookout for anything, and keep me posted," Jaway said while curling up the hose.

Then he walked toward his fydon to replace it, and entered to work at the control panel.

If I get this paperwork done now, I will be able to enjoy tomorrow.

While Jaway attacked his task list, the team finished arriving. They set up camp until all five fydons were in place in the first, about a thirty-second walk from the pool.

The campfire area was already assembled at the center of the basin, a few steps from the water's edge. Three unlit, chopped logs were propped up in a cone shape, and smaller kindling filled the space below. A trio of thin metal legs with grooves held up a large, round disk above the wood. This device, called a pargle, converted smoke into colorless gasses and prevented detection by heat-sensing devices. Two large rings around the pargle created enough seating for the entire crew. A pair of slim metal legs met at a point to hold up the contiguous round benches. Many of these were centrally fixed to the undersides. The crews ate meals here, and the campfire was the perfect location for fun evenings.

East of the seating area, farther from the water, an outdoor kitchen was constructed. A spacious, rectangular countertop with lower cabinets ran along the front. An equally wide section, also with lower cupboards, extended along the left side toward the water. This surface was used for placing dishes and showcasing food for meals. The end cabinet acted simultaneously as a dishwasher and storage space. After the dishes, cutlery, and towels were carefully organized, they were automatically washed and dried. Then they remained in place, disinfected and ready to be used again.

A set of cabinets on the right side of the front countertop also ran toward the pool. This section contained a cooktop with a cover on the end, and a lower refrigerator and storage. Next to the stovetop was a sink that ran purified water for cleaning and drinking. Many other cabinets were used to store emergency kits and items related to cooking. This kitchen created an inner space where culinary experts masterfully conjured delights and displayed food for the crew members to retrieve.

"Chow is ready!" Crumpler shouted while setting out plates and utensils.

A hoard of eager faces surrounded the area and fetched regional fare and drinks before heading to sit around the campfire, now blazing.

"Relish your meals, everyone!" yelled Krizzles, and then feasted on the plate of home-cooked cuisine in front of her.

The silence was not awkward, because everyone was elated to simply sit and absorb the surrounding beauty. The crew chewed and looked at the gorgeous foliage around the waterfall, illuminated by the jumping flames. The lush rainforest vegetation offered a canopy that almost completely covered their existence from above. As the troop's hunger became satiated, they began slowly discussing plans for the next day.

"Hey Price, do you think we can plan an expedition tomorrow?" M. A. Sickles asked. She was excited about the possibility of anything resembling a hike.

"Yes, Terrain Analyst Curtis and Terrain Analyst Roberts scoped out many locations, and if the weather permits, we should be able to have an afternoon trek," responded the excursion manager before taking another bite.

Price hummed with closed eyes and raised shoulders, enjoying the finely prepared dish. He had a trimmed beard and a very short haircut with a flat top. His lips curved up at the sides to create the appearance of an everlasting smile.

"Compliments to the chefs for a tasty meal and Commander Barbour for his speedy reflexes!" Price said while raising his glass for a toast.

Everyone chanted, "Cheers!" in unison and clinked their cups together in honor of the cooks and their talented leader, who kept them safe and earned incentives for the group.

After the culinary experts smiled with pride and acknowledged the praise, Jaway shouted, "My pleasure!" while clanging every cup in his line of sight. Just then, he looked around and realized that a gradual, deep, eerie darkness had surrounded the camp.

CHAPTER FIVE

After the dinner dishes were collected, everyone sat around the campfire and chatted as close friends.

"Krizzles, do you mind getting your drogger so we can sing some songs?" T. A. Roberts asked.

"Yeah no problem. I was actually hoping others were in the mood too!" A. P. Krizzles stood up and finished eating a piece of fruit. She loved playing her instrument because when she plucked and sang, she felt like every good feeling flooded her brain.

This was an indication for everyone to change clothes, take a break, and return to the campfire. Although attendance was not required, everyone shared the same quiet eagerness to return. Word had gotten out that they would get some black orchid elixir that night by the water, but they equally enjoyed spending time together.

The drogger was a popular instrument because it always stayed in tune and its small size made it easy to transport and store. The front and back were triangles with equal sides that were one and a half hands long. These were connected all around by a strip the size of half of a finger, creating a mostly empty box. Near the edge and at the center of one of the sides, a small triangle pointed toward the middle. The metal curved inward from the face to the back on each side of this triangle, creating walls so that the drogger remained airtight. A belt or rope could be tied through this three-sided hole for convenient carrying or hanging. Across from this hole, on the front side, were three parallel strings next to each other. The first string ran the entire length of that side. The second string was half the size of the first, and the third was half the size of that. Each string sounded an octave apart from the next and was stretched between two pegs. Perpendicular lines were etched into the instrument along the strings, as a guide for the musician.

Droggers were made in Sun City, which was part of the Mountain Region that ran along the entire west coast. It was almost in the very center of The Land, just south of the lowest area of the Rainforest Region. Sun City was located on the edge of a massive, round area of salt beds. The industrial town was smaller than most major cities and had originated to process natural resources like salt and unique metals. Droggers were made from elements found below the salt beds of Sun City. A special mixture created an incredibly durable, rare bronze with a blue tint. After mining the raw chunks, an ironsmith melted them in a stone cup over a raging fire. Then impurities were skimmed off of the top of the container, and the molten metal was poured into a triangular mold of a drogger. After the cooled piece was removed from the form, the craftsman smoothed the edges and cut off any excess, then cut a slit in each of the pegs.

Three strings made from a rainforest spiderweb were added after it was completely cool. Webs from the Tabot spider were carefully removed in the rainforest. The individual threads were cooked and spun into heavy-duty string. A musician carefully installed the strings so that they would remain in tune forever. This dependability was one of the reasons the drogger was so favored among musicians.

A drogger was played in the lap by plucking or strumming the strings with the fingertips and nails. Players initially followed the lines etched into the instrument to find notes, but A. P. Krizzles was so good she could play in the dark. The tone quality emulated the sound of the human voice, so it blended perfectly when used to accompany singing. The sound vibrated inside the drogger and created an echo effect.

Krizzles had learned how to play from her grandpa, and her technique was reminiscent of his style. He was known around the Highlands Region as one of the best drogger players.

By the time she returned to the campfire, the entire crew were sitting around, chatting and relishing the moment of complete freedom. Some members sat on the ground with their feet toward the fire while others sat on the benches. After removing the drogger from its fabric-lined case, Krizzles tapped the sides to listen to the sound in that humidity and heat. She plucked the strings with one hand and used the other to press down in different locations. As she examined the instrument in her lap, the entire crew became silent.

Her voice was like a smooth, soft knife that pierced the soul. She began singing and playing a traditional love song called "By Your Side."

"Along the way we see you going, down the path, everyone knowing. Take

your heart and let me lead you down the way. Down the way, my heart will lead you, where to go, I won't never leave you. In my journey in the path of life."

After nodding her head to indicate that everyone should join in the chorus, she led them: *"In the path of life, you'll be guided by and by. Never needin' nothin', never needin' nothin'. Everything's alright, always for tonight. Don't you ever miss me, cuz I'll be always by your side. Always by your side."*

She continued into a second and third verse, split by the refrains sung by the entire crew. Tears welled up in some of the young adults' eyes—they missed their families, but were simultaneously grateful for their new support system, and felt full of comfort and love. It was like each crew member had been covered from head to toe in a thick, slimy liquid, unable to escape the all-consuming goo. Even if they tried to resist the positive feelings, the reality was that their souls were covered in long-lasting peace and joy.

After they finished the last refrain, they took a few seconds to absorb the new, shared state of being, and then clapped and cheered. Krizzles stood up and bowed with a quirky grin as she waved her arm in tiny circles away from her body.

"Thanks very much, my adoring fans! No autographs, please." She giggled while sarcastically whipping her flowing hair to the back with her hand and tipping her neck to the side.

In The Land, it was common to share and express feelings openly in safe spaces.

Churchill said, "You know, every time I hear that song, I feel like I'm with my family. And seriously, though, your voice is amazing. When you were singing the verses all by yourself, it made me feel like the world was spinning!"

He placed both hands over his heart. "It literally makes me feel like my heart will pop out of my chest or like I started levitating."

"Aw, thanks so much. I'm glad you enjoyed it. It's my grandpa's favorite song." Krizzles smiled sincerely, remembering all of the hours she'd spent with him as they sang and played together after dinner on summer evenings, overlooking stunning rolling hills of violet blazing in a golden sunset.

After some silence, M. O. Kandova patted him on the back. "With all due respect, are you sure that wasn't from the beans at dinner, Churchill?"

All of the crew, including Krizzles, shifted from contemplation to sudden, uncontrollable laughter.

"That's a good one, Kandova!" said Churchill as he pointed at her, laughed, and threw his head back.

They felt free to make as much noise as they wanted because of a machine called an expadier. When it was turned on, it held all sound within the camp and notified the crew of any human activity within a two-hour walk's radius.

"Do you guys have any requests or dedications?" A. P. Krizzles asked after the commotion ceased. She understood how important certain songs were to her comrades.

"Do you know the one about the man from Grinzol with all the kids? I can't remember the name right now for some reason. It has a really cool Highlands Region twang, and it's super fast," M. A. Sickles said. She was from the same home town as Krizzles.

"Of course I do. It's called 'The Things He Did for Love.' For those of you unfamiliar with our city in the northwest part of the Highlands Region . . ." She broke seamlessly into song.

"There once was a man from Grinzol town. Never knew the time when to laaay on down. Stayed up all night, never had a fight, but oh, the love he gone and done. Kids all over Grinzol towwwwn! Kids all over Grinzol towwwwn! They look like the man who couldn't settle down. Good thing he was handsome, and good thing he was bright, or the whole town would be such a fright!

Ohhhhh therrre once was man from Grinzol town. He wanted love and love was found. Married her right, they never had a fight, but all the love he gone and done. Kids still over Grinzol town! Kids still over Grinzol town! More looked like the man who couldn't settle down.

Ohhhh therrre once was a man from Grinzol town. Had lots of kids within his vows. Years passed by, his wife soon found, that their kids were related to half the town! She chased him up and down and around, the purple-blue flax rolling hills. When she found him, she locked him away. Until they grew old and moved to Ezlay!"

They all shifted from tapping and moving their heads to the beat and burst into laughter once again after hearing the punchline. Each member of The Land knew that the man would not be any better in Ezlay, a beach town known for attractive ladies walking next to the waves. The Highlands Region was known for gorgeous hills that were purple and blue because of the flax that was farmed there. Grinzol was in the center of the hilly land, and Ezlay was the nearest large city on the east coast, just an hour commute away. Many retired parents liked to move there for the beaches after their children grew older, so their grandkids could visit the ocean.

Among the commotion, M. A. Sickles stood up and gave A. P. Krizzles a huge hug. They both squeezed genuinely.

"Thank you, my fellow Grinzolian! I really needed that pick-me-up after a day like today. It made me feel like I was back home."

"My pleasure! I love that one, too. It gets me every time." Krizzles smiled sincerely.

Next, she asked for requests, and she played five more songs before M. A. Sickles got up and walked around to her fydon, which was only a thirty-second walk from the edge of the fluttering nearby pool. She arrived back with a round tray of glowing, secured, sealed tubes, so bright that the campers squinted their eyes. The greenish-blue light bounced off of the water like tiny, alternating explosions. "All double-checked, we have two doses per person!" Medical Attendant Sickles said before handing out the anticipated thick, soupy liquid.

The process and labor required to produce the elixir made one dose worth an entire month's wage. Captain Serra carefully removed a filled transparent cylinder from its compartment on the tray. It was clearly labeled with his name, and a sticker indicating it was a double portion.

"Alright, cheers everyone!"

After he removed the seal on the top, a pungent, rich aroma flooded his wide nose, which gave him an immediate euphoric response. His face, framed by a short, carefully clipped beard, lit up in bluish tones as he inhaled only through his nostrils. The scent was powerful because it came from condensed orchids. According to the Royal Academy of Knowledge, smelling the elixir alone gave many benefits to the brain. As Captain Serra tipped the doses back, he looked up at the night sky and noticed the beaming, bioluminescent broth slowly dripping toward his mouth. His tall body seemed extended because his head was tilted back. While he waited for it to complete the journey, he noticed all of the beautiful foliage that created a colossal canopy.

After clearing the entire tube of its contents, Captain Serra looked at Jaway and said, "Over and out, Commander."

Other crew members said the same after they drank their portions. This tradition had started many years before, as the commander of the crew always approved use of the elixir.

They sat around playing cards and got water and snacks at the kitchen, waiting for the elixir to kick in. Jaway also liked the healing and mood-enhancing effects of the elixir, but he alternated sessions with Lieutenant Commander Pama. This way, someone would always be alert to handle a crisis.

About thirty minutes later, they started to feel lighter and happier. Their minds seemed to slow down, and they were able to observe more minute aspects of the surroundings. Sounds around them became crystal clear, and breathing was easier, as though the pressures of life had been removed. Their bodies demanded more healthy refreshments. Toxins exited the body through liquids because the orchid elixir increased thirst. A stronger appetite for healing foods provided exactly what each person needed for intense recovery.

"It sounds like I can hear every single drop of water falling from the waterfall, and every leaf that flutters in the wind." Serra spoke in a soft tone, sitting on a cushion on the ground.

He squinted to see in the darkness as the fire bounced and cast a flashing light around the camp. Then he looked inside the fire. It was almost like the flames became a pictogrammer with moving images. He saw a scene on a mountaintop with an active volcano. As he looked closer, he realized it was his family—they had gone on a pilgrimage to sacrifice valuable items. He fondly remembered hiking up a volcano with them, and he felt surrounded by comfort.

In between hauling tasty morsels into his mouth, Serra watched different therapeutic stories. One involved a monkey in a tree, and he watched as it collected fruits and stashed them away. He was reminded of the importance of planning for the future.

Then he heard a gentle, convincing whisper in his mind that said, *Forgive and forget. Move on.* He became open to granting a pass to those who had harmed him and focusing instead on a positive future. The captain thought back to the attack that day, but instead of being filled with adrenaline, as he had been earlier that evening when recalling images of the explosion, he felt completely safe and started to remember the hours differently than they had happened. According to his new memories, he'd woken up and the hours were free from potential harm. He now believed that they had simply collected information about the surrounding area and watched a quiet sunset, then prepared a luxurious camp.

The emotional repairs that they experienced would continue for days, weeks, and months after the night. Serra always liked getting up and walking around after drinking the elixir, because when he moved, he could feel the different state of mind more strongly. So he steadied himself and walked back slowly to his fydon to use the bathroom, get personal snacks, and gather some games. On the way back, he received a big hug from C. E. Didier.

"You know, you are one of the best guys, and fydonmates, on the planet." Didier remembered their sibling-like relationship. Serra had always been supportive in many ways and had helped her to advance professionally. Although he was only four years older, he was married with three kids, and he'd transferred this fatherly role to the crew. Building close friendships with lifelong bonds was common in The Land. And expressing emotions with dear friends was even more typical. People loved deeply, and they showed it.

"What games did you get? I'm super excited for anything right now." She smoothed her chin-length, medium-brown hair behind both ears and pressed her bangs down on her forehead until they reached the lower part of her eyebrows, looking up to check if she needed a new trim.

Then she looked down at the bag in his hand.

"Where did you get chocolate parrots? Us cooks can't even get our hands on these. Can I have a few?" Didier whispered, just in case the captain didn't want to share with everyone, because rare snacks went quickly with the crew.

If word got out, he might find himself with only one chocolate parrot left, instead of thirty.

"Yeah, grab some, cutie. I've had these stashed away for five months," Serra whispered. He slowly put his finger to his lips and curled his shoulders forward. "Shhhh." He giggled with wide eyes, like they were breaking the law.

They ate a bunch of the candies before returning to the campfire to play games.

"Who wants to play?" Captain Serra asked.

He saw many hands flying up in response.

"Okay great! Let's get started." He grabbed his favorite game from the sack, and they sat to begin.

They played while joking, carrying on thoughtful conversations, and planning activities for the next day. Then, one by one, they retired, until just Serra and Didier sat together. They looked at the stars and pointed out constellations and discussed stories associated with them. The captain had always been fascinated by C. E. Didier's tattoos, which cascaded from the midpoint of her thigh down to her ankle on one leg. In the past, he was careful because he knew they might represent something cultural from her Rainforest Region roots. But that night he felt as though they were close enough, as fydonmates, and he was feeling fearless.

"Can you explain your tattoos to me? I've always been fascinated by them." As someone without any body art, he spoke with sincerity and respect.

"Yeah, no problem. Well, I'm sure you know that in the Rainforest Region, we share the same genes as those who live here in the Wild Territory, but we have cities that are part of The Land, obviously. We are still highly influenced by our past, and part of that is the common practice of tattooing. As you can see, we use many different shades of purple because it shows up well on our very light tan skin." She moved her leg toward the fire so he could see better.

"Those of us living outside the Wild Territory decide how little or how much we want to incorporate our culture into our lives. So some people have just a few tattoos, like Churchill, who is from Albronder, which is the other major city of our region. I am from Kritziddle, and some of us choose to fill an entire limb, like me." She laughed softly, so as not to disturb their slumbering colleagues in the nearby tents.

Didier pointed down at her thigh and turned her head, showing the side profile of her tiny, perfectly straight nose perched on a flawless, twenty-one-year-old face.

"We like to keep our tattoos whimsical but with heavy content. So if you look carefully, you can see a skull here, but it's just swirling lines. Can you tell?"

"Oh, yeah, I can make out the eye sockets and the outline." Serra threw a small bunch of twigs on the fire, creating enough light to see more details.

"This represents my ancestors, who are always looking out for me. This one has girly decorations like a tiny hummingbird, so it represents my grandma, who is constantly with me and protecting me. We believe that love never ends, and I'm certain that, out of everyone in her life, she loved me the most. So even though we deal with loss in life through death, we are always with those who loved us. And if you look down here—"

Didier turned her long, lean, well-defined leg to the side, pointing her finger and waving her hand in a large oval.

"This entire area is a battle scene. Notice the curving lines; you can see an angel fighting ferociously at war. She is holding the head of a demon, and this represents the inner battle to always fight negative thoughts. The demon head is hard to see—you have to study it closely, because it is made with the lightest purple color that we have. That is intentional, in order to represent that the negativity in life may seem major; however, if you fight and conquer it, you will realize that it actually has little power, and is not the serious character we may have formed in our mind. We also should focus on the victorious positivity in life, which will always triumph over difficulties. And a lot of the others I just filled in because I thought they were cool. You can see that they are in many different shades of purple. I wanted to honor my cultural roots by covering most of my entire leg."

"Wow, thanks for sharing. And I'm really sorry about the passing of your grandma. Your tattoos are a really cool life lesson. I also believe that my ancestors are watching over me. I get small signs from my grandpa every once in a while. I never realized that your tattoos had such deep meaning. And you know that I grew up in the Nodgedrowde countryside, with plains all over. I honestly wasn't aware how much native life influenced modern people in The Land right now."

Serra had gained a deeper understanding of his close friend and countryman.

He continued, "Even though I'm only twenty-five years old, I can't help but think about my own kids. I hope to be an inspiration and support them as they grow up. I always told myself that I wouldn't start a family so early like everyone in my region, and I didn't plan on getting married so young either, but my girlfriend got pregnant and we just decided to make it work. I stayed in the military in order to pay for them, and now I have three children. One thing you will find out about anybody from the Plains Region in the south is that we have tons of kids."

He looked down at the ground. "My wife doesn't mind raising them while I'm here; she has so many siblings and extended family that are part of their everyday lives."

The captain paused, thinking about his children, who deeply missed him, and visualizing the last time he said goodbye. His eyes filled with tears, which threatened to break the dams and flood his face.

"I really miss my family sometimes, and I have to remind myself that I am here for them—to make their lives better and to take care of them. I didn't have the luxury of exiting the military after my three years were finished. I wanted to get out and become trained in something else, but instead of taking the risk and income loss, I just stayed in." His voice quivered.

"Yeah, we all can see that you take this very seriously. You have more on the line than just yourself, unlike most of us on this crew, who are single. I see you day in and day out, and I'm certain that your kids are going to honor you and cherish every moment they get with you," Didier said, fondly remembering her own family members.

Serra's tears started flowing as quickly as the waterfall that rushed into the reservoir in front of them.

"That means a lot to me. I try my best to make them proud. It's just hard to be away from them for long durations. Sometimes I'm just going about my daily work, and I see their faces crying because I had to leave and they love me so much. I also just want to be there for them in their struggles in life. I want to be there for my wife. But being here right now is the best way to be there for them."

The tears continued to run down his cheeks and over his beard, then drop off of his distinctive jawline onto the ground. He leaned his head forward, and his broad nose now hosted the rivers as they combined from each eye before falling off of the tip.

"Just a few more years and I should be able to get out and find something. Maybe I can go directly into a field that I'm qualified in, because of my military experience. It's also an option to save up enough to take the time to get training in something new. I don't know the details yet, but I do know I'll be with my family in a few years."

He used his arm to wipe the liquid from his face as he fluttered his eyes, as if he'd just realized exactly what he was saying and was snapping out of a trance.

"Phew, this elixir is amazing. I never realized I felt like this. Sometimes it makes me confront what is boiling underneath, far, far away. And I always feel healed the next day. I'm glad you're my sister and can keep this a secret from our tough crew members!" Serra laughed while still wiping his eyes.

The fire had become only embers and ashes.

"Is that an order, Captain?" C. E. Crumpler asked sarcastically.

Then she burst out in soft laughter, and Serra joined; they both knew he did not care. He pinched his fuzzy chin and gazed at the nearly extinct fire, then at the lowly lit, beautiful scenery, and took a deep breath.

"You know, not all of us are from places as gorgeous as this, like you. In Nodgedrowde, we have lots of plains, crops, and livestock—typical Plains Region, southern stuff. Every time I'm in the rainforest, my soul melts. It's like I'm in a dream world. Does it ever get old for you, since you grew up around stuff like this?"

"Well, only a bit. I mean, a lot of it is normal to us, but no, I don't think it gets old in the sense of taking it for granted. When you grow up with this nature, it is even more a part of who you are. We love humid air with lush foliage, bright and dangerous fauna, and breathtaking organic scenery. When we are outside, it is part of who we are, and we appreciate every second, all the time. It's almost like nature is our lover and we are eternally content to coexist with it." Didier was sure that the elixir was increasing her access to her true feelings.

They both took deep breaths of the fresh air and looked around at the moonlit surroundings. When the remains of the fire died completely, they cleaned the space and headed off to their individual tents.

"Good night, my spectacular friend," Serra whispered from his bed, which was located next to their fydon.

"You too, my amazing brother and fydonmate!" Didier whispered back, turning over under her covers.

Meanwhile, Jaway had been up organizing details in his fydon for the ascension back to the glider in a few days. When he noticed that everyone was gone, he walked down to the campfire, poured water on the fire pit as an extra precaution, and then headed to his tent. He always loved retiring at the end of the night at base camp. Not only were the mattresses incredibly comfortable, he also loved taking time to reflect about the day with nobody around.

Jaway stored his shoes safely and opened the door on the side of his personal floating accommodation and got in. After changing into his pajamas, he sat up and grabbed an elitser from the dresser at the end of the tent. He began taking notes about the day and writing a list of things to accomplish in the near future. With a grateful heart, he put his elitser away and turned the light off.

While lying in bed, he could hear the gushing of the waterfall, but the rainforest seemed silent compared to the daytime. He was thankful to have such a cozy place to sleep, and he started to imagine himself on his favorite vacation with his family. He envisioned being on the beach as he breathed in and out with a hissing sound.

Jaway tried a breathing technique his mom taught him. When he was young, she would tuck him in every night. He used to wait with his hands above the covers so that she could formally tuck him in and read a book. She would walk him through a breathing technique for relaxation, so that he could sleep well his entire life.

"Slowly breathe into your lower belly first, then expand your middle ribs, then into your upper chest until it is full. Leave everything expanded, and start to breathe out from the upper chest first, then the central area around your ribs, then to your lower belly. At this point, blow out all of the air possible. Pressing out all of the remaining air will flush out toxins. Repeat this cycle until you feel at peace. It will increase your oxygen levels and make you feel calm. While doing this, loosen up every part of your body, starting from the feet and moving all the way up to the top of your head, focusing on each part as you go. This will allow you to feel more at ease. Pretend that you are in a favorite place, like on the beach, for example. Really put yourself there to watch the dolphins and enjoy the sun. Imagine that you are surrounded by close friends. This will help you to unwind even more and sleep peacefully."

Each night, he became better and better at achieving full relaxation, and as he grew up, he continued the nightly ritual on his own. He became known for being able to sleep through anything. Jaway also knew that being well-rested would allow him to be the best version of himself. He aimed to be relaxed and make tasks as easy as possible, while never compromising on quality. This way, he had enough energy to handle anything.

So this night, he continued the breathing exercise with visualization until his entire body felt at ease. When he rolled over, he noticed that all of his muscles were tingly. Then he fell into a deep sleep to the sounds of falling water and a light applause from the surrounding leaves.

49

CHAPTER SIX

The next morning, each crew member woke feeling refreshed and exhilarated for the coming day. They all had gotten more than enough sleep, and a brand-new clarity filled their minds. The black orchid elixir was a special treatment that reset the brain for a new beginning. It was almost as if it shut the mind down for repairs, then restarted it like the trauma had never happened. Because the elixir was completely natural and non-toxic, there were no side effects, and it always left patients feeling clear-minded.

Price planned an unexpected breakfast above the clouds for the team. They all got ready to meet at the campfire an hour and a half before sunrise, so it was still pitch-black. Freshly showered and squinting soldiers arrived, rubbing their eyes and stretching their arms wide. They smiled and greeted each other with hugs and fun, personalized handshakes. When everyone was present, Price began explaining his plan.

"Good morning, soldiers. I trust in the power of the elixir and hope that you knocked out peacefully last night! I know I feel completely free and clear to start my day. As you are aware, we are here for you to regroup, have fun, and take care of anything you need to. Before we begin the day, we are all going to take a hike to a unique place. Thanks to Crumpler and Didier for preparing breakfasts that we can eat on the go."

E. M. Price motioned toward them, and C. E. Crumpler took off his hat and said, "My pleasure, everyone. We hope you enjoy. They're wrapped up so you can eat easily!"

Thanks and phrases of gratitude came from the crew.

Price said, "After a rainforest surprise, we planned a fun cardio session, and then you can eat your breakfast before we return. Be sure to take one before we leave. If you don't already have your exercise gear on, change now. Are there any questions?"

After waiting a bit in silence with waking, blank stares he said, "Okay, then after we return from the morning adventure, we will have lunch at the campfire, and then we can talk about your choices for afternoon activities."

Jaway said, "Thanks, Price, for guiding us through our itinerary for the day. I'm sure we will all have a great time! Don't forget to grab a breakfast wrap and meet in front of my fydon in ten minutes."

Everyone dispersed quickly after taking one of the delectable, convenient packages. The camp lit up with flashlights as crew members walked around.

Jaway addressed the crew, "Alright, it has been ten minutes. I see that you all are ready for an exciting morning. Take it away, Price."

"Thanks to Terrain Analysts Curtis and Roberts for clearing the best hiking trail. They will be leading us through the rainforest."

T. A. Curtis asked, "Did everyone remember their wongers? It looks like we will be traveling through some insect-heavy areas."

A few crew members had forgotten theirs, and ran to their tents to grab them quickly.

Wongers protected people from bugs. They were little coins that could be placed in a pocket, and they emitted frequencies that kept insects and bugs an arm's length away from any extremity of the body.

After they returned, Curtis began walking, motioning with her hand for the others to follow.

"If you really want to experience the rainforest waking up, then be as quiet as possible along the route," she said.

They began hiking through the untamed rainforest. Curtis and Roberts chopped carefully left and right, using a special machete. It had a brightly colored laser tip that cut through anything with ease. Each member wore a shirt that contained a flashlight near the top, so moving their bodies in any direction lit the path.

During the journey, they walked next to a scorpion breeding site and got to see an anaconda the size of three men by some overgrown tree roots in a pond. Forty-five minutes later, they arrived in a cleared area. The terrain analysts put away their laser machetes, and everyone gathered around Price.

"As you can see now, we are entering an ancient area. It has been abandoned for at least one hundred years," he whispered.

The crew could only see a path and a cleared area at first. But as they walked closer, their eyes strained to see the majestic building that towered over the trees. Most of them had no clue what they would experience. The forest floor was open because it was covered with stone bricks, although they were like miniature hills and valleys. Trees had grown randomly through the cobblestone plaza, haphazardly strewn throughout, with sparse foliage on the ground. As they walked closer, their flashlight shirts began to illuminate a block the size of five men. Shortly after, they could see the other cubes beside it.

As they walked up a ramp, they could only see enormous stone masses to their left. When they turned the corner, they finally got a glimpse of the impressive pyramid that they were climbing.

The crew felt dwarfed as they continued walking up a ramp next to the gigantic cubes. E. M. Price grabbed a cylinder, called a jipty from his backpack, and it turned into a ladder. The crew followed him up to another flat expanse. By this time, they were near the treetops, and they continued ascending until they reached a sunken bench carved near the edge, overlooking the canopy. They all sat down without talking, careful not to disturb the wildlife.

They waited in the dark and fought the urge to chat. It was so quiet that it seemed like nothing lived above or below. Soon after, the black turned into gray, and the crew could finally see the immense building they were on and how it jutted out of the rainforest floor. They looked up and could only see huge square stone blocks that seemed to reach the heavens.

At that moment, the silence ceased, and different animals called out after a long night of sleep. The crew heard a few monkeys screech and different birds caw. It slowly became a cacophony of mysterious, spirit-like sounds.

The sun poked only a sliver above the cloud-covered canopy. It looked like a sea of broccoli capped with an intricate spiderweb, with a blazing orange slice peeking through the edge of the earth. As the sun continued to rise, the sky became filled with every color imaginable: hot pinks, rich purples, burning oranges, and bright yellows. A few clouds appeared as floating cotton shelves that reflected different hues of the sky.

When the entire sun became visible, the smokey dew above the canopy revealed more pyramids in the distance. These empty, abandoned monoliths soared high above the forest and provided a sense of the area and where they were standing. Until this point, the crew had not had a clear understanding of the entire structure.

Then a flock of large, purple birds were spooked out of the trees and flew toward the heavens. They covered the sky and broke into two different entities, creating daytime fireworks. One group flew straight up while the other stayed near the treetops. There were so many birds that they looked like two huge purple lava lamps bubbling up and down and all around. The upper flock then flew down and to the right, while the lower flock flew up and to the left, creating two large blobs of purple on the outside, with a rounded, overlapping diamond in the center that changed to a deep purplish-black.

The sky blazed hot pink behind the contrasting gangs, and then the birds became one entity, changing shapes as they bobbed above the trees until they finally descended and were absorbed by the ocean of green. Other huge, multicolor parrots flew closer to the crew in pairs, catching a current in the sky and riding it higher and higher, like helium balloons. Many monkeys flung themselves from branch to branch, popping through the tops of the trees. The crew felt rejuvenated watching the sky turn blue and the animals in motion as the sun rose.

"And that is what we call a sunrise surprise!" Price's announcement signaled that the crew could begin talking.

Many started discussing how renewed they felt and how humbled they were to be on the ancient pyramid. Then one member started clapping slowly, until all of them cheered, applauded, and whooped like the monkeys below.

"And that's not all, crew!" Price pointed his finger.

He grabbed his jipty again, placed it on the end of the cubic platform, and proceeded to climb up the ladder. Krizzles immediately shrugged her shoulders and looked from side to side, then began to walk, trusting that something fascinating was sure to come. The crew followed, and member after member created a fugue of *whoas* and *ahhhs* and *ooohs* as they each reached the top. From this upper block, they could see the entire side of the pyramid. It seemed to be never-ending. The massive blocks continued up at an angle, and in the center met a huge rectangular structure that jutted to the highest point of the entire pyramid. To the side were human-sized stairs that led all the way to the top.

"And this, my friends, is your cardio challenge for the day. We are going to walk, jog, or drag ourselves to the top and back," said Price.

"Last one has to insert the drainage waste hose from the glider before we leave the site!" Jaway shouted as he and the crew threw their backpacks down and darted up the stairs, hoping to be any place but last.

The glider made waste into compost, which was then inserted through a hose under the rainforest floor. It was completely organic and did not negatively affect the rainforest in any way. It actually helped fertilize the soil by introducing organic matter with rich nutrients.

Each member of the crew counted to fifteen when they got to the top to enjoy the breathtaking views all around the forest. They saw a wide river that etched a deep, winding snake through the vast green expanse. Then they took off down the stairs to return in any place but last.

Jaway made it back first, with a considerable lead. One by one, they stopped on the platform where they'd started the challenge, panting heavily and bending at the waist with their fists on their knees. Some lay down and waited for the loud gulps of air to return to normal. After people caught their breath, they cheered on the others to make it back.

"Come on, you can do it, don't quit," they shouted as Mechanical Operator Dario, who was in last place, stopped completely.

Beads of sweat ran down his entire body, and he continued because of the encouragement. As he imagined draining the waste the next morning, he pumped extra energy into his spaghetti legs. While running down step by step, Dario focused on precision to avoid injury.

Just then, Churchill stopped—he couldn't continue any longer. He felt as though his heart were beating out of his chest, and his legs burned.

"I can't go another step," the man gasped.

"If only those extra snacks could run for you now, Churchill!" M. O. Kandova said, trying to lighten the mood.

This put a grin on Churchill's face. It was not insulting because they all could see that he was incredibly fit, but the others were just in better shape, and many were half his age.

M. O. Dario suddenly got a second wind and pushed any remaining energy into his muscles. As he passed P. G. Churchill, he pressed beyond the pain, remembering that it was temporary and would later relieve him of the impending extra duty.

With a head full of echoes from the crew, Churchill immediately forgot everything and began running down the stairs. When he hit a patch of moss, he fell back but caught himself with his hands. He rolled to the side, stood up, and then carried on. By this time, he knew there was no possibility of winning, but he wanted to finish the race, so he gathered his composure and took the last forty steps forcefully. His shirt clung to sweaty, bulging pecs and defined abs as his thick thighs flexed over and over again. He arrived at the platform with the entire crew, and they held him up with sweaty hugs because he could no longer stand. After he received at least a hand slap from each member, Churchill collapsed on the stone next to M. O. Dario, trying to guzzle as much air as possible.

"Great job, team! When you catch your breath, grab your bags and we can eat our breakfast here," said E. M. Price through intermittent light wheezes.

After the team replenished lost liquids and ate the protein-filled wraps, they sat in the sun to digest their food and relax from the morning adventure. They discussed the experience from that day and exchanged small talk.

As they retraced the steps they'd taken before sunrise, traveling down the pyramid seemed like an entirely different world. Earlier, they had only been able to see limited areas lit by the flashlights on their shirts. In contrast, on the return trip, they could see the surrounding structure and small details. When they reached the forest floor, it looked as if the cobblestone surface around the pyramid continued forever.

Price led the team, stopping every once in a while to point out different facts about the environment. They all had seen monkeys before, but he explained the behavior of a group of small gray furry monkeys with white-tipped hands, feet, and tails.

"As you can see now, the dominant one with the enlarged pectoral muscles is trying to catch the attention of a female. He does a special dance while picking fruit from the tree and throws it as far as he can. This shows that he is fit enough for passing his genes to the next generation."

After a few moments, the monkey changed the direction of the fruit flinging and began pummeling the staff with round orange fruits. Layers of feathery skin cascaded up and around the stem, which had frayed ends toward the top. Information Processor Hilton caught one and peeled it open to reveal bright-pink flesh and green seeds.

"You may not want to eat that, I. P. Hilton—it will probably give you an upset stomach," Price said.

"Ah, thanks. I've never seen one of these before." He dropped the fruit to the ground.

"Alright, let's keep moving team, so we can get out of the line of fire." Price ducked away from one of the flying projectiles and began walking quickly.

After they reached the edge of the stone flooring around the pyramid, they trudged along the path of slashed foliage from the morning. It seemed like an entirely different place, with interesting, sunny ponds, small rivers, and captivating wildlife. Price asked the other fourteen to gather around as they funneled into an area with a large tree without much growing around it.

"For those of you who don't know, this is a copaiba tree. You can punch a hole into the side, and a resin drips out. Many of you have used the resin but have never seen the tree. We know that it is a powerful anti-inflammatory, and an expectorant, and can fix digestion problems."

He presented more trivia about the tree and medicine, then led the gang back to base camp. Just before arriving, the team took a break to rehydrate. Lieutenant Commander Pama randomly gazed to the top of a tree while she tilted her head back and sipped. She wiped excess water from her full lips with her forearm.

Her short haircut was styled to bring different layers to the front of her face, and it accentuated her large eyes, full lashes, and swan neck. Long, toned arms and legs combined to complete a tall, fit body.

Suddenly, in disbelief, she squinted her eyes, curled her forehead, and leaned forward to one side. Almost everyone knew that she had hawk eyes. Her peripheral vision was so good she could see nearly everything happening next to her while still looking forward. They used to play a game where someone held fingers up, about an arm's length to the side of her, and she could say the correct amount.

"Is that what I think it is?" Pama said.

"What? I don't see anything. It's just endless greenery." said T. A. Curtis

"If that's what I think it is, this is a fantastic day!" Pama pointed to the treetops.

Her neon-pink laser machete made a steel-scratching whoosh sound as she lifted it from behind her backpack and over Curtis's head. It was made of metal and contained a brightly colored beam on the sharp side to aid in slicing through dense brush. She hacked at the vegetation to forge a new path leading to the base of a tree.

"Can you see it now?" she asked.

Only M. O. Kandova could at that point.

"It's a black orchid, in the shadow near where the tree splits into two." Kandova pointed to the towering tree.

"You guys can't see that? Everyone is here and nobody has a lensicator?" Pama was shocked.

A lensicator covered the eyes and allowed the wearer to see great distances or in low light. Nobody responded because they all knew they should have remembered to bring one. At age twenty-seven, Pama was the third-oldest crew member and ranked immediately below Jaway. Because of this, she deserved respect as one of the most seasoned colleagues, and she had chosen the military as her career with plans to continue for a very long time. It was evident that the others could learn a lot from her, and she was willing to hold impromptu lessons that demonstrated an entire slew of abilities.

In the crook of the imposing tree, a few thick green leaves spread from side to side, revealing three shoots. Each one had many blackish blooms.

"With all due respect, Lieutenant Commander, are you sure you're not seeing things?" said Curtis, a newer crew member who was highly skilled, but did not understand the scope of the skills that Pama had honed over nearly a decade in the military.

All of the other members looked at her strangely and remained quiet, almost in shock. Curtis's comment elicited a reaction nobody expected. Pama set down her backpack and took out a long piece of fabric with handles on the ends. After grabbing a wound rope, she flung it over her shoulder, then wrapped the fabric around the tree, gripped the handles, and used her kleck to make her shoes grow spikes.

She began climbing by setting her feet in place on the bark, then releasing the fabric by moving her arms forward and flinging it up on the other side of the tree. When the fabric had moved higher, she pulled her arms on the sides, then lifted her body up. She repeated this over and over. At one point, she became tired and looked down to take a break. The troop was astonished that anyone could have climbed that far after the grueling cardio workout up the side of the pyramid.

They encouraged Pama by shouting, "You can do this! Don't give up, Lieutenant Commander. Reach your goal!"

When she made it to the space where the tree split, she couldn't resist being captivated by the fascinating specimen before her. The flowers were the blackest color she had ever seen in a plant, and the shade cast by nearby leaves revealed vivid, illuminated greens and blues. Each flower had three large, curved, circular petals tilted toward the sky. The largest one grew behind two that connected in the center and mirrored each other as horizontal, smaller ovals. A spacious bell in the very center curved up and then turned down. This contained the famed bioluminescent innards.

From the ground, only the bottom part of the black petals could be seen, mostly blocking a view of the glowing center. This was one reason the crowd had not been able to identify the flowers. As she admired the mesmerizing glowing orchids, her nostrils filled with an overwhelming scent that made her body shiver. Without thinking, she began picking the roots away from the tree. Pama carefully removed the entire plant and lowered it down with a rope.

"Can you see it now?" she shouted as it descended near the crew. She winked at them, chuckling to herself while they laughed with her.

"Wow, I've never seen one of these in person before. They are absolutely stunning." Price placed the plant carefully inside its own bag.

"Look out below," the lieutenant commander hollered as she planted her feet one last time before a quick descent. She refastened the fabric around the tree and released it by moving her arms forward. When the fabric dropped to a comfortable spot, she pulled the handles and stepped down, allowing the simple device to hold her weight. She repeated this until she stood firmly on the ground.

"And that is how it's done, my friends! Dad would be so proud." Pama's face beamed while she gathered her sack for the short final walk to camp.

The lieutenant commander was always motivated and ready to attack any challenge. She had grown up on the Highlands Region in the east, but on the edge of the rainforest. Her father enjoyed taking Pama and her siblings on physically demanding adventures through the rainforest, so climbing a tree on a whim would have been normal for their entire family.

The squad said many supportive words to Pama while they strutted back to camp and passed the specimen around. Most of them thought it was really special to finally see the famous black orchid in person, as they had only enjoyed the healing powers of the elixir as patients.

Jaway instructed the crew, "Alright, enjoy your free time and get cleaned up before we meet at the campfire for lunch at midday."

A. P. Krizzles motioned to Pama silently. Her eyes danced from E. M. Price toward the pool, while nodding slightly in the same direction. Lieutenant Commander Pama looked at her mischievously and returned a wink. After Price set his items down by the campfire, they each walked up next to him, facing in the opposite direction. They locked arms with him at the elbows and lifted him off of his seat.

They carried him to the nearby flickering, luminescent water and dropped him in with a heave-ho. He flew through the air and converted his surprised, flailing limbs into a cannonball by curling his knees to his chest and wrapping his arms around them. With a huge smile on his face, he forcefully and purposely hit the surface to make the biggest splash possible. On incentive days, it had become a tradition to throw one person into the water during the stay. The crew members always chose someone who deserved to be recognized for doing a great job, so it was an honor for E. M. Price to be selected.

Upon hearing the commotion, those who had made it to their tents threw down anything of value and ran into the plunge pool. Some darted full speed and dove from the edge, as the reservoir lacked any shallow spots. Jaway showed off acrobatic moves by flipping with a twist into the turquoise relief from the heat. Then he jumped out, ran back to the edge, sprung from his feet, crossed his arms over his chest, and completed a spiral with a curl, hitting the water again feet-first.

After seeing Jaway's trapeze moves, Serra walked around the right side of the pool to explore the path that went to the backside of the waterfall. When he reached a small, round room behind the base, he stopped with a still soul to notice some unique ferns. The sunlight traveled through a moving liquid filter into the hidden shelter, illuminating it in a light blue tone. It smelled like fresh rain, and a fine mist floated in the air. The space had been carved into the stone by years of constant erosion, and Serra, with oodles of military training, noted that it could be an ideal hiding place in an emergency. It offered complete privacy.

A large, flat rock lay at the base. It spread behind to serve as the floor of the room where Serra had paused. He reached out, cupped both hands together, and took a drink that quenched a lingering thirst from the immense loss of fluids that morning. He could see three large, horizontal stones that alternated up the waterfall. After scooping a few handfuls of Mother Nature's chilly tears over his head, he continued walking on the trail that curved along the left bank at a consistent level.

This section was as wide as the length of an arm. As he strolled, Captain Serra ran his right hand along plants that grew in the hard-packed dirt wall, which rose to create a shelf above it. This embankment started very low at the front left side of the pool and gradually increased in height all the way to the left side of the waterfall. This created a raised walkway that extended to the same place, then wove to the left in front of a large rock. Then it turned right and ascended before weaving to the left again and around another boulder. It curved a few more times before arriving at the top piece of land, to the left side of a flat slab of stone next to the crest.

Serra paced along this path, and then dove. Soon, he bobbed up and wiped his eyes. While he chatted with the other crew members who were also swimming, he noticed an incredibly thick, tangled vine that swept down to the forest floor. It flowed from the top of the closest towering tree, which grew on the left side of the raised path.

He got out and stomped through the surrounding foliage and unwound the thickest vine from smaller, engulfing creepers. He held it in his hand and marched to the footpath above the wall. It fell perfectly on the embankment, but was long enough to reach far into the clear, sparkling waves. He pulled it first with maximum strength to see if it was stable before jumping into the air and grasping the vine, forcing it to carry his full weight. Just above ground level where he stood on the trail, he tied a massive knot.

Now that the soaring rope swing was complete, Serra gripped his hands as high as he could and ran away from the swimmers with all of his might. He pressed his feet together on top of the knot and swung back toward the action. After circling around and rocketing high into the air, he dove into the deep water in the middle of the basin.

The other crew members clapped for the captain when he arrived back at the surface. After soaking for a few minutes, the entire clan knew it was time to emerge to wash their clothes and clean up for some free time before lunch. They all dispersed to the tents and fydons, laughing and reflecting with each other about the entire morning.

CHAPTER SEVEN

Culinary Experts Crumpler and Didier prepared a smorgasbord next to the campfire for lunch. When Jaway got a plate of food and found a seat, he paid close attention to the conversations. Curtis was sitting next to Kandova, describing the impact of the morning excursion.

"I don't know what it was about today, but I've never experienced a sunrise like that before in my entire life. It seemed like the wildlife were active in a unique way, and I sensed everything differently. Maybe it was the elixir from last night, or perhaps, even though the glider is camouflaged, the creatures can sense that it is there. So when we watch the sunrise from our vehicle above the trees, they don't behave naturally. I don't know. I should ask Krizzles sometime and see what she thinks."

"She would definitely be able to give you some insight into that. Yeah, I agree. It was almost like a moment where our spirits were intertwined with nature. I think the surprise of also being on an ancient pyramid contributed to the overall experience. It was so mysterious and captivating. The transition from complete darkness and silence to vivid colors and full activity highlighted the contrast, and made what we saw even more intense." Kandova looked contemplative and took a bite of one of her favorite dishes.

"This food is so good, especially after all of that morning activity. Do you know what is going on this afternoon?" asked Curtis.

"No, I haven't heard any concrete details yet. They'll probably let us know what's available after lunch." Kandova bit off a chunk of bread from a miniature loaf.

Sickles gave Jaway a high-five and smiled as she said, "Great backflip, Barbour! That was insane! You gotta teach me that sometime."

"Thanks. Yeah, I would love to. I learned it when I was a kid and have been able to do it ever since." Jaway laughed with her.

Near the end of the meal, Price began to explain options for the rest of the day. "Can I have your attention for a few minutes while you finish your meals? I want to go through your choices for this afternoon."

The feasters grew silent and gazed attentively at him.

"First of all, Churchill is available for an hour for any of you who want help with your future plans—if you need help setting up training, or if you just need to chat. Next, you are also welcome to use the entire time for certification studies. As you can see, the waterfall and pool are available, and that is an option for more fun exercise. Serra found a vine if you want to swing into the water. Notice that you can walk up the side over there." He pointed his hand for them to look at the path above the embankment.

"Curtis and Roberts checked it out, and you can climb up the edge and dive down from the top. It gets deep quickly so you should be fine. There are some large eels right below the waterfall, but you should be alright as they are not aggressive. Are there any questions or additions at this point?"

"Just be careful when walking to the top," said T. A. Curtis. "As you get higher, it is kind of slippery. Oh, and don't forget that we have some inflatable swimming toys also."

"Great points. Thank you. Alright, I am in charge of an exciting surprise excursion that I have wanted to do for a while. Many of you showed interest, so we will be going on a hiking tour. There are lots of unique sights that are sure to blow your mind. Don't forget your wongers if you are going with me, and I would suggest bringing your lensicators as well. Thank you to Pama for the valuable surprise lesson this morning. It should serve as a reminder that if you don't also have hawk eyes, you need to remember your lensicator, and all recommended devices for that matter." Price winked at her and she lifted her hand and quickly curled her fingers down one by one, starting with the pinky, until her pointer finger was in his direction and her thumb was to the sky, to indicate she was happy to help.

"You are also welcome to do anything else you like, but check in with us and let us know where you plan to be so we can ensure everyone is safe. Bottom line—exclusively enjoy yourselves for at least part of the afternoon, because that is why we are here. Have a tremendous time, and relish the rest of your meals!" E. M. Price smiled and then sat down.

The crew liked being together so much that most of them usually chose group activities. Jaway stood to finish the announcement, as they had planned.

"I want to reiterate what Price mentioned—that you should really have a good time today, because this is a special reward for being stellar at your jobs! If you need anything from Churchill, he is going to be in his fydon beginning in about twenty minutes, but only for one hour, so he can get some personal time also. Waterfall folks, you should be all set, but let me know if you need anything. I will be around camp to hold down the fort if anybody has questions. For those of you going on the surprise hike, our esteemed excursion manager will be leaving promptly in thirty minutes from right here. Don't forget everything you need to be safe. Any questions?"

The onlookers chewed even faster now, and nobody said anything, so Jaway continued.

"Alright, I hope you all have a fun time. We will meet back here in the early evening for another home-cooked meal from our fantastic culinary experts. And thanks to Didier for staying near camp to prepare that. Make sure you get in some good time in the plunge pool and waterfall too."

Everyone offered appreciation.

Didier nodded. "No problem, guys. I got your back."

She usually provided light snacks from the kitchen in addition to preparing the dinner. C. E. Didier loved cooking. It was particularly fun because she could make preparations in the outdoor kitchen, which was located near the campfire and poolside action.

Any chance the gang had to break away from the carefully designed meal plans was a treasure. Each member of the team took a monthly body inventory test. The results revealed the perfect food intake for that person. A set caloric guide was created, as well as goal percentages of daily fats, proteins, and carbohydrates. From this system, each member had an individually curated meal plan and exercise regimen.

The gymnasium was located on the bottom floor of the glider in between the kitchen with its dining area and the engine room. This gym contained everything anyone might need in order to achieve their best fitness levels. Although meals were tasty on the glider, during rewards everyone could eat whatever they wanted, and specified workouts were not required. Didier enjoyed taking advantage of this and baked rich, decadent morsels that tasted even better because they would become unavailable after the crew returned to the main vehicle.

Roberts and M. O. Dario decided to stay back and get some career advice and work on certifications. They were close friends who'd both grown up in Ezlay, a city on the east coast that was part of the Highlands Region, which was known for endless rolling hills, beautiful beaches, and residents who took deep pleasure in every moment of life. They arrived together at Churchill's fydon. Because M. O. Dario was also assigned there, he opened the door himself. A section of the wall slid like liquid down to the ground as stairs, and they walked up through the opening.

"How's it going, P. G. Churchill?" Dario asked.

"Great. I'm just going through some busywork." He looked up and peered over his glasses.

"How are you two doing? It's good to see you here."

"We are great, but we wanted to do some future planning. We don't mind if you talk to us at the same time." Dario spoke on Roberts's behalf.

"Okay, sounds good. Let me go through a few general things before I gather your information. To begin, both of you are close to the end of your required three years in the military at ages twenty and twenty-two. As you may know, typical options are staying in to make it a career, finding a job immediately that is entry level or only requires your military academy training, starting a two-year technical degree, or beginning a three-year professional degree. Don't forget about less traditional options either, like working for a family company, if you are so lucky, or doing something like monk training and serving those on pilgrimages. Just remember that the sky is the limit." Churchill set up his elitser to find the documents he'd created for them.

"Alright, Dario, it looks like you opted for guidance in a non-military career path. Just let me know if you change your mind—I have some great ideas for different military jobs that you would love, but don't feel any pressure."

"Alright, thanks. For now, I'm just interested in civilian occupations. My mom really wants me to settle down back home in Ezlay." Dario was noticeably stressed by this strong-willed parent, as a twenty-year-old who was nearly finished with compulsory service.

"I completely understand, my man. You scored highest in mathematics, spatial ability, and people skills on your last marketable traits test.

Let me look up some choices that may be good for you." P. G. Churchill reached to a lower shelf to get an infogrammer.

He was trained to look up special information in the tiny pyramid.

"Let me see here. I inserted your specific scores and checked the data. You would be best in a technical field such as engineering or mathematics. And in the actual position, due to your high interpersonal skills, a niche for you could be to work one-on-one with clients."

"Okay. Can you explain how this would be different than just being an engineer?"

"Good question. Well, sometimes people are strong in mathematics and spatial ability but are not fluent in dealing with others. So for them, we would suggest just engineering or product design. It is actually quite rare to have such a high interpersonal skills score, so you would be perfect as a representative in an engineering company. In this circumstance, you would work in the office with design; however, your main purpose would be to explain the costs, options, and other necessary information to a customer."

"I've always thought operating machinery in the marble and stone quarries would be fun. And I think there are some in the vicinity of Ezlay."

"Okay. If you chose to go this route, you would learn how to operate the machinery and you could work in the field, but your main purpose would be to interact with customers to get them exactly what they wanted. You would know the parameters of what is possible, and you would be familiar with the materials available. Does that sound like something you might imagine doing?"

"Yeah, you're right. I do enjoy making friends and being around others, so I think it might be a winning combination. You know our Highland Region vibe." Dario laughed broadly and then grinned. "I would not be only working at the site all day, every day. I could also interact with customers and get them what they need. Thanks so much for your guidance. I really appreciate it. It gives me something to think about."

He was always interested in planning out his life and wanted to know the steps he could take to make that happen. These sessions also were fun for him, because he felt as though he were visiting a Keeper of the Stars for guidance, but instead, this was occupation-focused.

"No problem, M. O. Dario. We can follow up whenever you want in the future. Now, let's see what we have for you, Roberts, our other crew member from the breezy beach city of Ezlay. It looks like you are very close to finishing your three years of compulsory service. Are you also opting out of the military side of things?" Churchill wanted to offer the most extensive list of possible paths.

"Yeah, I'm certain I just want a civilian career as well."

T. A. Roberts was a twenty-two-year-old, one who knew exactly how the decisions made over the next few months could seriously affect the outcome of his entire work life.

"Alright, we'll just check out the civilian side of things. As always, keep me posted if you change your mind, and we can modify your results." Churchill switched the pyramids in order to check his elitser.

"Hmmm, I'm not shocked at all." He gazed intently, while rubbing the underside of his chin with his thumb, the other fingers resting in a fist. "Your tests show that you scored highest in creativity, scientific reasoning, and language. This is not surprising, because you do a great job as a terrain analyst right now, and it requires creative problem solving and science. Let me check and see what your specific numbers indicate about professions." He moved the other pyramid in front of them.

"Alright, as you can see here, you have many career options that would be a good fit. Acting would allow you to use creativity as well as language. Being a language specialist or translator could also be an option."

Although their technology could make blobes without live actors, the people valued the human element in performances much more than a digital version of entertainment. They felt the same about translating in real time. The technology could not convey emotions and feelings in the moment that influenced what was being said. Therefore, live translators were used for important situations.

"Have you ever thought of these top two?" Churchill asked.

"I knew that I excelled at language, but I have never thought about being an actor. And in school I studied just a few tongues."

"Well, that is definitely a start. First, take a few days to think about what you see for your future and if you think these are in line with your vision. If you are interested in pursuing information or starting training, then let me know. You can definitely focus on honing the most useful languages or begin some acting classes."

"That sounds great."

"Alright, touch base with me in a few days, and let me know if you have decided to follow any of the suggestions. I can help you get the ball rolling." Churchill set the devices back in their carefully selected spaces.

"I'm glad that you both stopped by. I think we are finished here. Are you guys going to the waterfall?"

"No, we are going to study for our certifications that are coming up soon," Dario said.

"Sounds great. I'm going to finish up some work and then head down and swim."

"Thank you for helping us. I'm looking forward to planning out my future after the military!" Dario said.

The close friends went to their individual tents to memorize facts and procedures.

After the campfire lunch, many crew members went back to their fydons to get ready for an afternoon of lounging near the pool. The water had many important minerals, and tests had revealed that it could provide multiple health benefits. A. P. Krizzles and T. O. Jeffers were so excited about the free time that they finished the rest of their lunches quickly and ran to their tents to get their swimming suits. Because they were assigned to the same fydon, they headed there together to make use of the shower area. Kandova was already in the fydon, preparing for the hike.

"Kandova, you aren't going to dive from the top of the waterfall with us?" Krizzles asked their fellow fydonmate. "We have inflatable swimming toys, and we will let you pick any shapes you want! Not convinced?"

"I had enough time in the water this morning. I need to get some more hiking in. And you know me, I gotta hang with my fellow jaguars, out where the large felines live!" M. O. Kandova joked with a straight face and wide eyes while hissing and curling fake claws toward Krizzles.

She had heard rumors of cats who lived in the area and wanted to see if they were true.

Then Kandova began purring and talking slowly. "Are you going to miss your big jaguar for a few hours?"

With a contorted face, she made fists, bent her arms at the elbows, and alternated bobbing her shoulders up and down in a hilarious dance move.

A. P. Krizzles laughed loudly, then unsuccessfully made an effort to recreate the comical low voice with an accent. "No, but I bet you're going to miss I. P. Hilton in the water!"

They all giggled together.

"Seriously, you almost had me with that one, but I can't be too eager." Kandova smacked her gums from one side of her mouth and winked sarcastically while leaning forward with that side of her body.

"A lady has to make him want more, if you know what I mean. We gotta be mysterious. I can't follow him around like a lost, hungry puppy waiting for some sustenance." She said this in her natural voice before pushing one hand with her palm smoothly through the air.

"And you know what?"—she switched—"I'm a *big* jaguar who don't need to beg."

Jeffers stepped out of the shower room in her bikini and joined the other two. All three laughed again and slapped their hands together in jest.

"You know it! Jaguars for life," Krizzles said in a deep, slow voice.

In all seriousness, Kandova had a slight crush on Hilton, but the entire crew was careful to stay professional. They aimed to foster sibling-like relationships; romantic connections were highly frowned upon. Because of this, feelings of attraction were often dismissed or only discussed among close friends. Although Kandova was a jokester, she would often freeze up whenever the information processor came around. If they were alone together, she did not know what to say and became a nervous wreck. Because she had never been in love before, she could not process the strong emotions that she felt for him. Whenever they got close, her anxiety morphed into a mixture of adoration and embarrassment, and made her even more confused.

This bewilderment created the most unexpected situations. For example, one time they were in the glider central common area, waiting for an elevator. Kandova attempted to speak to Hilton clearly, but instead, she looked up and said with a scratchy, wavering voice, "You know, we're supposed to have great glider weather. Not like weather in the glider. I mean great weather for glider flying. I mean . . ."

Her unintelligible babbling was interrupted by the arrival of the elevator. She was relieved to be rescued until she realized they would be riding up without anyone else. They stood in complete silence during the trip, both puzzled about the words that had just been spoken. As Kandova turned red, beads of sweat rolled down her face, which made her even more frightened. It was like a snowball rolling down a hill, accumulating more and more snow until it was a huge, raging, icy boulder. By the time they reached the upper control room and walked out, she was so relieved that she darted to her work station and attempted to return to her normal self.

Within minutes, she felt at home and was cracking jokes and throwing around mechanical operator terms with ease.

Because of experiences like this, she often avoided Hilton, although she also felt drawn to him. Kandova's fydonmates understood her heart better than even she was able to.

CHAPTER EIGHT

T. O. Jeffers and A. P. Krizzles headed down toward the water with towels, a small bag, and snacks. When they arrived at the campfire, they noticed that Jaway was relaxing while checking his infogrammer. This monitored the whereabouts of all crew members, and interacted with the expadier to protect the group from a number of dangers, including unexpected nomadic tribes.

"How's it going, Barbour?" Krizzles sorted her items next to the campfire near the edge of the water.

"I'm great. Just checking in on everyone to make sure we're all safe. I'm sure everything will be fine, but you never can be too careful!" Jaway looked up and noticed Krizzles in a bikini.

She'd developed a perfectly proportioned hourglass figure after years of sports and working on the farm, and her hair fell like a veil. When she started putting it up in preparation to swim, it was like an unexpected reveal. To this point, Jaway had looked at her as a little sister despite the fact that, at nineteen, she was only two years younger than him. One of the reasons why he viewed her as family was because when they first met, he felt as though he was relaxing at home with his two younger sisters.

This made the shocking surprise even more intense and confusing.

Her long, flowing mane lay over supple shoulders, a perfect swan neck, and a curvy yet perky chest cupped by a bright-pink bikini top. As she flipped her hair with her hands to the crown of her head, she exposed her beauty without barriers. She smoothed out the bumps along the sides of her head and pulled every strand to the top, where she held the masterpiece with one hand. Once she had gathered all of the long, flowing locks, Krizzles wrapped them and created a topknot by pulling out a seemingly foreign contraption from between her lips and securing it on the top of her head. By this time, her strong jawline seemed more pronounced, and her sparkly, grayish eyes glimmered over jutting cheekbones.

Jaway was enamored and puzzled by this mysterious new way of perceiving A. P. Krizzles. He had always admired her athletic prowess and respected her proficient workplace performance capability. But it was like he had been looking through smoky glasses and unintentionally ignoring the perfect specimen of the human race that he interacted with daily. When they first met, he was initially intimidated by her appearance, but that quickly faded when her personality came through. Her combination of outgoing spirit and dedication to the work quickly shifted his perception—he saw her as a valuable and necessary asset. They were also laser-focused on the mission and safety of the crew due to the serious nature of their job.

As the waterfall rushed behind them, the all-encompassing lush surroundings lifted the weighty burden of self-preservation like a raging wind unexpectedly hurling a window open. Suddenly, he felt the hair rise on the back of his neck and a warm fire burning inside his chest. Jaway's pupils dilated as his mind spun around and he recognized that he was attracted to the woman. In the same moment, he tried to reject his body's physical reaction by reminding himself of workplace protocol.

While he clenched his eyes shut and shook his head, Krizzles tapped him on the shoulder and yelled, "Last one to the top is a rotten egg!"

He dropped everything and began a mad dash with all of the others to the crest of the waterfall. He threw his shirt off along the way, running in a juvenile effort to avoid being the rotten egg of the day.

They ran carefully up the path above the wall on the left side of the shimmering green-blue oval. Then they zigzagged through different levels with flat boulders, mossy turns, and arborous obstacles. Youth kicked in, each member determined to finish in any place but last. Jeffers, Jaway, Krizzles, and Didier ran in a pack as they laughed and pushed their bodies for maximum effort. Hilton was three paces behind the other four perfectly sculpted bodies, but only because they'd started while he was still walking from his fydon. As they reached the top, one by one, they stopped to enjoy the freedom of the day.

"Hilton, you're the rotten egg!" C. E. Didier shouted over the booming rapids, panting through laughter and patting him on the upper back.

"Yeah, I may be the rotten egg, but only because I got a late start!" Hilton attempted to catch his breath.

"Is that why eggs become rotten? Because they lie around so long?" Didier asked as everyone chuckled together.

"Alright, who is going to be the first to make the plunge?" Jaway asked.

Krizzles started a slow chant that the others joined. "Rotten egg . . . rotten egg . . . rotten egg."

I. P. Hilton shrugged his muscular shoulders and smiled from ear to ear, revealing bright white teeth. He ran to the edge of a flat boulder on the left side of the river and then flew through the air, shouting, "At least I'm not too chicken to jump—cluckluck, cluckluck, cluckluck," adding to the childish banter.

While leaping, he managed to perform a flip before plunging feet-first into the sparkling ripples with his hands at his sides. As he plunged deep into the clear water, he opened his eyes to examine the area. Many huge, yellow eels swam near the base of the waterfall. They rushed away from Hilton, appearing as wide satin ribbons in the wind. He floated under the water, looking around at the piercing, bluish-green beams of sun. It felt like his heart slowed down, and he was at peace with the surroundings. When his ears started hurting, he engaged his feet and arms and headed to the surface.

"Woah, we weren't sure if you were safe down there, Hilton. We were going to give you two more seconds, then jump down to save you. How is it?" Jaway shouted from the highest point of the waterfall.

Hilton lifted his chiseled arms out of the water and gave them two thumbs up.

"There are huge yellow eels the size of my legs down there, just like Price said! But they swam away, so they don't seem aggressive. I bet they love eating chickens, though." Hilton tried to catch his breath as he licked his lips and swam aside so the others could take a plunge.

"Want to jump together, A. P. Krizzles? We could do a front-flip into a dive." Jaway motioned to a few points on the large rocks on each side of the stream, and waited for approval. He knew Krizzles was down for anything athletic.

After she gave a nod, they walked to the starting positions far from the edge, then counted back together slowly. "Three, two, one!"

They sprinted to the edge and quickly crouched down before detonating an explosive spring in their legs to launch off of the huge, flat rocks. While in the air, they sensed each other with peripheral vision and front-flipped in sync before gluing their straight legs together in a point, lifting their arms above tucked heads and plunged into the refreshing pressure chamber. Their ears popped as they descended as far as they could go. They rose immediately to the surface and met each other with a high five and an elbow bump.

"That was epic! Where is our chicken status now, Commander?" Krizzles pressed her arms on the bank to leap out of the water, where she secured a few locks of hair that had come undone.

C. E. Didier and T. O. Jeffers also wanted to show off, so they walked to the edge of the rocks and turned around.

"Check this out!" Jeffers said.

They completed synchronized backflips and a twist before hitting the sparkling waves, hands first. After everyone cheered for them, Churchill arrived from leading guidance sessions.

"I see we have made ourselves at home!" He walked over to a small bag.

It contained tiny, multicolored, coin-shaped diamonds that would soon become inflatable toys.

"What should we make these guys? Inflatables used to be my favorite when I was a kid." Churchill's face exuded sentimentality.

"Mine too! We were thinking about a jaguar, a black orchid, and a gold coin. What do you think?" Krizzles's topknot was completely refreshed, and she punched her fists against her hips.

"That sounds great!"

Krizzles used her kleck to turn the first diamond coin into a huge cat the size of three men, complete with black-outlined gold spots with a light orange-and-white background. The jaguar stood on a platform so they could lounge under the belly and it would stay afloat. She changed the next one into a gigantic black orchid flower. Three black petals curved around to create inhabitable spaces, and the center curved bell mirrored the surrounding liquid of the reservoir in glowing greens and blues. The shiny dark material floated along the surface and seemed to be illuminated from below as it bobbed above the crystal-clear waves. Then the third was transformed into a flat gold coin with upturned edges. It was complete with The Land's insignia and textured sides.

After the floating figures were set into place, the team began soaring through the air, taking turns on the vine that Serra had set up. A. P. Krizzles was the ideal daredevil for the setting. She ran and jumped while clutching the creeping plant. After quickly traveling through the air around the bank, she swung back and landed on the gold coin.

She steadied her body on the currency by holding the sides down to avoid spilling into the water, and then shouted, "Emperor of the coin!"

Krizzles loved underwater sports, so she asked the vacationers while circling, "Is anyone in the mood for a brief game of trudles?"

The smile on her face was an offer difficult to refuse.

"Trudles is the best," Jaway said immediately, almost tripping over his words. He surprised himself, looking back at the words as a reflex beyond his control.

Hilton and Jeffers also expressed interest, so Jaway said, "Perfect! We can have two-on-two. I call Krizzles."

They all knew she was the best. A trudle was a colorful, sparkly, and illuminated robotic fish that traveled under the water when sent by a player. The game originated from the Highlands Region in the east, home of the best beaches in The Land. Two teams faced each other below the surface, either standing on the bottom or swimming. The players used a vrimp, which covered the mouth and nose, to breathe oxygen for up to thirty minutes. It was attached to goggles so the players could see.

This pool was so clear that they could see across the entire bowl without any goggle filters. Each player extended a net with a long handle to catch the robotic fish as they were launched toward their team. After a trudle was collected, the player held it upright by finger notches on the side and used an underhand throw to guide the fish to the opposing team, which could have any number of players. The tricky part of the game was not only judging distance underwater, but also how the stealthy trudles could change speed or direction at any moment. Floating cones above alerted people in the vicinity of a game in session, defined the posts of each player, and lit the body of water.

After each member was in place, a server would send the first fish across. When it was caught, another member from the same team would send another fish, and then another, until three were in play. If a trudle was left uncaught by a net, it would automatically return to the player who served it. The idea was to not only catch and send, but also to anticipate the next trudle and successfully catch each one. When a player missed a trudle, the point went to the opposing team, and all fish returned to the senders on the winning team. When a team hit the decided amount of points, the teams switched places and played again, if they wished. Usually the vrimps would need to be replaced by that time. To keep everyone safe, a tiny light would flash inside the goggles when only five minutes of oxygen were left.

"Where should we place the markers? Can you see a level spot where we can all stand?" Jeffers asked. She squinted through the turquoise waves from the surface.

"There is a perfect location over there." Jaway pointed to the far side near the launching pad of the vine.

"Oh yeah, I see what you're talking about. We can play on the floor of the pond." Jeffers got in, and Jaway told her where to place the cones, like they were siblings at home leveling artwork on a wall.

She emerged from the room-temperature water and began suiting up for the game.

"Hilton's team starts last because he is the rotten egg. It's a rule." Jaway reminded them of the unwritten decree, and they all laughed at how he delivered the words.

Every player grabbed a net, and then Krizzles and Jaway took three trudles.

"Do you guys play up to twenty-one, too?" Jeffers asked.

They swam at the surface and prepared to affix the vrimps, clearing the goggles.

"We have different rules in Bingdole, but we can do twenty-one." Hilton helped Jeffers adjust her goggles.

"Thanks, man."

"No problem, teammate!"

Hilton was known for being generous and helpful. Effective teamwork naturally flowed from his magnanimous personality.

Now that the terms were set, each player placed a suction piece around their mouth and nose, then fastened the goggles before very slowly descending to the sandy pool floor, so their ears could adjust. Krizzles served first. The trudle glowed bright green, and its sparkles flashed as it wiggled back and forth. Bright yellow, flowing fins oozed through the water, creating a feast for the eyes. Hilton reached for the trudle successfully, caught it in the net, and passed it back as Jaway released the second fish, but this one was bright purple and green. T. O. Jeffers extended her clenched fist, which contained the handle of the net, and captured the wandering, violet underwater dragon. Then Jaway sent the third trudle.

The bright-red, sequined monster flashed crimson and magenta fins as it elegantly bobbed from side to side and passed the distracted players.

Usually it would return immediately to the sender, but this time it took a trip around the entire pool and illuminated a huge, prehistoric yellow eel. The swimming machine seemed to scream in horror, fleeing noticeably faster back to Jaway. Because these eels were not aggressive and usually were scared of humans, the team members were only concerned for the safety of their trudles from time to time. A. P. Krizzles motioned to Jaway that it was his serve for the next game. He gave her a simple nod, but the emotions from earlier returned.

Jaway looked at her for a second after releasing the toy, and it felt like his chest was in front of a blazing campfire. While he thought about what an amazing person she was, he tried to inconspicuously spy on her. A beam of light from a floating cone above revealed her features with an angelic glow, and he realized how much he loved her beauty, athleticism, kindness, talent, and sense of humor. At this point, the fire that raged inside his chest made him forget that they were colleagues.

A fin-flick of a trudle against his leg shook him back to reality. Thankfully, the fish were returning to his team, so nobody picked up on his daydream. Krizzles served, and they played until the vrimps notified them that five minutes of oxygen was left.

"I'm having a great time! Do you guys want to play again and switch sides?" Jeffers asked after each of them arrived at the surface, hoping to hear interested replies.

"Yeah, we're on a roll. Another thirty-minute session would be a lot of fun," Jaway said.

The other two agreed, so they played again, complete with daring catches and wit-flexing concentration, until they came to a near tie. Although Hilton and Jeffers were ahead, they motioned to call it a tie. As they slothfully rose to the surface, Jaway wished that he could spend every second of his life with Krizzles. The slow ascent was necessary for their body to adjust to the pressure, and he almost hoped it would last forever.

As they reached the surface of the water and breathed in atmospheric air again, Jaway realized that he had to snap out of the fairy-tale world he created. The reality was that he was the leader of the team and he had to lead by example. In addition, they were responsible for keeping each other alive. He understood that he was in a high-ranking position at twenty-one years old because he was capable enough to operate machinery at a high level, and mature enough to remain professional, calm, and focused on the mission at hand. Unfortunately, romantic relationships did not fit into the reality they faced. Because of this, pursuing a relationship with A. P. Krizzles, or anyone else he worked with for that matter, was completely out of the question.

As Jaway lifted his body out of the pool, it was like all of the dripping water was the love he'd felt that day, leaving his soul. It shed down, and he accepted that he was not allowed to feel that again.

CHAPTER NINE

They each got out of the water and began removing the simple gear and organizing the trudles equipment. P. G. Churchill helped them gather the items, offering towels to the four who played. Once everything was clean and packed away, they each set up an oversized towel so they could relax after exerting so much energy.

"It feels so good to be in the heat of the sun." Hilton stretched his toned, twenty-two-year-old body on the towel, his feet spilling past the bottom edge.

"Yeah, I agree. I didn't realize how cool it got down there. My lips are nearly blue." Jeffers laughed as they closed their eyes and soaked up the sun.

As they lay quietly, their fit bodies glistened in the rays.

Hilton got up and said, "I'm going to get some snacks and drinks—do you guys want some?"

The entire group asked for refreshments after being so active. Hilton went to the kitchen area and prepared a platter with many foods that were not in their normal meal plans. After taking the tray and water over to the other five, he took orders and began preparing drinks in the nearby kitchen.

"Can you please cancel mine and surprise me with a sweet and sour beverage?" Krizzles asked. "I love it when you just make something mysterious. It's always good."

"Order up, my good lady," he said in a humorous accent, and then winked at her.

Hilton's mother owned a specialty juice shop, so he knew how to blend and mix complementary tastes together. Because of the reward, they had syrups and alcohol that they usually could not access. Each creation was brightly colored and had an elaborate garnish made of fruit that flowed out of the top and looked like the most unique and beautiful bird of the rainforest. He arranged them on a tray and delivered them to the loungers as they absorbed the sun.

All military members exercised regularly according to a personalized program, and they followed equally regimented diets. The philosophy behind this was to gift each soldier with the most physically capable body for strength and endurance, so that they would have the best chance of survival in the most extreme and unexpected circumstances. They each were like a statue of a god— perfect specimens of the human race, and in the best shape for their individual body types.

"It's hard, but, ya know, they commanded us to relax!" Krizzles lay back after taking a drink of the luxurious concoction.

They sprawled in silence for twenty minutes as the gushing waterfall intertwined with shushing leaves blown by light breezes, resulting in thousands of layers of snaps, whisks, and plats.

"Do you guys ever miss home?" Didier did not make any effort to open her eyes.

"Yeah, I do sometimes," said Hilton. "It's so crazy that my family is moving on with life and I can't be a part of their growth. When we finally got messages the other day, I found out that my baby cousin just started walking, and he was born right when I left. I think that's normal, but it's not easy."

They only sporadically received communication from loved ones, and strict guidelines limited the content.

"I agree. I totally get you. I think it took a long time for me to get used to living my life away from my family because we are so close. We were always going places and hanging out and having big dinners together," Jaway said.

"Yeah," Krizzles chimed in, "I think that is a common way to feel. We spent every living second with our families, and then we left them. It can be sad sometimes. I'm really glad that I have you all."

"Agreed." Jeffers downed the last of her fruity nectar, then began working on the brightly colored garnish, which was almost as big as the jumbo glass it adorned. "You all are a pretty good substitute." She laughed to lift the mood.

"Can you guys smell that?" Krizzles asked.

"No. What is it?" Jaway asked.

"You really can't tell that it's going to rain?" Krizzles took a deep breath through her nose. "I always forget that other people can't pick that up. I don't know how to describe it, but it's a sweet, fresh, metallic scent. Not right now, but in a while for sure—maybe later tonight."

"Have you always been able to feel that? It's like you have an extra sense. I don't think any of us can even tell that the air smells different," Jaway wondered out loud.

"Yeah, I have been able to feel and internalize nature ever since I could remember. All of my relatives were also born with it; our DNA includes a heightened sense for reading the wilderness. As far as I understand, it comes from generations and generations of farmers spending their entire lives on the land. It is a special gift that my ancestors have passed down to me.

"When I grew up, we had to know when it would rain because our crops depended on it. If we could anticipate the precipitation, then we could save a freshly cut crop by processing it immediately, before the unwelcome weather arrived. If we felt a severe thunderstorm brewing, we also would herd livestock that were grazing in faraway fields, so they could be safe in the barn. So here I am, extending my DNA for the purposes of our mission!"

Krizzles laughed, and the others joined her as she continued.

"We also have a phrase, and it goes like this: 'Always leave it on the land.' It means to give your best. So if you work as well as you can and give it your all, the crops and livestock will show it. And in the end, you will make a good living. It makes me feel warm just accessing the memories."

Jaway said, "That's so cool. My mom grew up on a farm, and us kids always loved hearing stories about it. We used to sit around, and my Uncle Harold would tell us the coolest tales about living there. It seemed like such a fun existence, with lots of work but fascinating animals and entertainment all over. It also seems like everybody who lived there was really interesting. For example, they lived in an era without much technology, so they had to be super creative and funny to pass the time. And everyone knew everyone, so they had to be nicer to each other because you would always see people again. It was like any choice anyone ever made was etched in the brains of the people, and could be recited at any moment. Was it like that where you grew up?"

"Yeah you are making me miss my home. It is so cozy. And my little udringa is missing me for sure." Krizzles's head shifted to the side, and she looked solemnly into the distance.

She was lying on her stomach with her elbows on the ground to prop up her upper body.

"What? You're an udringa person too?" Jaway flipped from his back to his tummy. "They take so much attention and care that not many people can commit to them. What color is yours?" he asked.

"Mine is all white, and her name is Daisy. She is adorable and super sweet." A. P. Krizzles smiled, and her eyes sparkled.

"What is an udringa? I don't think I've ever even heard of that," Hilton said.

Krizzles laughed. "That's because you're a city kid. It's okay. An udringa is the cutest, most amazing animal on the planet. They come in different colors, but they are all super tiny and fit in your lap when fully grown. You should see how small they are when they're born. The best way I could describe it is that they are like miniature llamas. They have four legs and a long neck and are all wooly."

"Oh, I think I may have seen one of those a long time ago, but I'm not sure. Maybe one of my neighbors had one," Hilton whispered.

"We named mine Daisy because she loved to eat the daisies around the outside of the house. One time, she got into a patch of sticky weeds. You know the round ones that cling to everything? Well, her wool was so full of them that you couldn't even see her face. And after she got into the yard, her legs got stuck together so she couldn't even walk. Thankfully, I was on my way out to feed the chickens and saw her. On the farm, we like to have our animals as indoor and outdoor pets, so they can roam during the day then come home for the night. We had to shave off all of her soft wool, it was so full of the sticky weeds. I had to put a miniature sweater on her, so she wouldn't get sunburned during the day. She was so cute." Krizzles chuckled with a smile that revealed pearly teeth. She sat up with both legs to one side.

Jaway did the same and crossed his legs.

"That's very funny. Mine was black, and we named him Trashie because he would always try to eat the garbage. What a strange coincidence. I guess they like to eat weird things. He is an indoor pet, and they are incredibly curious, so I guess he always thought that we put the trash into the waste bin as a surprise or something." He laughed out loud with everyone else.

"Trashie also loves eating flowers. What is with that?" Jaway shrugged his shoulders and faced his palms to the sky.

"Maybe it's because the flowers smell so good, and they are as big as their heads. Imagine having an edible plant the size of your face around and not trying it at least once," Krizzles said with a tinge of wit. "Daisy spends all day with the cats and chickens. She actually thought she was one of them until recently, because they grew up together and are about the same size. If a chicken laid an egg under a bush while out during the day, she would sit on it like it was hers and her fuzzy wool was like a big egg cushion. She even tried to make a clucking noise, but it just sounded like a screeching, broken yelp. But the birds loved her as one of their own. I think the turning point was when a python tried to get one of the birds. We saw it later recorded as a blobe—the snake slithered around the birds and checked them out. Little Daisy went nuts and stomped the python's tail until he left. From that day on, all of the chickens treated her like one of their own. Ah, my sweet, tiny Daisy." Krizzles looked around at the beautiful foliage and took a deep breath to enjoy everything as she day-dreamed about her fluffy family member.

"Do you keep the wool? It's really valuable," she asked after a minute.

"Yeah, my mom spins it into yarn and dyes it. It can be stripped and colored into so many different shades. Do you guys?" asked Jaway.

"We trim it, but we don't do the spinning. We send it away and get socks, and if we save up a ton, we can get a sweater."

"Yeah, the fabric is super thin but really warm. I have a few long-sleeved shirts. Have you seen the price in stores? They are insanely expensive."

"Yeah, I've heard it's because the textile is toasty but light, and they produce such a small amount."

"What do you like the most about udringas?" Jaway asked.

"Hmmm. It's hard to pick my favorite feature. When I was growing up, we used to let them suck our pinky finger. It was so adorable. Their cute tiny hooves, their pointy ears, their teensy tails and loyal personality . . . There's so much that I—Oh! I know," A.P. Krizzles interrupted herself. "My favorite thing is when Daisy gets excited and jumps in the air and flails her front and back legs in and out. Her back bends over and she clicks her front hooves with the back. It's so expressive that whenever something thrills us, we call it a heel-clicker, after little Daisy."

"I'm the same. They are so fun. That's so cool that Daisy does tricks like that. We trained Trashie to play fetch, and sometimes he gets sticks as big as his body. He can barely lift them, and it looks hilarious," Jaway reminisced as he basked in the sun.

"Does anyone want some saturn fruit? They're perfectly ripe!" Didier said from the nearby kitchen.

Each soldier raised a hand to lazily indicate they would love some of the delightful green flesh.

"Alright, I would be more than happy to make a platter," C. E. Didier volunteered, then sliced the fruit with precision and placed it on an oval wooden platter with different nuts and cheeses.

She'd really made it for the others because she was craving the tasty snack herself. She brought it over with a carafe of water that held an emerald in the bottom. They believed that the gemstone would release different energy and minerals into the water. This was naturally filled with nutrients and filtered from the kitchen faucet for safety. The crew perked up from their near coma induced by the crashing and splashing sounds, the full sun, and their recent exercise. Quietly, they each ate and drank.

Didier broke the silence with some knowledge learned while becoming certified as a culinary expert. "Did you know that the saturn fruit used to be only eaten by the elite? It was really difficult to find."

"Is that so? If that is true, then today we feast like emperors and empresses!" Hilton raised a glass in honor of the miniature meal.

Everyone lifted their cups and said in unison, "To the emperors and empresses!" before sipping the mineral-rich water.

T. O. Jeffers got up and said, "I don't know about you guys, but I am going to enjoy this gorgeous body of water when I still can."

Everyone else wanted to relax.

I. P. Hilton said, "We still have diving hoops if you want to try to jump into them. They can be fun."

"Let's make it extreme hoop diving! I'll swing from the vine and go through the rings. I think I can do it!" Jeffers said.

"That is a great idea." Hilton got up to set the hoops in the pool.

The tricky part about this endeavor was that they became moving targets, so she would have to fly through the air on the vine and then release just right to enter at the center of the hoop, angling her body almost straight down. But she was up for a challenge.

It was also fun for the spectators to judge her success in the water. They liked the idea of having the entertainment while still being able to rest. Jeffers strutted around the left edge of the twinkling turquoise pool and walked up the path above the wall, where the vine came down. She held the plant tightly with her fists, ran back to swing in the air, then placed her feet together on top of the huge ball toward the bottom of the vine. She launched through the air and soared directly above the sunbather enthusiasts as they *oohed* and *ahhed* at her, hoping she didn't fall on their passion fruit hors d'oeuvres.

Jeffers let out a long, ululating shout while showing off through the air.

Three red hoops an armspan in diameter floated, bobbed, and drifted. Just after passing once over the water, she set her eyes on one of the rings. She released her hands, pointed her arms, and pushed her feet against the knot like a diving board. Her body slid through the middle of one of the hoops with long, stiff limbs and pointed toes. The crew reacted in disbelief, as if they had witnessed a miracle—none of them had thought it would be possible. When she came to the surface they cheered with wide eyes and dropped jaws, snacking all the while. She swam to the edge near the roaring fans and emerged with a huge smile.

"And that is how it's done." Jeffers laughed.

"I never thought that was even possible when you told us what you were going to do!" Jaway said, and the others agreed. "Kudos and accolades for your training. We gotta get ourselves together." He laughed.

"I actually think I can do a flip into a dive into a hoop. Wanna see?" T. O. Jeffers asked, remembering her years of training for competitive diving.

The adoring fans were all in for the daredevil entertainment of the afternoon, and she was met with thumbs up and hoots of approval for the new challenge. She easily repeated the previous moves, but with a flip before the dive, and the crowd went wild.

She took a break to get some drinks and snacks, then got up and said, "Let's try the inflatables! I've always wanted to fall into a huge gold coin."

Jeffers set the large, floating figure into the reservoir and made her way up to the launch station of the vine. She set off, but this time the wind flipped the large toy out of the water and onto the bank. While she was in the midst of a full swing, she decided to return to home base to reset the target. Hilton was looking in the other direction and saw the large jaguar figure picked up by the wind. When he looked back, Jeffers had disappeared. Every worst-case scenario rushed through his mind at that time. *Was she vaporized by the enemy? Are we under attack? What just happened?*

With a rush of adrenaline, he ran around the edge of the pond and halfway up the path to the base of the vine. The other crew members followed.

CHAPTER TEN

When he got there, he noticed that there was a hole in the path, and he yelled to the other members who had just arrived, "Jeffers fell through the ground! It looks like an abandoned hunting trap."

Hilton saw the layers of the old covered pit. Many bamboo poles were situated next to each other, parallel to the ground, concealing an enormous sunken room below. Soil and years of debris covered the bamboo so it appeared as simply part of the surrounding surfaces. When Hilton put his head through the hole Jeffers had punched out with her body, he could see a spacious room that was meant to entrap a huge animal.

"Are there any spikes down there?" Jaway was concerned that, if present, they could have pierced anyone falling in.

"Nope, I don't see any spikes. It looks like Grandpa Time took care of them for us."

Normally, hunters would have secured sharp poles into the base, facing up so that prey would fall through and be immediately stabbed in multiple places. Luckily, the pointed wood spears had all fallen over, and were now lying down, instead acting as a cushion for the fall.

"Are you okay, T. O. Jeffers?" Hilton shouted into the darkness.

She regained consciousness and looked up slowly with no idea where she was or what was going on.

"I'm here. Help!" Her voice was soft and scratchy as she tried to make sense of what had happened.

"We're here! It looks like you fell through a retired trapping pit. See the bamboo ceiling? Stay calm—we are going to make sure to get you to safety. Can you feel if you are hurt in any way? Are you injured?" I. P. Hilton asked.

"No, I think I just got the wind knocked out of me." Jeffers shook her head and sat up.

"Hilton, you have to go down there. We can't waste another second, and you are taller than anyone I know. You're the only one of us that can help her!" Jaway said. He wished he could save the day himself, but Hilton was two heads taller than the average man.

"Gotcha!" Hilton responded in a millisecond, then broke the sides of the hole so he could fit through, jumping inside.

Jaway beamed a light so they could see.

"How are you feeling, Jeffers? Do you feel pain anywhere?" I. P. Hilton hoped for the best and tried to assess any possible injuries.

"I think I'm good. Just my pride a little," she whispered, then coughed and sat up all the way.

A shadow revealed a piece of bamboo sticking out of her upper thigh.

"It's worse than I thought," she said, pointing down at her dirt-covered, punctured leg.

Hilton reacted immediately. He stood up and looked around quickly to devise a plan. Then he ripped his swimming trunks up the center seam and tore the entire portion off from the crotch to the side, leaving himself covered. To fashion a long strip of fabric, he ripped that piece in half from top to bottom, then tied the ends together, doubling the length. Next, he wrapped it around her thigh and around the puncture wound to hold it in place and help stop the bleeding.

He looked around in an effort to devise a plan and said, "We gotta get you out of here now. You know how we shoot you out of the water with our hands?"

"Yeah, we do it all the time when we swim."

"It looks like that is our best option. Are you down?" He acted swiftly, maintaining complete focus.

"I'm ready for anything," Jeffers said as he helped her stand.

"Barbour, she has a wound on her right thigh! I'm going to launch her up to you with her good leg, and you guys can pull her through," Hilton shouted at the top of his lungs, to make sure the other crew members could hear through the bamboo.

"Alright, we are here to catch her!" They lay down to distribute their weight, trying to avoid complete collapse.

Jeffers put her left foot in his intertwined fingers and placed her hands on his shoulders as he bowed down. Next, he threw her toward the hole with all of his might. The other crew members grabbed her torso and arms and carefully pulled her through the opening, trying to avoid any contact with her right thigh.

Thankfully, the hole that had been smashed through the bamboo cover still held the weight of the crew members. As they pulled her out, they made certain not to fall in. They laid her on a stable section of the path, while Jaway rushed to get a stretcher. He ran to his fydon, which contained an emergency bag. There, he grabbed what looked like two white sticks and dropped them on the ground. He walked closer to Jeffers and used his kleck to transform them into a gurney.

"Is there a jipty in the emergency sack? We could quickly throw it down to Hilton," T. O. Jeffers said weakly.

She was always thinking of others before herself.

"Good thinking," said Jaway.

He dashed over to grab a small cylinder from the bag. Returning, he threw it into the ancient trap so Hilton could activate it and climb up the rungs to freedom.

Jaway and Churchill lifted T. O. Jeffers carefully with the stretcher and brought her over next to the campfire area.

"I should be able to take it from here, Barbour," said Churchill.

"Alright let me grab the emergency materials for you," Jaway panted, then rushed away once more on a journey for the equipment.

Part of Churchill's personnel guide training included a medical certification, so he had experience dealing with wounds. He removed the makeshift bandages with his glove-covered hands, which revealed a crimson mud of blood and dirt. Jeffers hissed into her front teeth at the pain.

"It's temporary, it's temporary, it's temporary," she whispered to herself.

"Someone get me sterile water, please!" Churchill said as Didier was already on the way back with water and clean towels from the kitchen station.

"Thanks, Didier. Do we have anything to give her for the pain?" P. G. Churchill pointed his head toward the wound with wide eyes, in an effort to not alarm the patient.

Then he removed another device, called a dopridam, from an emergency bag. It transformed from a thick, flat, red triangle into a square box with an open end. The edges were covered in a round, squishy material.

"Let me check our kitchen kit," Didier said as she opened a cabinet. "Oh, I have some tikompay. That should do the trick."

"Okay, perfect! I'll administer that right away. Jeffers, try to relax.

We're doing everything we can to get you back in tip-top shape. You will be just fine."

Churchill tried to fake that he was certain of a full recovery. But just as the words left his mouth, he realized he should have put more effort into the performance. It definitely sounded robotic, unnatural, and unconvincing. In addition, the technology officer in front of him would understand the magnitude of the situation the most. Tikompay was a substance created by combining two natural ingredients: a sap tapped from a tree and a pod from a vine. The sap was boiled down until it was soupy and then mixed with the dried, pulverized pod. The result was a honey-like syrup that, when placed under the tongue, helped increase pain thresholds by blocking the sensation of discomfort.

"I don't need any pain relief. I can handle it by myself." Jeffers cried out, the words escaping the edges of her mouth.

She bit down on a stick and tried to fight back the urge to scream. The technology officer was well-known for having sewn up her own stitches with natural cordage on an outing when she was isolated from her crew. Jeffers had operated so well that there was only a minuscule scar.

"Come on, we have all the stuff. You're tough, but it will take the edge off," Churchill said, this time with an award-winning performance.

A final rubber glove snapped and hugged his fingers like an extra layer of skin. She moaned and curled her back as another jolt of pain shot up the side of her body. When it stopped, she smirked, trying to appear light-hearted. "Alright, you don't have to do much to convince me."

He squeezed a small amount of the tikompay under her tongue with a syringe, and she immediately felt calm and euphoric as her body relaxed.

After waiting for indications that the pain relief had set in, Churchill whispered, "You are just going to feel slight pressure. Before you know it, you'll be on the road to recovery, my good friend. We are here for you."

He carefully used a surgical tong to clamp the sides of the largest bamboo piece, then pulled. The surrounding skin lifted as the wood-like grain protested against the removal. He shook the skin free by pulsing quickly from side to side. It slowly unhinged, cell by cell, releasing its grip on the bamboo.

As it ascended from the wound, the open gouge flooded with fresh blood. When Churchill knew the majority of the giant splinter was removed, he pressed with a sterile cloth to stop the bleeding. Next, he poured water around the wound and began breaking up the coagulated mud before cleaning it with an antiseptic on sterile cloths.

"Alright, I have to remove another chunk before we can place the dopridam. How are you doing, Jeffers?" he asked with a soothing tone.

"I'm great! Don't worry about me." She wanted him to focus on the task at hand.

"You're just going to feel some more pressure, and you may want to look away for this," he said as she turned her head.

P. G. Churchill grabbed the second-largest piece of sharp bamboo with small forceps and shook it from side to side to keep the skin intact while releasing the foreign object. Afterward, he pressed one of the sterile rags onto the wound to stop the bleeding again.

"Can you pass the dopridam, Barbour?"

"Yeah, no problem." Jaway wiped dirt from Jeffers's face. Then he put on a glove and passed the box to Churchill, who placed the soft edges of the dopridam upside down and over the area of the wound. It immediately sealed to the healthy skin of the leg, like a large, square octopus suction cup. Churchill controlled the dopridam through his kleck, first taking an assessment by zapping different beams to and fro.

It created a slight buzzing sound, and they waited in anticipation to see the results. The water rushed and gurgled in the background, a reminder of their paradise vacation gone wrong. The reservoir surface sparkled from the sunlight and bounced bright streaks onto the underbellies of the surrounding canopy leaves.

Jeffers opened her eyes and noticed the snaking blue flashes.

"I don't think I've ever taken the time to notice how the light reflects off the underside of the trees. It's like it lights them up with a dancing blue fire," she said.

"Yep, the tikompay is definitely kicking in. Do you see any moving images? This would be the time to get a sign from the forest, as they say."

Churchill spoke slowly, guiding her gently. He had heard of experiences where people received prophetic visions, and was skeptical, but he wanted to keep Jeffers's mind occupied while they waited for the dopridam to finish the initial sweep.

A sound of dropping coins rushed from the device. This was an indication that the machine would be able to restore the wound to eighty percent of the initial healthy state, and the rest would naturally heal over time.

"Phew, that is a relief." Churchill wiped his brow with his bent wrist, careful not to touch the glove.

"It looks like today you will recover by eighty percent, T. O. Jeffers! This is great news." He noticed that her eyes calmly followed the underbellies of the tree tops.

She did not respond; she was in a deep trance, trying to decipher what the visions meant for her life. While the dopridam repaired the wound, she saw a chariot cart behind four horses, carrying a muscular rider along a beach. A volcano launched indiscriminate glowing blobs like bombs upon the sand and into the waves through a smoke-filled breeze. Jeffers could hear the deadening, molten explosions and feel the heat on her skin. The skilled rider guided the white beasts around the obstacles, away from the origin of the blasts. He looked behind and ahead as he made lightning-speed adjustments to the reins, which acted like an extension of his powerful hands. The horses followed each minuscule movement as their adrenaline-filled muscles fought for their lives.

He and the team of stallions eventually escaped the reach of the dreaded exploding inferno, continuing as fast as they could. Gushing tears flowed as he mourned losing the love of his life and his children. His parents and siblings would never be part of his life again. His entire culture may have been wiped out, but he had a mission as the city messenger, to reach the closest settlement and warn them of the coming horrors. It would be only a matter of days before the volcano chain would destroy the surrounding areas too. When part of the range blew, the others would follow—the underground magma rivers flowed without bounds.

He rode along the open beach, then abruptly turned off to a cleared road. The ghostly horses felt the emotional pain of their master and pushed every ounce of energy into each lunge toward the unknown destination. As he arrived in the center of the town, his horses collapsed and he darted up the stairs of the warning tower to light an emergency signal. *Please be awake, please be awake.* He pleaded in his mind as he imagined a young, sleeping soldier accustomed to years of endlessly peering into uneventful darkness.

"Come on man, come on!" he shouted into the pitch-black night, clearly aware that his voice would never carry that far.

Five seconds passed that seemed like years, and then another flaming watchtower burned in the distance, and one after the next in perfect rhythm. Each blaze calmed his pulse and relieved his anxiety. A woman and a group of servants arrived at the base of the tower and greeted him with water and supplies.

After he bounced down the stairs and collapsed on the ground, one of the women grabbed the scroll from his rucksack and read the guidance: "Our civilization has been destroyed by the volcanoes. You are next. Run!"

Two women poured water into his mouth, then lifted him by the arms and threw him into a carriage, which soon became filled with anything of value that they owned. Although it was becoming dark at this time, the people knew they had only a matter of hours before their homes and livelihoods would be destroyed, and if they were not careful they would share the same destiny.

The entire city packed up what they could and started off in droves. They rode into the distance, away from the rich volcanic lands that they and their ancestors had worked. Moans and crying announced the fast-moving caravan to the sleeping wilderness as they traveled in hopes of saving whatever possible.

Six hours into the journey, one of the children pointed back and shouted, "Stop! Look!"

As they turned around and noticed the land sloping up, the night transformed from pitch-black to early-morning dark gray. What appeared to be a tiny, glowing ember grew, and they knew their homes, shops, and fields were but a memory.

As they watched, it seemed like a dream. Their bodies ached from the rigorous demands of the trip, and sleep deprivation fogged their perception. It took a few minutes for reality to set in—that Mother Nature had demolished their worlds and anything that defined their culture. They numbly returned, one by one, and continued the brisk journey to safety, away from the chain of volcanoes that would soon erupt.

The moving story slowly looked farther and farther away, as if T. O. Jeffers were being launched into the sky. Vast oceans morphed into soft, bluish-green lights that flashed on the underside of fluttering leaves, and she made a conscious decision to return, in her mind, to the location in the rainforest. The first-aid box had used lasers to zap splinters and dirt, while a tiny vacuum removed any foreign remnants from the large gash. Generally, after an initial evaluation, the dopridam used lasers to scan and remove foreign remnants. Then it focused on stopping any bleeding and disinfecting wounds. It could even repair muscles. In about three hours, huge gashes could be mostly back to normal, and the rest would be left for the body to heal.

"How much time do I have left?" Jeffers whispered, trying to push up on her elbows and lift her torso from the ground.

"Woah, woah big soldier, give it some time. Just relax and stay still. The more you move around, the longer the dopridam will take. Commander Barbour, can you grab a pillow from one of the fydons?" P. G. Churchill's voice had a supportive tone as he crouched on his knees next to her. "You've been following the visions for about an hour. So you just have a few hours left here, and then you're good to go."

Hilton said, "Yeah, you're doing great. Just a little time and you're good as new. Don't let this ruin your day. You are still at one of the most beautiful places on earth, and we will have an amazing dinner tonight."

He delivered one of his famous drinks to her. A mixture of fresh, brightly colored fruits and sweet snacks poured over the rim on a curved skewer. Jaway returned with a uniquely shaped pillow that allowed Jeffers to sit up and place her arms on the sides, like a queen on the throne. This way she could stay still while relishing a drink and interacting with everyone else.

"I thought I would never get out of that trance. It's true that the tikompay not only takes away the pain but creates visions. I'm still wondering what it means. Do we know anyone good at interpreting them?" Jeffers unintentionally interrupted herself, indicating her next question was more important. "Does anyone have an elitser I can borrow? I want to write it all down so I don't forget!"

She squinted as she tried to keep all of the information fresh in her mind.

A. P. Krizzles, who had never left the area, quickly jumped up. "How about I do you one better? I'll run and grab yours from the fydon."

She gave Jeffers a wink and an elbow nudge into the air, so as not to disturb the dopridam, before rushing up to the vehicle.

"You're the best!" Jeffers's voice was back to full strength.

The dopridam then assessed the blood loss and the amount of repair the body would have to complete on its own. It produced recommended percentages of proteins, carbs, and fats to eat for the following day. An image popped up from the device, and C. E. Didier stopped by to read it and enter the information into a contraption for later.

"I got you, Jeffers. We'll work out the correct percentage of nutrients and vitamins for your meal tonight, but don't be afraid. I'm one hundred percent certain it will taste amazing, too." Didier knew the available inventory off the top of her head.

"Churchill, we'll have to check and see why the hunting pit wasn't picked up," Jaway said. "Maybe we didn't even think to check over there, or perhaps there was a problem with our equipment."

He was resolved to prevent similar crises in the future. They were the best of the best, and always accustomed to self-evaluation in order to improve.

"Can you explain what really happened?" Jeffers asked. "I'm still a bit fuzzy."

"Yeah, you were on the rope and went back to where the vine hit the path, but when you hit ground you must have crashed through an ancient, overgrown hunting hole. Thankfully, the spikes on the floor of the dugout weren't still upright. It could have happened to any of us." Jaway sat next to her and picked fruit off of one of I. P. Hilton's vitamin-rich kebab concoctions.

"I kind of remember everything just going dark. Well, at least we still have some time to enjoy the afternoon!" T. O. Jeffers was tough, and wanted to take advantage of the gorgeous surroundings with close friends.

"I agree. What matters is that you're safe and recovering. You still have the rest of the day to relax and recuperate. If you're interested, while you wait you can attempt to decipher the vision and what it means for your life," Jaway said. Many people believed these visions could serve as life guidance.

"I wouldn't even know where to start with that. Maybe we can ask around later to see who is gifted with interpreting," Jeffers whispered, then lay back on a temporary, yet comfortable, bed constructed next to the water.

She closed her eyes in an effort to encourage her body to heal. Now that she was relaxed and on the mend, the others posted warning markings above the ancient trap. It was time to continue the well-deserved incentive.

"I'm just glad you're okay, Jeffers. You gave me the biggest scare. It was like you were vaporized," Hilton said.

"Thanks, buddy. It's good to know that I'm surrounded by people who support me and always have my back. You know that I'm always there for you, too." Jeffers's eyes were closed now, and she focused on resting so her wound could heal.

Jaway sent a request to Central Command with an injury report through his elitser. Central Command approved more black orchid elixir for Jeffers in order to heal any trauma from the experience.

"Looks like we just got cleared for a small dose of black orchid elixir, T. O. Jeffers. Do you want to take it now or later?" Jaway looked into the distance and entered information through his kleck.

"Now is fine! We have many hours before nightfall."

Nearly every soldier loved hearing the news that they had been cleared for a dose of elixir. Although it was not addictive, it was a special feeling, promoting emotional healing so they could continue living free from the trauma that could negatively affect all aspects of life.

Everyone at the camp continued an afternoon of renewal near the water with Jeffers, after a long day of physical activity and unexpected, high-intensity, real-world emergency training.

CHAPTER ELEVEN

After lunch at the campfire, the crew members who were feeling the most adventurous headed back to the fydons to prepare for a surprise excursion through the rainforest.

"Don't forget your lensicator, Price. You'll never forgive yourself." Pama winked.

"Thanks for the reminder, my loyal fydonmate. You know I wouldn't trade you from our fydon if I was offered the world. You're a beast. Quite elegant, but still a beast!" He sifted through his possessions and got ready to lead the crew members on a predetermined path through the rainforest.

The word "beast" in this case meant that she was bold and fearless in the face of danger. It was a huge compliment, and meant to describe her character, while elegance was in reference to her beauty. Pama was as gorgeous as the other crew members, with long limbs and trained muscles. A short pixie haircut enhanced the angles of her face. Her pronounced forehead balanced out full lips and large eyes.

"Ah, I see. You were impressed by my laser machete and climbing skills? Well, I've got more where that came from!" Pama lifted a hot-pink machete from her backpack like she had earlier that day. It whizzed through the air at lightning speed, producing a buzzing sound.

The juxtaposition of her tough, rugged spirit with the hot-pink weapon reminded everyone that inside she was a tender and loving toddler. Each one had a case with a safety button that kept the blade covered. The user had to press the button, and then use their kleck to turn on the laser. Lieutenant Commander Pama showed incredible skill by pressing the safety button, turning on the laser with her kleck, and pulling it to her chest in an instant. Most crew members took at least three seconds longer.

After Crumpler came out of the bathroom, they all checked each other's backpacks and then headed outside of their fydon to meet the others.

"Did you guys realize that we are the only fydonmates to go on the excursion all together? We definitely are all searching for an adrenaline high today! Woo hoo!" Crumpler shouted as he exited last.

After he walked off of the final step and settled on the ground, the stairs slid back up to cover the door.

"That's bangin'! We must be the most adventurous team of all." Pama gave her fydonmates huge high-fives.

"Pama, do you mind being my right-hand woman on this trek today?" E. M. Price asked.

"You know I've gotchu, buddy!" She shouted, "Sir, yes sir!" as a joke.

They laughed together, amused by the fact that she was second in command of the entire crew, but choosing to follow orders from someone of significantly lower rank. Only Jaway outranked her among the soldiers in their glider.

Over the next few minutes the other four arrived and everyone sat in a circle, faced each other, and double-checked the safety gear. Even Kandova wasn't cracking jokes as usual; she knew their wellness was a priority. After the incident when everyone forgot their lensicators earlier that day, all of them had made sure to remember every piece of equipment that might remotely be needed.

"Alright, just double-check that you all have your wongers, lensicators, machetes, spike shoes, and climbing gear with ropes and clips," Price confirmed.

The excursion manager realized the importance of being equipped for their safety because they were about to embark on an adventure only fit for adrenaline junkies. They each indicated that they were completely prepared for the journey by making a fist and lifting a thumb.

"Alright, now that we are all prepared, remember that the main goal for today is that you have a good time. So take a minute every once in a while to enjoy the scenery, relish the fresh air, and most of all embrace the opportunity to participate in extreme activities. We have no clue what we might encounter along the rainforest floor, so when we are there, beware. Keep in mind that if you can make yourself invisible to the surroundings, you will be able to witness unique wildlife in its purest form."

Price wanted them to be surprised by what they would see, so he did not reveal detailed plans for the day.

"I'm not going to give away our activities, but I know you are all in the mood to test your limits, and I'm here to make that happen. That's even for you, Curtis. We are going on an uncharted course and won't be following the route you cleared for us, but I promise that you will thank me in the end. I have filled in Pama, so she will be helping me guide you through our rainforest adventure."

"Yeah I'm down for the trip of a lifetime, so if it is cleared with the powers that be, then I'm all in," Curtis said.

Price took out a device that created a map of the surrounding terrain, but he built a visual dam around it to block the view. He could see the beautiful teal waterfall where they'd set up base camp, the ancient pyramid from the morning training session, and everything else in the area.

"Keep your eyes peeled for any nature along the way. Remember, there are poisonous killers around every corner. Have a good time, but be aware of your surroundings."

They walked toward the edge of the trees. Price remembered that a few had grown up unfamiliar with the rainforest.

"Alright, activate your wongers to keep the mosquitoes and flies away."

They looked into the distance, in order to send an activation signal through their klecks. When everyone started looking around as usual, the excursion manager knew they were ready. Without saying a word, he put away his personal map and began walking to the edge of the clearing, where he pulled out his laser machete. His knife glowed bright green as he easily cut through the dense foliage to create a walking path. Price's long-sleeve shirt was ultra-thin, but it protected against even the sharpest thorns. After thirty minutes of hacking and hiking, the crew reached a part of the forest that was more open and didn't need to be removed. Price grabbed the safety case from his backpack, deactivated the laser, and slid the oversized knife into the thin, wide envelope until the safety button clicked.

"Now that it is less dense, we can walk strategically through the leaves, and we won't need to chop them down," he whispered.

He silently motioned with his hands and reminded them about thoughtful trekking etiquette as he walked forward. Then he gently released a branch to appear careless and hit Lieutenant Commander Pama behind him, who jokingly mimed injury and anger. The crew members held back laughs, remaining silent—they all knew the reward would be awe-inspiring.

In the thick forest, it was always important to hand branches to the next person, instead of releasing and snapping them. When the loud, violent cutting came to an end, the abrupt gentleness and peace ignited raging excitement inside the crew members. They knew creatures had been disrupted up to that point, but going forward, they would be able to become part of the natural world and one with the rainforest. As they walked through the forest quietly, each of them stepped carefully to avoid any cracking twigs or other sounds. They read hand movements from E. M. Price as he directed them around obstacles. Captain Serra and M. A. Sickles were committed wholeheartedly to the cause of silence, as they carefully passed branches to avoid whipping others.

At one point, the group of seven stopped unexpectedly, surrounded by regular brush. The miniature crew was confused—until this point, Price had explained transitions or mimed changes. In contrast, this time they just came to a stop, and nothing looked out of the ordinary. Echoes of bird calls wafted around them with intermittent whoops from unknown creatures. Sickles looked up into the canopy to see the beautiful foliage, untouched by human hands. She felt as though she were part of nature, like her everyday life did not matter. The animals operated under their own rules, and all of them simply survived off of the land.

What a dream world, she thought to herself. *I wish I could live like these birds, just waking up and eating easily accessible food, taking long naps, all while surrounded by family.*

She watched two birds that looked as though they were in love. They walked out of their carefully sorted nest inside a hollow knot in a tree with smooth, green-grey bark and tiny, bright green leaves. The birds had oversized orange beaks that jutted out from below their eyes with two small nostrils. The beaks curved down to pointy tips. Their heads were covered in bright-purple feathers, with vivid emerald fans that rose from the back of the neck and curled forward. From the breast down, the feathers smoothly switched to hot pink all the way to the ends of their ankles. Blue claws with long nails clenched the branch as the mated couple walked to the end of the tree to pick a perfectly ripe fruit. They processed the produce with their beaks, holding chunks with their free claw, while leaning on each other for balance. After the couple in love masterfully filled their bellies, they huddled next to each other with what seemed like smiles that radiated through the forest.

Although the team had only stopped for a few minutes, it was like an hour to M. A. Sickles, who relished in the moment, feeling one with nature. The breathtaking colors were like a feast for her eyes.

She thought to herself, *Oh, now I get it. We stopped for . . .*

As the medical attendant turned her head, she saw a spider the size of five large coconuts with huge fangs and ten eyes lunging toward her.

Then she saw a blinding pink beam of light as it split in two. Each half fell to the sides of her face, and she felt a tingle from her toes to her head as furry legs brushed each ear before falling to the ground. Without a sound, Lieutenant Commander Pama had unleashed her laser machete on the huge spider that wanted to enjoy Sickles for lunch. These were incredibly venomous creatures, and had strong muscles in their legs for clamping onto the victim while immediately eating the flesh with powerful fangs. If it had landed on M. A. Sickles, she would not have had a chance—wongers were of no help with monsters like this.

But for now, it would only be a story for camp after the adventure. Everyone remained silent, for their safety, and Price locked eyes with Sickles, who was noticeably shaken. He used hand signals to ask her if she was okay and wanted to continue. She shook her head from side to side, as if to say "Is this even real?", and then shook her head to indicate that she was comfortable moving forward.

At eighteen years old, her youth as well as her desire to be filled with adrenaline created the ability to recover quickly. The good news was that these spiders lived as loners, so there would not be more contenders. After confirmation that M. A. Sickles was not hurt and was ready to move on, Lieutenant Commander Pama turned the laser of her machete off with her kleck. She walked quietly toward the large arachnid and began gutting him. She cut off the fangs and their venom sacks, zapped them quickly with a hot-pink laser, and then threw them into the forest.

The eight muscly legs would be a tasty appetizer later on in the trek—one for each member and an extra for the hunter. Pama carefully removed any inedible parts and popped the heart out. It looked like a curved carrot. It was customary for the butcher to take a bite of the heart, and she did not like to shy away from a challenge; she knew she could hunt and live in the wilderness as well as anyone else. Pama placed the organ between her teeth, tore some of the flesh, and chewed quietly as she passed it around.

Normally, Sickles would have been disgusted by even the thought of these circumstances, but this creature had almost taken her life, and she was so angry that she also took a bite.

C. E. Crumpler motioned to save the rest and then pretended to use a frying pan. He pointed to his backpack, then closed his fingers to one point and placed them next to his mouth as he made a silent kiss to indicate it would be delicious. The culinary expert could cook it over an open fire when they stopped for a break later and include foraged ingredients if they found any along the way.

Pama nodded her head to indicate that she understood. She placed the heart inside the huge leaf that she folded to hold the legs and other morsels. This disgusting spider was a delicacy—people would pay up to five gold coins for one. It tasted like very tender chicken, and was thought to promote circulation and resistance to allergens.

Price took a moment to look at their location. Then he put away the map and they continued forward toward a surprise destination. The crew walked among the natural surroundings as spirits, maneuvering silently like smoke through open patches of air, ducking below branches and experiencing the smells and sights along the way. Fresh, dusty swathes of earthy scent tickled their noses from collections of rainforest mushrooms that exhaled fine particles and lured wildlife. They marched for twenty minutes past the fungi forest. Complete concentration was necessary to trek unnoticed through the vegetation.

All of a sudden, T. A. Curtis looked up from the mundanely passing branches and focusing on the fancy footwork needed to avoid loud cracks from stepping on twigs. She stopped with wide eyes and an open jaw, prompting the others to assess the surroundings. The terrain analyst's head slowly curved upward while she breathed in deeply and loudly, like the crashing of a wave on a beach. It was almost as if tens of thousands of blooming orchids jumped in the room and shouted "boo!" Some members were actually shocked with a sudden feeling of electricity down their spines, because their thoughts were so consumed with weaving in and out of the foliage.

The flowers flourished in trees well above the forest floor, reproducing exponentially with no apparent predators in sight. These orchids were bright yellow with black stripes, and the size of two coconuts. A large bowl on the bottom held tasty nectar, and petals curved around the sides and on top. Each of the surrounding petals hugged a furry white heart that adorned the center.

Pama motioned to look at a bat that was feasting on a bowl of the sweet juice while taking breaks to rub its head on the cozy, colorless core. Bats from nearby caves enjoyed luscious snacking and pollinated the plants. This contributed to the perfect conditions for the breathtaking natural feast for the eyes.

An unexpectedly heavy wind blew from above, and with it a sweet and deep new fragrance surrounded the crew. Each of their brains was immediately massaged, and their bodies relaxed, investigating the unique and robust floral scent. The mysterious smell made them forget about everything else in the world. Nothing mattered but being in that moment. Price waved his hand in a circle to gather the adventurers' attention. When all eyes were on him, he motioned toward a blossom that was straight above. The excursion manager lifted his nose up by the tip with one finger to impersonate a bat. He acted out the flying bats who visited the nectar cups and contributed to the orchid offspring. Many members nodded to indicate that they understood what he was miming.

With arms toward the sky, Price pointed two fingers on each hand and curved his arms forward to indicate the direction of their continued journey. He began carefully walking again, and everyone followed. As they continued, they were accosted by constantly changing visual masterpieces. A bird-filled tree appeared as a purple octopus with moving tentacles. The crew paced for ten minutes through a new species of trees covered in neon-orange bugs that fed on the sap and covered the bark entirely. The wongers prevented the sticky little critters from getting any ideas of pestering the crew. If any crew member had forgotten theirs, they would have been covered in gooey sap and tangerine-colored regret.

Just after that brilliant show, the crew members heard flaps above the canopy and witnessed thousands of bats flying in the direction of the orchid encampment. E. M. Price mimed that this meant the caves would be nearby. A few minutes later, they arrived at an extreme change of scenery. The dense, high canopy became a rocky landscape that rose quickly into a tiny mountain made of granite.

When they exited the lush greenery, the members felt a sense of freedom to move in the openness. Price consulted a device that revealed pathways through or over the gigantic formation. He motioned that the crew could either go through the veins that weaved inside the caves, or scale the side and climb over. In order to save time and enjoy a cavernous adventure, the members settled on the more dangerous trip. They walked along the outside border of the crag until they turned a corner. Then everyone froze, a few out of fear.

They stood before an intricate web of naturally created, open rooms on the side of the mountain, where hundreds of different jaguar families lived. The metallic sun shone directly inside the rooms, mimicking the countless golden eyes and patterns mixed with black and white. They were kings and queens relaxing on the balconies of exquisite apartments. A background of orangish-white gradient covered the inhabitants' coats. Some areas contained small, split, black spots while other spaces contained conglomerations of black splotches that outlined haphazard circles. These amoebic shapes were filled with a darker orange color and smaller, randomly placed blobs.

Kandova's face lit up—she considered herself a jaguar when joking around and had admired the creatures for years. Most of the large cats enjoyed this time of day by lying in the sun on their bellies with their heads up, their paws turned toward their chests, and their hind legs resting on either side of their bodies. Tails slowly flopped from side to side as the only visible movements. A few turned their heads from the direct sunlight to open their eyes and look at the strange humans. The beasts had no reason to stop their daily ritual; the people clearly presented neither danger nor benefit to the cats. Thankfully, these vegetarian jaguars posed no threat to the humans either as the crew members passed directly in front of the commune.

Price stopped the group in the sunlight and explained through actions that the cats survived on a diet of special large mushrooms that grew heartily under the nearby canopy. The bright-purple fungal ground covering could be seen from where they stood. When up to half of a mushroom was damaged or removed, it could be regrown within two days. The cats were careful to only eat half or less for this reason. Because of the freedom gained from an abundant, renewable food source, and reliable shelter from the elements, the felines focused on family life, cleaning each other and napping in the sun. The mushrooms induced deep relaxation, and the area was exclusively filled with positive and calm actions.

The cats liked the open air in each room and never used the bathroom inside the dwelling units or near their secret stash of limitless cuisine. They strategically dug deep holes near trees in the forest, nourishing the vast rainforest soil as a result. Their homes remained clean, and the open rooms lined the entire side of the structure that reached straight toward the sky. The cats collected grasses and leaves for soft bedding in the homes. The sheer number of inhabitants enamored each trekker.

Price mimed that despite the huge population of cats, there were hundreds of empty rooms above the already-occupied lairs. They looked above the countless cats and noticed the housing waiting for future occupants. Kandova jokingly mimed that she would be moving into one of the apartments after the trek.

CHAPTER TWELVE

E. M. Price led the others past the last feline abode to the entrance of a dark cave. They stepped inside and heard a huge drop of water echo loudly throughout the area. Pama activated her shirt flashlights, and the others followed. A few stray bats whizzed by the bouncing beams of light, each attempting to remain upright on the slippery surface. A small, stone-lined path led to the edge of an underground river. They looked around at each other and saw stunned faces, all feeling out of place in the strange environment.

Then Price took out a bunch of wax candles, one for each member. These were necessary because they constantly revealed oxygen levels and would immediately extinguish with a sudden drop. The fire also provided a more authentic experience than the technological alternatives, as well as a challenge. They each lit a candle, one by one down the row. The excursion manager took off his backpack, stripped down to his swimsuit and shoes, and placed his clothes in the rucksack. He sealed it closed with his kleck, connected it to his swimsuit with a small rope, and threw it in the water. It bobbed from side to side, keeping the contents bone-dry.

The other crew members immediately stripped down to their swimsuits, keeping their shoes on, and attached the airtight containers by rope. Each member felt the shockingly cool liquid attack every part of their bodies while they descended into the dark and murky challenge. The hot, humid rainforest was just a memory as they paddled with one hand and held the lit candle above the water with the other. Nobody could touch the bottom, and the current began to accelerate.

Price screamed, "You each need to catch the left corner of the next bend!" His breaking the silence indicated the gravity of the situation. "It's coming up here!" he shouted as the rapids pushed them violently down the river.

They each paddled to keep their heads in the air. Price was the first to swim to the left side. He pushed his candle into a crevice, where it lit a tunnel behind him. Then he grabbed the ledge and pulled himself onto mostly dry rock, immediately turning around and getting on his knees. Grabbing Lieutenant Commander Pama's arm, he pulled her up. She turned around, crouched down, and grabbed T. A. Curtis. Then she shoved the candle in between two boulders.

Curtis locked arms with C. E. Crumpler and M. O. Kandova, whose candles had gone out long before. They all got out of the water and untied their bags quietly while Pama and Price waited for two more crew members. M. A. Sickles and Captain Serra remained far back, as they had found ancient drawings on the walls and were trying to decipher what they might've meant to the people who made them long ago. They had just set off with a half breaststroke when a surge pushed them quickly down the river.

The medical attendant's candle went out, so she grabbed Serra's hand as they approached their colleagues, who were drying off and waiting for them. They locked eyes with Pama and Price, reaching out unsuccessfully as the two flew past, just out of reach.

"Ride your bags!" the excursion manager shouted to the pair as they flushed into the darkness and the unknown.

Pama asked, "Should we jump in and follow them?"

Price motioned to stay where they were.

"The current is too powerful right now. It would only put us in danger too. We'll have to hope for the best."

They gathered their items, relit the candles, and forged forward with worried eyes—they knew a broken team could be a recipe for disaster. While walking, Price noticed that the roaring echo faded more and more with each step. When they were finally in complete and awkward silence, Price opened his airtight bag and grabbed his elitser. He used his kleck to send emergency messages to the lost members of their group. At that point, he could only hope that they would reconnect in person soon.

He threw the elitser back into his bag and walked into a vein that created a domed hallway through the center of the structure. The black walls were smooth and wet with a microscopic layer of mist. As they trudged along, the crew lit the spooky walls with their candles. Price slowed down and raised his hand to point out more ancient human drawings on the ceiling of the pathway. They all welcomed the distraction and could not help but be enamored by the untouched markings from a forgotten past.

In the blink of an eye, E. M. Price fell forward, and Pama reached out as a reflex. She managed to grab his swimsuit and yank him back toward the group. He stumbled back into Pama and Kandova, who were next in the line, creating a chain of collisions. The crew had been distracted and did not realize that the floor of the path had ended; they were sitting on a ledge that led to only darkness. Price managed to keep hold of his candle, and he relit it as they stood up.

He took a deep breath, choosing to once more ignore the pact of silence. "You don't even know how thankful I am for you guys. You always have my back!"

Pama said, "We are a team, and we are always there for each other."

M. O. Kandova could not resist the opportunity to joke around. With wide eyes, a raised brow, and mischievous frown, she slowly turned her head until it landed on the lieutenant commander. The continued smirk on her face indicated she was being completely facetious to lighten the dark, adrenaline-filled mood.

She crossed her arms, lifted her chin and said, "I see what you're doing here, Pama—just looking for any excuse to nearly rip off a man's swimsuit, and simultaneously save his life from certain doom!"

"Yes, Kandova, you have foiled my plan to seduce all men around me by saving them from peril while executing my deepest desires!" Pama shared in the humor.

They all laughed hard, then took a minute to gather their composure after the much-needed break. Kandova had a way of delivery that allowed her to successfully explore heavy or borderline inappropriate topics in a joke. Usually her listeners felt freedom to welcome the humor no matter the subject or circumstance.

When Price was saved, he heard a stone fall into water, so he knew it was below, but did not know how far. Now that they had recovered, he began to refrain from speaking again, and motioned for everyone to be silent and listen carefully.

Looking around, he found a rock. He threw it and waited to hear the drop. Price could tell that it was a significant distance, but it could be manageable. He threw another stone out into the darkness, and it bounced several times, revealing that there was a flat surface and possible path on the other end. He used hand signals to explain to the other four that they would have to jump into the water, but kick their legs and use their free arm to stay afloat. If nobody had fire at the end, they would be unable to see without breaking the challenge and resorting to technology.

He boldly sat on the ledge, which almost consumed him, and imagined a lake below. Moving forward, the excursion manager slid his body over the side while holding himself up with just one hand above his head. He took a second to hang on before he dropped and slid down the wall until he reached the water.

Price kicked his feet together and cupped his free hand to push his body up. His bag flopped next to him in the water while he successfully managed his candle, keeping it lit. He swam to the center, fighting only a slight current, and placed the light in front, so he could see the floor that his rock had revealed earlier.

The others watched in awe as he boldly progressed, convincing themselves that they could do the same. E. M. Price reached the edge and lifted his swimming arm up to the new layer. He kicked his legs and pushed his body up with his left hand to stand on his feet, while his right fingers held the candle and lit an entrance to another tunnel.

The spelunkers roared inside with admiration and encouragement, waving fists and sending smiles to their successful comrade. Price looked up to them after pulling up his bag, smiled back, and waved for them to follow, as if it had been an easy feat.

Lieutenant Commander Pama was next, already on her way into the water. She tried to prevent complete submersion, but her candle went out. Thankfully, Price met her with a strong grip and lit her candle once he pulled her out of the water. They both grabbed her bag and prepared to help the next three.

Once everyone was back onto the moist cave floor, they continued through the path. More unique artwork explained ancient living. Crumpler found a reenactment of tribal members jumping from a high ledge into water, and then swimming across to find a path to complete the journey through a cave. He was convinced that this was what they had just experienced, and accepted it as a good sign that they were close to an exit. They walked swiftly to find a way out so that they could start searching for their missing colleagues.

The domed path got smaller, then larger, and morphed into new shapes as they entered a room the size of a house. Light shone in from a high hole to roughly illuminate different sculptures that had been created over thousands of years. One column was milky pink and white, swirling in a perfect spiral from floor to ceiling. Stalactites reached down from above in varying pastel colors. The members admired stalagmites that created a garden of stone figures; one looked like a hat and another a perfect mushroom. After they squeezed through a vertical vent and walked ten minutes, they began to smell strong fresh air, and they knew that freedom was near.

After they turned the bend, a bright new light in the distance surprised the crew. When they arrived, they saw a long, lit strip near the ground and could hear rainforest creatures on the other side. They each crawled on their stomachs and inched toward the exit.

One by one, they emerged victorious over the challenging cavernous terrain. They walked out to an open sunny area. Their cooled bodies soaked up the warmth as they fell to the ground to recuperate and regroup. A tiny brook of crystal-clear water bounced between rocks and provided an opportunity for the team to clean muddy dirt that had accumulated while they navigated through nearly impassable spaces.

Sitting with crossed legs, Price grabbed his elitser out of the bag and connected with his kleck. His worried expression did not change—the original message had never been retrieved, and he had not received a response.

"I just hope they made it out safely," he mused. "The current was really rough."

A large flock of miniature chartreuse parrots were shocked by his voice, and they fluttered from four large trees into the sky. They began floating like oil and water, swaying as a huge, bright, singular yellow unit against the dark-blue sky.

"Since nature has already been alerted that we are here, do you guys mind if we talk?" Curtis cared little about the challenge to remain silent.

By this time, the fractured crew was only concerned about their lost friends. Shrugging shoulders and unconcerned eyes gave them the go-ahead.

"I should have thrown my bag in to see if we could have stopped them." Price's eyes looked lifeless.

Pama said, "You did your best. There is no sense beating yourself up about it. They are trained for survival. Try to shake that off and believe that everything will work out fine."

"Yeah, you're right. I'm just thinking of the worst-case scenarios right now." E. M. Price took a deep breath. "Let's take a break and have a snack here to give them some time. I'll send our location."

They each took food out of their bags and sat in a circle in the sun, drying and warming their bodies from the chilly caves. The excursion manager quickly removed his elitser again, and began inputting information via his kleck. They sat quietly but on edge, trying to imagine the best possible outcome.

"Well, this was the most amazing trek I've ever taken, Price," said T. A. Curtis. "Thanks so much for putting this together. I grew up in Pragadol in the Mountain Region, and I have seen about a hundred new things today. And that cave was spectacular. We could never do that on the west coast because there is always a chance the mountain would get angry and fill with lava."

This was meaningful coming from her, as she had more of an analytical personality.

"I'm glad you enjoyed yourself today." Price's face grew less anxious, and then excited and relieved a moment later when he finally received some messages.

"Yes! They got out fine and are heading to us now!" he shouted. He pounded a fist to the sky, then breathed out loudly. "You don't even know. I was so worried that something would have happened to them, and I'm in charge of the trek. I would never have been able to forgive myself."

Pama gave him a heavy pat on the back. "And you are doing a fantastic job, and that is why they are fine. They probably had all of the items they needed because of our reminder!"

In fifteen minutes, M. A. Sickles and Captain Serra could be seen walking in the direction of the group, who were still reheating from the chilly cave journey. Crumpler jumped up and started waving his hands back and forth. The others ran over to greet the new pair, who appeared winded.

"The river spit us out halfway back to base camp! So we mostly ran. Thankfully, our bags helped us float above the rapids, and we linked arms until we saw daylight. We were only in the dark for a bit; the sun peeked through different openings along the river," Sickles said.

"It was still insane though," the captain added. "The open cave became a long, narrow tube, and the water rose almost to the top, so we had to lie on our backs. When we got out, there was a mangrove forest along the river, so we swam to the edge and grabbed the roots to get out of the strong current."

Price brought his bag over, which contained a first aid kit.

"I'm so relieved that you are both back. How are you both feeling? Do you have any injuries?"

"We managed to float on our backs to avoid dangerous debris or anything else in the water. Our bags were lifesavers. I feel great and have no injuries. What about you, Serra?" M. A. Sickles accessed information she'd learned during her intensive medical training.

"Yeah, me too. Physically, I'm great. Just some bumps and bruises. I was worried about you guys. Sorry that we got derailed from the group. We were wrapped up in the cave art, and then the river surged and swept us away unexpectedly."

"No problem. Believe me when I tell you that we are incredibly happy that you are safe and sound!" E. M. Price said. "But the real question is . . . are you ready for more?" He grinned.

Curtis turned slowly to him. "Are you serious? That was already amazing enough! You have *more* planned?"

"Yeah, if you guys still want to go. We have enough time to get there and hike back to base camp before sundown. There are a few things to see, but it may take a lot of energy." The excursion manager had a mischievous look in his eyes, still keeping his full plan a secret.

After the entire group approved of the extended journey, Price encouraged the two rejoined members to refuel with nutritious snacks. After drying off in the sun, hydrating, and eating a few tasty morsels, they dressed for the hike and organized their backpacks. Price sat with his private map again for a few minutes, planning out the trek.

"Alright, off we go, ladies and gentlemen!" he whispered, motioning in a circle above his head to indicate that they would return to muteness, leaving nature undisturbed.

They knew that when they left in the glider, their technology would repair all of the chopped brush with one simple zap. Every one of the adrenaline seekers wanted to see the animals in their natural state, and did not want to disturb the behavior of any other creatures.

They walked one by one into the rainforest along a path that had been created by local trongoles—deer-like animals that were taller than most people. The caravan was soon surrounded by lush green foliage and a high, robust canopy. They passed through a patch of the same edible mushrooms that were popular with the felines. The fungi had taken over a small area where no plants grew. The large, bright-purple, round masses looked like loaves of bread covering the surrounding ground. Kandova pointed in the opposite direction of where they had been looking.

Within the sea of purple, a mother and fawn trongole stood, carefully eating portions of each luscious fungi. Their vivid, majestic, vertical-green-striped bodies contrasted with the purple, erasing any useful camouflage. Together, they looked up with glowing emerald eyes at the silent humans, but after the mother began feasting, the fawn continued without care. Typical herds remained small, usually consisting of two families, as the dense brush of the rainforest restricted movements of larger groups. More were sure to be nearby, however—there would usually be two additional grown males, another female partner, and any offspring. Thankfully, their small furry horns posed no threat. These allowed the lean beasts to navigate thick brush without becoming entangled.

The bright-green stripes on black fur allowed them to blend in with surrounding rainforest foliage. If they stood still, they could not be seen among the huge leaves and shadows in a typical rainforest setting. From the knee down, trongoles were all black, so their feet disappeared under the shade near the rainforest floor.

The mother flicked her tail to the side three times and pointed her ears the same way, which communicated to the offspring that they would move in that direction. They stepped forward and began meticulously dining on more half-loaves of the bright purple mushrooms. The mother's long, black tongue wrapped around the fungi before she chomped down on the high-protein entree, careful to leave enough left so they could grow back.

Price got the attention of the crew. He mimed that the pointy ears indicated different states or instructions, like agitation or what they just witnessed—the direction they wanted to walk. He created a story with his arms and mouthed that the trongoles were known to dip their long, slender, black tongues into large orchid containers of nectar.

The mother yelped loud and deep, calling the other members of their herd. These large creatures commonly wanted attention from each other; they were incredibly social. A distant return call from a much deeper voice indicated that her partner would be arriving soon, an invitation for the crew to move on. Thankfully, the trongoles ate most of the thick plants and created a clear path that the crew could easily follow through the rainforest.

CHAPTER THIRTEEN

After a long, focused journey on the path, a wide opening through the green tunnel revealed a sunlit patch. As the crew stepped from rock to rock, they passed through to a new universe without a canopy. A towering mountain looked almost within reach, but was still far away.

M. O. Kandova stopped and looked up. She almost lost her balance as she observed the massive natural structure. It was as if a crystal had formed in the middle of the rainforest. Huge, gray, granite rectangles seemed to be huddled together, shoulder to shoulder, to create the gigantic mass with a level top.

"We can speak now. And that, my friends, is your real challenge for the day!" Price lifted a hand in the direction of the organic monument. "Take a moment to absorb the setting. I kept it a secret so you could gain your own personal perspective and not look at it through my point of view." He looked up toward the sky, feeling the enormous sense of majesty.

Flocks of birds appeared to be flying in slow motion near the top, painting sluggish circles and waves in a heavenly sand garden.

"I wonder if birds delivered the seeds that created the lush vegetation up there," Pama said.

As they moved forward, the other side of the mountain emerged slowly until a glorious waterfall was revealed. A river poured over the edge, the shaft of water stretching halfway to the rainforest floor. Then it flowed like rainbow silk in the wind before dispersing as a dewy, sparkling mist across the surrounding treetops. M. A. Sickles stopped, frozen at the sight of the waterfall.

"I've never seen anything more beautiful in my entire life," she said, admiring the multicolored, glittering lightshow.

After the group saw the mountain from that angle, they entered another patch of trees and followed the trongoles' trail. As they proceeded with excitement, they imagined scaling the formation, which rose from the ground at ninety degrees. The thick canopy once again covered most of the view to the towering structure.

The ground eventually changed, now covered in small pebbles, and then a huge granite wall appeared as the crew exited the edge of the rainforest, where different plants reached out to the sun in a tall green partition. As they left the forest one by one, each crew member found a space and looked up at the wall.

"It feels like I'm going to fall over when I look straight up! Every time I start a climb, it feels the same," Captain Serra said.

The others nodded their heads in agreement. Their jaws dropped; they felt like tiny ants looking up at the imposing natural phenomenon.

Price pointed out different features of the granite and the structure itself. Then he said, "Alright, let's get prepared for the climb of your lives. Time to make your dreams come true!"

They all sat and removed their backpacks to change into climbing gear. Price removed many items. He walked over to the stone wall, which soared straight up toward the sky, and pressed a device called a smidalia onto the smooth, sparkly surface. The black, three-dimensional, diamond-shaped tool marked out a climbing path for the team by shooting out a glowing green line. The laser beam shone all the way to the top of the structure.

Next, the excursion manager opened a bag of hooks, called hildents. Each oval device shone like silver with a blue tinge. One end was able to pop open when operated by a kleck. The other end had a suction cup that could secure the hook to any hard surface. Price threaded a light rope that resembled thin yarn through a few of them. He used his kleck to secure the first hildent onto the granite while he held it with his hand.

As the crew prepared for the climb, Lieutenant Commander Pama walked around and double-checked each climber, reminding them of climbing protocol. Price placed the second hildent, suction-cup-side first, on the cool gray rock. It traveled up the wall along the green beam and fastened itself while constricting around the twine so that it could no longer slide through. He pulled the string with all of his might, and nothing budged.

It was incredibly strong, spun from a Tabot spiderweb. Yet it remained incredibly thin and lightweight, ideal for carrying on long treks. The excursion manager pushed the round end of another hildent onto the rope that was hanging down, and it opened and closed around former spiderweb. He pressed the cup side onto the wall and it traveled up, even farther this time. It stopped and then squeezed the yarn just like before. This time, Price grabbed the rope and took a running leap toward the granite as he kicked off of the wall and swung around in a circle, landing on his feet.

"Well, it's great to see that everything is in working order and holding securely! It feels like Harvestium morning when I was a kid," he said.

Price repeated the process until it reached the top to create a safe foundation for the ascent.

He chose a simple configuration since the crew had already been incredibly physical that day. Each hildent spit out miniature ledges along the route that could be used to step on or pull up. On a different day, he would have chosen a more difficult level, placing the ledges much farther apart. Some even would have required a jump through the air.

While Price secured the path, each crew member stepped through the leg holes of shorts and pulled them up, then tugged their conjoined short-sleeve shirts to rest on their backs before placing their arms through the sleeves. Once they had their jurprodians on, they used their klecks to secure them closed on the front. The cuffs of the shorts-and-shirt combo tightened around the body of each crew member, and a series of oval metal loops popped out around the waist.

Lieutenant Commander Pama was the first to get outfitted, complete with her backpack, so she walked around and grabbed each climber by the shoulders and pulled each jurprodian up and down with all of her might to check that the suits were secure.

Jurprodians were the end result of continued studies using different natural substances; their fabric also came from the web of the Tabot spider. It was lightweight and impenetrable against fast-moving objects, and could easily be unfolded or stretched to a new form through the use of a kleck.

"Now you do me," Pama playfully demanded after her final safety test on her fydonmate, C. E. Crumpler.

"I got you, my good friend." He began tugging on her clothes.

"Looks like it's all secure!" Crumpler was excited for the climb; it was so close he could taste the adrenaline, rock dust, and sweat.

By this time, they had begun speaking freely, and they continued without care.

"Alright," said Price, "thanks, Pama, for your help with checking while I was setting up the path. Everyone, you can now click your safety ropes on your side loops, and we should be all set."

All seven members connected a leg-length string to each side of their waist. The strings had metal loops that opened and closed on each end. One side was connected to the climber, and the other would click around the rope that was fixed to the rock wall. Each adventurer tested the fasteners on a sample cable, then put their backpacks on. Bridges of material sprung from the sides of the bags, connecting around their waists and chests.

"Alright, after our pack check we can begin our ascent. Remember that only one person can be between two hildents at a time. And make sure that at least one of your loops is always connected to the rope. Both rings should never be simultaneously disconnected at any point in the journey. Are we clear?" Price asked.

Thumbs rose from each crew member.

"Wonderful. Alright, well as you can feel, the wind just picked up a bit, but it looks like we should have clear, sunny weather all day. Just be careful to notice any changes as we climb."

The plan was for Price to go first, and Pama would bring up the rear. If anything happened along the way, they were the most experienced climbers and could problem-solve most scenarios.

The excursion manager connected both of the loops, from the ends of the ropes connected to his waist to the first section of tight cable, and began climbing. After following a snaking path, he reached the second hildent. Price disconnected just one ring from around the tight, vertical twine and carried it to the other side of the hildent. After this was secure, he disconnected the second loop and did the same until both were connected to the second portion of line between the second and third hildents.

When he began completing the second stretch, M. O. Kandova clipped in both of her loops and began the joyful and exhilarating climb that promised to deliver more than what she'd been expecting from the day.

When she reached the second hildent, she took a look at the ground and was filled with adrenaline. Her body focused on the job at hand, and she was energized.

Each member continued joining until each person was on their own stretch of cable between two hildents. The perfectly vertical wall provided views of everyone at all times.

Forty-five minutes later, Price reached the midpoint of the climb, and passed his location down the line until it reached the lieutenant commander at the end. Immediately after relaying the message, a huge gust of wind blew the waterfall up into the air. The water rode a current around and into a circular pattern before thrashing horizontally onto the climbers. They had experienced bold waves of wind, but this surprised everyone. Kandova suddenly felt ice-cold needles all over her entire body as she lifted a foot from one climbing hold to the next.

She breathed in quickly, filling her lungs to maximum capacity before taking in a mouthful of water that bounced off of the wall in front of her face. In an instant, her body went from constricting muscles for the climb and sweating to stay cool, to confusion and drastic shock, and then to a refreshing new normal. She coughed the liquid out, squinted, and used the backside of her hand to wipe each eye.

After taking a moment to gather her composure, she shouted to the others, "What do we do if we have to go? I swear I can't hold it!"

She gathered the fabric of her jurprodian and squeezed until a gush of water fell on C. E. Crumpler directly below, shielding it from those under him.

Before the culinary expert had a chance to reason, he immediately reacted and asked, "Aw, you couldn't have waited until we got to the top?" But when he realized it was just water, he started laughing loudly. "You got me! I am reminded of the wise, ancient climber who once said, 'Never trust a yellow waterfall.' Well, today was my lucky day, because it was clear!"

He had pranked her the day before, so this was part of playful revenge. Crumpler welcomed the obviously merciful joke—it came with a quick recovery, compared to more elaborate tricks.

"Now we're even!" Kandova yelled, and they laughed together.

"Alright, let's tackle this mountain!" he said.

Crumpler looked around at his dripping body and options for the next steps of the climb. All of the climbers were keen on finishing, to see what interesting surprise awaited at the top. They had mostly only been able to see lush trees and plants from the bottom, and wondered what else was up there. They continued at a swift pace—the sooner they arrived at the summit, the more time they could spend exploring or hanging out in this virtually untouched piece of wilderness. The crew carefully lifted their body weight with their arms and pushed through their legs, making them acutely aware of individual muscles.

Twenty minutes later, Sickles stopped to look around at the vast rainforest. She saw an endless ocean of green treetops. Closing her eyes, she breathed deeply to enjoy the moment in the fresh air.

"You know, this is really special that we are all out here. Very few people ever even get a chance to come to the middle of the rainforest, let alone scale a gigantic mountain!" said Serra, who was just below her, as he also stopped and took in the views. "Wow can you see the flock of birds over there?" He pointed with his free hand, grasped one of the ledges with the other, and carefully perched on two holds with his feet while leaning against the wall.

"I wonder what kind of birds those are. When they fly in circles, the color changes from bright pink to vibrant blue. I bet their top side is pink and their bottom side is like the ocean. It looks like some psychedelic moving art from here."

They watched as the distant kaleidoscope morphed into different shapes and colors as the flock of birds split into two huge masses.

"Yeah, that is so breathtaking!" M. A. Sickles pointed, in case the others didn't know where to look amid the never-ending options of continuous terrain.

Just as she regained focus for the climb, she carelessly stepped on the next ledge and slipped on pooled water. Her foot slid off, and the other leg was already in the air, so she swung against the wall like a swimmer flying through the air on a vine. Instead of plunging into a refreshing lake, her body smashed against the hard stone while one arm still held onto a ledge.

Adrenaline rushed throughout the medical attendant's body, and it felt as though time slowed down. Her gripped hand lost hold, and she looked around, trying to grab any of the ledges that passed her as she fell through the air. Thankfully, they had followed protocol, and Captain Serra was still on the stretch of rope between the two hildents below her.

Her body slipped down the wall for what seemed like hours, but the seconds were halted as the ropes attached to her waist hit the hildent below. She swung from side to side, and when she sailed by the next time, she grabbed the vertical cable that connected the hildents and stopped.

"I'm alright. I'm okay!" Sickles shouted.

All of the other members halted and stared with concern. Sickles was visibly upset, but the training that they'd received kicked in. Though many parts of her body throbbed in pain, she held back the desire to punch the wall with all of her might. Each soldier received climbing training, and they learned that falling could be part of the process—it might happen every so often due to factors beyond their control. They were encouraged to trust the safety gear and let it do its job. After falling a little, they would expect to reach the hildent, where they could scan for injuries, calm down, and then continue.

They also learned that personal lessons could be gained from a trip like this. In real life, true rewards resulted from taking risks, and it was important to pursue a fulfilling life, whatever that meant for each person. These crew members had chosen a specific experience, full of excitement and possible danger, simply by going on the trek. People could overcome fear in order to live dynamic and thrilling lives, just like the adventure rewarded each climber with confidence to tackle many more challenges. And if they fell, they had the power to ask for help or regain their strength and complete the task as originally imagined. All of these concepts twirled through M. A. Sickles's head as she restabilized her feet.

"Have you scanned yourself for injury, Sickles?" Price shouted from three sections above.

"Yeah, I just have a few scrapes, that's all."

"That is wonderful. How are you feeling? Ready to continue, or do you want a break?"

His voice seemed to travel along the wall directly into each climber before dispersing into the vast, open sky.

"Thanks for checking, Price. I'm good to keep going."

The medical attendant reached for the next ledge and pushed up on her leg as she began reclimbing the same section. Although she'd experienced a minor setback, Sickles tried to forget about the pain, and was still excited to reach the top. She was thankful for the fresh splash of water that continued to keep her cool on the rest of the voyage.

The entire group pressed to the top, where Price greeted each soldier with a smile and an open palm to lift them onto the flat surface. He had tied his waist with a long rope to one of the nearby palm trees, which seemed odd and out of place so far from the ground.

"Woah, this is crazy! It's like a special tiny world up here," Sickles yelled as she popped her head above the edge, the fourth person to arrive.

"Yeah, it's bizarre that there's a mini forest at this elevation. Kudos to you for persevering and quickly recovering from your fall. That is a true test of courage and determination." E. M. Price looked in her eyes, and they locked each of their hands together while he pulled her up.

"Thanks. I'm just really excited that you took us on this exploration today!"

Sickles grunted while also pulling her weight up. Once on the top, she disconnected both of the ropes that connected her safely to the vertical cable held in place by the hildents. The other members clapped and cheered for her. She only had scrapes on her arm and on the back of one of her hands. Once all the members made it to the top, they sat around to rest and stretched their muscles while Price gathered the hildents and rope from the side of the mountain.

CHAPTER FOURTEEN

Because she arrived second, M. O. Kandova had time to make a fire with dried coconut husks and deadwood, complete with a pargle on the top—a round disk placed above flames and held up by three thin, extendable poles. It converted the smoke into colorless gasses and camouflaged the warmth from heat-sensitive devices, so that the team's location could not be revealed.

Each hildent released the rope and then slid up to Price, who collected them in a bag. Finally, he held the line in one hand and wrapped it under his elbow and the same hand quickly until the entire rope became one ring. Then he released the bottom side and tightly wrapped the last strip around the center of the oval. He threw the bundle in his backpack before joining the others for a break by the campfire.

"Doesn't this seem like something on another planet? It's like this little unique land in the sky."

They all agreed, looking around at the palm trees and the edge that melted into the surrounding sky.

"I'll give you a tour after we have some time to relax," Price offered graciously.

The fire had been burning for a while, and coals glowed brightly on the bottom. Lieutenant Commander Pama had been climbing trees and collecting the ripest coconuts. She walked back with another collection of the tasty harvest, placing them with the others in a neat pile.

"Crumpler, do you mind checking those spider parts? They should be fine since we stored them in a cooling bag." Pama started opening the coconuts with excitement, and drilled two holes in each top.

"Yeah, no problem. I've made them a few times before in training school, so I can cook them too!" The culinary expert stood up and stretched.

He walked over to one of the backpacks and opened it, then removed a clear bag that revealed a green leaf. He placed it next to the fire, then gathered cooking utensils, including an expandable pot with a cover, tongs, a paper-thin cutting board, and freshly sharpened knives with guards on the blades.

"I totally forgot about these! I guess we had a lot on our minds," Crumpler joked as he downplayed the death-defying trek. He took out some hot peppers that he had picked along the walk. "These will go perfectly with my dried spices and herbs. My dad, who was also a cook, always used to say, 'Never leave home without spices and herbs. They may save your meal, or your life, but at least your hunger, they will curb.' He had some amazing stories!"

After double-checking that the large pot was correctly assembled, he placed it over the fire by clicking it into the grooves of one of the metal pargle stands. Then he poured the water from a few of the opened coconuts and removed the bright white flesh.

M. O. Kandova asked, "Anything I can help with?"

"Perfect timing. Yeah, can you cube this coconut flesh?" Crumpler accepted her help with delight.

While she chopped the coconut, he diced some spicy rainforest peppers, then placed them inside the pot, followed by seasoning. Kandova sat next to the preparation station to hang out with Crumpler. He told a story while he stirred the sizzling mixture and adjusted the fire. A few pieces of peppers popped loudly as a divine scent rose from the pot and he stirred the coconut milk around.

"My dad was captured when they were on vacation near Kritziddle, in the center of the rainforest. This was long ago, before parts of the Rainforest Region had integrated to The Land. Anyway, they were on a nature tour, and this would have been really mesmerizing for anyone from Inablay on the east coast. Everything in the rainforest was fascinating for people from my city. I'm sure you can relate, growing up on the beachy coast, also in the Highlands Region.

"Well, that day, the men went on a forest tour while the women stayed back in the hotel for spa treatments. A tiny tribe from the north got lost just outside of Kritziddle, in the south-central part of the region. Because all of the buildings were constructed to appear as though they were part of the surrounding trees, the tribe didn't even realize they were near a major city. So the men were hiking with a guide and the tribe members captured them and tied them up at their temporary camp, mostly out of fear. Thankfully, their guide could communicate with their captors. He told them that my dad was a professional cook and had some special flavorings that could enhance the food they were preparing.

"They released him and let him cook. They were enamored with the exotic flavors and my dad's personality. Their fear eroded, and they invited the entire group to drink and eat with them. They hung out the whole day, joking and eating, and my dad gave them some spices and herbs when they left. The guide was able to explain to them that a large city was nearby, and then he directed them back to the north. That is why he always encourages me to never leave home without them. Like the saying goes, you never know when some spices and herbs could save your life!"

He smiled and checked on the progress under the lid.

"Woah, that must have been an amazing experience. I'm going to start carrying spices with me everywhere I go, too!" Kandova laughed.

Crumpler chuckled along with her. "Alright, we are ready for the pièce de résistance!"

He opened the chilled, clear bag along the top and removed the green leaf that had covered the spider parts and legs. After rinsing everything with water, he diced the heart and other bits and placed them into the pot. Then he bent each leg's knee and tied them together with a string to make a large circle. Crumpler brushed them over the fire to burn off the leftover fuzz, rinsed them again, and then placed each of them inside the pot under the liquid. He covered the concoction with the large leaves, which were used as wraps and added an earthy flavor, and then put the lid on.

"Alright, we just need to lower the heat and wait about fifteen minutes, and it will be all ready."

Each climber felt a rumble inside as their mouths watered. M. A. Sickles brought tested drinking water in a large, expandable bucket.

"It looks like the water that bubbles up to the surface has been purified by going through tons of layers of rock and limestone. So there are lots of great minerals in there too."

They sat around in a circle on comfortable cushions near the fire. Each crew member drank the coconut water, then sliced the fruits open and began eating the flesh. The empty coconuts served as bowls for drinking the fresh mineral water.

Curtis raised her beverage and said, "Props to Crumpler for fixing us this delightful snack, and to Pama for protecting us with your lightning skills. Now we will feast like kings!"

Each member took a drink after C. E. Crumpler and Lieutenant Commander Pama gave a nod to reciprocate gratitude. The spider flesh was considered a delicacy, and would have been incredibly expensive if purchased as a meal in a city.

"I hope you guys love how it was prepared. I've only done it a few times in culinary training school, but I think I remembered everything."

Crumpler was humble, but also confident that it was accurate, because he memorized every culinary technique and recipe he studied.

Each climber had an expandable tray with legs in their backpack, and they set them all next to each other to create a dining table in the shade of some nearby palm trees. Captain Serra squinted his eyes to look at one of the trees that was just past the climbers and said, "Is that what I think it is?"

He remembered that they'd grabbed all of their equipment and took this opportunity to show that off. He reached for his lensicator and put it over his eyes like a pair of glasses.

"Well, I'll be! That is a tree with miniature lemons. Let's go pick some!"

The captain walked over with Curtis and Sickles, returning shortly with a bag full of small citrus fruits.

"These will go great with the spider legs—like a lemony, coconutty, spicy herb dish!" Crumpler said. He began rinsing the lemons and then cut them into halves. "We can squeeze these into our water or onto the spider!" He placed a few coconut halves, filled with the yellow fruit, onto the makeshift dining table.

Each person had a large plate that curved up at the sides to additionally hold liquid. These were part of the rucksack-packing protocol items, as were the inflatable cushions they used for seats.

"Alright, we are almost ready. Everyone come sit down."

Crumpler grabbed Pama's plate. He used tongs to place two of the longest legs on her platter, so large that their ends rested on the makeshift table. Then he ladled some of the coconut spicy stew for her.

When everyone else had some spider and chunky soup, he served himself. The limbs had transformed from brown to bright orange, and now had a glossy shine. The climbers dove into the savory snack with fervor, starting with the stew. It was completely silent except for the sound of bubbling water, birds, insects, and chewing. Thankfully, Lieutenant Commander Pama started disassembling the legs first, because most of the others had never eaten them. They watched her carefully as she began by pouring the broth from the open end of the legs onto her plate with the stew. It was a buttery color. Then she snapped them at each knee.

"This is the best part here." She broke the silence to show everyone the white meat that easily slid out of the lengthy exoskeleton with a fork. The hefty morsel was the size of a large carrot. She placed it in her rounded plate and squeezed lemon juice all over. After she sliced it, she filled a spoon and closed her eyes to enjoy.

"Mmm, now that is amazing!" she shared with squinted eyes before ravaging the rest.

Everyone ate and remained quiet for the next few minutes, relishing the delicacy.

Eventually, Kandova leaned back and patted her firm and fit belly with both hands. With a satisfied yet sarcastic look on her face, she said, "I do have to say that hit the spot, but did anyone else think it tasted like chicken?"

They broke out in laughter because it was true; one of the most expensive dishes available tasted like something common. They chatted for a few minutes then discussed the weather and the trip. Sickles talked about what it was like to slip and fall and how the training came in handy in the moment.

When Price got up, they all rose, started cleaning, and set everything in the sun to dry.

"Alright crew, take some time to let your food settle and do what you need to do. Let's plan on being all packed and ready to go in thirty minutes. And convert your jurprodians to the flight setting."

Each crew member continued to clean, pack, get ready, and banter. The sky around them had suddenly become saturated with very large, bright-orange-and-green birds with huge talons. Everyone stood still and silent, and looked up. The creatures glided in circles, nearly blocking the blue from the sky. It was apparent that this flock's original plan was to descend onto the top of the mountain, but they remained in flight due to the current occupants.

A coconut fell near the campsite—one of the birds had dropped it.

Many others still held them in their claws. Captain Serra realized that this could be dangerous for them, so he released his laser machete and created a light show, waving it through the air to scare the birds away.

As it became clear that they would not be making a pit stop, E. M. Price said, "Well I was going to save this for the tour, but this is the perfect moment. These birds first introduced the palm trees up here long ago. Over time, they developed huge talons in order to pick ripe coconuts. By dropping them from a higher elevation on the surface of the tower that we are on right now, they easily crack open and can be eaten. Naturally, some of the dropped coconuts never split open, and instead sprout to create the palm trees that we see today. The birds like cracking them up here because it is free from predators—infinitely safer than landing on the ground somewhere."

As he took a breath, the climbers all heard a huge plop just a stone's throw away. One of the huge birds was still above them.

"Uhhh, is that what I think it is?" Kandova asked in a disgusted tone.

"Yes, that conveniently is what I was going to discuss next. The bird droppings that cover this area help to decompose all of the other matter and create soil over time. That is why so many things can grow up here. They also transport seeds, like those of the miniature lemons that we found earlier," Price said.

"I appreciate this little ecosystem, but I'm incredibly thankful that it fell far away from us. That would have covered my entire body!" M. O. Kandova laughed and held her hands out in a large circle to mimic the size of the huge droppings.

"Yes, that could definitely ruin your day!" Price laughed as he took a set of andoofers out of his bag and put them on his face, like spectacles. "Who would have thought that these might come in handy for more than just rain up here!"

Pama chimed in, "You never know when any device may be useful, or keep you from having a very crappy day!"

They all laughed. She was joking but also using the situation, as the highest-ranking member on the trip, to remind them of the importance of bringing every piece of required equipment on any trek.

Soon the birds were nowhere in sight, so the crew all suited up and gathered under one of the palm trees for a tour of the upper area.

Price began explaining, "As you can see, it is quite rocky in many spaces up here—basically a huge stone. Over time, though, a lot of soil developed."

He began walking to show them around, and they followed.

"It would take about twenty minutes to walk around the outer edge. We're not going to do that today, but that's just to give you an idea of how large it is up here."

They passed patches of bizarre trees, unusual ground coverings, and rock.

"Look up into this tree. Some of you may need a lensicator, but you should be able to see a uniquely shaped nest. It is a round oval and comes to a tip on the sides, and the opening is on one side. That's the nest of a fairybird. They are light pink in color and have ornate plumage. We might be able to see one because a nest is here, so be on the lookout."

"Oh yeah, I can see it. That's really cool!" Serra said.

They walked to the center, where water gushed to the surface and then created a winding river that poured over the side.

"This is a natural spring that travels through the very center of the structure we are standing on now. As the tests proved earlier, nature has purified it; it runs through different rocks like hardened lava and limestone. It has lots of good minerals that are said to benefit the health, so if you want to get some, now is your chance."

All of the members cupped their hands and took large sips of water. Then they followed the deep, winding river to the edge and looked over.

"Wow, it's such a rush looking down from the top of the waterfall." Curtis poked her head out as far as she could safely lean.

After the brook poured over the side, it remained a steady stream halfway to the ground. There, it split up and drifted into a dew that looked like flowing silk, sparkling and sometimes revealing the full color spectrum in the light of the sun.

"Do you see the open area down there? That's where we're going to land!" Price said, pointing down.

The crew had had an idea that they would be jumping over when E. M. Price asked them to convert the jurprodians into the version used for flying. In this setting, the short sleeves folded down to cover the arms and the shorts converted into long pants.

"It makes sense, right?"

"Yes, we can save a lot of time by avoiding another climb, Price. Good plan," Captain Serra said.

"And it should be an amazing drop to the bottom." Pama was noticeably concentrating on something else in her mind.

"It looks like the wind has died down enough so that if we jump off anywhere along here and kick out as far as possible, we will be fine." Curtis looked at a device in her hand as she kneeled on one knee.

"Alright crew, there you have it," Price said. "We are cleared for flight. Follow all of the criteria checks we learned in training, and you should be safe. Take the leap whenever you are ready, and be sure to space out so we each have enough room.

The crew stood looking off into the distance while carefully connecting their klecks to different devices. Pama went around to each member and pulled their backpacks hard to make sure they were secure.

After the last check, her face brightened. "I'm outta here, cheeseheads!" She sprinted toward the edge and jumped up and away from the structure.

The lieutenant commander stretched her arms and legs out as far as they could go, then clicked her heels together and patted her arms to her sides. With these movements, the jurprodian formed a flap of fabric between the inside leg seams, and did the same to create wings between the sides of her abdomen and her arms.

She steered into a circle above the rainforest canopy to ride a current of wind that slowed her down. When she flew over the open area for landing, she used her kleck to engage a parachute that shot out of the backpack. She then directed it to gently descend onto an open piece of soft ground.

Pama arrived back to the earth at an angle and ran for about ten strides before stopping completely. The peering crew cheered from the top. Everyone was so overtaken by adrenaline and excitement that they had forgotten about staying silent, or just did not care.

"I did it!" Pama shouted.

Her arms pumped up and down in exhilaration and a feeling of accomplishment.

Serra said, "Now let me show you how it's done, my kind brethren and sistren!"

The playful terms indicated he was joking around. He walked calmly toward the origin of the waterfall to get a running start. Then he turned and held his stance for one second before sprinting toward the edge and jumping up into a flip, which catapulted him farther away from the stone wall. The fabric appeared between his arms and legs successfully, and he rode a wave of wind in a large circle. After repeating the loop, he returned back to the huge structure and steered directly under the waterfall, where the stream had become mist. After surfing another round, he engaged the parachute and steered down to the open, soft space for a safe landing.

By the time he arrived, Lieutenant Commander Pama had already folded her parachute and was watching from the tree line.

"Way to go, Serra—that was insane!" she shouted after he stopped completely.

He extended his thumb toward her with closed fingers and then waved both hands at the others to indicate that he was safe. He began pulling the chute toward himself, then walked next to Pama to fold it with his kleck, placing it into the backpack pocket.

Next, Crumpler made the dash with no fancy flips, taking a much less showy approach to his dive. After he rode a few currents of wind, he activated his parachute, but nothing happened. Thankfully, he caught another gust with fully spread arms and legs, and it pushed him back up. After he finished the last lap, he engaged the backup parachute. The others did not even know he'd had problems until they saw the smaller chute open. By then, he was too close to the ground, so he tried to pull up on the cords.

At the same time, a powerful gust of wind pushed him to the side. Crumpler swung around. His parachute automatically regulated and balanced as much as possible, but it could not prevent him from sailing directly through the heavy mist created by the waterfall. At this point, his only option was to try to land.

Slick from the moist encounter, he aimed toward the open patch and got on course. It appeared as though he had regained control, but just when he tried to land, another strong gale blew him up into the air, and he flung about like a rag doll as his backup parachute turned inside out. Just as Crumpler was about to crash directly into the ground, his chute blew into the trees that outlined the space, yanked him up, and became tangled inside strong branches.

Thankfully, his backpack held him as he swung back and forth by the cords. Pama and Serra ran over to find him unconscious.

"Crumpler! Are you okay? Are you okay?" Captain Serra shouted.

The lieutenant commander had placed her laser machete in ready mode, and was about to hack the entire tree down. With the machete flying through the air, she saw the culinary expert start moving out of the corner of her eye and instead pulled her arm up and toward her body to avoid the tree. She followed through, but planted the machete in the ground. Then they heard a loud and long inhale. Crumpler opened his eyes halfway and looked around.

He spoke softly, with vocal fry. "I'm great. Just a light detour."

"You scared the living hell out of me." She sighed deeply.

With more power in his voice this time, Crumpler said, "I'm good. I think I just got the wind knocked out of me when my parachute snagged the tree."

"Part of me still wants to cut the tree down." Pama smiled playfully.

He laughed, but it came out as a wheeze.

"Naw, I'm just joking," she said. "Let's get you down from there and make sure you are really okay." They walked directly under him. "Alright, you are going to have to do something strange with your kleck. You have to send a signal to your backup parachute so that it detaches. Give us a minute though to get something inflated below you. Can you do that?"

"Yeah, I should be able to. I have no problem chilling out until you're finished."

Serra immediately took his seat cushion and placed it next to Pama's. With his kleck, he sent a message for the two to fuse together. They created a high landing pad in the shape of a square that protruded up on the sides. It was as long as two men. They moved it directly under him.

"We're in place. Crumpler, are you ready?"

"Let me give it a shot."

He tried to override the cords' safety feature and make them detach, but he could not figure it out.

"You have to go through the safety protocols—the default is that they will never disengage. Try it again," Serra said.

It still didn't work, so Lieutenant Commander Pama grabbed a jipty from her backpack and expanded it to lean against the branch.

"Don't worry man, we got you. I'm on my way up."

When she arrived at the top, there was no easy way for Crumpler to get onto the ladder.

"We are going to have to cut you down anyway now, I guess. Are you ready?"

"Yeah, ready as I'll ever be!" he said with as full of a voice as he could muster.

"Alright, just try to fall on your back with your arms crossed."

She whipped out her machete and sliced the cables. C. E. Crumpler hugged himself as he fell from the tree onto the inflatable cushion. He bounced into the air, and after making contact a second time, flew forward into a standing position on the ground, where he ran a few steps to maintain balance. Then he raised his arms to flex his muscles at his friends, who had watched the whole ordeal from above. They cheered him on and hollered words of encouragement.

He approached Pama and Serra and gave them a huge hug.

"Thanks so much for being there for me. I really don't know what happened. You even saw that I was cleared for the drop."

"Don't worry about that for now. We are just happy that you are safe. Let us double-check that you are okay though. Do you mind lying down on the cushions, out of the way, so we can check for any serious injuries?"

"Yeah, that's great. Thanks."

They dragged the safety contraption farther into the forest, away from the soft ground, and had him lie down.

"We are going to have Sickles come down next, and when she gets here, she can give you a complete checkup. For now, just relax and enjoy the view," said Serra.

The trees were sparse in that location, so the culinary expert could still see to the top of the structure.

Pama shouted up to the rest of the crew, "Send Sickles down next."

She purposely kept the sentence brief so that echoes would not make it unintelligible. The rest of the crew physically indicated that they understood.

"Tell her to have fun still." Crumpler rested on the cushions.

They relayed the message to M. A. Sickles.

CHAPTER FIFTEEN

It had been quite the day for M. A. Sickles. Although she was trained to withstand close calls, she still felt shaken by all of the extreme circumstances.

"I was hoping to wait a little longer, but I think I should be fine. Give me a minute to test everything. I've had my fill of unexpected derailments for the day," she said to the other three who remained on the top.

E. M. Price came over and helped check that she was fitted correctly.

"Alright, you're all set," he said.

She attempted to clear her mind of all thoughts, then looked around at the tops of the trees below the structure. Her stomach felt like she had just eaten something bitter, and she was full of anxiety. Sickles felt fear, but tried to focus on happiness by closing her eyes, taking deep breaths, and enjoying everything around her. She had always been enamored with waterfalls and in awe of their beauty.

"I am going to take advantage of this unique opportunity," she said after opening her eyes.

The medical attendant sprinted toward the edge and jumped high and away from the structure, spreading her arms and legs out to provide a lift. She decided to fall with the water at first, then rode the wind in a circle and returned to the waterfall. Sickles moved her arms, which acted as wings, until she sharply turned to face the ground, as though sliding down the waterfall on her stomach.

Remaining an arm's length away from the pouring mineral waters, she flew directly down. At the halfway point, she broke through a thick dew as the foggy liquid blew off to the side. To stop the direct fall, she carefully navigated her slightly wet body to fly perpendicular to the wall, then floated up. When she was far enough away, she deployed her parachute and carefully landed on the soft open area.

After running for about ten steps and coming to a stop, she shouted, "Yeah! That was awesome!"

Sickles did a happy dance that consisted of jumping up to the side and clicking her heels. Then she moved both fists through the air to create a rainbow shape and ended by pulling both elbows to her waist and opening her fists to imitate an explosion.

After the celebration, she quickly got to work securing her parachute. She removed a light foil fabric from her rucksack with a small, thin, rectangular object, then went over to Crumpler and began working.

"I know you already said you're feeling great, but we are going to assess if you withstood any internal injuries. How are you feeling now?"

"I'm feeling normal. That was an amazing fall, by the way!"

"Aw, thanks. I needed some success after the bizarre day I've had." Sickles laughed and covered Crumpler with the light foil.

"We are going to place this film on you from head to toe, and then my trusty glawtor will go to work. Just try to relax and breathe normally."

"Alright, sounds good," C. E. Crumpler whispered just before the last portion was fixed over his face.

"The glawtor is scanning for any serious damage, including your bones and organs. I see an image of your body above our small rectangular box, and we are looking for your whole frame to light up green. If you get any red, then we can investigate more by zooming in on that part. This won't start fixing anything, as it is just used for assessing harm," M. A. Sickles narrated with a soft, caring tone.

After a moment, she brightened. "Good news—you're all green on the top side! Okay, next I'm going to take off the material, and then you will lie on your stomach with your arms bent at the elbow and crossed so you can lay your head comfortably on them."

He flipped over, and she used the glawtor to assess any injuries on the back side of his body.

"All green here, too. Not even a scratch. You are good to go, my friend. Phew, that is a relief."

"Thanks so much, Sickles. Now I can freely enjoy the rest of the trek!"

He got up and replicated the dance that Sickles had done earlier, to show everyone that he was fine. At age twenty-three, he knew his fit and young body would be able to snap back from much worse, and the others knew it as well. Captain Serra and most of the other members laughed and cheered him on after the quick performance.

"Alright, so now that everything is fine, you have some time while the others jump to do a diagnostic and see what happened to your parachute so that it doesn't happen again," Serra said after giving him a high five.

"That's a great idea. I can get it done now and still watch the others jump."

Crumpler sat down with his backpack and equipment. He connected to the parachute with his kleck and ordered it to complete a report.

When she got approval to jump next, T. A. Curtis was stretching in preparation.

"All clear, Curtis—you are free to fall when you are ready!"

"Alright, thanks Price."

She finished a few more stretches, specific for the task, and then sprinted until she kicked off and rode the currents in the wind for three slow rotations. At the beginning of her third loop, a flock of humming-birds zoomed from far off into her zone, and she was surrounded by the curious, tiny, brightly colored flying creatures. Some of them flew next to her as she completed the end of the loop. Thankfully, they buzzed off in time for her to open her parachute and successfully land.

Kandova had been waiting anxiously. Normally, she would have avoided looking directly down from that height to suppress a natural reaction of fear. But she'd witnessed Crumpler nearly crash and had been watching activity on the ground over the period of time it took for the past jumpers to leap. Her body had begun sending messages to avoid the jump, and it showed on her face. She fought bouts of energy shooting through her stomach, and her head felt as though she were spinning. She broke out in an abnormal sweat. In her mind, she knew that once she jumped, it would all go away, and she would be able to build an exhilarating memory of a lifetime.

"Remember that you are going to be fine. You've got this, Kandova!" E. M. Price said upon seeing the look of terror on her face.

"Thanks, buddy." She smiled and attempted to clear her mind.

M. O. Kandova rechecked her gear, and despite her body's physical reaction, she ran and jumped anyway, remembering to kick away from the wall. She couldn't help but shout to the others below as she looped slowly around.

"I'm a flying jaguar!" she shouted, in the funny voice she used with her close friends, moving herself into the position of a pouncing cat for a millisecond.

They all laughed and cheered—they knew that she had overcome personal hurdles. Her mind slowed down, and Kandova took the time to appreciate the amazing experience and trust in the training she had received. On the next curve, she looked into the distance at the tree tops and could see different structures peeking through the deep shades of green that speckled the earth as far as the eye could see.

She took a deep breath as she flew back toward the waterfall. From far away, she admired the rainbow and wondered what it would be like to actually be inside it. Kandova looked at the wall behind the waterfall and noticed little ledges where soil had fallen from the top and small bundles of greenery had grown. The next time past, she floated through the space where she imagined the rainbow would appear from the ground, and felt the slight velvety mist caress her skin. By this point, her heart rate and breath had slowed down, and she was only focused on enjoying the beauty of the trip. She successfully landed on the patch of soft land and walked to the rest of the grounded crew.

"Woah, I got to fly through a rainbow! That was so cool!" Kandova organized her rucksack.

"Yeah, I made a blobe of it," said Sickles. "You gotta check it out. It's like you are circling into the rainbow! Look, you can see where you pass through it and you are on the other side." The medical attendant pointed out details while the moving image beamed through her pictogrammer. "I had to put stuff back into my sack and had my pictogrammer out anyway!" She operated it with her kleck to show a playback of a view from the ground.

"Yeah I had some anxiety at the beginning, but I put it aside and had the best drop ever! It is so gorgeous, and such a thrill!" M. O. Kandova shouted, full of adrenaline.

Only Price remained on the top, and while the others anticipated watching his voyage, they were at different stages of getting their possessions in order. Price walked to the edge and threw a bag far from the structure, then popped the mini parachute out and directed it through his kleck to drop exactly in the open area.

Pama successfully caught the bag, which was full of excess items that the crew did not want to carry while gliding. She opened it and set the objects on a rock on the edge to be claimed, then left the miniature parachute for Price to reconfigure when he arrived. Price checked the conditions, and he was cleared for a jump.

The excursion manager was the only person to have traveled there before, so he wanted to amend some choices that he'd made the last time. Although he'd had an amazing first descent, he'd ruminated for fifteen years, from ages eighteen to thirty-three, about how he could make it even better. After his initial jump off of the jutting mountain, he'd wished he had relaxed and enjoyed the experience more, so now he took a few deep breaths to become centered. Price had also only completed one loop before—this time, he wanted to try for more.

Heck, why not do some flips at first, too? I think I can pull it off, he thought to himself.

As the last member on the top, while walking toward the center, he looked around the unusual ecosystem as if to bid adieu. Price nodded his head to signal gratitude, then turned around and sprinted toward the edge, planting both feet to spring into a double flip that projected him far out from the cool granite. He dove straight down, viewed the surroundings carefully to experience the moment, took a deep breath, then activated the flaps between his arms and legs, which immediately made him float away from the structure. The trek leader wanted to get as many loops as possible on this flight, so he rode out and steered into his first circle, keenly aware of any currents he could utilize.

When he felt a gust of wind pressing from below, Price put his arms up to stop moving forward, then laid them flat to his sides, pushing him higher than the surface he had jumped from. The excursion manager looked around at the palm-tree-inhabited space before diving down with the waterfall. During the next few loops, he relaxed and breathed deeply, while appreciating the beautiful details of nature. After the third circle, he successfully landed and was met by the other six members of the trek, who were filled with gratitude toward their selfless guide.

The pack ran after him, each holding one hand behind their backs so he could not see what was there. They each had a container full of water, which they poured over his head, then lifted him up on their shoulders and carried him. The parachute dragged behind, into the shade at the edge of the open area. They set him down while chanting his name.

When Price was settled, Pama said, "That was a spectacular jump, man.

We wanted to let you know that we really appreciate the time you took to coordinate this amazing afternoon for us."

"Yeah, we know that it took a lot of planning and was quite the risk, but it was an opportunity of a lifetime! It meant a lot to me," Kandova said.

"That's great. And we got to use lots of our training along the way!" Serra pointed out, to validate the functional purpose of planned excursions.

The younger members had never done anything like this, and most of them were struggling with being away from home. The activity made them feel connected to one another, and also helped redirect their attention to something even more intense than their homesickness.

"No problem! I'm really glad that you all enjoyed yourselves, and I would happily plan it again. I hope that you got to hone some of your training and challenge yourselves to realize you can do anything, no matter how scary it may have seemed in the beginning. If there is a next time, we will try to avoid face-eating spiders and attempt not to lose members on rivers in caves." Price laughed loudly with the others as they bonded over the shared experience, which they realized would soon come to an end.

"But I still have my face, and we ate him instead! And that's what matters," Sickles joked.

Everyone chuckled hard with her as she made light of the challenges they'd faced on the trip. When they finished laughing, they began gathering the items that had been sent in the special drop. They each checked that their wongers were still engaged to keep insects away, then prepared for the hike back to base camp.

"Alright, I think I know what it was," C. E. Crumpler said to the crew. "The cooking pot in my bag stretched it too much and blocked my main parachute from coming out. So next time, I'll send it down at the end with the extra items that we don't want in our backpacks for the descent."

"You were right, Serra," Lieutenant Commander Pama said. "We did learn quite a bit on this trek, and hopefully we will be better equipped for future outings. You never know what will come in handy in more serious situations."

All members of this small group, as well as the others back at base camp, felt open to share shortcomings in order to improve effectiveness in the field. They all had the ultimate goal of working together to reach their maximum potential and to become more skilled. The life-and-death situations forced them to set egos aside and focus on the objective.

Each member double-checked their backpacks and changed their jurprodians to the most basic setting, consisting of simple shorts and short-sleeved shirts.

"Alright, so we will be taking a different route back, but we should arrive in time for dinner, and it will still be light out," Price announced while everyone was adjusting their packs and outfits.

After each member indicated they were ready, they followed Price onto a path that penetrated the lush, foliage-rich rainforest. Now that they were reentering, it was imperative to remain quiet and be on the lookout for any predators or dangers. To remind the group about staying silent, he made a hand sign by closing his thumb onto his other four fingers, which were straight and touching, symbolizing a sealed mouth. He also waved his hand around in a circle to remind the members to be on high alert for hazards.

They saw a variety of flowers and plant parts along the way that were used as medicines for different ailments all around The Land. The bark from one tree was used to treat stomach problems. E. M. Price quietly lifted his pictogrammer, which contained a photo of the plant and outlined the health benefits and common uses. A small, bright-orange orchid popped up on the pictogrammer. These grew in heavy patches high in the trees and were used to cure acne caused by a hormone imbalance. Many of the crew members were surprised—they had grown up in busy cities and had used one or more of the different remedies, but only purchased them in a store as dried powders or other processed forms.

The clan carefully stepped through the rainforest, holding branches respectfully for the next person and aiming to navigate without a sound. The path curved from side to side, and the ground coverings changed as they continued to the base camp. They walked up a hill on an incredibly slippery and steep slope. Trongoles could easily navigate the incline; their hooves dug deep into the ground when angled downward.

Price pointed to his shoes and made spikes pop out through the use of his kleck. The others followed suit. When they reached the top, they could see that the path went straight down the hill and then curved at what looked to be a body of water.

As they grew closer, they could see a clear, spring-fed pond with a deep, sandy bottom. Price already had his pictogrammer out, so he showed them a picture of a fish and motioned for them not to get too close to the water. On the sides of the pond, which dropped suddenly, huge, clear, flat fish slowly waved their fins and moved gently in almost-perfect camouflage. The pictogrammer's description contained a bright-red symbol that meant the animal could be dangerous. Price took two long sticks and placed them on the shore of the pond. He lifted them slowly as if they were the legs of a large bird walking around the perimeter.

After the third stride, one of the nearly invisible fish lunged at the sticks and dragged them under the water. Its teeth were the size of a human hand, and zigzagged in order to interlock inside a powerful jaw. Price pointed to the pictogrammer section that described feeding behavior. It clearly stated, "The objerner can pull an animal or person into the water with its powerful jaws and teeth. Once the prey is in the water, every other objerner begins ravaging until it is quickly consumed. If large bones are left, the objerners will use them to sharpen their teeth until the bones dissolve."

This was particularly fascinating for crew members who had never been exposed to the rainforest region while growing up. They walked carefully on the path near the beautiful yet unforgiving pond. When they were all safe, E. M. Price pointed out a tree that was dripping sap from an area where native fauna had scraped. Below the tree, a collection of the sap had pooled. And on the same tree, a vine grew with long, green pods. Price held up the pictogrammer with a picture of both plants growing near each other. It read: "Tikompay is made when this sap is boiled and mixed with pulverized pods from a vine that commonly grows on or near the same tree. Tikompay is a syrup used to reduce pain." These plant-based medicines were administered as a standard practice throughout The Land.

CHAPTER SIXTEEN

It had been a very long day for the group. They were ready to relax, and had worked up an appetite. They carefully and quietly navigated together until the trongole path turned in the direction of base camp. Pama and Serra took turns hacking through patches of brush in order to create the most direct pathway back to their destination, until they reached a portion of the rainforest that had very little ground cover, where the hikers could walk freely. Soon after, they arrived outside of base camp with daylight to spare and extra time before dinner. As the adrenaline-seeking bunch grew closer, the sound of the pounding waterfall became louder and louder.

"We made it back!" Kandova shouted to those she had bonded with so closely that day, and also to the others who were nearby.

Krizzles had been relaxing by the fire when she heard the announcement. She ran to the crew members and gave Kandova a huge hug.

"How was your trip? You have to tell me all about it over dinner! Didier has been cooking food from every region, so it's going to be delicious."

"We had the best time ever! We got to see the most amazing parts of the rainforest, and navigated through a cave river with a candle in one hand while swimming with the other, and we climbed a huge granite mountain with a gorgeous waterfall and got to jump off after. Oh, and how could I forget? We saw the most mind-blowing cats! I have to tell you all the details later." Kandova spoke quickly—she wanted to ask Krizzles about her own experience. "How was everything here?"

"We had an overall chilled-out day. We dived from the waterfall, played a game of trudles, and had fancy drinks and snacks. We can share the rest later. Let's go check in on Jeffers!" Krizzles said while grabbing her fydonmate's backpack. They greeted everyone quickly before walking over to the technology officer.

Jeffers was relaxing on one of the lounge chairs and watching a blobe on her pictogrammer, still recovering. A. P. Krizzles set down the rucksack and sat next to her, holding one of the woman's hands with both of hers.

Krizzles whispered slowly, "Our fydonmate is healing from an eventful day that ended with a small dose of black orchid elixir."

"I'm okay now, and that is what matters. We can explain after you're all settled, maybe at dinner." Jeffers's eyelids drooped. She was trying not to exert too much energy, so she could recover.

"I'm so glad you are okay. You can fill me in on all of it soon, Jeffers. There is no rush now." Then Kandova switched to her humorous jaguar voice, "And whose lucky day was it that they're passing out shots of black orchid elixir?"

Jeffers laughed, still noticeably returning to complete consciousness. "Alright, go get yourself a shower and come back here for dinner. Didier has been cooking like a madwoman for tonight!"

"Sounds good. You relax for now, and stay calm." Kandova gave her a big hug that exuded concern.

"Yeah, make sure you just relax, and we will be back down for dinner soon. I have to prepare some stuff for tomorrow in the fydon." Krizzles grabbed Kandova's rucksack, and then they both gave Jeffers a long hug and headed back to the fydon.

The other members of the trek also excitedly checked in before heading back to their fydons to shower and change for dinner. When everyone came down to the campfire, they each grabbed a drink to make a toast.

Jaway addressed the group. "I know we all had an eventful day today, filled with adventure and your choice activities. I hope that each of you feels inspired and encouraged to continue doing an excellent job. Thanks to all of you for your fantastic support. So many of you stepped up to take responsibility wherever it was necessary. Price, thanks for heading up the adrenaline tour. I look forward to hearing about the fun time you all had. Much appreciation to our fantastic culinary experts, Didier and Crumpler, for preparing amazing meals for us. It is really heartwarming to have regional cuisine. Here is to the crew that earned these additional few days, and to many more good times together. I really love spending my time with you guys, and I couldn't ask for better soldiers!"

Everyone raised a glass of wine from the Mountain Region and took a sip after saying, "Cheers" in unison.

"C. E. Crumpler can you fill us in on the outrageous spread?" Jaway asked.

"No problem, Barbour. As you all know, Central Command really wanted us to enjoy the evening, and they sent different cuisine from each region. Of course we have interesting food from the Rainforest Region where we are now—some gathered this afternoon by yours truly in the surrounding area. Let me give you a brief overview of what we have. We are just now preparing the freshest seafood from the Highlands Region's famous waters, flown in by a mokdon this afternoon."

This prompted a playful regional phrase from Kandova: "But how fresh are they, Inablian brother?"

She'd grown up in Owantay, which was a beach town on the east coast, and Crumpler had grown up in Inablay, on the same coast but much farther north.

"Well, as a fellow coastal highlander, I can assure you they caught these recently. They arrived alive, and were treated with care."

He touched the huge feet of many clams that were partially paralyzed by of bed of ice where they rested. The previously still feet flinched and then retreated at a slow pace back into the shells.

The Highlands Region consisted of rolling hills, many covered in purplish-blue flax flowers, that ran to a gorgeous, beach-lined coast on the east, in contrast to the jutting cliffs on the west coast that made fishing difficult. Therefore, the Highlands Region was the premier seafood producer. Self-navigating vehicles, like the mokdon, could easily transport food, as well as any other goods, throughout The Land. Mokdons whooshed high above most other air traffic and guaranteed that a catch would arrive happily inside an aquarium, for the freshest-tasting seafood possible.

In addition, the boats housed devices that identified sea life species and estimated the age. This way, the ideal target could be surrounded by a wall of bubbles like a cage, which avoided accidental harm to other creatures. The bubble cage calmly delivered fish to the ship, where they were captured and logged into a database. This prevented overfishing for healthy and thriving populations. The nonviolent act kept the aquatic life unharmed and calm, leaving the flesh untampered by adrenaline or other stress-related factors that could negatively affect the taste.

"And I can assure you, they chose the peak age!" Crumpler added.

After laughing and sharing a moment to appreciate their regional influence, he said, "My fellow highlanders and I are also very excited to share in the bison that just finished roasting, and we are thankful that they were not delivered *alive* by a mokdon. Now that would have been the surprise of *my* life!"

C. E. Didier walked over to a huge container of roasted bison meat and lifted the lid to reveal a mist that spread to the nostrils of every hungry crewmember and made each mouth water incessantly.

"Obviously, this is from the Plains Region in the south. We also have a special corn that some of you may have never tried before. And last but not least, we have turkey, passion fruit, wild chokecherry products, and wine from the Mountain Region in the west. There are lots more different dishes, so enjoy!" She beamed with pride to show off her culinary training. "And thanks to our fantastic sous chefs, who helped guide us in making your regional cuisine, with tips about how your grandmothers would have prepared the ingredients!" Didier was also excited to dive into the spread of covered dishes and large pots.

The group clapped with salivating mouths and impatient stomachs.

"Alright, the sun is setting, so dig in and enjoy, and let me know if you need anything. We are finishing up the freshest dishes now, and they'll be up soon," Didier said.

This was the indication to begin filling plates with heaping portions of some of the best cuisine the land had to offer. Each of the fifteen crew members took a plate and sat among the rings of seating around the fire. At first, nobody spoke as each person fulfilled their hunger and enjoyed the carefully prepared food. The long day also contributed to the silence. They were tired and ready to relax for the night.

"While I have everyone's attention, I want to propose a toast to I. P. Hilton, who saved me earlier today. I'll fill those of you in later if you didn't hear. You are a true comrade and friend. Thanks for being there for me." Jeffers raised a glass of nectar high in the air.

Everyone lifted their drinks together, followed by another synchronized, "Cheers."

"I would also like to thank Pama for cutting me out of a tree. I know you will always be prepared, wherever we go! Here's to Pama!" Crumpler said.

They agreed with naturally supportive responses. When everyone had eaten one plate of food, they began chatting and explained the details of the day, so that each person heard about what happened with the other activities.

Jeffers shared details about her experience—how she had been relaxing and having fun one minute, and then in the next she was surrounded by a mysterious darkness. She continued to applaud Hilton as the giant who'd saved her.

The information processor shyly accepted the praises, and Kandova took note, watching his reaction. While he spoke, she gazed into his eyes, which reflected flickering flames that seemed to jump out more and more as the rainforest darkened to night and became silent and still, except for the sound of rushing water. She noticed that she had never felt this way before. It was as if their bodies were being pulled together yet remained out of reach, like gigantic, powerful magnets that, once connected, could not be easily separated. M. O. Kandova noticed his calm demeanor and brilliant teeth as he smiled every so often. She loved his tall stature and was drawn in when the others honored his efforts to save Jeffers. She strangely desired to have been the person who fell into a deep, dark trap so she could experience his strong energy, lifting and catapulting her into the air after his ear brushed against her lips to listen for signs of breath.

Because these feelings were new, Kandova didn't understand how to process them. She knew that she felt a more immense desire than ever before, and that it was directed toward him, but she did not know whether to act on it or let it be. Sisterly love toward her made her incredibly thankful that Hilton had risked his life in order to save her. Because Kandova trusted Jeffers's opinion, she was convinced that I. P. Hilton was a good man, with the best intentions to care for others, and she felt secure.

Jeffers made a joke in the midst of seriousness. "If you weren't such a giant, and also like a younger brother, I would have to marry you!"

It gave Kandova relief that her close friend saw him only as a sibling. When she looked over at her other fydonmate, Krizzles, she saw gorgeous wide eyes aimed at her, and then the gigantic sparkling gems looked intensely at Hilton with a raised brow, to indicate that she could see that Kandova was taken by him.

Then A. P. Krizzles laughed silently, smiled, and raised her shoulders just enough so that nobody else would notice, as if to say, *I see the way you look at him and I approve!*

Kandova's face turned bright red. She knew that romantic connections were highly frowned upon among the crewmembers, because they were ultimately responsible for each other's lives. She winked back at Krizzles quickly and subtly. She also was unsure if Hilton had any interest in her, and did not want to let others know how she felt in case she was rejected. This was a rare situation where she became completely shy.

Thankfully, the other members did not pick up on the nonverbal communication—they were distracted by the elaborate and exciting stories filled with death-defying leaps and exotic rainforest creatures. In an effort to appear completely normal, Kandova enthusiastically explained her love of the jaguars. The bouncing amber glow from the campfire provided camouflage while she softly yet intensely scanned Hilton's face and body. She tried to look away, but she could not until Krizzles whisked her attention back into reality with all of the other members. The mechanical operator wondered why her chest felt warm, like it was too close to the fire. Her body was energized from head to toe.

Curtis and Roberts started discussing what had gone wrong with identifying the old trap below the ground.

"We looked back at our equipment records, and it appears that we were able to pick up the eels in the water, and the slip hazards, but we forgot to turn on a setting and thus missed the hollowed-out earth there," Curtis said.

"Now we know, and next time we will double-check to make sure that it is on, so we can warn you of all potential dangers. I've never seen an ancient large-game trap like that around our previous base camps, but now we know to search for everything. I really hope we can avoid anything like this in the future," said Roberts.

"Well, thanks," Jaway said. "We really appreciate you both looking into that. You know, this is one of the things that I love most about my crew—that you all are willing to reassess anything in order to strive for perfection, especially when it comes to keeping each other safe."

"Yeah, isn't that normal?" Curtis asked.

"Actually, it is not, but we won't go into a discussion about other battalions right now. My point is that you guys are the best, and I really appreciate our climate." Jaway briefly chuckled.

After the short discussion, they all felt better about their safety moving forward.

Darkness had swiftly descended on the camp by the time dessert was served. The surrounding areas looked completely black, while a full moon rose slightly as the canopy filtered the little light that entered at a low angle. A clear night sky promised to eventually allow moonlight onto the camp and illuminate the waterfall area.

After the sweet course, Krizzles and Kandova helped Jeffers back to the fydon that they shared together, to freshen up and change into cozier clothes. As they approached the vehicle, the door slid down to form stairs, and they all boarded.

"Have you ever felt so good that it seems like your chest is on fire, and everything is okay and there is nothing more you want to do than be with a person all the time?" M. O. Kandova looked at the ceiling and fell into her seat, flailing her arms and legs in a relaxed motion.

She looked sedated, bobbing her head to the sides and taking a deep breath.

"Sounds like someone got bit by a love bug! Who is the lucky guy?" Jeffers asked. The technology officer felt giddy because she knew they were breaking the rules.

Krizzles asked, "You didn't notice how Kandova was looking at a certain someone in the firelight today? A certain someone who valiantly saved you?"

"No, I was distracted by the stories of murderous spiders and near-death experiences from the other group!" Jeffers laughed. "It's Hilton?" she whispered. "Well, just so you know, I completely approve, but I would never encourage you to do something outside of regulations. As long as you keep mechanically operating, whatever you do is fine by me, and I'll keep it a secret. But you shouldn't let anyone else know besides us." She paused. "And if someone fell in love with a guy who was as caring, and sincere, and handsome as I. P. Hilton, they would have my unabashed support."

Jeffers smiled and then went to look outside in both directions before closing the door so nobody would hear the conversation.

"I guess I never thought of it, or I didn't realize how I was feeling, but do you ever wonder what it would be like to make a romantic connection while we are completing our compulsory service for The Land? I know it is not allowed, but what if it was possible within the guidelines?" M. O. Kandova said, louder now.

Krizzles peeked her head out of the shower room, speaking through her toothbrush, "I think it is totally *possible*. You just couldn't let anyone know. Why, Kandova? Do you like someone more than friends?"

Krizzles poked Kandova's arm before going back into the bathroom to spit into the sink.

"I'm not quite sure. I just feel a way I've never felt before."

"What? You've never been in love? Or are you a virgin? You are, aren't you? Your face is turning red. You're always so high glamor with your makeup—a cosmopolitan girl from Owantay. I just assumed everyone there were east coast lovers because of the beach life, sun, and aphrodisiacs from the seafood!" Krizzles's playfulness was characteristic of a nineteen-year-old, youthful, fresh point of view.

Kandova, who was the same age, stayed confidently relaxed and appeared to look into the distance before asking in her jaguar imitation, "Maybe?"

She shrugged her shoulders jovially and switched to a serious voice.

"Actually, my dad has always been super overprotective, and I always tell my parents everything that is going on in my life. So that is probably why. He always got to them before I could." Kandova laughed loudly.

"There is nothing wrong with you never going all the way." A. P. Krizzles carefully chose her words. "I'm just saying that I'm certain it is okay to start a spark in our line of work, as long as you make a concerted effort to stay focused on the safety of the crew, and keep it under wraps."

"Hey Krizzles, can you bring your drogger down and play some songs by the fire tonight? I always love hearing your tunes," Jeffers asked after finishing in the bathroom.

"Well, you know me. I always love playing. Sure, I'll bring it down." Krizzles placed the bluish-hued, metal, three-stringed triangle into its carrying case, which she removed from a drawer near the back of the fydon.

"I always bring it from the glider just in case! Ya know, I'm feeling extra silly for some reason."

CHAPTER SEVENTEEN

The girls left the fydon one by one, and the door slid up. Krizzles and Kandova walked on each side of Jeffers, and they hugged each other tightly to show sisterly love and support.

"You are the best fydonmates ever, and I love you guys," Jeffers said. "And I swear that is not the shot of black orchid elixir speaking either!"

They all laughed as they strolled down to the campfire, looking forward to spending time together that was free from any obligations or distractions.

They each sat down in the inner circle, where T. O. Jeffers got comfortable, knowing she had to heal.

"Let me grab some heavy firewood, because we all know what that means!" Krizzles said in a mischievous tone.

They knew that a lot of firewood would require them to stay out longer. Krizzles walked to the edge of the camp and squatted down on one knee in order to fill one arm with many different heavy logs. When she'd stacked a load past her line of sight, she placed the other arm under the wood and walked carefully toward the campfire, feeling with her feet as she moved, her face turned to the side.

"Phew, I made it! That one piece was poking my arm something awful. But at least I just had to do one trip." She dropped the wood just outside the two rings of seating with a crash.

M. O. Kandova got up and helped her place the logs on the fire so they formed a pyramid. Soon they began to burn, and high flames flashed the surrounding area, flickering off of the water.

"So what's this I hear of you taking tikompay, Jeffers? Did you have any dreams?" M. O. Kandova asked.

"Yeah, it was really strange. It was like I was in another world. Are you good at interpreting tikompay visions?"

"Yeah, my grandma was great at reading, and she taught me what she knew."

The symbols of the dreams were passed down from family to family, but it was becoming a lost art.

"Would you be able to tell me what it meant?"

"Sure, let's try to get through it before anyone else gets down. And if somebody comes, we can continue it later, okay? Don't forget that they are incredibly personal and should be kept close to your heart. That's what my grandma always told us," Kandova said, while Krizzles started strumming her instrument to check that it was in working condition.

"Yeah, I'm really interested to hear what they mean. I wrote them down in my elitser when it was all fresh in my mind. I could see an unfolding story for about an hour."

"They must have given you the standard amount of tikompay for one hour. Was it like you looked at something and then it changed into shapes?"

"Yeah, it was the leaves for me. It was like the wind blew in a way to make them look like a moving story."

"That is quite normal when you are in or around the rainforest. So, what did you record in your elitser?" Kandova asked.

Jeffers explained from her records, "A muscular man operated a chariot along the beach while a volcano erupted all over, including the sandy area where he rode. So I guessed he was in the mountain region because of the volcanoes. And I thought it was long ago because there were still a lot of beaches. I also assumed that the volcanoes created the cliffs that we see today on the western coast, where I grew up.

"He was the city messenger. I even felt hot and could hear the lava crash in the water and sizzle. His horses were white, and there were four of them. The rider had to carefully navigate around the falling lava that dropped all around them. After they escaped and reached clear land, he cried and cried while riding, because he'd lost everything he knew and his culture was destroyed. In order to get to the city, he rode along the beach, then took an open road, then turned off to a different route. Somehow, I sensed that the horses could feel the anguish of their master, and it motivated them to push their bodies as much as possible. The city messenger arrived at the nearest neighboring town to warn them, because the same fate was to come their way, as well as the other surrounding cities. His horses died when he got there, and he ran up the warning tower stairs to light the emergency signal.

"He pleaded to himself that the next tower guards would be awake to see the signal. He knew that the underground magma would travel to them soon. The next warning towers ended up lighting also, far off in the distance. He was greeted with water and supplies by a woman and a group of servants. After this, he nearly fell down the stairs, and then he collapsed. That was when one of the women read the scroll that was in his bag. It said that his entire civilization had been destroyed and they were next and that they should run. They helped the messenger into a carriage and heaped their valuables in with him.

"All of the people fled in the dark, away from the place where they and their ancestors grew up. After walking six hours, a child shouted for them to stop and look. They saw their city in the distance burning from the lava. Their bodies hurt and they couldn't think clearly, so they numbed the pain and stayed on their journey to safety, away from the range of the erupting volcanoes. And that was when I kind of forced my mind to return to reality here next to the waterfall. Do you have any idea what that could mean for me? I don't even know where to start."

Throughout the story, Jeffers tried to stay relaxed so she could finish healing.

"Yeah," said Kandova, "I think a lot of it was symbolic for your life. My grandma always said that before you start to decipher a vision, it is important that you are in a state of mind to handle a difficult message. Do you think you are?" She was calm and completely serious.

"Yeah, I think I'm fine. I just want to know what it means for me. I am clueless." Jeffers matched her fydonmate's level of reverence.

"Okay, well I'll do my best to remember. My grandma always used to tell me stories when I was afraid because of a storm or something, to calm me down. And it worked every time. I would get engulfed in whatever she was saying. Little did I know that she was passing down interpretations of visions that had been in my family for generations. After the tales were finished, she would tell me what the individual parts symbolized for our lives and explain the guidance that it might give to someone." Kandova flipped her hair and licked the corner of her mouth with the very tip of her tongue. "Well, I'll see what I can remember."

She interlinked her fingers and flipped them around and away, to snap her knuckles. In order to entertain her friend who was still healing, she gestured as if she were someone famous who was dealing with overzealous fans. She felt the interpretations from ten generations flowing through her veins, and she dove into explaining what she thought the vision meant, according to her family's teachings.

"First of all, this man represents your life and the paths you may take. He had big muscles, right?"

"Yes, he was ripped, as if he worked out every day with heavy weights. He was like our guys, but ten times more fit, if that's even possible."

"Okay, well muscles are an indication of being powerful and strong. So you are a solid and firm person. And usually the beach is your mind— where the two levels of consciousness meet. The sand is your logical thinking, and the waves are your emotions, which can lack sensibility sometimes and can flop around. Don't forget that your feelings can be unpredictable and unreliable.

"The fire from the lava next to the water stands for something in your life that pulls you from one side to the other; maybe there is an internal struggle with how you feel. And the steam from the lava going into the ocean could mean that you need to literally let out some steam. The horses are strong and resilient objects around you, maybe actual solid bodies. Because they are white, whatever they represent is also clean and innocent and will help to bring abundance and goodness into your life. The volcano stands for times when you lose control and are bursting. Be careful, because the results of outbursts could harm those around you or yourself. You will want to find out how you can regulate anger to prevent this.

"In general, a road is your understanding of navigating life and how you can make your goals into reality. Because he switched to an open road, this means that you will eventually, but consistently, improve in some way. It could also be that you will slowly but surely move up a social ladder. You are twenty years old, so this is quite common for your age group, given that you have to eventually decide on a career. You may want to get a real-world job after this obligatory service is over.

"It could also mean that your future is open to many options. We are all making choices that could determine the trajectories of our lives, so that could be completely true. When the man chooses a different road, this most likely signifies that you will choose a new path soon. And perhaps you will pick nontraditional work, in opposition to your family's expectations. He was greeted by the women with drinking water. This represents what you believe about your soul and that you will feel quenched and fresh inside."

Kandova paused suddenly before continuing.

"So right now, I'm kind of putting it all together. Maybe you will have a battle between your logical mind and emotions, like the beach scene. You might be angry and blow up like the volcano, but in the end you will be wise and inside you will feel at peace. You'll be invigorated, like when they gave him the water.

"Signaling the watchmen meant that you should keep your eyes open for a person or thing that can hurt you. And the tower represents your lofty dreams and life goals. So those together may mean that you should be aware of people or things that could tear down what you want to do in life. The fact that he climbed the tower represents the inner journey of your soul and hidden thoughts that may be revealed to you. You should forcefully follow your desires for spiritual understanding.

"The scroll can mean two things: that you carry hidden wisdom or that you have the ability to be great, but you cannot see it yet. Remember that the sky is the limit, as far as what you can do with your life. I think the fact that the contents of the scroll warned the city and saved them means that when you share knowledge and experience with others, you will improve or save their lives.

"You might have heard the saying, 'Wisdom sets you free.' It could be that you help others to think logically, and only base conclusions on what you can see and hear and taste and touch. When your followers do this, they will not be swayed by random ideas, and it will keep them safe. For example, sometimes people enjoy controlling others with fake arguments. If someone carefully investigates the statements for validity, they will keep their money, time, and resources safe from those moochers. That's just my spin."

She laughed before continuing.

"The destroyed city could mean that you have let your friendships or connections go and allowed them to crumble. I think because it burned, it is important to keep those who love you close and to nurture those relationships. Because all of the people went to a safe place in the end, you should keep a positive outlook on life—when all is said and done, no matter how bleak it may have seemed, deep down inside be assured that it will all work out for the best. Hang in there and stay motivated to live your life to the fullest."

Kandova let out a deep sigh. "That is mostly what I can recall. What do you think?"

"I'm kind of processing what you said," said Jeffers. "It was like taking a sip from the base of the waterfall."

They both laughed.

"But on a serious note," she continued, "I agree that I have been strong and resilient, and I am powerful. I need to own this. I like what you said about the two parts of my mind joining. For example, it is important to be emotional and deal with feelings, but also just as critical to be logical and maintain a balance. And continuing with the same idea, I need to find ways to let off steam so I don't end up exploding. I have not dealt with that so well in the past and kind of kept things to myself, then blown up and hurt others in my life. I think when I can manage my feelings, then I can avoid self-sabotaging my close relationships and keep those that I love in my life. I like to think I'm a pure person who is loyal and kind, and I want to continue on this path in life. Perhaps I can incorporate that into my career. I've always been searching for a spiritual purpose and have been interested in being devoted somehow.

"I like how you mentioned basing beliefs on things you can see and hear, on concrete proof and real evidence. Because especially when dealing with spirituality, it can be easy to be led astray by people with selfish motives. They can use any argument to create self-doubt and control others to take their time, money, or anything else they want. If I follow a spiritual calling, I want it to be because it is what I desire and need in my life, not because someone else is benefiting from it or controlling my thoughts or manipulating me.

"I'm excited to be reminded that my life journey is open and I have multiple options, and in the end I will have a bright future. I'm also looking forward to making my own path, which may be different from the norm or what is expected. I mean, let's be real. I'm the girl who gave herself stitches with natural materials in the wilderness—with no scars, might I add!"

Jeffers laughed boisterously with her girlfriends. After taking a breath, she became more introspective.

"That's super cool that the vision means that my soul will be quenched and I'll feel fresh inside. So even though I may have been a hothead and blown up, I can become wise and at peace and learn how to manage that. And by learning that skill, I will keep loved ones close. You know, the vision was spot on, in that I think I usually assume the best in others. With this positive outlook, I have to be careful and watch out for shady characters. It's just a reality of the world."

She took a minute to carefully and slowly look around the rainforest as the moonlight began to illuminate portions more and more.

"Speaking of dangers in an interpersonal sense, there are many aspects of the rainforest that may want to eat us or cause severe harm to us, like poisonous plants, animals, and insects. It is kind of like a metaphor for life—that ignoring threats can lead to huge consequences. It's a priority to live in reality while believing I am safe, and to navigate through life while preserving myself as much as possible. It can also be a good strategy to keep special dreams to myself and beware of others that want to take these away.

"When I reach these personal goals and I have arrived at whatever career I choose, I really want to do something to help others—to spread wisdom and not keep it hidden in a scroll. You're right, though, we are just starting our lives in the real world, and it's critical to consider life after our compulsory service for The Land. I'm twenty, and you guys are nineteen, but the reality of coming up with a plan for my life is serious.

"Even though the military is required, I still love what we do, but I think I want a different life. I just don't see this becoming my forever job. There's gotta be a field more peaceful, where I can help people and live a pure life with loved ones around. You've given me a lot to think about. I may visit Churchill soon and get some ideas."

The sound of voices approaching made the women turn their heads until they could clearly understand the words. The full moon light shone at its brightest of the night, but not enough to reveal which crew members were walking down to the campfire.

CHAPTER EIGHTEEN

"Quick, throw on some makeup! They'll never know." Krizzles said under her breath.

While looking in the direction of the walking voices, she slipped a pradimptor over to Kandova along the ground. She quickly bowed her head down onto the pradimptor and waited until the count of three. The other two faced the noise, in order to cover up the impromptu makeup session. When M. O. Kandova returned to a sitting position, she was almost the same, which shocked the other girls, who peeked only out of the corners of their eyes.

"Oh man, I kept my usual, natural setting on. Quick, try it again," A. P. Krizzles whispered.

She hoped that the talkers would take a little longer to arrive. This time, when Kandova recovered, she was in a high-glam look, typical for her home city of Owantay. She had defined eyeliner, lash extensions, bright eye shadow, dark brows, and matte-red lips.

"Okay, now you are a true Owantian girl!" Jeffers whispered out of the side of her mouth.

The chatting people came within sight.

"Before we knew it, the jipty extended and punched through the bag, ruining it, and crashed out our huge upstairs window! It was the last time my parents left us home alone for an entire year," Jaway said.

He was confidently joking about his and his sisters' first experiences trying to use their klecks to extend a jipty into a ladder. The others with him laughed hysterically and didn't pick up on the last-minute makeup application.

"Step one is always the same. Take it out of the bag. Step two is to *look out*!" Pama quickly related to Jaway's story about learning to use a kleck on a new device at home with siblings.

Jaway arrived at the campfire with Hilton, Price, Pama, and Crumpler.

"What do we have here? All three fydonmates together, just like us," C. E. Crumpler said.

"Yeah, we can't get enough of each other!" said Kandova.

"Well, we are here to crash your fydonmate party, and we brought nobter ingredients. I see you ladies already got lots of wood for the fire. Way to go! Looks like it could last for at least five days." Hilton laughed.

"Well, we wouldn't normally let you join us, but because you have ingredients for nobters, we'll make an exception," Kandova joked back, surprisingly relaxed from the bouncing fire, the sounds of rushing water, and conversation with close friends.

This was the first time she was completely uninhibited around I. P. Hilton. She hated freezing up—out of everyone, she wanted to be the most genuine with him.

"Ta da!" Crumpler revealed eight miniature pans and skewers from behind his back. "We have everything you need for nobters: miniature pans with lids, skewers, caramel, grains, and cocoa cream!"

Nobters were made by placing precooked, dried grains in the bottom of a pan. Small caramel balls went in next, and then a cocoa cream made with coconut milk was scooped on the top. The tiny skillet was then covered and placed over the fire by clicking it into a notch on one of the legs that held up the pargle, which filtered any signs of smoke from the fire. The mixture heated until it created a semi-solid cookie that was poked with a skewer and eaten after cooling.

"Let's get this started!" Krizzles stood up and handed out the components to the crew members, who had already made themselves at home around the fire.

After delivering the items, she sat next to Jaway. They each talked about memories of making nobters while assembling luscious individual skillets of delectability above the fire.

"Do you guys mind watching ours cook? Price and I are going to head back up to the glider to get the chilnor and some ink. I'm in the mood to finally get a new tattoo that I have been considering for some time! It will be the perfect ending to our adrenaline-inducing day," Pama said.

"Yeah, no problem, we're watching our own, so a few more is not a big deal. How do you want them? Crispy or gooey?" Hilton asked.

"We're both gooey all the way, right Price?" Pama asked while nudging him with her elbow.

"You know me so well, my fydonmate!"

"Alright, we got you then," Hilton said.

They walked swiftly back to their fydon and flew up to the glider that hovered above the rainforest, camouflaged from any angle. Then they embarked onto the bottom level, parked, quickly grabbed what they needed, and descended back to base camp. They were thankful that each fydonmate went to the campfire so they could take the vehicle up to the glider. If someone had gone back to their tent or was working in the fydon, it would have been impolite to move it. The two walked back to the edge of the pool of glowing water to find their snacks sitting peacefully, resting and cooling.

"Thanks guys, we owe you!" Pama said.

"No problem. I think they'll be exactly like you requested," Hilton said. He was sitting comfortably next to M. O. Kandova.

Price held a box that contained everything he needed in order to give Pama the tattoo that she had been envisioning. He took out a pictogrammer, and a design he'd created popped up into the air.

"What do you think of tweaking this by adding a small, inconspicuous spider to represent you saving a life today? Poor M. A. Sickles. I'm glad she's relaxing after everything that went down."

"She's a tough little cookie, so I'm sure she will be fine. Yeah, let's add a tiny spider, maybe within the details. Like you have to stare in order to see it. Can we make it look like it's part of the vine?"

"Yeah, that's a great idea." He used his kleck to add a spider to the current sketch of the tattoo. "Alright, what do you think of this?"

"That is perfect. Let's do it!" Lieutenant Commander Pama said.

The design was a climbing plant that would wrap around her ankle and then down to her toes. Small, hot-pink flowers that matched her machete danced around with green leaves, thorns, and a group of shoots. An arachnid was hidden within the vines.

With the approval out of the way, Price slipped gloves on and started to prepare the canvas. He wiped some disinfectant and a numbing cream on Pama's ankle and foot. As he moved a device around her skin, an outline appeared in dark gray. Then he filled the chilnor, which looked like a pen with lasers, with the first color. He seemed to be drawing with a writing utensil, but he actually was depositing the ink beneath her skin. The lasers created enough light to see in the moonlit darkness, and also promoted the healing process, just like the beams in the dopridam that had repaired Jeffers's injury earlier that day.

In about fifteen minutes, he drew everything in different colors with careful intricacy and extra attention to the fine lines. Pama sat still, visibly trying to ignore the pain.

"Alright, what do you think?" Price asked.

"Woah, it's amazing! Thanks so much, buddy. I've been wanting this for what seems like forever." Pama peered over the new artwork that might accompany her throughout her lifetime.

"No problem. Alright, so we just have to do the healer and it should mend within two days."

Price took another pen-like device and passed over the lines again. This one sealed the skin and promoted restoration with plant-based emollients.

"You are all set—now we can enjoy our nobters." E. M. Price removed his gloves, washed his hands in the water, and grabbed a tasty fireside snack.

Everyone else joined in, munching on the treats while chatting and watching the flames bounce. After they finished eating the nobters, Hilton collected all of the dirty dishes and took them to the kitchen area nearby, where he filled the automatic cleaner.

"Do you mind playing some songs for us, Krizzles?" Jaway asked.

"Sure, I would love to. Let me get my hands clean first."

She walked over to the water's edge and washed her fingers carefully. Then she wiped them on a nearby towel to make sure all of the sticky lusciousness would not transfer to her drogger.

She took her drogger out of the case and sat back next to Jaway to start singing and playing her instrument.

"Ever since I was a young girl, I loved hanging out with my family and being musical, however I could." Krizzles reflected back on the joyful memories that had speckled her entire developmental life. "Is there anything you guys want to hear?"

"Do you know any ruduhkoms? Those are my favorite." Pama knew they shared a similar culture, both coming from the Highlands Region.

"What is that? I've never heard of it before," Price asked as an outsider—he'd grown up in the southernmost city of Fowdleck in the Plains Region.

"What? You haven't heard of ruduhkoms? You have been missing out. They are very popular with everyone in our area. It is usually a slow song and has a common formula and topic—a love story that follows a person through their life. It can be reassuring about romantic relationships or heartbreak. It can include any emotion that is a result of caring about another person, depending on the type of love exchanged. So it could be about friendship, family, a lover, or something like that," said Lieutenant Commander Pama. "We consider ruduhkoms to be like folk music because they were originally only passed down by relatives. Only recently have they been recorded. Mostly, they were only learned by rote, and are part of our ancient past that survived." She was thankful to share part of their regional culture.

"Exactly," Krizzles said. "I know a bunch of ruduhkoms—my grandpa taught me some that he learned from his grandpa. What about a sad love story? It's called 'Jamie and Clyde'!"

"Yeah that sounds really deep. I'm game for anything you want to do!" M. O. Kandova said.

"Alright, here is 'Jamie and Clyde,' how I learned it from my grandpa. Listen carefully to the chorus, because it changes just a little each time."

A. P. Krizzles looked down at the instrument, lined up her fingers, and strummed a few practice chords. Then she plucked a beautiful melody as an introduction, and started singing in a clear, angelic tone.

"Well one day she walked by his side
He said, 'How's it goin'? Are you showin' all your life?'
Well one day she stayed up all night
Worried where he'd gone and who he was with, all her strife.
Jamie sat by the water's edge, looking at the stars
Lonely and hungry to belong
Jamie cried by the water's edge, singing all the bars
Wondering what she had done wrong
Another day, she walked by his side
He said, 'How's it goin'? Are you showin' all your life?
Well many days she stayed up all night
Worried where he'd gone and who he was with, all her strife
Jamie sat by the bed's edge, lookin' at the dark
Shouting and trying for the truth
Jamie cried by the bed's edge, singing all her scars

Moaning from the depths of her soul
Well one day she woke up by his side.
He couldn't say, 'How's it goin'? Are you showin' all your life?'
Well one day she buried her Clyde
Worried where he'd gone and who he was with, all her strife
All her strife
All her strife"

Krizzles had begun the ruduhkom gently, then increased the volume gradually until she sang, "buried her Clyde" the loudest, emphasizing that the love of Jamie's life had died. She carried the tune and placed each crew member into a trance. They noticed the graceful tone of her voice, accompanied not only by her string instrument, but by the gushing waterfall, insects, frogs, and occasional gust of wind that made the leaves hiss.

She looked down and around periodically, and Jaway saw inside her spirit, through the sparkling gray eyes. He felt one with her. Despite Pama's tough exterior, she welled up with tears. The folk song from her home region sounded similar to others that she knew. She was touched by the story and reflected about her family back in Wratshide, who also loved singing together during holidays.

"And that is how it's done," Pama said.

She lightly clapped, proud to share her culture, and the others softly applauded for Krizzles as she smiled.

While Krizzles continued to play many different kinds of ballads, Kandova noticed Hilton staring at her multiple times. She would look away, and then look back again, and he was still locked onto her. This gave her confidence to feel free with him, because she knew that he must like her. Nobody else detected this; all attention was fixed on Krizzles as she unlocked their hearts and invaded their souls with angelic, otherworldly sounds. It was like she was a window, where everything good from another dimension was funneled through into the spirits of the listeners.

Jaway was just as taken as the others, and he followed A. P. Krizzles's dynamic eyes, which opened and closed intentionally, sometimes looking off into a faraway land that only existed in the lyrics. He watched her perfect fingers strumming, extending from beautifully formed palms and soft arms with glowing skin. Her swan-like neck, free of any imperfections, drew his heart to her. Jaway admired the high cheekbones that jutted from under the most dazzling eyes he had ever seen in person. He noted a charming smile and sense of humor as she played quick, comedic songs that even made *her* laugh.

Jaway struggled inside to only remain platonic. Parts of who he was, parts that he did not understand, wanted so much more. It was almost as if he could not control himself against the powers that she had over him. During the course of the performance, he allowed himself to feel more than he ever had for any other woman in his life. There was nothing strange about staring deep into her eyes, because all of the other crew members did the same, singing along with the well-known tunes.

"I'm so glad we are all wearing comfortable clothes. It's truly a night where we can just relax and hang out!" Krizzles said as she walked over to her instrument case and situated the drogger back inside.

"I completely agree. And on that note, I am tired from a very long day, and probably should sleep as much as possible. Thanks to Hilton for always taking care of me. You are a complete star and saved my life today. I will be forever grateful!" T. O. Jeffers gave him a huge hug.

"No problem. I'm sure you would have done the same for me," he said. "I hope you sleep well tonight and heal a ton! Because we have to get back to the daily grind tomorrow, and we are going to need you to be close to one hundred percent."

Jeffers, Price, Pama, and Crumpler all said goodnight to everyone while Jaway, Krizzles, Kandova, and Hilton stayed back to clean up. After the kitchen was sparkling again, and the miniature pans and accessories were gathered from the washer, the remaining four sat by the fire.

"Can't let a good fire go to waste!" Hilton argued convincingly.

They played a few games, and then Jaway started talking with Krizzles, while Kandova and Hilton connected separately.

"The last time we gathered family communication, I got some blobes from my mom of my Trashie. Do you want to see them?" Jaway was certain the answer would be affirmative.

"Oh *would* I? Anything you have related to udringas is on the table," Krizzles flirted, but careful to make sure that it could also be interpreted as simple friendliness.

She put her chin on her fists and her elbows on one of the seats, sitting on the ground next to Jaway.

Jaway took out his pictogrammer and started playing short clips of Trashie.

"That is my mom, and the little black one is Trashie. We have two udringas now. Oh, there he goes. This is our yard, in the back. He is trying to play fetch with a stick he found that is twice as big as him. He never finds a proportionate twig. It's always out of his league!"

"He is adorable. His wool is so dark. I'm probably used to Daisy's white coat. How old is he?" A. P. Krizzles asked, completely enamored by the miniature pet.

"He is ten, which as you probably already know, is nearly ancient for an udringa. We got him when he was super small. I think he was only six months old—he could fit in my hand, and I was still pretty young." Jaway's smile beamed from cheek to cheek.

"Daisy is five, so she is much younger than Trashie. I love your house. It's very different than homes in my region. Ours are like a pointed sideways oval shape on a huge pole, and they twist if there is a hurricane or tornado."

"Wow, that's so cool. I would love to see your parents' place sometime. Yeah, ours curve up so that they can handle earthquakes; ours is a typical Zander, Mountain Region, west coast home. That is the top-floor window that my sisters and I blew out with the jipty when we were practicing on different devices." Jaway laughed and pointed to the third story, which had a floor-to-ceiling window in an odd shape that continued the curve of the house.

"Woah, they must have been angry. That is an *enormous* window!" Krizzles laughed with shocked, wide eyes.

"Yeah, they didn't leave us alone at home for about a year afterward." The pair chuckled together as responsible citizens looking back at past mistakes.

"So tell me more about yourself. I know that you are at the top of your field, or you wouldn't be in our crew. And you are a great musician from the Highlands Region. What else?" Jaway asked, his voice calm and organic.

"Thanks." Krizzles laughed. "Hmmm. Well, you already know about the love of my life, Daisy. She is so sweet. We have a farm, and I have five brothers and two sisters. I grew up playing sports, so I can get a little competitive sometimes. I don't know if you've been to my region, but it's really picturesque. We are known for beaches on the coast, but the farmland is gorgeous too. Just envision rolling hills as far as you can see, but the most beautiful bluish-purple in existence. We grow flax, so when it's in bloom, it is really breathtaking. Our nearest beach town is Ezlay, and we can get there in about an hour by vrodilop for fun with the family. We are ten total, so we fit exactly into a standard vrodilop—no more, no less. We usually go for the weekend or take a day trip. The people are relaxed and chilled out, and there are nice restaurants on the beach."

Krizzles shared openly, with a sincere heart. She felt a deep connection and wanted to take advantage of the moment to tell Jaway about the things that were most important to her, which included cultural influences, family, and hobbies.

The pictogrammer shut down.

"Let me get this charged so it's ready for tomorrow," Jaway said.

Krizzles noted his strong biceps and protruding pecs as he grabbed the pictogrammer from the seat and put it into a nearby bag. When he got up, A. P. Krizzles also registered once more how tall he was. Her chest warmed, and she felt good from head to toe.

"Wow, so you guys have a huge family that fills an entire vrodilop? How perfect! I bet you all have good teamwork skills because of that. I just have two younger sisters, but we are close with our extended family so we were always busy with them." Jaway tried to not get distracted by his feelings.

"Aw, that's great. So you definitely know the nature of women then, because they outnumbered you and your dad!"

They laughed.

"Yeah, they are great, but you're right. I imagine it is much different than having brothers."

Jaway breathed deeply and looked around to appreciate the forest, as the moonlight illuminated his amber eyes. Krizzles gazed deeply into them while his focus was elsewhere.

"We are so lucky to be here right now in this exotic setting. Ah, look, the full moon is out now," she said.

The pool created an open circle in the canopy, offering a view of the sky.

"It's amazing how the moonlight makes the water glow a surprisingly brilliant blue, as if something is shining inside," Jaway said.

"Yeah, I love the way the falling water sounds. We don't have anything like this where I grew up. The moon is so bright tonight that there is a dark shadow." She lifted her hand to show the replica it created on the ground next to them. "It almost seems that the waves are twinkling just like stars."

They sat around and pointed at the constellations and discussed what they stood for, as random clouds periodically swept in front of the moon. They were filled with peace and tranquility. It was as if they were only able to be grateful and nothing else was allowed into their thoughts.

"I love looking at the stars. Of course I expect them to twinkle, but when I focus on one and see it sparkling, it always catches me off guard," Krizzles said.

"Yeah, it reminds me that we are a tiny part of the universe. The fact that it's full of other planets and endless space makes me feel so insignificant, but also in touch with whatever else is out there."

Both of their bodies were energized with a low vibration that hummed from head to toe. They breathed deeply and slowly, without even realizing it, and both had a revelation that in the end, everything would be okay.

"You know, sometimes I have to remind myself that after all is said and done, and we move on with a chapter in our lives, everything will be fine. No matter the problems we may have had in a situation, as long as we are alive, peace is waiting. After all, every circumstance will finish," Jaway said.

"Wow, I never thought of it exactly like that before. You are exactly right. I was strangely just thinking something along the same lines."

They were in a trance, watching the flashing stars that extended through the universe.

"It's almost like how at night, there is no pressure because daily life has ceased to exist. And we are removed from what is going on in the world and in our circumstances, because it has all been temporarily put on pause."

Jaway continued explaining his personal understanding of why he was so thankful. Fresh gusts of wind washed over their bodies as they spoke and peered into the night sky. They connected deeply and felt comfort with each other as more than just friends.

Krizzles knew that Jaway was a caring person, and that she could trust him. She also was attracted to his physique and leadership skills. All of the things she loved about him flashed through her mind as they stayed awake and talked. She hoped he felt the same about her, but she could not read his intentions completely.

"It is so nice to get a break from our regular routine. We are usually working so hard to operate at a high level, and our lives are in each other's hands, so it can be a lot of pressure. But here, it is almost as if we can put that on hold," Jaway said.

"Yeah, this feels like when I go to the beach with my family. I wonder if the beauty and power of the rainforest forces us to become one with it. We are guests, witnessing the daily routines of the powerful creatures here, but also part of *that* reality," Krizzles added to Jaway's observation about their mindset.

"I couldn't agree with you more. I feel so relaxed."

These conditions put the crew members in a state of mind where they were more open to love, and the surroundings continually whispered softly to each of them, deep within their souls.

CHAPTER NINETEEN

When Jaway started sharing udringa blobes from his mom, Hilton and Kandova began talking to each other, sitting on the ground at the other end of the campfire.

"Thanks for helping my good friend T. O. Jeffers today. That means a lot to me. She is incredibly grateful to you, too." Kandova looked at Hilton intensely, but innocently.

"You are very welcome. When it comes down to it, it was no big deal to help in that moment. I'm sure we would all do the same for each other."

He was shy at first, but then snapped out of it. He realized that this was his big chance to get to know M. O. Kandova one-on-one, in the perfect relaxed setting.

"Is it true they asked you to go into the huge pit because you are the tallest?" she asked.

"Yeah, I don't think the others would have fared as well as I did. I'm used to it. When you grow up two heads taller than most guys, you get accustomed to doing things like helping older ladies get cans from top shelves at stores."

He laughed, and she calmly joined in, then said, "I don't usually feel nervous around people, but I have to confess that I haven't really been able to relax with you until now. Maybe it's because when I look up you seem like a *tower*, and I'm working on a phobia of heights." Kandova chuckled and nudged him with her elbow. "In all seriousness, today I was really proud of myself. I overcame my fears and jumped off of the mountain and had a lot of fun! It was amazing, and I got to fly through a rainbow on the way down." She was still at ease.

"I'm just a normal guy, so you don't have to be nervous around me. But let me know whenever you want to jump off of all of this mountain, and we can make that happen." I. P. Hilton paused—he felt the rambled joke might have traveled through unforgiving territory. He tried to come back with a recovery. "Ya know, in the water. I'm a great spotter."

They both chuckled.

"Do you want to go sit by the edge of the pool?" he asked.

"Sure, why not?" She tried to cover up her excitement.

Hilton stood first and offered his hand. Kandova reached up, and he lifted her short and curvy body into the air, helping her to stand. He took the chance to hold her hand before they arrived at the water, and he realized it was his responsibility to make her feel comfortable.

"Oh, you want to put your feet in? We can totally do that," Kandova said after she saw him taking his shoes and socks off.

"Yeah, why not? It's not every day we get to enjoy a moonlit night under the stars in front of a waterfall."

After they both sat down and submerged their feet, they looked around at the breathtaking scenery.

"I don't know about you, but we don't have the rainforest where I'm from. Owantay is in the southern part of the Highlands Region, which is the farthest large city from the rainforest in my region. It is beautiful because we have the beach, but it's mostly rolling hills and coastline." Kandova was opening up to him like never before.

"No, I can totally relate. I'm from Bingdole on the northwest coast, and we have cliffs and mountains but nothing like this."

They both sat quietly for a minute, taking in the beauty and breathing deeply.

"It is really nice to get to know you a lot better." Hilton broke the silence and redirected the conversation back to building trust and exploring each other.

"Yeah, I agree. We haven't talked a lot before about our personal lives. It's fun getting better acquainted with you."

M. O. Kandova flipped her extra-long, straight hair over one of her shoulders. It flew through the air as she flicked her head to guide it toward her back, exposing long eyelashes that had previously faded into the background of flowing, silky tresses.

"I have noticed that you are a fan of the elixir. You always know how to get everyone to laugh."

"Yeah, I'm a firm believer in self-care and recovering from trauma, so I try to make it seem cool to encourage everyone to take the treatment. There are so many benefits from it, and some people get out of military service and have to undo years of damage. The way I see it . . ." She paused to gather her words carefully. "You have fun and also get to repair emotional damage, so it's a win-win situation."

"Wow, I didn't realize you were such a caring person," Hilton joked, and she slapped his bulging bicep. He pretended to be offended that she'd tapped him.

"Hey, what do you mean?" she said, pretending her own offense. "I am *always* caring."

She looked up at him with innocent eyes and lifted her shoulders to appear angelic, which made him laugh until they were both giggling together. Their large smiles flashed sparkling teeth and projected an image of jubilation that emitted from their souls.

"No, I'm just joking. But I also really appreciate that you do such a good job. I mean, as a mechanical operator, you are probably more necessary than I am, as an information processor. We know that even though you banter from time to time, you take your job seriously, and the rest of us sleep better because we are in good hands."

He was trying hard to compliment her from an authentic place.

"Wow, thanks," she said. "I never realized that. I mean, I hear it often and see the results, but I forget to process how much everyone appreciates me. But, yeah, I respect that we all have to do our jobs at the highest level possible in order to keep ourselves safe."

"I have to be totally honest. I was shocked that you could see the orchid this morning on the walk. Not only was it already dark, but it was far away in the shadows. I gotta give you props for that too." Hilton knew that his compliments were being genuinely received. He was feeling the situation and could tell that he was connecting with Kandova.

"Aw, thanks! Yeah, ever since I can remember, I've had good eyesight. It has served me well in life." She laughed.

"So tell me more about yourself. Who is Kandova really? So far, I know that you are nineteen years old, just three years younger than me. You are from Owantay, a comedic jaguar sometimes, and you love a good adrenaline rush. What else?"

He listed these specific details in order to prove that he cared and listened intently. Kandova accepted the effort and opened up to him as someone who would value what was important to her.

"Well, I have one sister, and we are typical Owantay girls. You know, we can't help but love a high-glam look. My mom actually only had two kids because she wanted to keep her figure into her later years. She is even more stylish than me and my sister combined."

They laughed together before she continued.

"Even though we are a relaxed beach city and us highlanders are known for enjoying everything about life all the time, Owantay is the largest city of the region, so we have access to lots of high-quality things. Loads of artists of every kind flock there, where they can make the most money in our region. We Owantians love fresh seafood, because it comes straight from the nearby ocean. My family likes to go to the beach together, and we are super close. Hmmm, what else?" She paused. "My sister is my best friend, and we can tell our parents everything. I really miss them, so I'm glad to have been assigned to an amazing crew. This is the longest I've ever been away from home, so I'm still, ya know, adjusting to life without them every day."

Kandova shifted her confident gaze to the gorgeous moon, beautiful waterfall, and sparkling water that sloshed below. Tiny, residual, inconsistent waves lapped onto her legs, which were partially immersed in the deep, moonlit, green-blue pool.

This gave I. P. Hilton the chance to peer deeply into her prominent eyes, which were framed with long eyelashes and fluttered from time to time, as she took small breaks from the surroundings to look at him. He made sure to appear engaged in the conversation whenever her gaze landed on him, as he sat beside her.

"Yeah, that sounds like it would be difficult. I think we all have had to adapt to life away from our families. It was also tough for me. I learned to take advantage of the moments I get with them, and to make it meaningful, but I've had a few more years of practice than you at being separated. My family is very close as well. I have two brothers and two sisters, and my parents are really cool. My dad's a teacher," Hilton said.

"Wow, that's big compared to mine. I'm curious to hear what your mom's like."

"She's a lot of fun, and I hate to admit it, but I'm definitely her favorite."

They both chuckled.

"Naturally," Kandova replied.

"She owns a drink shop in Bingdole, so I grew up working there. We blend lots of fresh fruits, and they are tasty—and healthy, too. The job was a blast, but I ultimately liked helping out mainly because I got to spend more time with my mom. She is super cool and an overall wonderful person."

He continued, "You know, it's interesting hearing about Owantay. I actually only know small details about the east coast, so you are schooling me as we speak. I loved the seafood that was delivered for dinner today. That was a special treat. I can't imagine always having that at my disposal." Hilton's mouth started watering as he thought about the luscious spread they'd eaten.

"We have it all the time. The fish is way easier to get from the ocean, because we don't have as many cliffs right up against the sea like you do."

"Yeah, that is the hurdle for our fishing market. Those pesky cliffs. Hey, isn't trudles originally from your coastline?" Hilton was proud that he knew some geographic trivia.

"Yes, we actually invented the game because we have so many beaches with crystal-clear water. I love trudles."

"We played a really fun match while you were getting filled with adrenaline and flying off of your mountain today." He gathered his thoughts, making sure to share about his own life as well. "We are the second-largest city in the Mountain Region. Bingdole is fantastic, but I'm a city kid through and through. If you get a chance to go, you should visit. We have the second-largest volcano in The Land, so lots of people take a pilgrimage there. It is fun hiking up and practicing the religious ceremonies. It's so powerful, and makes you realize how insignificant we are on earth."

Hilton was meticulously trying to put his best foot forward.

"I would love to go," she said. I've heard about the pilgrimage hikes, and it seems like it would be fun with the whole family."

"Yeah, it is. You know, I absolutely appreciate going to the beach and enjoying the entire day there, so I think I would fit in well with your culture on the east coast. That's why I stayed behind today. We got to relax and play some trudles. Apart from the minor incident, it was amazing. And seriously, how often will we get the opportunity to be in a place like this?" I. P. Hilton whispered. "If you're into artistic stuff, we are multicultural on the west coast, and the metropolitan cities also produce a lot of fashion and design. We are much more formal because we don't have the resort vibe like the east coast, but we have great artsy stuff too. Have you ever tried our wine?"

"Have I?" M. O. Kandova pretended to hold a cup, and she hiccupped like her uncle at large gatherings. He laughed at her impression.

"That's my uncle at every Harvestium." She giggled. "But honestly, your wines are so good. I love a nice glass of artisanal west coast wine. They're all unique, but so much care goes into producing them."

The frogs wailed to a crescendo around them.

"Sounds like the toads also approve of your regional wine," Kandova joked, and then the frogs croaked softer and softer, almost as if she had coordinated with them in advance. "I initially considered staying and enjoying a relaxing day by the water, but then I realized how much I needed a high-energy adventure, so I went on the trek instead. For me, it was the event of a lifetime, in a world that feels like another planet— I wanted to explore and see the animals and plants that I had heard so much about in class during school. We have nothing like that back home, and it was everything I envisioned and more. Right after we started, Pama saved Sickles from being eaten alive by a deadly attack spider, with her magical lightning reflexes. Then we took the body on the hike, chilled of course, and ate it on the top of a mountain!" She exuded a look of disbelief about the day.

"Wow, that *is* the epitome of being adventurous. What did it taste like to you?"

"Surprisingly, and I was a little disappointed, it tasted a lot like chicken. We found some small citrus fruits, so at least it was a lemon version."

They both laughed.

"You're a regular beast of the rainforest now, Kandova—eating murderous spiders and defeating mountains."

They chuckled again.

"Yeah, that was one of the highlights, too—jumping off of the top and then flying through a rainbow. I always wondered what was inside them when I was a kid. It was a real challenge to stay silent for most of the trip, though. I instinctually wanted to talk constantly about the exotic plants and animals. I was so relieved when they decided to give us a break. I owe Price big time for coordinating that whole trek."

Kandova stopped talking to avoid speaking in her jaguar voice out of habit. Collecting herself, she continued, "I bet you have seen tons of that stuff by now though." She was making an effort to learn more about the handsome gentleman who continued soaking his feet next to her.

"Yeah, I have been on lots of treks, but it sounds like you guys had multiple rare encounters. Your one hike was, hands down and honestly, better than all of mine combined."

They both quickly pulled their legs out of the water as a reflex, because something large brushed against the bottoms of their feet.

"What was *that*?" Kandova asked.

"It seemed huge, whatever it was!"

"I bet it was an eel. They are supposed to be humongous, but I don't think they would do anything to hurt us. The brief they gave us said they weren't dangerous. But why don't we chill out over there and dry off just in case?"

Hilton led Kandova over next to the campfire and offered her a towel.

"Good plan, especially after what I saw today! You know, I think you might be right. I heard that eels are nocturnal," Kandova said.

As she walked with him to the seating area around the campfire, Hilton's entire body filled with warmth. He tried to act normal but realized, with much more experience under his belt, that he was falling in love with Kandova. The mechanical operator was funny and sweet, serious when she needed to be, and full of personality when appropriate. He also was very attracted to her physically. He liked that she was close with her family, and that she cared about others deeply.

"You know, even though we haven't talked a lot, I feel like I've known you forever. Like maybe we knew each other in a past life or something. Do you feel the same?" Hilton whispered, trying to speak quieter than the other couple that was talking nearby.

"Yes, I feel the same way. I'm really glad we had the chance to get to know each other better tonight." Kandova tried to match his whisper, because in the back of her mind, she knew that they should not reveal any hint of romance, due to the conduct rules.

The comments of the other girls from earlier that night ran through her mind, and she decided to push it as far as she could without getting in trouble. This was the first time she had ever felt this way about anyone. She was pretty sure he reciprocated her strong feelings, and was giddy that they actually had a lot in common.

Hilton, meanwhile, had desired companionship for a very long time. From his youthful, twenty-two-year-old point of view, it seemed like ages since he'd left the home where he was raised, and he longed for a solid family life. He sometimes felt alone in the world, and many years of solitary nights had amplified the fact that he'd been single for an extended period of time.

That evening, he realized that Kandova was the one for him—that he yearned to spend the rest of his existence with her. He had seen her interact with friends, and she was incredibly genuine, so Hilton trusted that everything she shared about her family and what she thought about the world and how she felt about him was all authentic.

As they sat on the benches, he decided that they would be together forever, if she also wanted it. He hoped that he had impressed her enough to take an equal interest in a future with him. I. P. Hilton's new goal was to thoroughly investigate where she stood, and to leave the campfire that night certain of a possible future with one another.

CHAPTER TWENTY

Sitting side by side, I. P. Hilton and M. O. Kandova turned and looked deeply into each other's eyes for a few seconds, which seemed to last a lifetime. Then Kandova glanced away; she felt shy and was not sure if she was revealing her deep desire and budding love for the man.

He pointed to the full moon and started discussing interesting facts about the phases and tides that were affected by the glowing, majestic sphere in the night sky. At this point, with his new conscious understanding of his desires, Hilton was purposely putting her at ease. He decided to make a move to be catapulted out of the possibility of being romantically separated because of a strong friendship. He emphatically knew that it was necessary to make it clear that he wanted to be much more than just buddies, while balancing the burden of staying within the guidelines.

"I can't help but look around at the beautiful setting that we are in and appreciate the gorgeous waterfall that is flowing into a glowing turquoise pool that sparkles like the stars in the sky. I can only hear rushing water and nighttime rainforest sounds. Even though the leaves are saying to me, 'shhh, shhh, shhh,' I have to keep speaking. I'm not sure if this is the most beautiful scene I've ever laid my eyes on, or if my mindset is helping me to take it all in. Look over at the waterfall. It's like transparent fabric sheets, with pointed hems on the bottom, falling one on the other. One quickly drops out of view, only to be replaced again and again. I'm astounded by how bright the moon is here and how many stars we can see. The amount of light that is coming from the pool is incomprehensible; how can it not be lit from below?"

Hilton took a break to breathe deeply and close his eyes.

"And that fresh breeze of humid air that's caressing our skin, it smells so crisp that it must be Mother Nature exhaling. This may be the most stunning sight I have ever seen in my life—but you are even more impressive because of who you are inside. Don't get me wrong, you are gorgeous on the outside too, but I want to be clear that it is my wish to get to know you much better, and not just as friends." Hilton spoke softly enough to stay under the radar of Jaway and A. P. Krizzles, who were enthralled in their own conversation.

He paused to wait for a response, and just then the wind blew a huge gust into the camp. The trees hissed, and the almost-extinct fire blew into waves of bright orange and yellow. Hilton waited in agony—he had just exposed his heart, and possibly created a very awkward work relationship.

Kandova looked up into his eyes and wanted to kiss him, but instead she stepped over the inner bench and walked up to the raging fire. I. P. Hilton got up and stood next to her; his body blocked the view of Kandova from the other crew members.

She said, "This is how I feel about you. A blaze ignites inside me whenever we are close, and I can't help it. I simmer down and the fire seems to go out until a breeze blows and sparks another inferno. I'm still new to this, so you'll have to bear with me, but I am picking up what you are putting down."

They stood next to each other, pretending to get warm by the fire, and did everything in their control to hide their true intentions from the other two. After all, the highest in command from their glider was just a few paces away, thankfully distracted by his own exchange of words.

"I have spent years of lonely nights, longing to meet someone and have a partner," said Hilton. "I am sincere when I say that I want the best for your safety and overall well-being. But I also would like to get to know you better, and I want you to be my special person."

He was afraid of scaring her off, so he left out the extended plans to be linked forever. His objective was to clearly draw a line in the sand to avoid simply being friends, and he had accomplished this. Hilton needed to be vulnerable and make his intentions clear as an honest man. This way, if she liked who he truly was, Kandova could accept him into her life. She squeezed his hand, which was hidden between their bodies, then stared up into his eyes, breathing in and out calmly.

"I also want to get to know you much better, and I am sure we will have a lot of time in close quarters to be able to do that. I think we can manage to stay focused on our jobs and become acquainted at the same time."

She winked at him and smiled, then flashed pearly teeth and squeezed his hand once more. Her chest was a vortex of hot energy, but her mind was at ease.

"I think we might get caught if we stand here staring into each other's eyes, even though the other two are preoccupied," Hilton said.

He tried to push the growth of their relationship as much as possible while remaining within the constraints of the rules.

"You're exactly right, my west coast emperor." Kandova grabbed a stick nearby and jabbed the logs to make the flames higher. She added in a somber tone, "Well, I do have a problem."

He gazed at her pensively and realized that this could be the moment that he proved to be a good listener. Then he imagined multiple worst-case scenarios of rejection, and tried to fight the images off without revealing the inner battle on his face. He tried to replace the negative thoughts with positive ones as she continued.

"I've been dealing with a deficiency that has really prevented me from giving all of myself, especially when I'm at home." Kandova poked the fire and looked into his eyes innocently.

"What is it? Do you think we could work around it?" Hilton felt a heavy urge to fight for his dreams, but tried not to act desperate.

M. O. Kandova took a deep breath and looked to the ground away from him. She appeared to gather all of her strength before opening up to the captive audience of one. She started slowly.

"My problem is..." She paused, then quickly divulged her truth. "...that I can't reach cans at the top shelf in the grocery store. So when I get home, I can't even cook what I want, and my parents get concerned. And since you are taller than nearly everyone, and you have sufficient training in helping my kind with our problems, I just may need help for a very long time, starting now."

Kandova smiled, and Hilton's face immediately transformed from grave concern to relief. They laughed together. He realized in a split second that, first, he was not being rejected but was in fact being presented with quite the opposite, and second, Kandova now felt comfortable and relaxed enough around him to express herself, even with pranks. She had finally let her guard down, and he understood that it was his job to continue to fan the flames of what they had started. He gathered himself from what seemed like the possibility of a broken heart, feeling it evolve to a renewed vision of their future.

I. P. Hilton spoke while peering down at the ground. "As a matter of fact, I have been helping old ladies since my growth spurt. Here's a funny thing that I bet you did not know about me. I actually plan an extra fifteen minutes for each grocery stop, simply to help the less vertically fortunate." He looked at her directly, relieved that he did not have to grieve a death to his dreams. "So I think I may be able to set aside an extra, say, ten or twenty years for you if you need, solely out of a desire to be helpful and serve my fellow human."

They laughed together, and he was happy to convey that he could handle her sense of humor, even when discussing weighty, life-changing plans.

Kandova tried very hard to not take life too seriously when possible, although she was not always successful.

"Well, I do have an actual problem, but we won't have to deal with that right now. My dad is super overprotective and always drove off anyone I was even slightly interested in. But he's not here, so you are in luck! And you should be thankful we are not allowed to communicate with our families much now."

They laughed, and Hilton responded in jest, "I'm not exactly sure what that means, but yes, I am very grateful because it sounds like we won't have a lot of resistance."

Personal communication was limited for the crew, sometimes completely prohibited, because the enemy's technology could uncover their location. In addition, the military did not want crew members to accidentally reveal their whereabouts to family or friends, as that might jeopardize the lives of everyone on the mission. "Loose lips sink ships" was a common phrase heard among the military.

The crew was allowed to receive family messages when in a safe space, as determined by advanced technology. Sending messages to loved ones was even more restricted. Outgoing correspondence was permitted only when the glider returned to a protected place outside of the rainforest, after completing a mission, and when no information had yet been provided about the next assignment.

They both sat down, and Kandova poked the coals in order to pretend that they were just enjoying the campfire, which she had been purposely refueling to delay the inevitable end of the night.

"Hey, do you guys want to play a quick card game?" Jaway's voice startled the budding couple.

"Yeah, that's a great idea," Hilton said, certain that he had already completed the goal of becoming much closer to the woman he desired from the depths of his being.

All four of the crew members sat together on the ground outside the benches, where they played three rounds.

"Alright, this was a fantastic night to end an equally wonderful day," Jaway said, indicating that he was ready to go to bed soon.

"Yeah, I think we all had an extraordinary time." Hilton got up and started to completely put out the fire for safety purposes.

They situated the cards and returned the entire area to a functional space for the next day. As they did, it began lightly raining.

"Since you are both fydonmates and we are too, let us walk you back." Jaway wanted to build trust and show that he was looking out for everyone, especially the girl who made him feel on top of the moon.

Jaway and Hilton walked Krizzles and Kandova back to their fydon, where each wished the others a good night. The men returned to their fydon to take showers, then headed to individual tents. The girls talked with love in their eyes, while brushing their teeth and getting ready for bed. Then they went down to their tents and quickly fell asleep, filled with burning romance, as the rainforest dripped soft droplets from leaf to leaf.

When Jaway returned to his tent, he looked at information about the next steps of the mission before turning his lights out and meditating. Normally, he would imagine being in a place that made him feel calm and at ease, like a beach scene that he'd experienced, or time with his family. But tonight, he was already surrounded by the most beautiful sounds of gushing water, light rain on the leaves, insects, and frogs. He was thankful for the relationship that he hoped would grow in the future.

Fresh gusts of air blew every once in a while, reminding him that he was already in one of the most relaxing places possible. He began breathing deeply and slowly, like his mom had instructed when he was a child, and he quickly fell into a deep sleep.

All four of them were physically exhausted from the day, and all slept soundly.

The next morning, the rainforest began waking. As the light gradually increased, the quintessential regional sounds grew louder and louder. The crew members woke and began preparing for the day they would return to life on the glider. Each of them, but especially the youngest, knew they would fondly look back at this adventure throughout their lives. Many took advantage of a morning swim in the turquoise pool, diving down with the waterfall to investigate the eels, while others planned the day or organized their belongings.

Crumpler and Didier prepared a spread with luscious ingredients, and soon rang a bell to indicate that the food would be ready in ten minutes. Everyone finished whatever they were doing and prepared for the nice breakfast in paradise. M. O. Kandova sat next to I. P. Hilton. They had a pleasant meal and gently chatted on the outside, but burned with love inside. In the same vein, Jaway and A. P. Krizzles enjoyed each other's company as they slowly emerged from a deep sleep, trying not to seem obvious about their inner desires.

In the middle of his meal, Jaway stood up to address the dedicated bunch.

"It is great to see all of you enjoying our last few hours in this pristine rainforest. Thanks to our culinary experts, who whipped up another phenomenal breakfast with these tasty ingredients."

Everyone snapped their fingers to create an applause that also seemed to be emerging from slumber, and then continued eating as they listened to their commander.

"I just received a report from Central Command this morning that a battalion similar to ours in a different part of the Wild Territory experienced extensive damage to their glider and personnel, and I want to remind you all to remain serious about every single decision you make. I also wanted to commend you all for laboring together with motivated teamwork and resolve to continue focusing on the end goal and keeping each other safe."

He was referring to the other crew, the one that did not exist in unity like theirs did. The dissonance in that group had been responsible for the failures that ultimately ended in serious harm to the ship and workers. Other battalions did not have the ability to operate machinery at the high level that Jaway's had, and many lacked professionalism among colleagues. This was a reminder for Jaway that their circumstance was special and unique, and he had to fight to continue to function at a high level and to have great interpersonal relationships.

"Okay, so we will be returning the tents to our fydons soon and then flying back to the glider. Once we get all settled, we can unpack into our living quarters."

He purposely did not mention that Churchill would be draining the waste with a hose. Everyone knew, and he did not want to highlight the personnel guide's loss in the race.

"As usual, we will be zapping the area to return it back to the original condition, so don't leave anything behind. Does anyone have any questions?"

Nobody responded.

"Okay, enjoy the rest of your breakfast, and we have two hours until we must be back at the glider. I'll be around if you need any guidance."

When Jaway finished speaking, he sat down to eat the rest of his meal. The crew members all completed whatever tasks were necessary to dismantle the kitchen, campfire, and benches. The individual tents were organized, minimized, and placed inside the fydons. Once the small vehicles were completely reoccupied, the crew flew to the glider, parked in the lowest level (designated for fydon storage), and began to take personal items to the nearby living quarters.

Lieutenant Commander Pama placed the black orchid they had retrieved into the central common area next to some couches, as a trophy of her expedition and a reminder for the squad to bring everything required for every excursion.

After the fydons arrived in place, each connected a hose to an area below the vehicle storage floor, where the waste was converted into organic matter and reduced to ninety percent of its original mass. Just before leaving, P. G. Churchill flew a fydon down to the rainforest floor, and inserted a hose from the glider under the surface. The waste was injected deep inside the ground, in organic form, where it would serve as fertilizer to help enrich the surrounding soil. Thankfully, Churchill did not have any problems and remained free from any contact with the organic matter. After he finished with the extra duty, he flew back up and parked in the fydon storage room.

"Alright, Churchill is here. Each crew member is accounted for, so we are cleared to run the zornpa," Jaway said from the upper control room, while most of the rest of them sat at desks and worked independently.

A zornpa was an integral part of keeping these missions as secretive as possible. When the glider was first parked, the zornpa took a scan of the entire area and stored the information, even down to the individual leaves and soil patterns. Upon departure, the zornpa used laser technology to return the area nearly to what it was before it was transformed by the humans' presence. It restored the soil to its original placement, erasing all tracks made by the crew. Even the black orchid was replaced high in the tree, and minor twigs were repaired. Any foliage that had been hacked by a laser machete was returned to the condition it had been in before the troop entered the space. Twenty minutes after the zornpa began its work, all parts were reconstructed to a very believable original state. Only a sophisticated machine would be able to detect that something had been repaired.

"Alright, I have just received an all-complete indication from the zornpa, so our presence is done here! Kandova, we are all clear to leave. Can you please turn the expadier off?" Jaway yearned to stay even just one day longer, but he fought to stay focused for himself and his subordinates.

When the expadier was switched into operation mode, it constantly scanned an area for human activity, within the radius of a two-hour walk. It was important to have ample warning in case any people approached them who chose to continue to live in the Wild Territory, in opposition to the united Land. Because these people were experts at silently maneuvering through dense terrain, they could easily surprise anyone. In most cases, those who lived in the Wild Territory would consider citizens of The Land to be invaders, and it would not end well for the captured. This was why the expadier not only could notify the crew about native people, but also prevent manmade sounds from leaving a temporary village, like the base camp that had been created for the incentive days.

"No problem. I am working on that now," Kandova said, sitting at a desk and working through her kleck in order to deactivate the expadier. "We are all set. The expadier is in standby mode now," she reported professionally, having completed the task much faster than most other mechanical operators would have been able to.

"Perfect. You're the best, Kandova. Alright, we are now cleared for takeoff to our next destination. Prepare the crew," Jaway said.

A message was played throughout the vessel, using the voice of an actor who worked and lived in Central Command, located in Zander on the west coast.

The recording said, "Attention, crew members—congratulations on your successful defense against an attack on The Land. We acknowledge that your efforts to operate at the highest level possible, and quick thinking, have saved not only your lives, but an immense amount of property. We hope that you enjoyed your incentives and that morale is high. The glider will now depart in five, four, three, two, one."

They took off.

"As you are aware," the message continued, "projectiles from the forest floor explosion caused damage to the front right end of the glider, and it must be repaired. Thankfully, it was minimal, but your next stop is Kritziddle, to dock and receive repairs and maintenance."

For security purposes, the location of the next destination was usually kept under wraps until just after departure. Didier was excited to go back to her home city, the second-largest of the Rainforest Region, and shouted a loud, "Woot, woot!" that rang throughout the glider on the lowest level as she prepared vegetables and personalized meal plans for the following week.

Each crew member knew what to do, and set out to work at their job in order to maintain daily life, advance the mission of gathering information, operate the vehicle carefully, or support the mission through a specific position.

CHAPTER
TWENTY-ONE

Six hundred years before all of that technology was available, people had lived just as comfortably without the elaborate devices that had been developed since the emperor's founding of the Royal Academy of Technology. The academy had only been around for about 150 years before Jaway's base camp experience.

Crawldsay was the capital city at this time, and was located farther inland and north of Zander, the capital during Jaway's life. Crawldsay was a fortified city right on the edge of the rainforest. It had been built over the span of two thousand years, from when The Land originally began. The rainforest had been depleted over that time, and farmland acted as a buffer between it and the city.

When The Land was originally established, it only contained three prefectures that spanned the entire west coast from top to bottom. Although the North, Central, and South Prefectures were distinctive in many ways, the western volcanoes and cliffs united them in a common experience. Over time, the other regions joined The Land to create Jaway's world from coast to coast.

As you can imagine, Crawldsay was drastically different than the futuristic modern realm. To begin, vehicular transport remained on the ground and was dependent on animal strength. Among many other differences, although the royal family's clothes contained the best materials and workmanship, nothing compared to the transformative jurprodians that were available to everyone during the time of Jaway.

"How much longer do we have, my kind sir?" Emperor Henerinni shouted through a tiny opening that was created when he unlatched a miniature door that faced the carriage driver on the outside.

"Looks like we have about thirty minutes until we make it to the gates," the driver yelled back with a bounce in his voice as they hit a bump in the road.

"Alright, thanks my good man." The emperor closed the small communication pathway by latching it shut. It sealed the royalty away from the outside world.

"Well, we still have a little time to kill on the way back home. What are your plans for the week, my love?" he asked.

"I would really like to finish a textile project that I began a few weeks ago," Empress Virginni said. "The fine materials just arrived yesterday. When it is finished, we can hang it in the bedroom."

"What is the subject matter?"

"It is a scene from the Zander volcano with pilgrims traveling up the side." The empress was proud that she was including a ceremonially themed piece that would live on the castle walls forever.

At that time, Zander was known as the destination with the largest volcano; however, the city remained smaller and less established than Crawldsay. Empress Virginni had grown up with the best embroidery teachers, so although she was just twenty-five years old, she was highly skilled at including exotic and valuable materials in her tapestries. She knew how to create fine details with real gold and silver string, precious gems, and the finest, most vibrant threads available.

The emperor and empress continued discussing personal hobbies until they noticed a considerable ascent and then a steady pull to the side as the vehicle made heavy, 180- degree turns in order to gradually climb the hill that protected Crawldsay from unwelcome guests, or even worse, rainforest people who wanted nothing more than to destroy the entire city.

Two muscular twarpens pulled the carriage with increased gusto. They knew that momentum would be on their side to make it up the hill, even though the speed made the turns more drastic. A twarpen was one of the most useful animals in Crawldsay at the time. Massive, rounded, furry hooves acted as their base, and they stood at twice the height of an average man when fully grown. Four strong legs allowed the beasts to pull heavy loads, or to be ridden as a form of transportation.

An elongated, flat back led to a long tail of very straight hair. The neck was thick, and a mane flowed from behind it to the ground. Pointed ears and large eyes with bushy eyelashes provided a way to communicate feelings to a master. Two spiral horns jutted out from the forehead, and a very long nose with a velvety tip led to plump lips and a mouth full of substantial teeth, perfect for grazing.

Unleashing these eating giants onto an overgrown, rolling hill produced a finely coiffed and manicured bump of earth, not to mention full twarpen bellies. The females produced milk rich in nutrients and taste, while young twarpens were prized for their tender flesh on tables throughout Crawldsay. Because of their gentle spirits and strong connection with the herd, they were also utilized on the nearby farms to pull plows, making them one of the most versatile beasts of burden.

In general, twarpens could be multicolored with brown, black, and white hues, as well as solid in any of these colors. The royal twarpens were bred from the strongest available studs and mares, and were solid in color only. The two that pulled the emperor and empress that day were pure white males.

The operator yanked reins attached to the magnificent white creatures to maneuver along the winding road that ascended and curved up to the city gates. Sweat dropped from the beasts as they pushed their bodies to pull the carriage to the top. After making the last huge turn, a wide road led up to two iron gates that, together, created an expansive half oval with a split down the center.

"Permission to enter!" the driver shouted to the lookout towers that flanked the huge doors while flashing a coin with the emperor's seal that was the size of his hand.

"Permission granted!" a voice boomed from high above the wide stone street.

A series of levers and locks began removing the extensive, interwoven seal between the two gates. The scent of oiled metal wafted in the air. After twenty seconds of scraping and wiping sounds, muffled by heavy breathing from the recovering twarpens, the gates began to swing open from the center. The slow pace revealed their immense weight. As the carriage leisurely traveled through the entrance of Crawldsay, the driver looked far up to the lookout towers, which seemed to reach the sky, and waved exaggeratedly to one of his friends, whom he imagined was stationed at the top. A distant hand waved back, affirming his assumption.

Barn animal yelps and hollers faded from very soft to loud as they entered the city and slowly followed the road around the left closing gate. Two colossal barns with curved roofs that extended nearly to the ground were located to the right of the entrance, reminding those entering the city that it was self-sustaining and could provide necessities for citizens for up to a year if necessary.

The entrance gates and towers were attached to two very long walls that extended far to both sides and were parallel to an equally lengthy rear wall that ran from west to east, with two lookout towers located along the stretch. A cylindrical lookout tower rose from the ground at the end of the front wall that traveled east, and then another straight wall started at the back side of that tower and traveled northeast to another tower. An equidistant wall ran northwest from there to a final lookout at the end of the rear wall. These walls created a point on the far eastern edge. A mirror image of this stood on the western end as well.

A total of ten towers surrounded the city along the walls and provided security as well as vantage points for defense if necessary. Outside the walls, all around the city, were steep stone drop-offs, virtually impossible to climb. These added security and an intimidating natural deterrent to any foes interested in compromising the safety of the castle. This was a major reason that the capital had remained secure for the two thousand years up to the time of Emperor Henerinni and Empress Virginni.

The vehicle followed the stone road past the barns and swung a left curve, moving west along a street that ran parallel to the front wall, then took a northwest turn with that wall. After meeting a small cluster of homes and shops, the road followed the next wall, which pointed northeast. Then they turned right toward the infamous palace of Crawldsay. The twarpen happily and slowly pulled the carriage up the much slighter slope, which seemed like nothing compared to the grueling Crawldsay mountain route that they'd just endured. This road only curved once, to the left, while ascending another stone base. It led to much smaller doors than those of the city, though these too created a half oval with a split down the center. A thin tower rose on each side of the doors. Very small vertical rectangles provided a complete view and almost fully protected anyone on the inside.

The driver again flashed the large coin and lifted it three times. "Permission to enter? All clear?"

This meant that the emperor and empress were in the carriage and was a way of double-checking that it was safe to enter the palace.

"Aye, aye. All clear," a voice boomed from the top of one tall, thin stone tower.

More levers and mechanical components scraped and slithered to unlock the gates and reveal the grand entrance to a giant, round, four-story building, complete with two major towers on the sides, with countless small, medium, and large turrets randomly distributed around the entire structure. The palace building contained four floors with thirty-six bedrooms, as well as thirty-six bathrooms with plumbing and fresh water. The main hall and ballroom were on the ground floor. The second floor contained the past emperor's room, known as the parent's room. A library with spectacular views was on the third floor, as well as the current emperor's bedroom.

Bedrooms and other useful spaces were scattered throughout the floors, separated by stone walls. Servant quarters were in the basement, and contained twenty bedrooms and five bathrooms. A stone floor provided very cool temperatures to store food, as the kitchen was also in the basement. Freshwater springs rose as a pool near the center rear area of the city. These provided flowing water that ran into the palace building as well as into a crystal-clear pond on the eastern side of the grounds. A section of it was stocked with seafood.

Sewage ran under the western side of the walls into the city sanitation system, to be converted to fertilizer and other useful substances. Palm trees dotted the landscape, and a palace garden filled with fruit trees was located at the west end inside the circular palace walls, beyond the barn.

After passing through the gates to the grounds, the driver parked the carriage in front of the palace doors, then tapped two times on the carriage wall. The doors swung open, and Virginni adjusted her dress and stepped down the stairs to the ground with the help of a doorman who greeted her.

"I trust your trip was productive and interesting, ma'lady."

He spoke with the formality and warmth of a worker who was treated with respect and care.

"Oh yes, Trube, we had a truly fantastic time, but we are so glad to be home. Can you make sure that my belongings are available in the bedroom by dinner tonight? I brought back some exotic delights and a cape that I want to wear," Virginni said as she planned out the rest of the day in her mind.

The empress knew each servant's name and treated them with dignity and respect. She waited as Henerinni descended and held her hand to walk into the palace together. They were known for their warm relationship after four years of marriage; they were very fond of each other.

"So I'll see you at dinner, right my dear?" Henerinni asked.

"Yes, I look forward to it, sweetie. Enjoy your xyloblut training." She gave him a kiss on the lips.

Henerinni was a well-known athlete in many sports, and took personal lessons in order to perfect his technique and train for endurance. Xyloblut was a sport that took place on a special court with two opposing teams, with five in play for each at any given time. The xyloblut court was located behind the palace, on the grounds.

A game began by players assembling in the middle, in front of a very high wall. One player stood in the center, with two participants behind on each side, and two more behind them, making a V formation. The opposing team mirrored the shape.

After the bouncy rubber ball fell through a chute, the center players tried to gain control of it. Then the members could bounce, pass, or carry the ball around one of two poles that were located in the back zone, which was farthest away from the start zone, next to the tall wall. Each team was assigned a different pole, and it was on the side of the court where they started, in the back zone. After reaching this area, a competitor could choose to climb the pole by stepping on wooden pegs and shoot, or travel back and shoot from anywhere on the court, as long as it was outside of the start zone. After a shot was made, players returned to starting positions and then restarted.

The athletes could choose to shoot into many different shapes—a circle, two triangles, and two squares—that were attached to the high wall near the start zone. In the middle of this, near the top, was a metal bar that held an empty flat circle, one and a half times the size of the ball. The disk was perpendicular to the ground, so proper technique was to throw the ball with a spin at the wall so it would bounce off, and horizontally travel through. This ring produced the highest points possible.

A triangle was placed on each side of the circle, but much lower and closer to the outer edge. Below each triangle and farther from the center was a square. If a player climbed the pole successfully to the top and threw the ball through the round ring, they gained fifty points. This was the most challenging shot, and it required perfect technique. If a competitor climbed the pole and made it through one of the two triangle, twenty-five points were earned. If a player shot into one of the lowest shapes, the squares, it was worth ten points. The squares were the largest, so shots could be made into them without as much precision.

If someone decided to take a shot from the court after running around their team pole, a circle yielded seven points, a triangle five, and a square three. After ten shots had been made, the squad with the most points won. A wait zone lay behind the pole area in the back zone, containing long benches. Extra athletes who were not yet in the game waited here, and after a point was made, players could switch out before creating the starting position with five participants per team again.

In addition to xyloblut, Henerinni loved aldroot, which was a safe, blade-based training sport intended to hone skills and reactions for sword fighting. He also participated and prepared for kurjintel matches. Kurjintel was a mostly no-contact martial art where players used kicks or punches to touch ribbons that were placed at different points on the body. The idea was that the exercises would improve muscle memory for body combat, working on precise movements.

Because Henerinni enjoyed all of these different sports, his twenty-nine-year-old body reflected the arduous workouts and matches. His pectoral muscles were prominent and framed by large biceps and beefy, chiseled abdominal muscles on a tall frame. His lower body was equally fit, and he was incredibly flexible in order to be able to participate in kurjintel matches. He was known for a prominent hooknose, and his full lips balanced his face with dark eyes and full eyelashes. Outdoor activities created a dark tan, which enhanced his tough look.

Henerinni arrived at the xyloblut court, where his trainer was already preparing for the lesson.

"Ready for another grueling but oh-so-good training session today? I'm certain you'll have a successful day," Paujee spoke in a deep tone.

"You know it, Paujee. I've been sticking to the meal plan you put me on. No snacks on the side at all. I just hope it pays off in extra endurance." Henerinni showed off his six-pack abdominals, which had recently become more defined.

"I've been tracking everything, and we should see the full benefits in one week. Hang in there—your body has been showing great improvements along the way. Imagine it just happening easily."

He led the Emperor through a warm-up involving a series of kurjintel stretches and specific routines on the xyloblut court. Then they worked on a collection of precision-enhancing exercises, followed by movements that used body weight for resistance. Finally, they practiced proper technique for throwing the ball with a spin through the different shapes on the wall. After the workout, they planned the next training session, looked at the data from the past month, and measured different parts of his body for the records. Emperor Henerinni was motivated because he wanted to win.

"Woah, I never get tired of the workout it takes to get up to the third floor. Just when I thought I couldn't get any more from my training, I show that I can," Henerinni joked between deep breaths as he entered the bedroom.

He looked up and saw Virginni at a seating area, working on a textile, and noticed that her face seemed solemn. The emperor walked over, careful not to sit down before he took a shower.

"How has your cloth come along, sweetie?" he asked, trying to gauge her emotional state.

"It's actually going well. I have bad news, though. I lost another baby." She looked numb, her eyes dead with disbelief. "The prenatal doctor stopped by and confirmed immediately after we arrived back from the trip this afternoon." Her beauty radiated endlessly, even through the toughest times and when she was in pain. "At least this one was early on, so I should have a quick recovery."

The emperor sat on the couch next to her, still glistening with sweat and smelling delightfully sour.

"Aw, baby, I'm so sorry. What can I do to help right now?" He wanted to comfort her like she needed.

She broke down in tears, careful to move the valuable textile she had been working on out of the way. The anguish in her soul didn't allow her to speak. Virginni only felt a tugging in her chest, and her tears poured out as she slid onto the floor with her face to the ground. Trying to speak, she realized that she could not.

When she fell on the rug, the emperor wrapped his arms around her and told her, "You are my world, and I am always here for you. No matter what we are going through, we will always be stronger in the end. I love you, baby. I love you. I love you."

The empress cried so hard that it seemed like air could only exit, and she couldn't take a breath. She bounced in agony as tears flowed from her gorgeous eyes. The emperor held her as she mourned the loss of the future she had planned as a mother. All of the dreams of what could have been had been shattered in a single visit from the doctor.

After a few minutes, she came to terms with reality and was able to breathe again, though she still wailed in beats for a while after she could take in air, followed by a huge breath and then silence. Finally, she spoke.

"I just thought this would be different, and that we would be welcoming a future heir into the world. I dreamed of the possibilities of who that little life could have been. There were so many, and now it is gone. I won't be a mother like I had planned."

Virginni sat up with the emperor's arms wrapped around her shoulders. She took a deep breath in and felt a rush of calm move over her body, like the tears that had streamed down her cheeks. The emperor noticed the peace she felt, and he aided her gently back into a seated position on the couch. They sat in silence as he held her hands in his.

The emperor looked deeply into her sparkling, light-tan eyes and said, "I am here for you. You are safe, and I love you more than anything you could ever imagine. You are my partner, and I will be here until the very end of life. What you are feeling is normal, and I can't say that I understand what you are going through because I can't, but I've been here through thick and thin, and you have a right to be sad. You have a right to grieve what you wanted . . . what *we* wanted."

Virginni was unable to speak, and felt as though her already completely numb body was engulfed by an equal amount of sedation. She tried to say something, but a lump in the base of her throat ached.

The empress took a deep breath and squeezed out, "I love you too, baby, and I wouldn't have this journey of life with anyone else. You are my rock, and thanks for being here for me. I feel so devastated right now."

Henerinni leaned in and kissed her on the lips. Her face, arguably the most beautiful in all creation, still looked breathtakingly stunning as she wiped her eyes and flipped her immaculately straight hair behind her shoulders.

"I think it is just that I come from a huge Bingdole family, and I want the same. You know I grew up with three sisters, four brothers, and my parents, so I imagined filling the bedrooms of this palace with our children. And we have been trying for the past four years, since we were married." She spoke more clearly now.

"I get that," said the emperor, "but I want you to know that for me, you are everything I need. The reason we chose each other for marriage is because we wanted someone who was enough. And you are enough for me. You and I are a small family, and whenever, or if ever, we add to our family, that is okay."

"Thanks so much for being my rock. I love you the same, and love having you as my family." Virginni meant every word from the core of her being. "Why don't you get out of that xyloblut gear and take a shower, sweetie? I'll play some harp—I know it will make me feel much better. Your mom and dad will be expecting us soon for dinner." She began to breathe more normally.

"I do smell a bit ripe, don't I?" Henerinni lifted his arm and sniffed, raising his eyebrows to lighten the mood. "Are you sure you don't want to cancel dinner tonight with my mom and dad? We can see them at any time. I mean, it would be totally fine if you wanted to."

"No actually, I feel like I want to be around people now. Let's not mention it, and just spend some great time with them. Your parents always know how to put a smile on my face." Virginni stood up and walked across the expansive room, which was one quarter of the entire huge cylindrical palace building.

She sat down on a chair that was behind a bluish metal harp of about her height, took a deep breath, tuned the instrument, and began playing the Tabot spider strings. They hummed and comforted her, spreading love throughout the space.

Henerinni walked over to the bathroom while removing his athletic rubber-bottomed shoes and a stretchy, form-fitting xyloblut shirt-and-short combination. He took a shower while listening to the skillful music that comforted his mourning wife. The empress played four of her favorite songs before standing up to get ready for the meal.

The emperor's bedroom was always inhabited by the reigning emperor and his wife. Exterior security doors swung outward to reveal inner doors that swung inside the room. A security guard stood outside at all times to ensure their safety. High walls were characteristic of the third floor, which was the highest story with full ceilings. The fourth floor had many rooms with lower, tilted ceilings.

In the room to the right, a sitting area with couch, tables, and chairs invited the royal couple to enjoy the space. Just behind the right door was a smaller closet that ran along the wall to the expansive bathroom. The bathroom walls created a completely separate space with toilets, showers, a bath, and a separate closet. The window above the bath looked over the land. Double doors that swung outward welcomed generations of royalty to take advantage of the facilities.

The outer wall was a gradual curve. Large stones of many sizes created an unpredictable pattern. Three balconies with double doors opened into the room, and blackout curtains hung patiently, waiting to slide over the arched doorways in order to provide complete coverage from every ray of light. A small, kidney-shaped pool with two long benches contained mineral water, opposite the entrance doors and to the right side. Bookshelves lined the stone walls around the room. A harp station was set up for the empress to the left of the pool against the outer wall, complete with a small table and chair. The bed was five pillows long and pushed up against the farthest left wall.

Beautifully crafted, brightly colored textiles covered the expansive bed, which was raised off of the floor, and three long benches waited at the foot. Tables flanked each side of the bed, and the largest closet was built out from the wall that ran to the inner doors. The closet contained full-length mirrors and a complete dressing area, as well as sufficient storage. Clothes were also kept in reserve in another part of the castle and brought to the emperor and empress for different occasions.

Tonight's dinner was considered a formal event, so the emperor was obliged to wear royal clothes, which included elaborate capes made from very expensive, rare materials, which displayed elite craftsmanship. Many of the formal clothes were passed from generation to generation, and new items were added regularly. A staff of clothiers worked in the palace, trained by their parents to have the highest sewing and construction ability.

Because it was a particularly warm evening, they brought the emperor a pair of pants that were baggy in the waist area and became tighter around the calves, with a cape that could be removed. This outfit was meant to be worn shirtless. For the empress, the clothiers brought a new cape that had been a gift from the last trip to the countryside. Stretchy silk stockings with elaborate designs stopped midthigh with a sophisticated lace band and matched her dark skin tone. A silk magenta dress flowed with many layers and highlighted her perfect arms with a neckline that covered her entire chest area. The wrinkle-free dress was decorated with intricate patterns and designs.

The cape from her most recent trip clipped onto the dress at the shoulders and could be removed if desired. In a heavier material, the cape flowed from the back to the floor and then created a very long rectangle that would pour down the stairs like a jellyfish fluttering in the sea current. A bright-green border of palm fronds framed a scene of a pair of soft, pink birds with intricate, lengthy feathers, kissing with closed eyes. This scene represented love, bonding, and lifelong companionship, just like the birds who mated for life. Colorful flowers and fruits surrounded the birds, who perched in a tree with silver bark. These stood for a bountiful life and continued health for the empress.

After the stunning couple dressed in their fine dinner attire, they walked hand in hand down the stairs in their rubber-soled, flat, slip-on shoes. Their capes clung to each step behind them as they strode down the curving single staircases from floor to floor until they reached the main hall.

CHAPTER TWENTY-TWO

The main hall was located on the ground floor and took up one quarter of the entire level in the northeast end, which made it very expansive. Because the palace was one large cylindrical building, the stone outer wall was a gradual curve. Square and rectangular blocks randomly interlinked, the corners carved out to fit like a puzzle. The bright-white quartz contained crystals that sparkled at diners as they moved around the room. Upon closer observation, tiny red and blue veins ran through each block, creating enough variation to interrupt a completely white backdrop.

Five large, rectangular windows were adorned with brightly colored fabrics made from valuable resources. Outer shutters could be closed in order to provide security against enemies or extreme weather, and bars were embedded in the center of the stones above the windows that could immediately drop to provide added safety. That day, the bars were raised and the outer shudders were open, for an unobstructed view.

The middle window was surrounded by a bright-blue, heavy silk fabric that seemed to whirl whimsically around a curtain rod and swoop in perfect, oversized spirals before pooling on the floor in an intentional bundle. Clear crystals hung from real silver thread around the entire window dressing, casting rainbows on the shiny floor, tiled with oversized diamond shapes. Each tile was the size of a man, and the light-gray, polished marble made the room look like it was floating on a pool of mercury. The matching-style window coverings provided sound absorption to remove the echoes that erratically bounced around in the huge space. On each side of this blue, silky central work of art, magenta versions of the same drapery framed views to the outside. Bright-yellow, shiny silk was used on the end windows.

Embroidered wall hangings that contained fortunes worth of materials like pearls, precious metals, rare jewels, and costly threads covered different patches of the curving wall. Unique situations were depicted in many of the intricate pieces of art, including pivotal historical events, such as the founding of Crawldsay two thousand years before. One of them outlined details about the formation of the three prefectures along the western coast that compiled the entire Land at that time. Royal family members throughout the prefectures of The Land had been trained in the art of creating these breathtaking tapestries and meaningful reminders of the past.

Virginni had completed four of the current pieces on display, and was known as a skilled master in that field of artwork. Not only was she was the most competent artist at integrating valuable materials into the tapestries, she also had an eye for creating lifelike depictions of humans, animals, and scenery.

The entire room was a quarter of the circular palace, so two long, straight walls traveled from the center of the ground floor to the outer curved wall. Double doors, opening on the insides, created an expansive entrance on each wall, perfect for elaborate fashion or displays. Enormous bookshelves rested on the sides of each entrance; four in total. The corner at the far right, yellow window contained spiral stairs that led down to the kitchen, which was located in the basement.

On the other side of that wall, outside the Main Hall, were three elevators next to each other, each half the size of an average man. Items such as food or plates could be sent down to the kitchen, or up to the ground floor. Staff would place items inside, close the door, then crank a round handle, which pulled a series of ropes that would send the contents through the hollow walls to the desired level. Each story had a room around the small elevators, meant to receive food from the kitchen. The station rooms, surrounding the dumbwaiters, contained anything a servant would need to create a table setting, including glasses, dishes, eating utensils, napkins, and trays.

In the main hall, an ingenious tube of mirrors inside the walls refracted light from candles that were set up in the corner where the two straight walls met. The rays were amplified and then beamed from the ceiling's five large, adjustable fixtures, creating columns of light to the floor. Levers on a control panel offered options to change the intensity, location, and size of the shafts. This invention in itself boasted the ingenuity of researchers who sought practical and minimalistic options for illuminating the most important dining space in The Land. Lighting was the most important factor in creating this delightful visual feast.

Most viewers had never seen anything like the main hall outside of the natural world. In the middle of the floor, a round table was set up for the two couples. A cylindrical ray of light shone from the ceiling and covered the very center of the table in a perfect circle. The space was capable of serving over two hundred people easily; however, that day it held just an intimate setting for four. The beautifully decorated wooden tabletop, which had been polished with a clear wax, glistened under the huge beam of light in the center of the imposing room. For a cozier feeling inside the immense area, three lush trees in pots were lined in a row behind the table, opposite the spectacularly treated windows. In front of the middle tree, twisted twigs rose from a large soil pot and formed a column with a sphere on top. Grape vines had grown up and around the perfect globe. Bunches of bright-purple, plump, sweet grapes hung down inside, fresh for picking.

The deep-golden evening sun shined through the windows and sprinkled endless moving, amber-tinted rainbows around the room, which flickered as the curtain crystals spun in the wind. A fresh floral scent of the plants from the palace grounds wafted through and mixed with the rich, mouthwatering aroma from the meal that was being prepared for the royals.

The setting would enamor anyone entering the grand room, and it was famous for making attendees gasp. Without realizing it, they would immediately release emotional inhibitions. This was not by chance, as the space had been prepared for thousands of years to strike the soul of any entering beings, and could catch anyone off guard, even the emperor and empress, who dined there often.

"I can't believe the hours and hours of workmanship that went into making this cape. It is really special," Virginni said.

She was talking to the emperor about her new article of clothing, partially in an effort to distract herself from the grieving process, but equally thankful for the artistry, and looking at her love for comfort. The double doors to the main hall opened, and when she looked up at the sight, she lost her train of thought as she saw the dazzling spectacle of light and the new window coverings that had just been installed. Her long, straight hair blew back as if it were ocean waves in slow motion revealing the neck of a goddess, and she took a deep breath as she stopped in her tracks and admired the setting. Then the wafting, fresh-flower fragrance and cuisine scent mixture forced her back into reality, and her body felt surprisingly hungry.

"I have never seen the main hall look this spectacular." Virginni spoke calmly and softly.

Then, a gust of wind caught one of the window dressings. It took flight and bowed from the center until the pooled fabric on the shiny, silverish ground lifted like a kite in the air and flowed directly toward her as a silky, jewel-toned welcome. The crystals fluttered and clung to the silver threads like flies on the back of a bucking bronco. The recovering couple stepped into the room and the double doors closed, blocking the current of wind. The spiraled creation immediately and mysteriously returned as a panel next to the window with an elegantly pooled satiny base, in the exact place it had been before. The young couple were reminded that they were at the capital of a powerful and plentiful land, and they were grateful for the good in their lives.

A smiling, aging woman with hair the color of the mercury-tinted floor walked up to them, reached out her hands, and gave them each a kiss on the cheeks.

"How have my beautiful daughter-in-law and son been doing? It is so wonderful to see you and spend time with you tonight. We have been talking about it all afternoon."

The former emperor and empress, who lived in a room on the second floor, served formally as advisers to the current rulers; however, they really just loved spending time with them. Henerinni's mom was entertaining and full of adoration, and suddenly filled Virginni's heart with peace and comfort. The former empress, Margorinni, knew how to talk to anyone and make them feel at home, because she truly loved those around her with all of her heart, especially her children.

"We had a nice trip to the farms near the rainforest line this afternoon, Margorinni. Did you notice my new cape?" Virginni smiled and winked as she held the sides and flipped it with one of her arms while spinning.

"It is absolutely divine, Virginni. Look at the fine embroidery and the scene of lovebirds. It reminds me of you two on a regular day—so in love."

"Yes, I had it taken immediately from the carriage just so I could show you tonight!" Virginni gave the former emperor, Arturinni, a kiss on the cheek and then sat down.

Emperor Henerinni greeted both of his parents lovingly, with kisses and hugs, and took a seat at the largest chair at the round table.

"Well, it looks like the rainforest line is backing up farther and farther every day! The farmers have been hugely successful."

He spoke out of concern for the security of his citizens. Because the people of the rainforest had been at war with Crawldsay for hundreds of years, the policy had been to replace the rainforest with farmland, and create distance between the capital city and their foes.

"That sounds like fantastic news. And the farmers are secure?" Arturinni's fatherly, interested voice rang toward the current emperor.

"Yes, I'm proud to say that they have not had any problems recently."

Shortly after they all sat down, the head of the kitchen staff came out.

"Tonight, we'll have seafood that was raised in our very own pond, with garden vegetables and cassava in cream, also grown on our palace grounds. If you would like anything else, just let me know and we'll whip it up." She smiled confidently.

"Thanks so much, Jeloot—you and your team are the best!" Virginni smiled to reveal sparkling white teeth.

She called the servant by her name in order to show respect, and extended her appreciation for the palace staff. Jeloot smiled widely, then poured wine and water into glasses for each person before walking away. Trays of breads, brightly colored spicy sauces, fresh fruits, vegetables, and rich cheeses appeared on the table. The beam of light made the vivid colors stand out even more. The room continued to emanate as a spectacle of beauty, with goldish rainbows dancing around from the window dressings, reflecting off of The Land's best artwork.

"How divine is the new main hall decor? I have no clue how they created such breathtaking silk window treatments. Did you notice the miniature bouncing rainbows all over?" Margorinni gushed over the setting as she shifted each diner's attention to the soul-piercing ambiance.

"I noticed it right away as we entered. It is absolutely a feast for the eyes." Virginni's light-tan irises sparkled along with the entire room.

After a moment of taking in the space, Henerinni immediately grabbed different items and placed them on his plate. He had worked up an appetite and could eat anything he wanted that night, as instructed by his trainer.

"How is your conditioning going, son? Are you still playing xyloblut?" Arturrini asked, as a former accomplished athlete himself.

"Yeah, it is going great. We're working on my endurance, and I'm on a strict nutrition plan. Tonight is my cheat night, so I can eat"—Henerinni pointed his hand to the ceiling as he paused with a grin—"and drink, anything I want. We are tracking my progress, and I should see the most impact over the next few weeks. I'm hoping to be in tip-top condition for any matches available during the Summer End Celebration."

"That is fantastic. You're a chip off the old block!" His father reached over and gave him a gentle pat on the chest with an open hand. "And have you started any new textile projects, Virginni?" Arturinni winked toward the empress.

"Yes, actually—some new materials just arrived today, and I started including them in a piece that I have been working on for the bedroom."

Her father-in-law's eyes grew big, and he tilted his head slowly while eating, showing amazement at her fine skills. The dinner was filled with laughter and enjoyment of the fine food while they chatted and the former emperor and empress told captivating stories about living long ago. Virginni was immensely thankful to have a close family who loved her deeply.

"Believe it or not, there was a xyloblut match yesterday in Najeeram, and your friend Pogger's record was broken. Can you believe it lasted so long?" Arturinni was astonished.

"Yeah, good old Pogger. Oh, to be sixteen with unlimited endurance on the xyloblut court!"

"If I remember right, you guys were on the same team for years. What ever happened to good old Pogger?" Arturinni asked.

"Yeah, we were best friends for a long time. We've tried, but we can't find anyone with huge arms like his. That was really what set him apart for climbing and throwing with precision during fatigue. We spent so many hours training and drilling different configurations. He was such a good guy. I haven't seen him in a long time, but he has been living in Bingdole." Emperor Henerinni fell silent, remembering his friend from many years ago.

"Oh, wow. Bingdole is so far north. Maybe he knows the same people as you, Virginni, since that is where you grew up. What is he doing all the way up there?" Margorinni asked.

Virginni had a mouth full of food and nodded politely.

"You're never going to believe this, but he has ten children already," Henerinni said.

"You were the same age, so he has been incredibly busy at twenty-nine years old!" Margorinni said.

"Yeah, he married his wife at eighteen. I don't know if you remember, but he also had many brothers and sisters—ten total. It's probably just in the family. From what I hear, all the kids look the same too, like his gang of sisters and brothers," Henerinni said.

"That is quite unfortunate, I have to say," Arturinni shared unabashedly, now that he was older. "He had the most unbalanced series of extreme features. Remember his long, narrow face with a strong widow's-peak hairline? And the poor guy's ears flapped out. I mean, one time didn't he get his ear stuck on one of the pegs when climbing down the pole in a xyloblut match?"

"Yeah, I felt so bad for him. We were losing already, and he went up for a shot but dropped the ball. We got it back to him, but he was being pulled down by the opposing team. His ear wouldn't let him descend because it got stuck on the walking pegs. That was a rough, rough game. But we managed to have a blast anyhow." Henerinni looked back at his glory days fondly.

"And he had the strangest combination of tiny eyes, with bushy eyebrows that met in the middle. What are they calling that nowadays, Margorinni, a unibrow?" Arturinni proudly kept up with the latest trendy terms.

"Yes, that is all the rage now. Girls are painting a unibrow even. Imagine that!" Margorinni was shocked at how fashion had changed over the past few years.

"Well, he and all of his kids are very current then." Henerinni winked. "It is hard to keep in touch, though, when he has moved on with such a busy life and they live so far away." He said this in between bites of the cheese as he got up to approach the fresh grape vines.

His ripped arms, midsection, and pectoral muscles bounced and flexed accidentally as he reached for the highest and brightest fruit, the cape covering only one of his shoulders below where it was tied around his neck.

"Honey, can you snip off three grape bundles for the table, please?" Virginni was surprised by her healthy appetite, wondering if she was still in denial, but also welcoming a temporary, dream-world point of view.

Henerinni clipped three bunches of grapes off of the inside of the sphere on the top, then placed them in the center of the table in the beam of light.

"You should see if he can come for the Summer End Celebration. I'm sure he would like to get away for a weekend from that huge household," Margorinni said.

"That's a great idea, Mom, I will definitely send an invitation. It would be fun to reconnect with an old pal."

Margorinni then discussed harp songs with the current empress. They spoke in detail about technique and connected by using harp-specific terminology. As a mother, Margorinni sensed that Virginni was going through something, and she comforted her deeply without acknowledging anything was wrong. She understood that sometimes people simply wanted to lose themselves in a beautiful distraction for a moment.

Virginni took the night as an event where she could delay grieving and just enjoy being alive. The couple knew that they would address their new loss in due time, and in their own way. The former Emperor Arturinni poured sincere compliments over the hearts of his beloved son and his wife all night; he knew that the messages of approval would continue playing as background chatter in their minds. He shared witty jokes and stories that captivated the couple and filled the main hall with laughter as the window coverings absorbed the joy and delight, preventing excessive echoing through the expansive and mostly empty space.

As the sun set, hot-pink rays shot through the hanging crystals and projected magenta-tinged rainbows throughout the room, morphing to different burning colors, until the quartet sat in a hall only lit by the five beams of light while cooler breezes danced through intermittently. Food and drink flowed just as freely as the hours-long conversation that drew laughter and information about an array of topics. The couples bonded deeply, with warm gratitude for each other.

By the time the conclusion of the night drew near, the emperor was excited for dessert, because saturn-fruit sweets were his favorite. After the kitchen staff presented a baked creation, with heavy cream on top, they all broke into it with delight. Margorinni took a bite, then closed her eyes and breathed in while holding a spoon to the side with her elbow on the table.

"One of my favorite desserts of all time!" She shook her head back and forth.

"Mom, you are so right, but it is not as good as the empress's saturn-fruit bars," Henerinni whispered with his hand next to his face as he winked at his lovely wife.

"Aw, thanks. It's my favorite dessert to make for you, honey."

When pressed to give out her recipe by friends or family, Virginni left at least one ingredient out so that nobody could recreate the fruity invention that came to fruition by trial and error. It was a silly inside joke with herself, and she was clearly amused by the reports of subpar desserts by those who refused to take her "no" for an answer.

After the last course, the couples took a small drink of strong liquor for digestion and stood up from the table. Henerinni fell to the side before grabbing the heavy wooden table.

"Whew, I guess I may have had one too many tonight." He laughed and gathered himself as he acclimated to a new sense of balance.

The couples walked arm in arm around the main hall to see Empress Virginni's pieces of artwork, which added pizazz to the white quartz blocks.

"Let us walk you to your room, Mom and Dad," Emperor Henerinni said.

"Why not? It's on the way. Off we go to the second floor!" Arturinni said.

They strolled out of the double doors and over to the stairs, which hugged the curving wall. Henerinni and Virginni sauntered after their parents because of the capes that flowed behind them. Upon reaching the second floor, they walked to the door that led to the much smaller room reserved for former emperors and empresses. They hugged each other, kissed on the cheeks, and wished each other fond dreams. Then Henerinni and Virginni walked up the stairs to their room on the third floor, laughing and joking along the way. It was almost as if they had delayed the pain that was waiting, needing a fun night before dealing with reality.

A security guard stood outside the outer double doors and opened them for the cooing couple. The inner set remained locked. As the security guard unlocked these doors, the couple poked each other and giggled like teenagers in love.

Upon entering, the emperor stumbled straight to the bed and sat on the side while Virginni went immediately into the large closet, where she removed the precious clothes and changed into something more comfortable. When she returned, she saw that the emperor had fallen onto the bed, exhausted from the day, filled with food, and more inebriated than he had been since he began the new nutrition plan.

"Oh honey, how are you doing?" She stepped over to him on the bed.

"I'm so tired I just can't move." He laughed slowly, the sound muffled in the blankets.

"Well, let me take off your cape and get you ready for bed, sweetie-pie." Virginni realized that he was in no state for serious conversation and met him where he was.

She untied the cape and pulled it out from under his side, then rolled his legs up in order to get him into the bed and shift his weight off of the rest of the cape. After hanging it up, she returned and sat on one of the benches that were placed at the edge of the huge bed that could have comfortably fit five people.

"Why do we even have a bed this big, anyway? Have you ever thought of that?" Virginni asked the question to test if he was still functioning.

"Maybe it's because their dreams used to be *enormous*! You know, they needed the extra room!" Henerinni chuckled slowly at the images that popped into his mind.

Virginni laughed out loud; she hadn't been expecting any sort of coherent response.

"You might be right, honey."

"Speaking of dreams, can you believe Pogger lives in your hometown of Bingdole? You moved here and he moved there. What a coincidence, right?" Henerinni clearly was talking with no control at this point.

"Yeah, I wonder if we know the same people." Virginni spoke as someone who needed to entertain another person who was only half conscious.

"I don't think so, because he is an executioner, honey. Those big arms just hack off heads. There is no way he would circulate with your family's social circle up there."

Virginni wasn't expecting to hear anything like that, so she sat up extra tall. Usually executioners hid their identities for obvious reasons, and this killer-for-hire's former best friend had just revealed the secret.

"You don't say? Why do you think my family wouldn't hang out with an executioner?" the empress asked, curious for more information.

She usually stayed busy by practicing instruments, creating textiles, and fulfilling other duties of a noble lady, and had never been exposed to the darker side of reality that lingered silently inside The Land.

"Well, maybe they would, but he has tons of kids and wouldn't have time anyway. I've heard they are all a rough bunch. You know, he may be coming through after the Summer End Celebration to anonymously chop off some heads for his job. I just didn't want to say anything to Mom and Dad to freak them out." Henerinni was practically talking in his sleep.

"Alright baby, I'm going to let you slumber." Virginni moved to where he was lying and caressed his head, giving him a kiss on the lips.

"You smell so good, baby." Henerinni turned around on his other side, clearly already in a deep sleep.

The empress knew she was all alone, and looked around the room.

"Sweet dreams, my love. Fill the huge bed with them." Virginni amused herself.

Sitting in the silence, she realized that she had time to gather her thoughts and deal with the reality that she had had four miscarriages over the four years that they had been married. Virginni had once thought it would get easier, but she'd never mastered grieving for her unborn. If anything, the pain was worse because of all of the rest that came before. She looked over and saw the moonlight shining through the large curved window, and as she did, a tear fell down and surprised her.

The empress stood up, full of energy from the sugary dessert, and walked past the conversation area of couches and chairs to the bathroom. She entered the doors that swung out and stared numbly into the moonlit room. Then she paced to the closet and changed her clothes again, but this time she wanted to wear black to represent how she felt inside. When she grabbed a shirt from the farthest shelf, she noticed part of the wooden wall swing open with the article of clothing. She thought that the fabric had gotten snagged on the wood backing of the closet and torn part of the wooden panel.

"We can just get that repaired tomorrow," she said out loud, and then wondered why she was speaking to herself.

When she stepped back into the bedroom, she thought she would soak her feet in the mineral waters of the pool that was just outside the bathroom. Instead, she stood still, looking at the moonlight beaming through the three massive, curved windows. Standing in the moon's rays, she looked at the shirt and could not find the snag she was looking for, which would have been impossible. Her eyes moved to the sides, and she turned around slowly, in careful thought.

Virginni walked back into the bathroom closet to inspect the damaged wood. She lit a candle, shoved the clothes away from that area, and examined the wall, but saw nothing out of the ordinary. After wondering if she was drunk and seeing things, she felt the wall and noticed a faint line that ran around it. When she pushed, a lever popped out, revealing what must have been accidentally pulled with the shirt. Then she could see a stray thread on the bottom that probably wrapped around the strange lever. She pulled the hidden handle, and it swung out while a small panel below the shelf moved back and slid to the side, creaking just loud enough for her to be concerned that the emperor might hear. After reminding herself that he was passed out, she got on the floor and put the candle inside the wall, looking in both directions at the empty space.

CHAPTER
TWENTY-THREE

Virginni felt an energized bolt of curiosity in her chest. After placing the candle inside the wall, she crawled in and stood up. This was the same space where the food elevators were located. She could either take stairs that went above and around the dumbwaiters, which was cramped, or she could go the other direction, which looked like it would involve a much lower risk of becoming stuck. Thick spiderwebs hung with years of dust, reassuring her that the walls were free of any of the critters that created the obstacles long ago. As she ducked under and walked over the webs, the outline of a door gradually appeared. On the third floor, she was high above the ground and tried to move carefully and slowly. If anything happened to her in the space at that time of night, nobody would be able to help her.

She lifted a latch and pushed the door with all of her might. It slowly opened, revealing that she was on the bottom of a mysterious outdoor turret. These randomly speckled the cylindrical palace, but she had never been told about any hidden spaces. Virginni cautiously stepped up the stairs that lined the outer wall of the spooky, vertical tunnel. She reached another door at the top.

When she forced it open, it was like another planet. A balcony floor hung out over the side of the outer edge of the turret and was open to the sky. A small, coned rooftop covered the area where the stairs were, but she could walk out to a platform that seemed to be elevated into the sky. She immediately stepped over to the edge, forgetting about her safety, and looked at the stars and the moon that flickered brightly. The empress put the candle under the covered area and returned to the terrace.

She sat near the knee-high railing at the edge and simply peered into the heavens while hugging her bent legs to her chest. In that position, she rocked back and forth and cried periodically for two hours while thinking about the latest tragedy that had happened inside her body. She recounted all of the plans that she had made for the past four children who had never made it into her world, and she grieved for the future that she so dearly wanted and imagined.

Empress Virginni had moved away from her family to be with the one that she loved. Therefore, she did not have the support system that she wanted as a twenty-five-year-old. As such, she had become used to being her own best friend. She also leaned on her new family, although they were not a substitute for the three sisters and four brothers she had grown up with. With them, it seemed like she always had someone to turn to for any problem, who also could understand her perspective and experience. She longed for the comfort of her parents and siblings, but remained strong in her ability to get through the challenging times.

The empress was unable to figure out the root of the problem. None of her family had had challenges conceiving. If anything, they had too many children on accident. She thought about her older sister, who already had six children, and her parents, who'd had eight by the age of thirty.

Suddenly, she realized that her husband must have been the factor that led to the miscarriages. Talking that night about all of the children Pogger had and his ten siblings, and thinking of her own family, made her realize that fertility was passed on, and her relatives had no issues with successfully having children. She reminded herself that the emperor only had one brother and one sister, which was quite small for royals.

Up to that point, Virginni had felt a lot of guilt and blamed herself. Now, she shed this burden like a snake sheds its dead skin. The shame slowly peeled off and lay on the terrace floor under the stars in the moonlight. She was renewed, for the first time in many years. In this calm state of mind, the empress sat up tall and took in a deep breath. She looked over the fortified city of Crawldsay and pondered all of the good things in her life that she cherished. She remembered all of the stories her mom had taught her about being resilient and persevering through tough times. The empress reminded herself that she was her own best support system and that only she could grieve and feel the pain, and decided to focus on positivity.

Tomorrow will be another day, she thought to herself, *and I will honor my experience and ensure that I heal.*

When she stood up, she felt as tall as the palace. With resolve, she returned through the walls in the dark, because the candle had burned out long before. She managed to make it back into the bathroom, but was covered in centuries-old, dusty spiderwebs. After taking a shower and leaving no sign of her secret passageway excursion, she carefully pressed the lever back into the wall, and the lower section slid into place. Virginni completed her usual beauty regimen and then closed all of the blackout drapes, because she planned to sleep for much of the next day.

Hours later, the emperor and empress woke up at the same time, stretching and yawning.

"Do you want breakfast on the balcony, baby? I don't even know what time it is." Henerinni spoke with a scratchy voice as he lay in bed, looking into the eyes of the love of his life, barely visible in the dark.

"Yeah, let's do it. We can relax and have an easy start to our day." The empress felt surprisingly alive and refreshed after the deep sleep. "Last night, I dealt with a lot of difficult emotions, and I had this really refreshing experience. It's not that I don't care, but it's like I was able to cope with how I've been feeling for a very long time, and I am ready to start the healing process again." She shared openly about her emotional state and how she had been navigating their latest challenge.

"Wow, that is great that you are healing. Was it my mom? She does have a way with people."

"No, I stayed awake last night just looking at the stars, and took some time to myself." She wasn't sure if she should ask about the secret passageway yet.

"Well, whatever you need baby, I am here for you. Just let me know and we can work through this together. Your struggle is my struggle, and you are the love of my life." His voice was hoarse.

"Thanks, sweetie—that means a lot to me." Virginni's eyes were half open.

Together, they slid the drapes and light flooded the bedroom, forcing their eyes to adjust to the midday sun.

Virginni broke her silence about the secret passageway over a spread of breakfast food on one of the balconies.

"Have you ever found any strange tunnels through the palace before, honey?" she asked while moving utensils around the table.

"Oh, like the one in the closet in the bathroom?"

"Yeah, I took a shirt down and all of a sudden there was a latch that popped out of the wall. I was really shocked."

"Oh, I thought I mentioned them to you before. They're all over the palace. I grew up finding them and playing in the walls as a child. One time, I got stuck pressing my way through a tight opening. Thankfully, it was so hot that sweat dripped on my skin and I was able to slide away to freedom." Henerinni laughed while remembering his childhood. "Did you go up to the turret there? It's really fascinating. I haven't been in any of them for years. I actually even forgot they were there."

"Yeah, it was late and I figured, 'What do I have to lose?' so I went up to the terrace area and just spent some alone time. It was really nice."

"Yeah, it's a really beautiful view over the entire city from there. I don't think I've ever been there in the middle of the evening before, though. I always had to sneak into my parents' room during the day and get out before they came back at night." He paused. "Even though we've been together for many years, I feel like we are always getting to know each other better." He looked into her sparkling eyes, which reflected the colors around them from the sunny day.

She smiled, and they leaned in to kiss on the lips.

"I'm going to visit the Keeper of the Stars today. Maybe he will give me some clarity," Virginni said.

"Ah, tell him I said hi. I hope he has a lot of good news for you. Do you mind if I head out for more training today? It sounds like you have a busy day already planned." Henerinni was willing to cancel everything for her.

"Yeah, that's no problem. I'm fine if we catch up at dinner."

"Okay, well I'm going to head out and get to my training session then. Have a great afternoon, and you know where you can find me if you need anything. I can't imagine how devastating this could be to process."

"Thanks for always supporting me, my love."

He got up, gave her a kiss, and walked into the bedroom. After he left for training, the empress's doctor visited and quickly provided an examination. He declared that she was in good health and could continue her daily plans, but recommended more relaxation over the next few weeks. After he left, she dressed modestly and was met by the carriage at the front doors of the palace. The Keeper of the Stars never made house calls, no matter how important the person. It was a long-held tradition that any Keeper of the Stars only provided guidance inside their own home.

"Let's take the long way around today, Grong. I'm in the mood to view the city," Virginni said as she climbed into the carriage.

"Sure thing, ma'lady!" He opened panels that allowed her to see out, but mostly were for securing the carriage.

She rode outside the palace ground gates, descended the elevated stone mound, and followed the road that ran just inside the city walls. They traveled past the massive entrance gates of the city, the two large barns, and many lookout towers along the way. They followed the road that continued just inside the walls, then took a left on a street that led to a building that housed government offices on the right and a neighborhood filled with single-family homes and shops on the left. They turned into the area that was clustered with houses and rode around the outside of the buildings until the carriage stopped at a home that looked different than all of the rest.

All of the homes appeared generally bright and airy, with pointed rooftops and clay shingles, but this building stood out. A unique, green-gray rainforest moss, one that did not grow much in Crawldsay, covered the dwelling. It grew in tiny bundles that floated above the reddish-brown clay shingles, beginning from the highest point and flowing over the edge and all the way to the ground.

A gust of wind blew as the empress walked up the stone path. The moss flowed like long hair underwater as the empress approached the door, located in the center of the home under the peak. She knocked on the door, which had a large star to indicate it was the house of the Keeper of the Stars, as had been tradition for many generations. Inside she heard pots and pans clattering, and she peeked at the windows that somehow managed to direct the moss around to allow uninhibited sunlight inside. A middle-aged woman opened the door, and her curly, gray-laced hair flowed in every direction. Scents of concentrated plants wafted and slapped the empress in the face.

"Good afternoon, Empress Virginni, come in, come in! Begrol will be with you soon. We are processing some plants that just arrived from a far-away land."

Begrol's wife was just as eccentric as her husband and home. She was also very gifted in lending useful advice, and had a background in mixing incense and working with essential oils from plants.

"No problem, Sobaniop, I will wait until he is free."

The empress always remembered names and was kind to everyone she dealt with, and people gave her special treatment because they felt that she cared—and she did. She walked down a few stairs past a bookshelf with many academic books that Begrol had written, some about healing with unconventional methods, and entered the small living room, where she sat on a couch to wait. Sobaniop brought her tea.

"This is very hot, so give it a few minutes. We just got the leaves yesterday from very far east. They are incredibly aromatic, as you can smell."

The mug sat on the table in the middle of the room and dispersed a licorice scent into the air as the divine steam rose like a fine mist flowing over a mountaintop. After finishing the cup of tea, Begrol entered the room slowly and greeted Empress Virginni with a kiss to both cheeks and a huge smile, revealing yellowish teeth. He was thin, and his hair was cut very close to a balding scalp.

"How have you been doing, my favorite empress from Bingdole? It is so great to see you!" He continued smiling and examined her facial expression, sensing that she'd had a miscarriage.

"It's a pleasure to see you too, Begrol. Today has been refreshing so far. I love the tea Sobaniop brought me." She smiled back.

"Yes, it is from far east. We can't even find it around here. So, tell me why you came to see me today," he said, with a tone that suggested he already knew, but wanted to hear her state of mind and how she was dealing with it.

"Well as you know, I've had many miscarriages in the past, and I just had another one. So I wanted to stop by and see if you had any guidance." Virginni looked at him with unbroken focus.

"Alright, let me grab your records and we can first check to see your history."

Begrol left the room and came back with details that he had compiled from previous meetings with the empress.

"Before we get started, you have already been seen by your doctor and are in good health right now, correct?"

"Yes, we just saw each other this morning. He said I am healing, but I was cleared to be out and about."

"Alright, that's great." Glancing down at the papers, Begrol said, "We have your cycle listed here, along with all of the past times you came to visit. We seem to have been able to predict your highest fertility windows, and you've had success getting pregnant, but there is a problem with completing the pregnancy. What exactly are you looking for today?"

"I want any guidance you can give me about the situation. As you can imagine, it has taken an emotional toll on me, and I've had to deal with a lot of disappointment over the past four years." She continued to look at him with a strong, concerned gaze.

"Yes, I can feel that you have been going through a lot of emotional pain. That is to be expected when one is dealing with the life circumstances that have been handed to you. I do have some questions. First, I am curious, do you come from a family with many children?" Begrol asked, as though he knew already but wanted to make a point to her.

"Yes, I actually have many siblings. I have three sisters and four brothers." Virginni looked seriously inside herself for any sort of clues she could gain from the words that came out of the man's mouth.

"And have they had many children yet?"

"Yes, they have no problems conceiving."

"The reason I ask is because I can sense in you that you want to have a large family as well."

"You are correct. I grew up with that, and I want that for myself . . . lots of kids running all over and supporting each other through each stage of life."

"I have a feeling in my gut that you will have twins at some point, but I have a warning for you. Don't look outside of your home or family. Have faith that fruit will grow from inside your home. Let's meet again when you have healed if you want more direction at that point. I have some plant extracts and oils that will help you recover from the emotional pain you have been through. Every day, I want you to drink a special tea that Sobaniop will mix for you."

On the ride back to the palace, Virginni tried to piece together what she had just heard. She could not understand why Begrol would warn her to stay within her home and family, because it had never even crossed her mind to be with anyone but her husband. She thought back to the transformative moment on the terrace the night before and realized that her husband's physical body was most likely the problem. The empress couldn't bear more miscarriages and wanted nothing more than to be a mother to many children, to create for them what she'd had while growing up. She didn't know what to do and decided to put her plans for a baby on hold.

Upon returning home, following the doctor's orders, Virginni stayed in her room most days, where she worked on new harp songs and completed different textile projects. Every so often she took a leisurely walk on the palace grounds to inspect the garden or visit the pond. She reflected often on the four miscarriages that had happened over the past four years, and decided, through the pain, to never go through that again.

Three weeks went by and she completely forgot the warning that the Keeper of the Stars had given her. One night, after the emperor fell asleep, she walked through the secret passageway in her bathroom closet and up to the terrace under the stars.

At this point, she had lost hope, and feared that she would continue with unsuccessful pregnancies. In her mind, she could either have a future with no children, or look outside of her marriage for a donor who could provide a healthy baby. Gazing at the twinkling stars that night, she decided that she would have to stop playing by the rules in order to get what she wanted in life. Virginni concluded that she had to take her future into her own hands. Although she did not know what that would look like, she was intelligent and came from an incredibly fertile family, and had confidence in her ability to have a successful pregnancy.

The next day, she started formulating a different way of looking at the world, and realized that she could never tell a soul anything about what she was ready to do. This would be a circumstance where she would have to continue to be her own support system, as she had grown accustomed to in the past. The empress also understood that she would have to rely on her intelligence to cover up even the tiniest hint of what was to come.

Although she had never imagined pulling off a stunt like becoming pregnant by someone else in secret, Virginni knew that if she put her mind to it, she would be able to figure it out. While she was working on textiles, she dreamed of different scenarios, usually ending with thinking to herself, *I'm not sure I even want to follow through with that.* Although she was still uncertain about the route she might take, she knew she had to begin by becoming aware of every single molecule in the palace, including all of the secret passageways, as well as the schedules of anyone coming or going.

She oversaw the servants, so the empress secretly compiled each of their schedules. When she talked with her parents-in-law, she paid special attention if they mentioned any time they would spend outside the palace. Every chance she had, she waited for her husband to fall asleep so she could explore the secret passageways throughout the entire palace, based on facts she'd garnered skillfully from Henerinni during breakfasts on the terrace or in casual conversation, careful not to seem as though she was seeking information.

One day during dinner, a block on the outer wall of the main hall popped and scattered white crystal stone and dust on the light-gray floor.

"Looks like we are settling even more than I expected," Arturinni said after walking over to investigate the surprisingly normal foundational problems. "Over the years, I have seen many of those get replaced. We'll have to ask someone to schedule a stonemason to come out and take care of it."

"There should be lots of masons in the city that can replace that, right?" Virginni was fishing for any sort of information possible, trying to sound as though she were interested in the repair process.

"You know, the difficult thing about this wall is that it was made using a special technique, so installation is a challenge for most. However, repair is a completely different animal. Especially that low on the wall. You are going to have to get an expert, possibly from Bingdole." The former emperor had years of knowledge stored up from living in the palace.

The empress's brain started racing—she would be able to do research from connections back home. She thought that asking how many children a stonemason had would not sound very fishy if asked correctly, and to the right friend in Bingdole, especially if she took a surprise holiday to see her family.

The future repairman seemed like the perfect candidate for the job— he would just be through for a moment, then return to a city far away forever, unaware of the outcome of their meeting. Her sister had just delivered a baby boy, which was the perfect excuse to travel back home for a few days.

Virginni made the journey, explaining that it was merely to spend time with loved ones. Upon arrival, she was greeted by her entire extended family, including all of their children. When she saw their faces and fit bodies, she was reminded of the attractiveness that linked their gene pool.

While she was enjoying time with everyone, she spoke with the servants that she'd grown up with as usual, but she was particularly interested in chatting with the master repairman. She struck up a conversation with him while relaxing in the basement kitchen like she used to as a child. After talking for a while, Virginni slipped in the actual objective, camouflaged in casual conversation.

"You know, we have a brick that has nearly completely ejected from the wall in our main hall. We were just eating a few days ago, and it literally made a big popping sound and cracked onto the floor. Have you ever heard of that happening, Towpilk?" The empress slowly introduced the general topic.

"Yeah, that happens all the time when it's settling. In a normal wall, it would just crack, but the stones sink, and sometimes one of them pops because the others are shifting around it, and it's just a little weaker."

"They said that it is a special job that someone from another city may have to come fix." Empress Virginni did everything to hold back from appearing too eager for information.

"I imagine they don't deal with repairs for that so much down there. We have much more wall that is laid with that stone in that particular style here, so that makes sense. They might just send me to fix it. I've done over four hundred repairs just like it before." Towpilk looked excited to take a trip, even just for work.

"Well, find out if it would be you and let me know—we will roll out the royal welcome for sure." Virginni encouraged herself inside her mind and realized that manipulation was way easier than she had ever imagined it to be.

The next day, Towpilk confirmed joyfully that he would be the repairman to visit Crawldsay and fix the stone in the outer wall of the main hall. Virginni had done her homework and asked about his wife, and found out that they had four children and came from large families. Everything lined up perfectly, and Towpilk seemed young and healthy, so on her carriage ride home to Crawldsay, she came up with a plan.

Virginni could gift a holiday to her in-laws to get them out of the palace, then make sure the mason stayed in a room that had easy access from the secret passageways. She would have ample reason to invite her fellow Bingdolian to dinner and keep the wine flowing so he would be drunk in the guest bedroom. She went back and forth in her mind about the dishonesty and the impact she could have on another person, but it all came down to her strong desire for a large family, and this seemed like her only option at the time.

The night before her countryman was bound to arrive, Virginni practiced special royal beauty treatments that had been passed down from generation to generation between the gorgeous women in her family, putting centuries of knowledge and wealth to work. After a bath in rose petals and milk, she applied expensive creams and balms to her entire body. From head to toe, she used twenty-eight different plant extracts, mixed creams, and blended oils. These were known as the "perfect twenty-eight." Each one was for a different part of the body, and the mixture provided the best night of sleep, which was known to also enhance attractiveness.

Virginni woke the day of the repair, feeling like there were tiny monkeys bouncing in her stomach, screaming and running around. This was new territory for her, after all. That morning, she executed a completely different regimen of beautification treatments. She outlined her eyes in a special baby-blue powder, enhanced her long black eyelashes, and created red lips. After perfuming herself with the most valuable plant extracts, she was ready to finally follow through with her plan. Towpilk was to arrive at midmorning, which gave her time to prepare and make sure everything was in place.

When Virginni went to greet the stoneworker, wearing fine robes, she was disappointed to find that he had come down with an illness and sent a colleague, who was a woman! Thankfully, the wall was repaired perfectly, but Virginni realized she would have to be even more tactful to secure a child. She still entertained the replacement for Towpilk, although the empress did not know her well. That evening, she sat under the starry sky and recognized that this must not have been her destiny, and she would have to start fresh and new.

CHAPTER TWENTY-FOUR

Two weeks before the Summer End Celebration, the royal couple had dinner with their parents. During the meal, Emperor Henerinni shared that his old friend Pogger from long ago would be visiting and participating on his team in a xyloblut tournament. In fact, Pogger had been exercising with a royal athletic trainer for the past few weeks in Bingdole. Virginni knew that because the man would be traveling from far away, and because he'd grown up as a family friend, he would be staying in one of the thirty-six bedrooms in the palace. She immediately thought about Pogger's numerous siblings and the impressive ten children that he had fathered over nearly a decade. She naturally started considering the secret passageways and how she could find out his room location from the staff that she managed. Her mind began concocting a plan to start a family.

Over the next few weeks, she made sure Pogger would be housed in a room that had easy access through the passageways. She also ran through different scenarios, in order to consider every single angle so that she could get away with a covert mission.

At this point, The Land had not adopted many laws that were later introduced to avoid capital punishment or protect human life. For example, human sacrifices were an accepted part of the pilgrimage to the varied volcanoes. When someone was found guilty of murder, treason, armed robbery, kidnapping, rape, or many other crimes, the punishment was death. Executioners by trade traveled from place to place, and their identities were hidden. They received years of training to skillfully deliver anything from a quick, easy death, to a long and arduous ending of life.

One night, after the emperor had another cheat day including lots of wine, he mentioned in a half-asleep state that Pogger would be completing the executions that took place one week after the Summer End Celebration, but the athletics were being used as a coverup. He would be staying in the palace until the day of the executions, then would immediately return home that night in the dark. With this new information, the empress revised her plan.

On the first day of the Summer End Celebration, Emperor Henerinni presided over the opening ceremony in the party hall of the town square, where a traditional parade showed off the harvest, music was played in honor of the emperor, and fireworks blasted off after it became dark. Because of hundreds of years of tradition, not much coordination was required; each person knew exactly what to do having grown up with the practices. Lots of wine flowed from a summer of impressive growth, and everyone ate food that was made communally.

Day two included animal shows that displayed the best maintenance and breeding of creatures, which were paraded from the barns during different times of the day. Craft competitions included common textiles and other homemade traditional items—nothing like the empress's creations, given the rare and expensive materials she used. Many fun, simple, two-person games like frog racing and ribbon unravelling occurred all over the city grounds, with prizes for the victors. Serious sports events were also included on day two, in order to encourage physical fitness, and Henerinni welcomed being an example for his people. He had strictly trained for weeks, and in the morning, he played a match with his Xyloblut team, including Pogger. They were victorious.

In addition, the emperor participated in an Aldroot match, which required wearing a jumpsuit from head to toe, shoulder guards and breastplate, and special shoes with steel tips. A lightweight training sword with a small ball on the end was used in the sport, ultimately to train the participants in different moves for actual sword battles. Henerinni received the most points after thirty minutes, the customary length, and won his match.

In the evening, he also fought in a kurjintel match. In this sport, ribbons hung from each tight body suit, and the competitors won points by touching the ribbons with their feet or hands. Henerinni caught his opponent off guard and managed to trip him with a low squat and extended kick to the leg. Athletes were victorious either by getting the most points after fifteen minutes, or tripping the challenger off of their feet. These matches helped the citizens with hand-to-hand combat, increasing awareness and reaction time as they planned intricate moves to outwit the other competitor.

At a special dinner in the main hall with guests who had been recognized for outstanding acts, Emperor Henerinni and Empress Virginni each stood and presented thoughtful and witty speeches to the audience of two hundred that had the honor of enjoying the spectacularly designed banquet venue. Because the empress was arguably the most beautiful woman alive, the people loved simply being in her presence. That night, everyone observed an even more elaborate fireworks show. Those on duty in the watch towers fused into the outer wall had the best views.

That evening, the empress knew that Pogger would be exhausted and possibly drunk, so it might be an opportunity to pounce. She carried out her usual beauty routine. When the emperor had passed out, she got up and changed her clothes into nearly indestructible silk robes and snuck into the secret passageway in her bathroom. She squeezed carefully through the walls, above different spaces, and walked to the room where Pogger was staying.

Virginni waited behind a bookshelf and listened for him to go to bed and fall asleep before she pressed a latch. The shelves swung open, just like she had practiced over the past few weeks. During careful research, she'd learned that his wife's nickname was Loo-Loo, and she wore Loo-Loo's favorite perfume, which filled the space.

As Pogger took a deep breath, he felt like he was at home because he smelled his wife in the room. He mumbled before turning over in his bed. The empress stood still, hoping he would remain enthralled in dreams. She used his wife's nickname in order to trick him into believing he was at home and that she was Loo-Loo. Then her master scheme to try to get pregnant was a huge success. After she had completed the assault, she reentered the secret passageway behind the bookshelf and quietly navigated through the walls until she arrived safely back to her bathroom entrance. However, instead of going back in, she decided to watch the stars from the terrace on the turret. Virginni held her fists to her chest and looked at the starry sky.

"This could not have been more perfect!" she whispered while reveling in victory.

She sat down and looked at the stars, went through the entire plan, and concluded that everything had been successful—that nobody would ever be able to tie anything back to her, including Pogger, who was in another state of mind.

The next day, the maid noticed uncharacteristic dirty sheets but assumed Pogger had taken a young lady who slipped out under camouflage of the evening darkness.

Virginni continued relations with her husband over the following week, so she would be able to convince him the baby was his.

She visited the Keeper of the Stars in the city to make it look like she was actively seeking support to become pregnant. Although she was certain Begrol instinctively knew what she had done, he would never say a word. During the days, she imagined every single possible scenario going forward, working to avoid any sloppy mishaps and to keep everything a secret.

Because of the prior four miscarriages, Virginni knew it would be acceptable to not mention a few missed ovulations, so she kept quiet about the life growing in her body for four months. Then, she went to her favorite place to spend time alone. From the secret turret terrace, she remembered back to the night when she had cried out in pain, but that evening she cried out in happiness. She had full faith that her plan would go through without a hitch. All of the lost children, broken dreams, and destroyed hopes hit her at the same time. She remembered the pain, humiliation, disappointment, and anger, and she wept as she envisioned closing a chapter in her life.

From that point on, she imagined getting away with the assault and moving forward with good fortune and continual love; the kind that, in her mind, could only be provided by having kids and a large family. The empress applauded herself for the manipulation she'd displayed in order to execute an airtight scheme. Before leaving the terrace that night, she was hopeful for a future with a large family like she'd grown up in. She imagined dreaming again and moving on with her life after producing an heir.

When she returned to her bedroom, Henerinni was winding down for the evening by taking a dip in the small pool, which was filled with healing mineral water. Virginni wanted to approach him quietly in order to have the most impact, and create suspense that could draw him in, before divulging her reality. The empress knew that the method of delivery about any news could change the reception, and she wanted her husband to be open and enthusiastic about the possibility of children, and to be completely invested in every future moment together.

She nonchalantly passed by in all of her glorious beauty, spreading her fine perfume throughout the room. With his head laid back and his eyes closed, he took a deep breath, as well as the bait, realizing she was in the room.

Henerinni was reminded of his one and only love and fluttered his eyes open, moaning, "Hey, sweetie," as though waking from a long nap.

The empress had processed that this brief encounter would define the way her husband viewed the rest of their lives together.

"Hey babe, how is your bath?" Her robe flowed around the room while she walked over to her harp, pretending she was going to practice.

"It has been great for my muscles. They were aching a lot. I'm not eighteen anymore, and I can definitely feel it. How's your day going? You're going to practice the harp? You know, it's always been one of my favorite instruments." Henerinni relished in the relief that he needed.

The empress assessed that he was in the perfect state to peacefully take in anything she had to say.

"I'm okay. Yeah, I'm learning a new piece, and I've been trying to get through one section that has been particularly challenging." She sat down with a concerned look on her face, purposely making sure her love was watching.

The emperor noticed her expression. "What's the matter, sweetie? Is something wrong?"

She paused as she sat in her practice chair, prompting her husband to get out of the pool, put on a robe, and walk over to her. Water sloshed and flower petals scattered around the floor.

He put his hands on her shoulders and said, "You know I'm always here for you baby, and you can tell me anything."

"You know how much I love *you,* right sweetie?" Virginni asked.

"Yeah, and I love you too—to the seas and back." Henerinni's concern grew.

She strategically waited for a comfortable moment.

"I have been keeping a secret from you."

He pulled up a chair next to her. With wide eyes, he sat and waited. The intended terror ran through his body. The empress understood that this conversation could tie their bonds even stronger for the rest of their lives, so she started slowly.

"Well, you know I love you. And we both have had a difficult time with the miscarriages." She paused to give him time to think, knowing that he was fighting to ignore worst-case scenarios in his mind. "You know that I always share every detail of my life with you, and we never keep anything from each other?" She looked into his eyes.

"Yes, my love, what happened? Is everything okay?"

His eyes squinted downward at the sides, and his eyebrows rose. He looked like he'd just received a blow to the gut during a xyloblut match and was trying to cover it up.

She slowly whispered, "Well, for the past four months, I don't think you noticed that I have gained a little weight. And I didn't want to tell you, but . . ."

As she paused, he imagined that she might want to leave him—maybe she had been incredibly unhappy. He beat himself up inside for the possibility that he had been completely clueless as he looked into her sparkling, khaki-colored eyes. In the flicker of a second, he second-guessed all of his actions over the past few months.

The empress stood up and looked away from him, closing her eyes for dramatic effect. Then she turned toward him to draw his attention to her beautiful face and flowing hair as it twirled through the air on a breeze.

"For the past four months, I have been hiding that I missed my ovulation."

She carefully made her face shine like the sun while revealing her sparkling white teeth, and his terror transformed into utter joy. Upon hearing the news, Henerinni elatedly jumped off of the chair, shouting, "Yes!" to the universe in relief.

He walked up to her and wrapped his arms around her, placing his nose onto hers. After a kiss, he carefully lifted her off of her feet and into his arms. He brought her to the bed and gently placed her on the oversized cushion, jumped on it, and gazed into her eyes as they both smiled and enjoyed the life-changing occasion. This was the furthest they had ever gotten with a pregnancy; they'd been told that if they reached four months, it would most likely result in birth.

Virginni placed her hands on her chest and said, "I have been seeing the Keeper of the Stars often, and he said that everything is in our favor!

Every single day I had to keep the secret from you, my heart ached, but I knew it was necessary. I am so sorry that I kept the news from you, my love." She paused. "I thought it would be wise to wait to tell a soul until I had passed three months. Remember our second miscarriage that we lost at the third month?"

"How could I forget? It was really difficult for us all, and I thought I was going to lose you."

"Well, I wanted to spare you the disappointment and pain until the baby was more developed. And the Keeper of the Stars just declared that this time, my baby will be carried to term. I wished to get his approval before mentioning anything to you." Virginni swaddled her tiny tummy, now accentuated as she held her robe around it. "And when I passed the four-month mark, with extra confirmation from the Keeper of the Stars, I was finally ready to commit to revealing my secret to you."

Suddenly, she started to weep. She could not tell which tears were strategic and which were real—it was an equal combination of both. The empress was so relieved by the idea of finally carrying a baby to term that she genuinely felt as though she needed to express it. She was sincerely happy to share this experience with the love of her life, but in the back of her mind, she kept thinking that she also needed to remain in control so that she could pull the stunt off without being caught. It was vital to put on a show and appear as genuine and innocent as possible.

Regardless of her motivation, it made the intended impact on the emperor. He watched as the tears poured, and his heart equally melted to liquid. Henerinni was filled with relief, relaxation, adoration, and empathy. He felt safe to dream of a future that included an heir.

The empress could sense that he was completely convinced and that anything she said at that point would be wholeheartedly accepted. After gathering herself with one deep, slow breath, she closed her eyes as her chin moved toward the ceiling and her hair slowly passed over her shoulders like a waterfall. She looked her husband straight in the eyes and knew that this was the opportunity to regain any trust that may have been lost for the future from keeping such a huge secret.

Virginni continued with a whimper in her voice, "I knew that if I told you earlier, you would be thrilled, and all I want is for you to be happy."

"And that is what I want for you too, sweetie."

"With the possibility of another miscarriage, I was willing to take the entire emotional journey myself to save you from dealing with the pain. After all, why should both of us have to mourn and grieve? I hope that you understand and that you forgive me for keeping this one secret from you." The empress gave a believable performance.

"Of course, my love." Henerinni gazed deeply into the colored part of her eyes and examined the tiny bits of sparkle and the faint ring around her iris. Her dilated pupils made him feel even more connected to her, and he remained fixated on her gorgeous face. "You know that I am with you to the moon and back. I would give you my all, and I adore that you are so thoughtful to me. Thank you for thinking of me and for trying to save me from possible pain and disappointment. I know how loyal you are to me and how much you love me. And I want you to know how much I love that my heir is growing inside you."

"And I love having your baby inside me, dear."

"We are a team to the end, and I am your biggest fan. I will always be rooting for you, through thick and thin."

Then she wrapped her arms around the back of his head and pulled his face to her bosom. She began to pass her nails over his scalp, massaging the back of his head as they swayed gently in silence. The emperor listened to the beat of her heart with closed eyes and smelled her unique scent. He wanted that sensation to last forever. Every single swipe of her fingers made him relax more and more.

"I am the luckiest man on the planet right now." He lifted his head from her chest.

"And I am the luckiest woman." Inside, she reminded herself that she'd set everything up to make him believe he initiated the interaction. "And don't worry, baby, I have been taking all of the prenatal care. You know how many times I have been through this. I'm an expert by now."

She chuckled to lift the mood and move things to a more celebratory tone. In that moment, she realized that the more time passed, the better chance she would have at getting away with the overall plan.

"Did you know that the regional emperor and empress from Najeeram waited until the fifth month for the official celebration?" Virginni asked.

By mentioning this, she was hoping that he would claim the same idea as his own. If she planted hints, the emperor would feel ownership over the process, while she was really calling the shots.

He gazed into her eyes. "Yeah, I heard that. You know, it might be a good idea for us to be cautious as well. What do you think of waiting one more month before telling a soul? I'm sure everyone would understand."

Henerinni felt especially calm after realizing he was in a much better situation than all of the other possible scenarios that had run through his mind just a few minutes earlier.

"That is a great idea, honey! You are so brilliant. How do you want to reveal the pregnancy?" she asked.

"What if we threw the celebration along with springtime activities? It would send a lot of positive energy into the entire process. We could make it easy and calm for you but fun for everyone involved, and by this time we will be close to the new spring season." He tried to be considerate to his wife, as she was dealing with a lot of different emotions.

"You're so brilliant, sweetie!" She smiled while patting his shoulder gently, as if to reward him for a job well done. The empress felt relieved that her plan might be successful, with no consequences.

Henerinni kissed her on the nose and squeezed her hand tightly in his, reassuring her, "I'm here for you baby, and your struggles are my struggles. We are in this together."

"I'm very thankful to have you in my life."

They got up from the bed and completed their nightly grooming routines. She played two of his favorite songs on the harp before they got back into bed.

They kissed, and then Henerinni said, "Sleep well, baby," to which Virginni replied, "Think of me in your dreams, sweetie."

They closed their eyes and fell into a deep sleep, grateful for the many good things in their lives.

One month later, the entire town celebrated the pregnancy with a two-day party that included many special meals all around the city. The citizens played many different games and enjoyed the festivities and welcomed spring. The last four months had been the most joyful time for Virginni, and she lived her life as though she could forget the scheme that was responsible for her current state of happiness. Her in-laws supported the couple with wise advice about raising children, ranging from simple tips about the logistics of dealing with a baby to how to handle different problems that might arise, as well as royal protocol.

During the last month of her pregnancy, the empress gained a lot of weight—much more than normal for someone of her height. After she gave birth, a second baby came out shortly after. They joked that Mother Nature had sent twins to make up for the previous incomplete pregnancies. She named them Dalinni and Joelinni, and planned everything for Joelinni to be the next in line as emperor, because he was born first.

After a little over two years, the boys could walk and run all over. They were very curious and enjoyed the summer days on the palace grounds in the garden, as well as the animals in the barn.

One hot day, Virginni was watching the boys play on the lawn in an enclosed area. A fire broke out in the palace kitchen, so she ran inside to make sure everyone got out. Although the boys were in a penned-off area with a small fence, Dalinni found out how to open the latch, and he led his brother to the pond.

When Virginni returned, she saw only Dalinni in the baby pen. He'd managed to return and secure the gate again. She searched all over the palace grounds, eventually finding Joelinni floating in the pond. The empress tried to save him but was unsuccessful.

After she realized he had passed, her wails were heard all through the city. She screamed at the top of her lungs. Nobody could figure out how Joelinni had ended up in the water, and Virginni never forgave herself.

Dalinni had led Joelinni to the pond and pushed him in, then ran back to the fenced area and pretended he was innocent.

By age seven, Dalinni's facial features became prominent. He had a pronounced widow's-peak hairline with a long narrow face. His brows were bushy and met in the middle to create one long eyebrow. Dalinni's ears bent away from his head and flapped out. He was successful on a xyloblut team with others around his age, because his arms were more powerful than all of the other kids in the game. He had to be admonished for being particularly cruel to other children during matches.

At that point, it was not uncommon for people to comment secretly with shock that Dalinni had come from the most beautiful woman in The Land, yet he did not favor Henerinni either. One day a maid looked at Dalinni, and Pogger's face flashed in her mind. She never forgot a face.

After a few weeks of remembering Pogger every time she saw Dalinni, she wondered if there was a chance that the other man was the father. She figured out the timeline from his birthday and realized that nine months before had been the Summer End Celebration when Pogger had stayed in the palace. Pogger's children had earned a reputation for being heartless, and this same personality was present in Dalinni. People had already believed for centuries that if parents experienced trauma, it was passed down to their children. Although Pogger's profession remained a secret, this philosophy also linked Dalinni to Pogger.

Over time, the maid became certain that Pogger was the father. She knew about the multiple miscarriages, because the servants were made aware of nearly everything in the palace. But Virginni had always treated her with kindness, so the maid kept the information to herself. Still, rumors blew throughout The Land like leaves flying on whimsical breezes.

The problem with Dalinni was that he enjoyed sadistic behavior and had inherited his mother's high level of intelligence, which was a recipe for disaster. When he grew into adulthood, he used his wit to cover up elaborate lies and manipulation. Upon being crowned emperor, he chose a wife who was equally self-absorbed and approved anything he did as long as her interests were appeased. Empress Suzinni was from Najeeram in the Mountain South Prefecture. She was the same age as Emperor Dalinni, so they shared knowledge of common events and had grown up similarly. She was known to be passive aggressive with situations involving her three brothers and three sisters, and she'd learned how to inflict pain without getting caught.

Empress Suzinni used her looks as one of her most effective tools to control others. She had fair skin and lengthy limbs, along with high cheekbones and long, silky hair in a simple, natural wave. Big eyes and full lips accentuated her prominent straight nose. Her curvy body with its large chest, small waist, and big behind were apparent even under modest clothing. In contrast to the previous empress, Suzinni had no empathy for the palace servants and never addressed any of them by name. She did not view them as worthy of respect, because of their stations in life.

One of the main reasons Emperor Dalinni chose her was because of her powerful family. It was the highest-ranking family of the Mountain South Prefecture, and an alliance like that opened an entire swath of power, lending him support for anything he wanted to enact, including military resources to brutally invade the nearby people of the rainforests. He attacked them like no emperor before, and committed atrocities and cruelty that had never been imagined.

He knew that his parents would not approve of all of the overt vio- lence that he had planned to implement in the city of Crawldsay, so he had them banished. Instead of living in the second-floor quarters, as had been tradition for thousands of years of former leaders, his parents moved with Virginni's family to Bingdole with their daughter, who was just a bit younger than Emperor Dalinni, and looked like an exact mix of Virginni and Henerinni.

Nobody realized the immense destruction that would overtake The Land after Dalinni started to slowly unleash his tyranny. His wife encouraged any sick violence as long as she was safe, and everyone else around him learned by example that he must be obeyed at all costs. He had little patience for dissent and took every opportunity to feed his desire to see pain in others. Death sports and new forms of inhumane punishment for minor infractions of the law were introduced. One of Dalinni's first actions was to abolish help for the poor so that the least of their city suffered the most.

From that moment on, the people of The Land knew the importance of a good leader, and they prayed for kind and empathetic rulers. The impact of everything he introduced lasted far beyond the scope of his reign; however, the new leadership after he left was surprisingly kind.

His children had been raised by servants who knew the importance of instilling values and respect for human life. From a young age, the servants used therapy techniques to heal any signs of trauma. When they were installed as leaders, the new generation naturally had personalities that valued relationships with people. They were hardworking, kind, compassionate, and loyal.

The tradition of the Keeper of the Stars remained intact, because Dalinni viewed him as merely an odd, boring person with strange practices. Because the ancient texts outlined protocol, the new leadership also had strong guidance. As this new power took root, it laid the foundation for reexamining human sacrifice in the volcanoes and the concept of capital punishment.

CHAPTER TWENTY-FIVE

About four hundred years after the cruel Emperor Dalinni, and around two hundred years before Jaway's time, an emperor and empress reigned over Crawldsay named Bobbinni and Marilinni. Many of the same practices and traditions remained since Emperor Henerinni and Empress Virginni's time, such as the Keeper of the Stars. Generations of trained family members kept the institution alive and well in all of its eccentric glory. The regions of The Land also remained constant, including the three western prefectures.

Emperor Bobbinni and Empress Marilinni lived in the palace of Crawldsay on the third floor in the same room that had been reserved for all of the reigning emperors, and Emperor Bobbinni's parents lived in the room on the second floor that was reserved for the former rulers.

Empress Marilinni chose to redecorate the bedroom, replacing the immense bed with something more practical. The former harp station became a reading area, and other small upgrades had been done over the years, but the secret passageways stood the test of time.

The main hall had managed to sparkle through different eras, because each emperor agreed that the breathtaking white stones should remain. Many of Empress Virginni's precious and valuable tapestries were hung around the palace, and she was remembered for being a master of the art. The pond was still stocked with fresh seafood. Crystal-clear water continued to flow into the freshwater springs in the middle of the fortified city, and into the palace. The homes and shops had mostly been handed down to heirs and remained quite similar. The two large barns still stood near the same imposing entrance gate, and the lookout towers continued to provide security and instill awe. Most importantly for Bobbinni, though, was that the xyloblut court was in mint condition.

"Pass it this way, behind you toward the palace," Bobbinni shouted to his xyloblut team as they ran formations against another squad.

The five pushed their bodies to the edge to try to win. At twenty years of age, the emotionally mature emperor enjoyed staying physically fit by practicing sports. He had a gentle smile and was shorter than average. At first glance, he looked quite plain, but he was not concerned with changing his image for others. He valued being a person of substance, which, to him, included being academic. Although he had a fit body as a natural byproduct of playing royal sports, he was not concerned with outward appearances.

His nineteen-year-old wife, on the other hand, was known for her allure all around The Land. Her beauty was more innocent, understated, and pure, as opposed to sexy and obvious. She also shared a desire for knowledge, but she focused more on her appearance than the emperor. She saw it as a fun hobby that was passed down within her family. She'd grown up in Zander, which was a much smaller city at the time and not yet the capital, southwest of Crawldsay but not too far away. Because the couple both loved learning, they bonded heavily over long, stimulating conversations that covered a myriad of topics they had been exposed to during formal education. Empress Marilinni's kindness and beauty drew her husband closer to her every day, and encouraged him to be more charitable in creative new ways. The newlyweds gained insight into the world by remaining close to their families and spending a lot of time with the former emperor and empress.

"Honey, we'll have dinner with your parents tonight in the main hall," Marilinni said when she arrived on the side of the xyloblut court with one of her girlfriends. The emperor gave her a quick kiss on the lips and ran back into the game.

She blushed and smiled as she chatted with her friend about the game, which was nearly finished.

"Nice job, honey, keep up the good work!" she shouted during a break from the conversation with her pal.

After the emperor's team won the match in a close call, the young and passionate couple walked up to their bedroom and got ready for dinner.

"Woah, that was a great match. What did you think, sweetie?" He scrubbed himself in the small pool in their room while she sat reading a book on a comfortable chair.

"You guys did great. I came a little late, but you had wonderful form on the winning toss at the end!"

The couple chatted until they dressed and got ready for dinner. Marilinni wore a brand new cape that had been gifted to her from their wedding. It was light pink and had a scene of the volcano in Zander, because it was her home town. The emperor put on a traditional cape that was worn without a shirt, the expected attire at the time.

They enjoyed dinner in the main hall with Emperor Bobbinni's parents and then retreated to their room. Upon returning, they discussed the ancient texts, which had been followed even closer after the violent reign of Emperor Dalinni. These were seen as guidance for a just and moral leader, though they still contained requirements for human sacrifice. At the time, the ancient texts were interpreted to mean that every seven years, each family was required to sacrifice a male or female virgin. The wealthiest families would purchase virgins or steal them from other lands, which understandably was not good for government relations. Many other requirements were listed in the different provisions, and if citizens chose to not follow the guidelines, they feared the wrath of the gods and wanted to avoid living lives of terror. As the couple discussed different topics within the ancient text, Bobbinni looked lovingly into his wife's eyes, with a gentle and content expression. Because he was wildly in love with her, he couldn't help but get lost in her gaze.

"Well what do you think, honey?" she asked as he stared at her, snapping him out of a trance.

"Oh sorry baby, I lost my train of thought. What were we saying again?"

The empress was not only beautiful, but she was also overflowing with kindness, and this completely enamored the emperor. They stayed up late discussing world topics, nature, politics, health, philosophy, and anything else that felt interesting. In addition, Marilinni was an amazing storyteller. She could hypnotize any listener and knew many stories that contained wise, valuable life lessons. Her mother had passed down the tales, as well as the special gift of dynamic storytelling.

They slept deeply as usual that night.

The next day, Marilinni scheduled a carriage ride to visit the Keeper of the Stars, because she had missed her cycle and wanted guidance to see if she might be pregnant. She visited the same house that Empress Virginni had frequented centuries before. The thick, exotic moss continued to flow over the edge of the roof, and the mysterious man inside was just as unique and gifted as Begrol had been. He checked her ovulation charts and concluded that there was a high chance that she could be pregnant.

Marilinni felt elated when she left his home that day—she was excited to be a mother and start a family. She told the emperor immediately, but they waited to mention anything until they were certain, around the third month.

During this time, the empress began having strange and specific cravings. One day, she shared that she was disappointed that they did not have any saturn fruits in the city, as she had an intense appetite for them. The emperor loved her so much that he assembled a group of hunters to go to the rainforest and find some. They traveled with three friends who were highly skilled guards, in case they met any hostility. Taking a carriage, they rode past the farmland and to a dense green space where they thought some of the fruit may have been growing.

The problem, and the main reason that it was so rare, was that the saturn fruits grew on a vine and appeared at the top of the canopy, but still under the leaves. So they were difficult to track. Fortunately, the emperor had a specially trained female chameleon who helped locate the fruit. Pookey was a loyal and smart pet.

After leaving the carriage, the group hiked through dense brush with large machetes. Once inside the rainforest, they took Pookey out of a small cage and placed her on a red glove until she transformed to the same color. This was an indication that the hunt had officially started.

As they were walking along, the sweet, vivid pet suddenly curved her back and turned green. This indicated that she smelled the saturn fruit above the trees and that the entourage could stop and set their eyes on a prize high in the sky. It was a waiting game for the group, so they set up camp while Pookey climbed a tree. Typically, it would take a chameleon an hour to get up to the treetops, so the men could take some time to make special foraging snacks, sing songs, and play games while encouraging Pookey with cheers. She was well trained to find the saturn fruit and was on her way up the largest tree.

After about an hour, Pookey made it to the top, where she found a cluster of the sweet treasure. The hunting reptile hissed four times to indicate the target was in reach. As the men congratulated her on a skillful find, she assessed the booty. Tradition was that the chameleon always got to eat the third-ripest saturn fruit, so she found it and bit through the outer purple layer of the sweet treat to reveal green meat and seeds on the inside.

She took a minute to revel in the glory of finding the rarities, looking down on the crew as if almost to say, "Look! I did it!" The ripest and second-ripest fruits were reserved as part of the harvest, so Pookey just had one. After her victory meal, she bit the stem of the ripest fruit, and they all fell into the net that the crew installed below. The cluster that day had had seven total, so Pookey dropped six for harvest.

After the crew packed everything up and Pookey climbed down the tree, they exited the rainforest and took the carriage home. They arrived after dark, and Marilinni was ecstatic, because she'd been feeling strong cravings all day long. Her mouth watered heavily, and she only dreamed of a saturn fruit.

So when they arrived home, she went to work quickly to make her favorite dessert, one both sweet and salty. It was thought that pregnant women craved the food because of the high protein and vitamin content. After just one bite, most people loved it, and it was nourishing to the body. While sitting up late at night and enjoying the delicious dessert, the happy couple decided that if they had a boy, he would be named Saturno, and if they had a girl, her name would be Saturni.

When Saturni was born, the entire city of Crawldsay celebrated with festivities, and the family received gifts from far and wide. She had a very unique eye color that looked like the turquoise sea. The family assumed that after four months, her eyes would change to a shade of brown, but the time came and went, and her eyes were still as bright as any blue-green flower in the rainforest. At six months, the family became concerned, and they began hiding her to avoid public knowledge, remaining hopeful that the natural process was simply delayed.

Saturni stayed inside the emperor's room on the third floor of the palace from the age of six months to around two years old, until one day when an attendant left the room during naptime. The witty child crawled into a laundry basket and managed to be taken down to the ground floor. As the basket waited to be transported farther, baby Saturni noticed that the coast was clear, and she ran outside through the smaller door that was just beside the grand entrance.

She ran and ran, following butterflies and fluffy, floating seeds to the garden, then off to the nearby barn, which was filled with fascinating sounds and creatures that she had never seen. Saturni almost got away with falling under the radar, but then she was approached by a woman in dazzling clothes.

"Well what do we have here? A baby with eyes of the sea?" The royal woman, who was visiting from Najeeram, was notoriously the most active gossip in her city, and loved to pit person against person in order to watch fights.

When the woman picked up little Saturni and put her over her shoulder, the baby immediately threw up on the cape, which was worth a small fortune. The rich woman did not care about the clothing, but she was concerned about her appearance for the day. As she contemplated how she would change for the afternoon, the empress walked up and grabbed Saturni.

"Beautiful day, isn't it?" Marilinni said, trying to avoid any talk about her precious daughter.

"Yes, it's gorgeous. If only my cape could enjoy the day as much as me." She removed it and showed the empress what had happened.

"Let's get this straight to the cleaners. I'll take it to them immediately so it doesn't get set in. Let me know if you need anything for the day. I know you are traveling." Marilinni walked away with Saturni.

The royal woman was in town because her husband was participating in a xyloblut match with the emperor, one that was ultimately meant to improve bonds between faraway cities. Without delay, the queen of gossip had concluded that Empress Marilinni was hiding her daughter, who had eyes of the sea.

She did not say anything until she returned back to Najeeram, with the exclusive morsels for her captive audience. Word spread throughout The Land, and Empress Marilinni and Emperor Bobbinni were forced to deal with the reality of their situation.

From then on, Saturni was treated as a future sacrifice to the gods. The ancient texts stated, "When a child is born with the eyes of the sea, they should belong to the gods and me. If you keep them from our grasp, you shall experience all of our wrath." This was translated literally at the time, and everyone in The Land knew that any child born with turquoise eyes would live a life to be an offering. Up to this point, no royal had ever been born with this physical characteristic. The idea was that the child would be near the gods, and would always convince them to have mercy on the family. The people believed that if they did not follow through with the requirements, their lives would be filled with terror as a natural consequence. Every day when Bobbinni woke, his heart sank as he knew the destiny of one of the loves of his life.

It was customary that a child like this would live under twenty-four-hour surveillance in order to preserve their virginity, and Saturni was no exception. Until this moment, not one person in The Land had defied the requirement, so the family reluctantly followed what had been done in the past. The emperor and empress loved their young girl so much that they gathered the most exquisite materials for her ceremony.

Over the years, Saturni made her parents fall madly in love with her. She had passion for life and enjoyed learning new things, just like her parents, and she constantly surprised them with her understanding of the world. She was also very kind and thoughtful. Saturni had obtained the ability to tell stories from Marilinni, who'd received it from her own mother. It was not uncommon to find innocent Saturni sitting outside near the pond, surrounded by a gaggle of kids who were intently listening to one of her inventive tales. The fondness that the family shared was deep, because the emperor and empress were madly in love before they had a child, and Saturni seemed to naturally intensify this adoration.

When the family reached the seventh year of obligation for a sacrifice, Saturni's fate was sealed. The ancient texts demanded requirements, and the family was not allowed to complete their volcano pilgrimage at a minor mountain; they were required to go to Zander, which was the largest volcano in the region, and happened to be relatively nearby.

Over the years, the family had gathered the finest required items from far and near, sparing no expense. Personal friends who labored as craftsmen offered special workmanship that they normally saved for only family. The jeweler made certain that each gem was of the highest grade and cut. The ceremonial silks were the most valuable around, including the most revered textiles from Empress Virginni's famous historical collection.

The morning of the first day of the pilgrimage was quiet and somber. Marilinni sobbed while she gathered the most prized items available in The Land, but she thought only of the love that she had for her daughter.

She stepped in front of the window, and a ray of sun bounced into a bowl of gems, sending multicolored laser beams around the room.

After the carriage was filled with everything for the journey, they met Bobbinni's parents at the palace entrance. They all fought to maintain composure; they wanted tiny Saturni to remain calm. Over the years, the family had successfully shielded Saturni from any knowledge of her fate. They told her that they would be going on a trip to walk up a great big hill and that it would be fun. They took the carriage to the city of Zander to spend some time together as a family, and then rode to the base of the nearby volcano.

They loaded a twarpen with the required items as well as anything they would need for the four-day journey. It took everything inside Marilinni to keep her composure in front of Saturni. They set off on foot and traveled up the black, volcanic-rock-lined road with the twarpen.

As they hiked up the side of the volcano, passing over large veins that had been formed from place to place, they had a lot of time to evaluate the situation and were forced to view the atonement as human, but felt obligated by the pressures of their world to continue. This was the first time that a royal had birthed a turquoise-eyed baby; only lower-class citizens had been in this predicament before. It was always assumed that the royals took the journey with a human sacrifice that was purchased and came from another land, while lower-class citizens did not have that luxury.

That day their beloved Saturni, who told captivating stories and frolicked along the winding roads up the volcano, was the only option. Four hours later, they arrived at the midpoint and were greeted by monks and their families, who lived there in service to The Land. They took care of the twarpen and brought him to the stables. Saturni quickly became friends with the children, and the couple were shown to simple yet clean rooms for the evening. They tried to eat dinner with the family, but they could not under such heartbreak. They were only able to dine after being secretly counseled by the monk family; it was clear they would need extra strength for the long physical journey the following day.

After waking from a sleepless night, the couple entertained their beloved Saturni during breakfast, trying to appear normal to her. They packed up their belongings onto the twarpen and walked up the volcano. When they arrived at the top, they paced along the edge of the opening in order to get to the ceremonial ledge. The expansive, round crater hissed steam and blew hot breaths onto the family, making them sweat profusely. They numbly walked to the preparation building next to the ledge, where they adorned Saturni with brightly colored silk garments and textiles that had hung in the palace for centuries. Under this layer was a sheet of flexible gold that contained precious gems. They placed an intricate silver crown on Saturni's head and fitted her with the finest amethyst and gold butterfly earrings. A ruby-and-silver nose ring clipped to her septum. She was covered with more pieces of elaborate gold and silver jewelry as well.

After outfitting little Saturni, the parents said together, "Gods of the land which we fear, please take this sacrifice that we hold dear. Our child is covered in gold, silver, gems, and silk. Please grant us peace by keeping our child near."

They walked up to the massive ledge that hung over the edge of the crater. Red lava flowed inside the volcano and sloshed back and forth, with large bubbles popping at the surface. Ash clouds blew into the air and were ushered away with breezes. Upon viewing the scene, the empress lost control of herself. She held Saturni with all of her might as they stood at the end of the long platform that jutted directly above the bright-red, molten destiny. The emperor joined and wailed loudly as they mourned the future loss of their precious love.

"Why?" Bobbinni screamed, and it echoed back five times over.

A confused and frightened child stood between them, soon realizing her fate. They froze in silence, then kneeled and looked Saturni in the eyes.

They both knew the expectation and understood the importance of following the laws. After all, they reasoned that Emperor Dalinni had been a result of not following the ancient texts. As the couple stood up in order to prepare emotionally for the push, the weight of the materials finally bore down on little Saturni, and her weak legs gave out. She fell onto the ledge and bounced over the edge, holding on with a tight grip. Before the parents could do anything, her sweaty palms delivered the sacrifice into the molten rock below.

She immediately vaporized, and a heavy breeze blew the ashes of what she once had been into a small tornado that traveled around the inside of the gigantic crater. The spiral wind spun back around and finally ended at the platform, where the parents stood. The empress's hair blew all over, and the gusts nearly pushed the couple into the lava below. The emperor fell to his knees, where he evaluated what he was doing and why. His heart was filled with pain, and he tore his shirt, pulling both fists out as far as they could reach, and arched his back to the skies while screaming at the top of his lungs.

The empress existed numbly next to the now-shirtless emperor. She could not believe what she had just seen.

In that moment, gold dust covered the couple from head to toe, and Bobbinni decided that he would do everything in his power to stop the human sacrifices. The metal thickly painted every surface of the couple, and they walked down over the rest of the day, returning to the monk family, but did not spend the night.

They walked in the dark to the bottom, where they were met by the carriage and taken immediately to the palace, still covered in gold, except where the rivers of pain flowed from their eyes.

In the following years, Bobbinni tasked a branch within the Royal Academy of Knowledge with evaluating ways to reinterpret the ancient texts in regards to human sacrifice and capital punishment. This team eventually produced justification to interpret sacrifices as symbolic rather than literal. Going forward, different materials could be used in place of human life.

From that point on, all human sacrifices were banned in the land. In addition, the branch produced a multilevel plan to shift the common mindset to save lives as much as possible. After sending multiple material sacrifices into the volcanoes, the people were never punished by the gods and experienced no new catastrophes.

Capital punishment was banned through The Land—when Saturni died that day, she saved countless future lives.

Around fifty years after the time of Emperor Bobbinni and Empress Marilinni, the capital city transitioned from Crawldsay to Zander. Zander was southwest of Crawldsay, so it provided even more of a buffer between the capital city and the people of the rainforest, who were still resistant against The Land. This new location was also closer to the ocean, and nearby the largest volcano. This provided more access to freely practice traditions while living and functioning in the most influential city.

During the same year of the capital city change, the emperor funded and established the Royal Academy of Knowledge. Most notably, within this academy, the Royal Academy of Technology began eight years later and was responsible for researching and developing the advancements that would ultimately transform The Land and create advantages over its neighbors.

Because of the undeniable progress in food production, product development, transportation, materials, and the like, foreigners were convinced that they would benefit greatly from peacefully joining The Land. Weapons created by the same academy also provided incentive for less-armed people who were unsure about merging.

As a result, twenty-five years after the Royal Academy of Knowledge was founded, the Southern Plains joined The Land by choice. They were convinced that incorporating all of the advancements into their way of life would be beneficial. After all, the endless plains of grasslands, crops, wild bison herds, and alpaca as livestock were no match for the obviously innovative and motivated emperor of the Mountain Region. Although they were required to pay taxes to the emperor's Tax Department, the banks all belonged to the emperor, and were converted to the monetary system designed by the experts in Zander.

After twenty-five more years had passed, the Eastern Highlands were also invited to join The Land. At first, different parts joined willingly. The people of the Highlands varied, as this region contained expansive rolling hills as well as many large, cosmopolitan beach cities. Understandably, some areas and cities refused to join because strong-willed farmers and others resisted. Surprisingly, the greatest defiance came from the sophisticated sects that were infamous for enjoying the pleasures of life at a slow pace.

This region was too full of resources for The Land to provide a pass, so The Land issued warnings that if they did not join, they would be considered enemies. Over a one-year process, these strong and heavily resistant groups slowly compromised, realizing they would never be able to fight against the much more advanced military. Soon, the entire region incorporated as part of The Land.

Ten years after the Eastern Highlands joined, many parts of the Rainforest Region were forced to meld. This region had experienced thousands of years of mistreatment that was often incredibly cruel. The times of Emperor Dalinni had been particularly horrific, and The Land had only stopped stealing Rainforest virgins for sacrifices a little over a hundred years before. As a result, these people would never be lured by simple promises of a better and easier life. They all fought back until The Land defeated huge portions of the region, forcing the last of the resistance to the north, which became the final uncontrollable space from coast to coast.

The rainforest people in the spaces that had become part of The Land were considered residents of the Rainforest Region. They conformed to a culturally influenced way of life that kept many traditions, but ultimately mimicked the lives of those living in the Mountain Region to the west. Those who continued to resist, keeping living traditional lives that were characteristic of the original rainforest people, were forced to the northern area, which was named the Wild Territory. This held strong as the last area to not bend to the will of the Western Mountain region emperors, and they lived defensive lives within the cover of the dense forests.

These resistant people remain untamed and out of reach of The Land by covertly researching the latest technology, and creating equally destructive counterattacks. The pressure of continuous battle had a stressful impact on these communities, yet they stood their ground and remained independent. This made emperors of The Land even more interested in controlling and defeating them. As The Land expanded, new regional emperors were considered colleagues to the Mountain North Prefecture emperor, the Mountain Central Prefecture emperor, and the Mountain South Prefecture emperor; however, the emperor of The Land retained ultimate control.

Sixty-nine years after these parts of the Rainforest Region joined The Land, Jaway was born, during the height of continuously morphing and developing technological advancements. At the time of Jaway's birth, each region's home designs had adapted to include different technology, yet they all retained qualities that made them uniquely suited for their topography and surroundings. For example, the typical Mountain Region house was three stories or more, along with a basement, and constructed in a wavy shape that allowed the building to sway during earthquakes. The Rainforest Region homes were built into the surroundings, with trees actually growing through the floor and exiting the rooftop. These single-level dwellings integrated nature because the rainforest people needed to feel as one with their surroundings, and the canopy above the homes provided a cooling effect in the hot climate.

Highland Region houses were oval in shape, with pointed ends. A thick central pole held the weight. A circular encasement began as a circle around the pole on the ground, and grew gradually until meeting the base floor. These features allowed the building to rotate during hurricanes in order to provide the least resistance to the heavy winds. Plains Region homes all had basements for safety and were usually four levels above ground with a top viewing floor. Because of typically huge families, up to twelve bedrooms were common.

Twenty-one years later, Jaway was in charge of the most elite military information gathering group of The Land. Zander had been the capital city for quite some time, and human sacrifice and capital punishment had been eradicated from society.

CHAPTER TWENTY-SIX

Upon arrival in Kritziddle, each crew member stopped what they were doing and watched as the large glider parked in a huge, open space just outside of the main town. The military used this as a repair center, as it was centrally located in the Rainforest Region. Open fields in the surrounding areas made it ideal, and the site was far enough south of the Wild Territory that complete security was expected.

After parking, the group clapped and encouraged their leaders and those who'd operated the glider.

"Thanks for all of your fine work, team—we have successfully landed, and we will receive a message from Central Command in a few minutes. Be ready for anything," Jaway said.

The crew waited in anticipation to find out how long they would be there and any other details of their stay. Each worker made their way to the lower or upper control rooms to hear the message.

They had started chatting about random topics when a fashionable woman beamed out of pictogrammers to start the blobe from Central Command. "Keep in mind that each of you serves a special role in gathering information for The Land. And this is vital in the quest to unite us completely. Your efforts encourage peace and safety for all people, and your families are very proud of your hard work. Listen for the following guidance."

They stood by quietly, ready to pay close attention to the instructions as their vehicle was assessed.

"Not only does your glider require outer repairs, maintenance is necessary, and it will need to dock for a total of . . ." They waited for the calculation. "Fourteen days. Please check with your commander for details. Remember that everyone at Central Command is very proud of everything you do, and we will continue to support you all as much as we can!"

Based on previous maintenance docking periods, any sort of working schedule was possible. Jaway connected to an infogrammer in front of his work station. He looked at the requirements for the crew and was surprised by the findings.

Jaway's voice was cast to each floor of the glider: "According to the information that was sent to me, we have been granted fourteen days of leave, for everyone."

He was surprised and relieved, and the crew was equally so. With this uncommon news, they cheered, clapped, and jumped for joy.

When they became silent again, he continued, "This means that you just need to check in daily with me and let me know where you plan to be. We must all remain within forty minutes of the glider in case an emergency mission call is issued. You are authorized to live in the barracks here. This is a great opportunity to study for the certification exams that many of us may have coming up. I know that C. E. Didier is local, so reach out to her if you are interested in staying in a hotel. For those of you who are not sure, I suggest taking a room in the barracks and setting up there, and then finding something later. She is always so hospitable, so I'm certain if you have any questions about the area, she is your woman. Because we have arrived in a secure zone, you will be able to communicate with friends and family in the next hour or so."

Jaway calmly sorted out details about the next few weeks. Due to security protocol, crew members were only allowed communication from the outside at certain points during a mission. The past objective had been completed, and no information about the next assignment was provided, so communication would be opened. This was a very special time for them, because other than being on call for an emergency mission, they could all live like normal civilians for the next couple of weeks. If they wanted to sightsee and enjoy the ecotourism that Kritziddle was famous for, they'd be able to. They could use the time any way they liked.

Some of the crew members teared up at the news of the unexpected freedom. In this scenario, battalions typically would take their personal belongings to rooms in nearby barracks, and figure out plans from there. In the past, small groups had rented accommodation together to split the cost, and spent at least a week on vacation. The excited clan packed most of their personal items, then sat around chatting in the central area on the bottom level until communication was cleared. At that point, most sent messages through their elitsers to loved ones and friends. Didier received news immediately that her mother insisted on cooking for the entire crew that night.

She projected her voice to all floors with Jaway's approval. "Everyone, you are invited to my house tonight, and my mom, Srondi, will be cooking for us. I really hope you can all make it and meet my family and experience a traditional Rainforest Region meal. She already started preparations at my place!"

For many of them, this would be their first opportunity to spend time with locals in the Rainforest Region. They all thought highly of Didier, and she was very close to many of her colleagues, so every member planned to enjoy a night at her house. They were curious about what it would be like.

After the company messaged family, they each gathered personal items and checked into a room in the barracks that were not far from the glider repair field. Pama made certain to place two ice cubes in her black orchid in the central common area on the bottom level before leaving, treating the glowing black and green-blue plant like a pet.

About thirty minutes after everyone went to the barracks, two vrodilops pulled up next to the building.

"My family is here to get us all—be in the vrodilops within ten minutes, or you are dust!" Didier lightly joked, then headed out to see her dad, who drove his transportation, and her sister, who drove Didier's.

A vrodilop was a vehicle that moved like a glider, but made for civilian use. Most families had one, and they were similar in all regions. These usually fit ten people and were composed of a clear material that could be made solid for privacy if desired. They were shaped like large rectangles, but the front-end roof sloped down and the bottom sloped up, gradually making a point for aerodynamic purposes. A leg on each bottom corner released during parking to keep the vehicle off of the ground. One door in the back morphed to create stairs, similar to how it worked with fydons.

C. E. Didier's vrodilop had a standard, large, cozy, U-shaped couch in the back that could fit seven people. A sofa at the front fit three people near the control panel, where the mechanics were stored. Didier's mom had made miniature curtains that were hung along one of the walls.

For safety, each passenger wore a bicktrude, a bracelet that provided protection. The thin yet wide bands came in many different colors, and would connect to the kleck of the wearer and automatically create a mostly transparent suit around them. The impenetrable suits provided complete safety for any rider in the case of an accident.

Didier's dad and sister looked similar to her—they also had tiny noses, were tall and fit, and had different shades of purple tattoos on light-tan skin.

"Shoomklat," her dad said, using her first name, "your mom and Cruld stayed home to clean your place and cook up a storm." They all cried and hugged each other.

"This is my dad, Blute, and one of my sisters, Nrode." Didier introduced her family members to the entire crew one by one, explaining tidbits of information for them every so often.

She presented Captain Serra and shared that they were like siblings. Hilton joked around with her when he was introduced, because they got along so well. Jeffers shared sincere appreciation, and Sickles smiled the most and thanked them for sending such an angel to her fydon.

"Shoomklat, who we always call Didier, is the best fydonmate ever!" she gushed.

At age twenty-one, C. E. Didier was old enough to live on her own, but she still relied heavily on the support of her family. The group of seventeen boarded the two vrodilops and distributed bicktrudes. Then, Didier and her dad drove them all to their neighborhood by ascending above the trees and following an intricate set of light beams that outlined roads in the air.

In the Rainforest Region, it was common for families to live next to each other in neighborhoods. Initially, two homes were usually built side by side. Then the next two houses would be built at ninety-degree angles on the ends of the original buildings so that a plaza remained in the center, with seating and art as a focal point. Many more dwellings could be added next to the end homes as they expanded.

Didier's family came from means, and her parents had built homes for her and her sister next to their abode. Hers was a large, standard home with four bedrooms that was built into the natural surroundings. These single-level buildings had high ceilings. The entrance door typically opened to an elevator that ascended into the living quarters, then to a rooftop terrace. Below the main floor was a space for vrodilop parking in the center. On the opposite side of the house from the door was a column that contained plumbing. Because the rainforest people were still close to their roots, they designed homes that incorporated available ingenuity but also natural surroundings. It was standard practice to build a house with trees that grew down through the floor and continued up through the rooftop. A special contraption sealed around the tree, stretching as it grew. The trees provided shade and kept the space cool.

Didier's home consisted of a kitchen, a large dining room, and a living room, with four bedrooms and bathrooms. The rooftop terrace contained lounging areas, outdoor eating spaces, and a pool. It had transparent walls from floor to ceiling, and these could be tinted to provide privacy in any location. Because there were no roads built on the ground before the modern structures, family neighborhoods followed any pattern or layout. The crew enjoyed the drive from the repair station to Didier's home. Many of them were in awe of the way the entire city was built into the surrounding nature.

Blute acted like a tour guide, proudly explaining his region to many of the first-time visitors. "Kritziddle is the second-largest city of the Rainforest Region, and ecotourism is a huge industry. We also produce many medicines with the natural plants that you can find growing everywhere."

Didier's dad had a very calm demeanor, which was characteristic of their culture. Individuals from other regions commented on how the people were tall and lean with light-tan skin and purple tattoos.

"On the right up here, you will see a rehabilitation center. People from all over The Land come here to heal from mineral waters and our natural medicines."

Blute continued explaining facts for the outsiders. Churchill struck up a conversation with him, because he was also from the Rainforest Region, but from the largest city of Albronder.

As C. E. Didier's vrodilop pulled up to a home, the crew members' eyes grew wide—it looked very expensive. She parked in the vrodilop space under the house in the middle, and her dad parked under his place next door.

They all entered through the front door and took the elevator up to the living quarters floor. Didier's mom, Srondi, was cooking in the kitchen and ran over to hug her daughter, and kiss her on the cheek. They embraced, and her mom cried. Then her other sister, Cruld, came from the bedroom area with cleaning gloves and also gave her a huge squeeze.

"Shoomklat, we are just tidying up your house a little bit. It has been sitting empty for a while, and it's not every day we get the pleasure of an emergency visit from our sister!" Cruld said.

They hugged and jumped in the air, happy to see one another. Didier walked around and explained the layout of her house, because she knew it would be interesting for those from different regions, and they needed to kill time before the food would be ready. She led them through the dining and living room, past many large couches and a very long table that could seat all of them comfortably.

They walked farther and she said, "Here are four bedrooms and bathrooms. Three of them are available for whoever wants to crash as long as you like."

The home was outfitted with a variety of the latest, most innovative appliances for cooking, dishwashing, laundering clothes, styling hair, other personal grooming, and floor cleaning. Then they all went up to the rooftop terrace. Most of the crew members were astonished by the pool and seating areas that lay directly under the lush canopy. They could see through to the sky in certain patches, and were eager to swim in the exotic pool.

At dinner, the entire crew enjoyed many typical dishes that Srondi whipped up, with local wine. They reminisced about the adventures that they had at base camp and joked politely to entertain Didier's family. Srondi and Blute were very proud of their daughter, and made the entire group feel at home. They even re-extended the open invitation to stay at their house, as they had many extra bedrooms.

After dinner, the crew and family went to the rooftop terrace to enjoy drinks around the beautiful pool under the canopy. Fascinating and vivid wild creatures joined them, providing an otherworldly experience for many of the crew members. Srondi and Blute said goodbye to all of their daughter's friends and then went back to their house, leaving the others to relax and enjoy the night. Some of them went down to the living room to play games, and a small group stayed on the rooftop.

While Hilton and Kandova swam in the water, everyone else left so they were alone when they got out to sit by the fire pit.

"I really liked getting to know you better last night. And I feel good when I'm around you. Do you feel the same way?" Hilton whispered, also aware that nobody else could hear.

"Yeah, I agree. I feel like we get along well. And I can't reach cans on the top shelf." She continued the joke they'd created at the fire at base camp.

"I was serious when I said that I want to be there for you. I have really wanted a relationship for many years, and I was hoping that we could at least start while we are civilians for these fourteen days," Hilton said as they huddled close to the fire.

"Are you saying you want to be my boyfriend?"

"Yeah. I feel like you are the person for me. I see us growing old together," Hilton shared honestly from his heart.

Kandova did not say a word. Because they were alone, she replied by leaning in and kissing him on the lips. Their chests burned with love for one another.

"Is that a yes?"

"There is nothing more that I want than to be your girlfriend. Let's do it."

She smiled and looked deep into his eyes, trusting the goodness that would be there for her through thick and thin. They chatted about how happy they were and laughed together. Then she checked a device quickly for any messages.

"Do you remember why I'm a virgin?"

Hilton nodded with a confused look.

"I just got a message from my parents, and you get to meet them tomorrow. They were on a pilgrimage in Zander, and they'll make their way here. What do you think?" she asked, waiting to see his reaction, which would reveal how serious he was about being together.

"Yeah, I would love to meet your parents." The muscular and tall man of her dreams smiled, revealing bright-white teeth and a beaming aura.

"Alright, let's do it. Technically, we are just civilians right now, so it is not against the rules, but let's try to keep it a secret, because I see us lasting forever, baby."

They found a place to look at the stars through a break in the canopy. They lay on a cozy, padded surface on the floor, and Kandova snuggled up to her man. She looked to the sky while her head rested on his shoulder and pectoral muscle.

They kissed and talked there for an hour before going downstairs with the rest of the crew. When they got downstairs, the rest of the tired travelers were making plans for where to sleep. The girls decided to stay at

Didier's house, while the others were going over to Srondi and Blute's place next door. Thankfully, the entire battalion was still there.

"Can I have your attention, everyone? I have a confession to make. I ate way too much good food tonight!" Kandova joked as her usual self.

Everyone laughed and also sincerely described how much they loved the hospitality.

She addressed the host while the others listened. "Thanks to the Didier family's generosity. I am in love with your place. I just got a message from my loved ones. They were on their pilgrimage to Zander and are being tourists in Crawldsay now, and will be here tomorrow. They want to take us all out to see some stuff. Didier, your whole family is invited too."

Kandova was met with encouraging positive responses. Most of the troop wanted to enjoy the sights and freedom, and her close friends were interested in meeting her parents and sister. The crew members finalized sleeping arrangements and had a cozy night in the unique surroundings.

The next morning, many of them woke early and swam in the pool. Their youthful, sculpted bodies decorated the space like a painting of gods under the canopy. Didier made a huge breakfast for the troop and her family, and they devoured it on the rooftop terrace with vibrant, magnificent birds, tiny monkeys, and fascinating brightly colored insects. They enjoyed the shade under the canopy and how nature lived freely among the people here. Jeffers commented on the distinct differences between this style of living and what she'd grown up with on the west coast.

Didier explained, "Our people lived in the rainforest, and it was part of our culture for thousands of years. So when we made structures and integrated into The Land, we made sure to keep nature intact and live as a part of it."

M. O. Kandova received a message from her family that they were staying in condominiums famous for providing tourists with an experience based in nature. Because they were not too far away, Didier's sister Nrode offered to drive her over after breakfast to spend time with them. Despite the recent advancements in technology, a movement had made its way through the upper class where anything of the earth was considered trendy. Using natural products from the land, decorating with organic elements, and using plants as medicine were very popular. Kandova's mom, Yordup, was a devoted follower of this trending philosophy.

Kandova's parents and sister were waiting outside when the vrodilop descended through the trees. They accosted her with hugs and kisses before meeting Nrode and thanked her for dropping off their loved one. The Kandova family was very close, and they were used to telling each other nearly everything, so they had a lot of catching up to do. They discussed many topics that she'd missed during the time apart.

"Praldeze, we have to show you the place we are renting. It is amazing!" her mom said. It had been a long time since she'd been called by anything but her last name and military title.

They gave Kandova a tour and gushed over the beautiful apartment, which was built into the surrounding nature. They took snacks and went onto the rooftop terrace to sit, chat, and enjoy the pool.

"So, tell me about your trip. How has it been so far? I wasn't expecting you guys to be around here!" Kandova addressed her mom, who was motivated to talk about everything.

"Well, we started by going directly to Zander for our pilgrimage. This was our first time hiking up the Zander volcano, because we had just gone to more minor ones before. It was magnificent, and I wouldn't have traded it for anything in the world. We got to the top and threw in the precious items. The whole process felt cleansing and like a new beginning, just to spend four days reflecting on life and being one with powerful nature. For me, it felt as if I were throwing our old habits into the volcano and we will start fresh and new." Yordup shared this all freely, as they were open about nearly every single detail of their lives.

During this time in history, the people considered the practice of throwing virgins into lava to be antiquated. Many believed in the symbolism of starting anew, and not as much in gods practicing mercy or vengeance, though most of the oldest generation still strongly desired to appease the gods.

Jaway's generation, in general, held a much more recent point of view toward religious practices. They believed in respecting human life and that it was an option to follow the pilgrimage, and throwing objects into the flames as an offering was symbolic. These offerings commonly included fine foods, precious gems, new devices, silver, gold, and expensive fabrics. It was typically a four-day experience to hike and acclimate to the elevation. Some folks mixed different chemicals with the material sacrifices to create a vibrant fireworks show that sparkled, banged, and popped. Spiritual vantage points throughout the land were also created in order to see very far over the scenery, often all the way to the sea.

"Then, yesterday, we spent the entire day in the ancient city of Crawldsay," Yordup continued about the trip.

At that time, Crawldsay Palace was a museum, and remained breathtaking with the original walls and artwork.

"Look at these, Praldeze, I got some cute plates with Crawldsay Palace paintings. This one has the entire fortified city. It really was a sight to see."

Yordup collected tourist mementos and displayed them around her home, partly to brag to her friends about the vacations.

"Since we were on a journey of self-reflection, we visited the Keeper of the Stars there for fun. It was a very intimate setting, like we were the only people in the world. He was in one of the most unique houses you've ever seen. I got sage from him and some life advice for a new start with better habits." Yordup was excited just to speak with her baby, who had grown up and been far away for so long. Although Crawldsay was an ancient town, people still lived in the homes, with updated interiors.

"Wow, that sounds like an amazing trip! I would *love* to go there some time!" Kandova said.

"Yeah, I think you would really love it." Yordup paused. "So yesterday, we also visited the farms between Crawldsay and the rainforest. They had a lot of local produce, and we bought chokecherry jam, unique wines, and crafts made with regional materials. The girls are going to love these when I get back!" She was excited about the treasures.

"That's really cool that you guys found so many local items. You know, our Commander Barbour is from Zander, and his family members have farms where you were. I think he grew up going there."

She felt relieved and at peace to unexpectedly spend time with her sister and parents.

Her mom continued, "Praldeze, I'm so glad we got to see you, and being able to explore the Rainforest Region is just an added bonus. You caught us at the perfect time, too. We were going to drive straight to Owantay today, and Kritziddle is just a jaunt out of our way. All the ladies are going to be so jealous that I could come to the west coast and experience the Mountain Region, and then I also got to spend some time in the Rainforest Region! Everything is so different from our beach lifestyle on the east coast. Okay, I want some input from you girls—let me know what you think."

Yordup was a typical high-glamor, Owantian girl through and through. She put her face into the pradimptor and waited a few seconds until her lipstick was finished.

"This one is a new shade of red. It has some orange in it, and it's a bit more glossy but stays on all day." She showed the girls the first option. "Or do you like this one better?" She lowered her face into the pradimptor and came up with a new color of red with a more matte finish. "This one is a totally different shade of red."

Yordup moved her face from side to side and tucked her large curls behind her ears to model the new shade of lip stick. The girls discussed the differences and talked about her eye shadow, which went better with one of the shades. They decided they liked the first option better, so she changed it back to that color within a few seconds.

It was clear, looking at Yordup, where Kandova got her style. She wore clothes that were modern yet sophisticated and was not shy about showing off her curvy body.

Kandova's dad, Dlamp, looked up from the book he was reading to interject, "You know Praldeze, your mom wore her wedge heels up the side of the volcano, and she still passed most of the other people, who couldn't even keep up with her." He laughed and patted his wife on the back before giving her a kiss. "That's my girl."

Then he continued reading his book.

"Have you been able to do anything fun on your missions, Praldeze?" Jussol, Kandova's sister, hoped for some adventurous stories.

"Yeah, we actually just got off of an incentive time in the middle of the rainforest. We hiked into the depths, swam through a cave with candles, climbed up the side of a mountain, and then jumped off with parachutes. Oh, I almost forgot. One girl almost got eaten by a spider, but another colleague slashed it with her machete, and we ended up eating it," Kandova proudly announced to her adrenaline-thirsty family.

"Woah, that sounds amazing!" said Jussol.

She looked up to her big sister and imagined the most exotic pictures in her mind. M. O. Kandova had originally received her appreciation for extreme activities from her parents.

With a book in his hand, Dlamp asked inquisitively about each event.

After listening to her responses, he explained more from their hike. "When you get up to the rim of the volcano, you can either ask a monk to walk out onto a platform and drop the offerings into the center, or you can do it yourself. I'm sure you're already thinking that, yes, we did it ourselves. It was a total rush looking down into a lake of lava. We could only handle a few minutes and we had to get out of there. We were dripping in sweat within seconds." He paused. "After the first day, we walked halfway up the volcano, and there was an incredibly nice monk family there. We stayed with them that night, and the last. There was also a monk family to stay with near the top for the second night, but they weren't as hospitable—still sufficient, though."

Kandova had learned to interpret visions through her mom, and Yordup always could sense what was going on in her life.

"So what's new with you, my baby girl? I can feel that there is something wonderful and fresh."

Kandova's face beamed as she smiled. She was cautious to share, though, because her overprotective dad had scared away any interested suitors in the past.

"Okay, Dad, try to take this gently. I met a guy, and we get along really well, and yesterday he asked me to be his girlfriend." She could not hold back, but now she waited for an interrogation from her father, who would certainly do everything in his power to make sure his daughter was never disrespected.

"Well, what did you say?" Jussol asked with wide eyes.

"I said yes. And you all get to meet him today."

CHAPTER TWENTY-SEVEN

Dlamp carefully approached the topic because of his past reactions.
"You know, sweetie pie, I had a lot of time to soul-search over
the past week or so, and I came to the conclusion that I have been blocking your ability to grow as a person and explore your own relationships.
You are a full-fledged woman and will possibly want to start your own
family soon, and I need to get with the program." Dlamp had a concerned
look on his face. "I owe you a big apology, Praldeze, and I am going to try
to work on being more inviting to anyone you bring around the family
from now on. I'm sorry."

Kandova looked at her dad, and felt validated as an adult. She was living away from home and making serious, responsible choices by herself;
she wanted nothing more than to be treated as a grown-up.

"Wow, I really wasn't expecting that, Dad. I totally forgive you for anything in the past. I was hoping that you guys would see me more as an
adult since I'm living away from the house, and that means a lot to me."
Kandova walked over and gave him a huge hug.

"I hate to be the bearer of bad inquiries, but how is that going to be
possible with you guys working together? Isn't that not allowed?" Yordup
asked the most important question.

"Well, we are good to go while we are on leave for these fourteen days,
and after that I guess we just have to not be overt. I imagine we actually
have to be inconspicuous during these days on leave also. But we should
be fine. I've heard of people falling in love during military service." Kandova was serious but had an excited smile on her face.

"Alright, just be careful. We want you to have a good experience. And
we will be sure to wait to grill him on his entire life until we are all alone."
Her mom winked at her and smiled.

"Well, I appreciate you guys keeping this low-key. I'm sure we can get some time today alone, just with all of us together. Maybe we can come back here at some point," Kandova said.

"That's a great idea. We have to have him over for dinner tonight. I won't take no for an answer." Yordup smiled from ear to ear, raised her shoulders, and inhaled to indicate that she was in heaven to be part of this possibly life-changing event.

"So while we are at the waterfalls today, he is the guy that is taller than everyone else. Oh, speaking of that, he saved one of the other girls' life by jumping into a huge pit and throwing her out." Kandova nodded with wide eyes to emphasize this.

"Woah, he sounds like a superhero. I can't wait to meet him," Jussol said.

"Well, his height comes in handy, but I really like him because he is so sweet. He is genuine and kind, and I hope you get to see that."

They joked around and made puns about falling in love before getting ready for the day. Kandova wore her sister's clothes; she loved the new trends that she had not gotten a chance to keep up with.

After lunch, the Kandova and Didier families met back at the barracks so the crew could get their personal items and change. Kandova introduced her family to her colleagues randomly, but made sure not to forget anyone. Jeffers was one of the first to have everything ready, so she approached the Kandova family.

"We are so happy to meet you, Jeffers, mostly because we have heard so much about you. It has been really difficult to have a slice of our family missing, but it has been reassuring to know that Praldeze has close friends around who will look out for her." Yordup said.

"Aw, thanks! That means a lot to me. I also have told my family a lot about your daughter, and I am really thankful to have her in my life. It's nice to know someone has your back!" T. O. Jeffers said, equally excited to meet people she had practically already met through the stories M. O. Kandova told. "And thanks so much for passing on your knowledge to her. She gave me a reading, and it was incredibly helpful. I'm still trying to figure it out, but it was great guidance."

"My pleasure. You know, we grew up with that as a family tradition."

Yordup was impressed when she met Hilton, and gave her daughter a wink when she was certain nobody was looking. C. E. Didier also drove her vrodilop so there would be enough room for everyone. The tourist-minded group in fresh clothes buzzed with excitement as they filled the vrodilops with themselves and their personal belongings.

"I am super excited to see the Grigogg waterfalls in person. I made a report about them in school last year! Did you know that they are the largest falls in The Land?" Sickles said, as the crew member closest to school age, at eighteen years old.

After the twenty-four members boarded the three vrodilops, Mrs. Kandova handed out tickets for each person, which they had purchased for the group. They set off as a caravan, flying above the treetops, following the beams of light, on a mission to be enriched by seeing one of the most powerful sights in The Land.

On the trip, Jaway met and spoke with the Kandova family and thanked them.

"I have to say, your family did a great job in raising your daughter! She is one of the best, if not the best, in her field," Jaway said.

"We are very proud of our young woman being out in the world and making a name for herself!" Yordup said with tears in her eyes, trying to not get choked up about her daughter living so far away from home.

"Mom, did you know that Jaway's family grew up on a farm in the area you guys traveled to yesterday?" Kandova said, in an effort to distract her mom, and herself, because she also was getting misty-eyed.

"I loved seeing all of the different products that are only sold locally. The farms are so quaint, and the land is like something out of a book." Yordup spoke highly of the farmland they'd visited between Crawldsay and the rainforest.

"I'm glad that you enjoyed it. My mom actually was raised on a farm there, and my uncle used to tell us the best stories about growing up. We loved everything about the farmland when we were kids." He paused and thought fondly about his memories. "They used to pick chokecherries and sell them for extra cash when they were kids."

"Really? We got some chokecherry wine and jam yesterday. It looks delicious, and it's really special that the berries grow wild." Yordup was proud to share tourist knowledge of the trendy natural products.

Dlamp drove the vrodilop and led the way as the other two followed. The vehicles hovered at a height of over three Rainforest Region homes and traveled between the purple lines that indicated the path and became visible through the transparent walls and windows. The Rainforest Region people loved looking at the stars, so they approved that these lanes were only visible through the vrodilop walls, and not to the naked eye. Other vehicles followed orange lanes that were below the purple lanes and traveled in the opposite direction.

The vrodilop mostly controlled the journey, but Dlamp carefully monitored it while sitting toward the front of the vehicle, ready to interject at any point if necessary. They passed by one of the massive towers that sent out the network of light for traffic lanes, then curved and turned above the rainforest below, unaware of homes that were covered by the canopy. Because this was so far from the Wild Territory, no threats were expected from the ground.

"Alright everyone, look over this ridge and I think you will see the magnificent Grigogg River—and maybe the waterfall!" Dlamp said while pointing toward the translucent walls of their family's vrodilop.

The riders all grew quiet, shifting their gaze in that direction, and were amazed at the majestic and wide river that slowly appeared as the vrodilop floated toward the parking area. They smiled and made excited noises over the beauty.

Each vrodilop entered the main parking area, then descended to the ground. The entire gang of jubilant tourists high-fived each other, their voices drowned out by the massive, crashing sound of water gushing over the edge of a fall into the continuing waves below.

Next to the parking area was a museum dedicated to the power source. The river ran from northeast to southwest. On this side, the shoreline curved around, creating a massive bulge in the river before the water plummeted over the edge. Along this southern bank, an old road ran along the entire shore. The water churned powerfully in this upper level, then fell over a half-oval indentation and crashed far below, creating white clouds and violent waves on the lower part. Stone cliffs held up the power plant, which was located on the far end of the waterfall. A small bank lined the bottom of the stone cliffs before the large river sloshed chaotically about. The energy plant was an expansive building next to a thick pole, with a hefty cable on the top leading away from the harvesting space.

The upper river had many unwavering rocks near the crest of the waterfall, which required the water to flow around. Two rock islands bathed farther up. Across the sizable river was also a road-lined shore that curved around and morphed at the crest of the waterfall into an overlook above stone cliffs. The base of these had a bank that ran along the lower portion. A power plant stood on the tip of the land that swung to meet the edge of the waterfall. An identical, large pole held up a massive cable to send energy away from the location. Two sturdy poles stood on both ends of the enormous half-circle drop-off, and a tight cable connected them from above the cliffs on each side. The cable ran directly above where the water crashed below, and six fixed, large cones hung along the thick cord.

"Woah, it's so far to the other side!" Hilton said.

He walked with the group to the museum, remaining inconspicuously next to his girlfriend. As everyone entered, they found it to be a cooled building that was lined with artifacts and scientific paraphernalia associated with creating power. A giant banner greeted them that read, *Welcome to the Rainforest Region Blatdrof Buzz Museum.* Blatdrof Buzz had originally discovered the energy source that The Land used to operate nearly everything at that point. After handing their tickets to an attendant, the group was ushered into a spacious, low-lit room with amphitheater-style seating.

"The show will begin in approximately five minutes," boomed a low professional voice from somewhere out of site.

The thrilled vacationers all sat down, got situated, and chatted civilly until the lights went out. In the front of the room, music began, and a vast blobe played that highlighted the Grigogg Waterfall. A professionally dressed woman who was obviously from the Rainforest Region spoke about the history behind the power. She was very tall and fit and had a few light-purple tattoos on one arm.

"When Zander became the new capital of The Land, after Crawldsay, the emperor established the Royal Academy of Knowledge. Who would have thought that just eight years later, Blatdrof Buzz and his team would have made the most transformative discovery in history? Well, shortly after, the emperor saw a need for a specific Royal Academy of Technology. Many of the devices you use in your daily life would not be possible without these findings," the charming woman said.

Then a visual of a large cylindrical cone replaced the host. Floating arrows indicated that something entered the wide end of the cone and then went through to the tip on the opposite side. Then they were funneled into an echo chamber cable. This led to a large box inside the power plant building next door, and then the arrows continued to circulate through an energy grid that went to neighborhoods and entire regions.

"As you can see here, sound waves entered the specially designed cone, where they were harvested through the cable into the power conversion box, then sent through above-ground and below-ground cords to homes and neighborhoods around The Land." The host spoke calmly and confidently. "Originally, this was discovered using the crashing waves on the west coast near Zander, but we also have a loud source of frequencies in the form of a waterfall. Today, we know the power that you use every minute of the day as 'buzz.' Buzz was named after the man who discovered it. If only he were alive today to see all of the useful gadgets that resulted from his research!"

At that point in the speech, it seemed like she was selling the idea of something, but that was the end goal—to create understanding and uniform acceptance of the past as told through the eyes of the winners. The entire history lesson failed to mention that the devices that had been created using buzz as a power source had enticed the other regions to join The Land. In addition, the immense gliders and quick-death lasers also intimidated many groups to merge. At that point, The Land wanted to make everyone only feel proud of "their" ingenuity and advancement as one people. For example, the kind woman left out the facts that the very first inventions using the technology were military weapons, vehicles, and communication mechanisms intended to intimidate less-advanced bands of people. Gliders were used as a display of strength, and thousands of fighters were immediately eliminated by the lasers on these fear-inducing, levitating machines.

"Blatdrof Buzz used buzz to power many different devices, and the Royal Academy of Technology continued researching and creating. Eventually home items, personal communication capabilities, and information storage solutions were realized and made ready for your use," said the lady in the blobe.

These items were provided to the separate groups of people to try to entice them to join The Land. For many, this was successful, as they understood the benefits for future generations and were lured by the promises of a more comfortable life for everyone.

"As you can see, the natural progression from discovering a steady power source led to even more advancements in technology. During the early stages of development, the first users wrote out characters to input data. The kleck, which was originally recharged by a wire, provided a way to upload information at lightning speeds. Eventually the Royal Academy of Technology found a way to recharge the kleck by movement. Now it is completely embedded in the ear without any wires.

"Today, buzz is used to energize user-friendly machinery to not only intricately cut heavy stones, but also move them over long distances. Architects can create exact plans and transfer extremely heavy blocks—marble, for example—very long distances with minimal effort. Levitation powered by buzz has removed the obstacle of transporting items on the ground. Buzz is also responsible for the purple and orange illuminated lanes that appear while driving and guide you and your vrodilop wherever you freely go."

The woman disappeared, and many images of different devices floated inside the blobe. Her voice continued to ring out as the various obsolete items appeared, "As you can see, the journey from these antique units to what we have today has been immense. But one priority that has been constant is that buzz remain safe for every user. Even at the beginning of the movement, all products for personal use have charged carefully without any safety issues."

The lady stopped talking, displaying how easy it was to place portable devices in pyramid shapes on a pad to charge with buzz. Next, she was talking to her family and parking her vrodilop under her Rainforest Region-style house. The blobe zoomed in on the charger that she parked next to, while her husband and children smiled and exited the vehicle. She broke from the cheerful moment as her kin blurred into the background.

"I've never have any concerns about buzz harming my family!" she said enthusiastically as they followed her out of the parking area into the elevator that transported her into her home.

On the wall, she looked at many photos of vacations.

"Even on remote holidays, our vrodilop, just like other large mechanisms, charged itself by the sound of a gushing waterfall or the noisy rainforest creatures."

She highlighted the ease and safety of the buzz, because early on, many people lost their lives at the hands of the energy in the power plants, while they were still learning how to safely extract it and send to society. She made no mention of these early calamities, but rather focused on a fictitious record that it had always been safe for personal use.

"And although the buzz is created by sound frequency, the energy produced in the form of buzz has never been detectable by the human ear, and hearing has never been damaged by this power in your items of convenience."

The relatable woman smiled and spoke calmly. Then she took the audience on a tour of her house, which looked cozy and spotless.

She walked into the kitchen and her daughter asked, "What's for dinner, Mom?"

The actress looked at the camera and said, "Sometimes there is no plan, but I have the perfect tools to create a delicious dish at the last minute." She grabbed some home appliances and began making a traditional Rainforest Region recipe. "And even if you need a quick refresher, I always have my handy pradimptor close by just in case."

She reached down and pulled up a device, holding it in front of her face for a few seconds. Her makeup was now in vibrant shades and a huge contrast to the muted tones that she'd worn until this point of the family tour.

She left the kitchen and went into the living room.

"Even when I feel a little chilly, it is easy to adjust the temperature in my home." She increased the heat with her kleck and smiled. Then she moved to the laundry room and snapped her fingers. "Laundering our clothes has always been as easy as one, two, three." She grabbed a beautiful dress that had no wrinkles and appeared to be newly cleaned as it fluttered over her shoulder on a hanger. "Our homes are filled with every kind of innovation to make daily life as easy, comfortable, and secure as possible. We have also developed ways to share and compile information quickly and easily." She walked into her daughter's room and picked up an infogrammer, which projected words into the air. "This is such an interesting report, sweetie," she said in a supportive tone while her teenage daughter smiled and gave her a hug.

"But this life has to come from somewhere." The woman snapped her fingers and appeared inside the Grigogg power plant, wearing a protective hat on her head. "Today, you will get to see what makes all of this possible for residents of The Land. We hope that you enjoy your tour and take a moment to be thankful for everything that stems from this innovative discovery!" She smiled and waved to the audience.

The lights turned on, and an attractive lady dressed in formal attire entered the amphitheater, announcing in a friendly tone, "Next we will visit the viewing area, so get ready to take pictures!"

The employee directed the group to follow her. They walked outside the Buzz Museum and onto the old road that ran along the edge of the river to a viewing area over the water. A clear, chest-high fence provided a direct view of the top of the cascade on that side. The half-circle waterfall also provided views of the bottom from that area, as white clouds and rainbows plumed at the base and rained a light mist onto the attentive crowd. They stored pictures and stood close to their friends for memories until the employee coordinated a group picture, over the roaring noise of the falling water. Kandova made sure she was next to Hilton in the photo with her family.

After the woman told them about the amount of water that poured over the edge, she directed them toward the nearby power plant, just a few minutes away by foot.

They walked to an entrance area, where each person received a head covering for protection and a pamphlet of information that seemed to advertise the concept of buzz.

"As you saw from the viewpoint, a cable stretches across the top of the waterfall and collects the sound waves and sends them through the cord and into one of the power plants on both sides of the waterfall. After it is funneled under one of the old roads, it is harvested inside the power plants and sent to the people of the Rainforest Region. Any excess buzz is sent to other regions in need of more buzz. As you are aware, there are many different power plants throughout The Land, and they are each located next to a noisy source for the most consistent flow of buzz."

The group walked through the plant and saw the machines that converted the sound into energy. Each person appreciated that the buzz they used every day came from this process. Upon leaving the building, the group was directed to keep their head protectors on, and each was also given a belt. Many of the members looked confused but took them anyway.

As they were walking out and back toward the museum, M. O. Kandova's mom said to everyone, "We planned a surprise for you all!" She paused for dramatic affect. "Do you see that tower there with the cable? It is a zip line, and we are all going to slide directly across the lip of the waterfall!"

Yordup looked thrilled at the sound of that.

"Now I see where you got your love for adrenaline, M. O. Kandova! Thanks, Mrs. Kandova!" Hilton said, and then celebrated with his friends. He addressed the love of his life formally in order to hide their relationship.

There was a spiral platform with stairs that got smaller at the top, and a thin, tight, heavy-duty cable ran from the highest point, over part of the river, past the center of the waterfall and, due to the curve, back over the river to an identical spiral platform on the opposite side.

The entire group put belts around their waists and connected their klecks. They converted the belts into harnesses that wrapped around each leg, and then two straps swooped over their shoulders like suspenders. They walked up the stairs that curved around and around until reaching the top, where they each connected their belt to a clip on the sturdy cable. One by one, the members of the large group whirled directly above the waterfall to the other side. It was so magnificent that every person's face lit up with joy upon completion.

Once the entire group made the adrenaline-rushed trip, they all walked over to a second overlook to see the view from the other side. This one was special because it was like a peninsula. On one side, it held back the river; in the center, water dropped to its fate far below; and stone cliffs held up the strip of land from the halfway point. This was where the cable met the other side and the massive cones could be seen along the cord. The designated viewing area showed the entire waterfall, which roared so loudly that members of the group were shouting to be heard. The cliffs dropped down to a bank, and the view showed an enormous river winding through vast, wooded areas and beaches full of rainforest life, complete with hanging vines. The crew walked around a similar power plant that also had a soaring, thick pole with a cable that sent the harvested power off to the grid.

The entire group soared back over the zip line again to return to the vrodilops. While waiting in the queue for everyone to go, Yordup was standing next to I. P. Hilton.

She said, "You are very tall. I'm sure people comment on it all the time."

"Yes, ma'am—I am the designated top-shelf reacher for all vertically challenged folks back home in Bingdole grocery stores." Hilton smiled.

"You know, we actually got a frisbee and a pool toy stuck in the tree above the rooftop deck in the rental, and could use some help getting it out. Are you free for dinner tonight?"

"Why yes, I have no plans. I would love to join you."

"Great! I'll be making a home-cooked meal from our region. I know I shouldn't have been eavesdropping but, when we were at the power plant, I overheard that you saved a girl's life. I am looking forward to hearing the details . . . well, whatever you are allowed to reveal."

"I'm sure anyone would have done what I did." He paused. "But yeah, don't worry, I can tell you all of the specifics except how we got to the location." Hilton laughed.

Then he leaned in and whispered with his hand next to his face, "Well, as long as nobody from Central Command is listening."

He smiled then winked, and the mother of his new girlfriend laughed loudly and threw her head back.

Before they had left the condominium that day, Yordup had taken the time to throw items into the trees above the rooftop pool, in order to have an excuse to get him back for dinner that night alone. She'd heard how tall he was and needed a believable reason, so that her daughter's new relationship remained a secret. All of the vrodilops went to the barracks, and Didier brought many crew members back to her place. Kandova planned to return with her family to the barracks to pick up Hilton later.

M. O. Kandova and her family told everyone goodbye and began the drive to their rental home.

"Honey, can we pick up some of the groceries now, while we are on the way back?" Yordup asked. "I'm not even certain they'll have exactly what I need, but I'm sure we can find substitutes." She enjoyed crafting large meals.

They stopped at the grocery store to purchase items for their stay and for the dinner that night.

"Honey, do you have cash? I left everything in the vrodilop," Yordup said as they were walking through the store.

"Yes, I do—I've got enough I'm sure." Dlamp always made certain to carry extra cash during vacations.

The Land offered a digital currency, as well as hard currency that consisted of metal coins and carefully crafted gems. The coins were laser cut and contained an official insignia. One gold coin was worth one hundred citrine coins. The citrines, as they were referred to casually, were flat and transparent yellow or orange, and also cut by lasers. A silver coin was worth fifty citrines. An emerald coin was worth twenty citrines. Emeralds, as they were commonly called, were vivid green. Amethyst coins, or amethysts, were worth ten citrines, and were transparent and violet. Finally, the aquamarine was worth five citrines and was baby blue in color.

They chatted just like old times while walking through the grocery store. Yordup also spotted and gathered special, unique items that would sell for a small fortune back home.

While they were walking, Yordup said, "You know, Praldeze, I was very impressed with Hilton. He seems like a very thoughtful, humble, and handsome young man. I approve."

M. O. Kandova blushed and was reminded of the love of her life.

"I know that we have just become official, but we have spent a lot of time together while working, and I have had the chance to see him in many different circumstances, and I am convinced that he is the right person for me." She spoke carefully in front of her dad, which was unusual because they felt open to share everything about most other topics.

"Well, like I said yesterday, we support that you are an adult and that you will naturally be making your own family soon, if that's what you want to do. This is a fun part of life where you get to explore relationships. It is a learning experience, and your mom and I are really happy for you," Dlamp said with a new perspective.

"It just feels like he is the only person that I want to be with all the time. And I feel like this surprise, two-week holiday came at the perfect time for us to get to know each other on a deeper level," Kandova said, visibly relieved that she could share her feelings without caution, with the most important support system in her life.

"Who are you and what have you done with my daughter?" Yordup joked, and the family laughed together, because they knew that Kandova had grown guarded toward her dad about disclosing information about interest in the opposite sex, and she had never been so sure about a relationship.

"Have you never felt this way about someone, or is it that you see a future with him?" Jussol asked. She was curious as a sister, but instinctively already knew the answer.

"I think he is just the right person to bring this out in me. I feel secure because he is thoughtful, sincere, humble, and caring. I just wonder if this is what falling in love feels like," Kandova shared without reservation. "And now that we are exclusive partners, I am looking forward to exploring what that means. I mean, I can't stay fifteen years old forever. I'm a very responsible nineteen, and it's about time that I had a boyfriend and started learning what it means to be in a relationship." She placed some vegetables into a basket that she carried around. "I mean, I have the opportunity to start a romantic connection with someone that could last my entire life, and I think I should be completely invested. That is my goal, because I can see myself with him, long term."

"Well, your father and I see a certainty that we have never witnessed before, and we trust that you are a good judge of character. Now that we know how serious you are, we will do our best to encourage your new relationship to grow and become a lifelong love, like your father and me. You know, I was nineteen when we first started dating, and we have been together all this time."

Yordup thought fondly about the many years filled with adoration, security, and laughter.

"And you have seen firsthand that we cherish each other more than anything in the world, and that we have always been there for each other, through thick and thin. We are loyal forever. Don't forget that only love is real. Only love is true. I look back at my life and what things used to be. When I grew up as a little girl, my grandparents had a farm that we used to visit on the weekends. It was such a happy place. Now they have both passed away, and the farm was sold and converted into different buildings. They even tore down the barn that we used to play in, and where the animals used to live. All of those people, all of those buildings, and all of the situations that seemed so real at the time are gone. When I remember my life, nearly everything has passed from what it used to be when I grew up.

"But the one real thing that has stood the test of time is love. The love between your father and I has bonded us as one, just like the devotion that we share as a family. And like the love that keeps our siblings together over the years. Just remember to be open to love's whisper, and take advantage of your heart's compass when it tells you to go. When you find the one, never let them leave, because, like I said a million times, only love is truly real and stands the test of a lifetime." Yordup had tears in her eyes as they paid for the groceries.

The cashier gave her a tissue because she knew exactly what Yordup was saying.

"I can't help but overhear your conversation, and I completely agree. When love calls, and it is with the right person, you have to take advantage of that moment, because it can be with you forever. Alright, that will be one hundred and fifty-eight citrines."

The cashier was in no hurry. She was a grandma who had experienced a life of joy, security, and adoration with her partner. Dlamp handed over a gold coin, a silver coin, an aquamarine coin, and three citrines. As they walked out to the vrodilop, Dlamp and Yordup reminisced about all of their happy years together, and talked about how thankful they were to be there for each other.

CHAPTER
TWENTY-EIGHT

After they returned home, Yordup and Jussol started cooking up a feast while Kandova and her dad took the vrodilop to the barracks to pick up I. P. Hilton. Thankfully, the other crew members were already out, enjoying their plans to explore the area. When the couple got into the vrodilop, they embraced each other tightly and kissed on the lips.

On the way back, Hilton opened up to Mr. Kandova about how much he had wanted a partner and family, and how serious he was about being there for M. O. Kandova.

"Do you love my daughter?" Mr. Kandova asked.

"It's funny that you ask this question . . ." Kandova listened intently to the answer, and her heart yearned for affirmation. ". . . because I have been exploring myself, and I definitely see a future with your daughter. I am in love with her. We have had a lot of time to get to see each other working in a professional environment and to find out if we are comfortable with each other, and I am extremely happy to have her as my exclusive partner."

The driving father reached over and gave him a hug.

"Well, you have my blessings, and I wish you and Praldeze the best. I'm here for you if you need any support or advice. Yordup and I have been together for a very long time, and we have been through many highs and a few lows, and I think you both can get through anything together if you are committed to making it last. I can see that you have wanted a serious relationship for a while and desire to start a family, and that puts me at ease. I can see that you are serious and careful in your approach to life, and that you will treat my daughter with care and be there for her." Dlamp noticeably embraced his new role naturally, compelled by the secure relationship he saw in front of him. Hilton was well mannered and thoughtful. He took very good care of himself and was strikingly handsome.

"And it is clear that you will fit in well with our family. I hope that you feel as though you are one of us and you feel comfortable around us as your own parents." Mr. Kandova extended the offer only because Hilton was undeniably a good person.

They returned back to the rental home, where Hilton removed the pool toy and frisbee from the trees above the rooftop terrace. Then they sat down at a carefully decorated table under the breathtaking rainforest setting, for a home-cooked meal served by a glamorous mom. I. P. Hilton meshed well with the family as they all joked around at the same frequency and felt comfortable together.

"So, tell us a little about yourself," Yordup said to him, because she knew their time would be short.

"Well. I grew up on the west coast in Bingdole. I'm kind of a city kid, so I'm learning about the countryside as I go." They all laughed together. "I'm twenty-two, just three years older than Praldeze. I have two brothers and two sisters, so we have a big family. There was always something fun to do when I was growing up. I'm my mom's favorite, though." They all chuckled again because of the way he said it, with a slight wink and shoulder raise. "She owns a drink shop, so I learned how to make some killer fruit juices with fun garnishes, and my dad is a teacher, so we were always expected to be invested in our education. Most of all, I want you to know that I am a loyal person who is thoughtful and caring. Like I said earlier, probably because of working in the military and being transient, I have really wanted a family and relationship over the past few years. Don't get me wrong, I love what I'm doing, but it has been an opportunity for me to reflect on what I ultimately want in life."

He paused, and Kandova interjected, "That is what I like most about you—your character and how I feel when we are together."

She held his hand, looking at him with unbroken eye contact and calm wonderment, like gazing out from a refreshing scenic overlook.

"We can see that you both are head over heels in love, and that is why we are so supportive of your relationship," Dlamp said, looking his daughter in the eyes.

"Thanks for sharing all of that about yourself. We think that you are a great addition to our family, and we look forward to seeing you after this trip," Yordup said.

"Thanks, it has been really great meeting you guys too."

After being prompted by Jussol, who was interested in adventurous stories, Hilton shared the details about saving Jeffers, who the family had grown fond of because she was Kandova's fydonmate.

Yordup asked Kandova to join her in the kitchen, to bring some plates and get something sweet, but she really wanted to discuss her daughter's newfound romantic interest.

"Your father and I highly approve of him. I can't believe he literally saved Jeffers's life. And to believe that we may not have met her today. You know how much we have come to appreciate her as your close friend," Yordup whispered while washing her hands and getting the dessert ready.

"Yeah, I figured you would. He is a really great guy, and he is the person of a lifetime. I think I'm in love. I just feel like there are fireworks going off inside my chest when we are together. I only want to be with him, more than anything in the world." M. O. Kandova paused. "I seriously can envision myself with him for the rest of my life."

"It is clear that you have opened up and you don't have any anxiety. Usually, I would have seen you super nervous around someone you like, but you are not at all around him. I think that is a sign of compatibility." Yordup gave her a strong hug. "I am so thankful that everything worked out for all of us to meet up. It was not by chance. It must have been meant to be. Do you think the same?"

Kandova looked out the large window. She said slowly, "Yeah, I really do think that this was destiny. Everything has fallen in place for us to be together forever." She explored her inner feelings and the coincidences that had happened recently. "And it is important to also recognize that the heart wants what the heart wants. Sometimes you don't have a lot of control over where your love lands. But I'm glad that it took a pitstop on such a good guy."

They returned to the rooftop terrace and began joking as they enjoyed the traditional east coast dessert, while the new couple sat next to each other and held hands. Dlamp shared a story about when he met Yordup and they fell in love. He winked at his beautiful partner.

"I don't think we ever told you girls this, but, ah, when I met your mother it was forbidden for us to get into a romantic relationship. Those times were very different than today. It's no secret that your mom's family came from a farming class, and my family was close to the ruling class. At that time, we were not allowed to date, and it was definitely socially unacceptable to get married. I didn't care. We fell madly in love, and everything that I adored about your mom came from her family's humble background. She was caring, hardworking, selfless, obviously beautiful, loyal, kind—and of course, I have to say again, she was gorgeous.

"We didn't care. We followed our hearts and knew that we meshed for a reason. We also felt as though fate brought us together because of many different coincidental events. But, most of all, we were one hundred percent certain that we could trust each other. So we met in secret during our first year of dating. We did not tell a soul, because if our families had found out, they would have done everything in their power to separate us. So we covered up our relationship for a year, and then we just told our families to come to the wedding because it was happening anyway, and thankfully they all came. At the time, it was extremely controversial, and we were looked down upon. Now people don't care as much, so I like to believe we were ahead of our time or we were trailblazers for love." He laughed with all of them.

It was much darker at that point; candles flickered in the middle of the table as their faces were illuminated by the warm light. The faint glow from the pool dimly flickered on the underside of the trees of the canopy, directly above the table.

"I just want you both to know that we support your relationship, even though it is technically not allowed. And we encourage you to spend as much time getting to know one another as vacationers as possible, while you have these two weeks together. There is an old saying from Owantay, and it goes like this: 'No matter how hard we try to evade the magnetism of love, what's meant to be is meant to be—your paths have been sealed by fate from above.'"

Dlamp continued, "We don't believe that you were put in this situation by chance, we bless your relationship, and we are here to support you."

His wife squeezed his hand tightly and kissed him on the lips.

"That was one of the reasons I fell madly for your father," she said. "Because he fought so hard for us to be together. He didn't care about society and what people thought. He knew that I was the only one, and the right one for him, just like it seems you two have found. Am I correct?"

"Let me attempt to speak for both of us first," Hilton said. "We definitely see a future together, and we are not reckless with our hearts. We are in love and want to be with one another for a very long time. Do you agree, sweetie?" He sat back in his chair, holding Kandova's hand.

"Yeah, I agree. I think that it was not a coincidence that we met, and . . ." Compelled by the romantic setting, she continued, "To be honest, when we first met, I told myself that we were going to get married. I just knew, deep down inside, that we were perfect for each other, forever. That's probably why I was so nervous."

Her parents stood up and gave the couple a huge embrace.

Dlamp said, "We are very happy for you two, and we support your decision to be serious. We encourage you both to spend as much time alone as you can. And follow your hearts." He paused. "We wanted to keep it a surprise, but we booked the house next door for you guys for the next couple of weeks. I know that you won't have much privacy on the terrace while we are here, with us peeking over and asking for you to come get our pool toys out of the canopy." He laughed at his own joke. "But we thought it was crucial for you lovebirds to have some private time to get to know each other." Dlamp had a glimmer in his eyes.

Kandova's face lit up.

"What? That is amazing, Mom and Dad. You guys are the best!"

She gave them both a hefty hug.

"Well, you know, you wouldn't get much opportunity to just relax and be yourselves at the barracks, so you just have to come up with a cover story and you are set," Yordup said as she waved her hands in the air and shrugged her shoulders. "Your first evening is tonight, and it is stocked with food already, so you should have breakfast and enough for tomorrow. We tried to stay longer, but it looks like we will be heading back to Owantay tomorrow afternoon—maybe we can have lunch together before we leave."

Yordup looked sad that she would have to say farewell to her daughter soon, but also content that she would be able to spend a little more time with them.

"That sounds *fantastic*! You guys are the best," Kandova said.

"Yeah, thanks so much, Mr. and Mrs. Kandova. I feel like it was destiny that you both just happened to be in the area and everything fell into place. Thank you so much for everything."

"No problem! Why don't we go over and check out your new place for the next couple weeks?" Dlamp asked.

They blew out the candles and went downstairs. After M. O. Kandova gathered her items, they all went next door for a tour of the entire home. It was almost a replica of the place that the family had rented. They all sat around upstairs, told jokes, and laughed for a few hours.

"Your father and I wanted to make sure that you both have the best time here, so we have a little something more for you."

Yordup passed a gift that had been decorated with ribbons and brightly colored paper. Upon opening the present, Kandova revealed an embroidered purse that contained six gold coins. This was more than enough to cover expenses for anything they chose to do.

"Aw, thanks. This means so much to us." She got up and gave them both a hug and a kiss on the cheek before sitting down again. "We are definitely going to be able to enjoy our lives as free civilians. *Maybe* we can even rent a vrodilop and go somewhere we weren't expecting!" Kandova said.

"That was what we were thinking, honey." Her mother leaned in and put her hand on Kandova's knee. "If you guys wish to take some day trips away from the city, or get some nice food for meals, you can do that and not worry about breaking the bank."

"That is incredibly special to us, and we are even more thankful for your blessing. I am really grateful that we were able to meet." Hilton sat up tall and confidently.

Dlamp, Yordup, and Jussol all stood and hugged Kandova tightly, relishing the experience they'd had while gushing about how much they loved her. The young partners walked her parents and sister back to the house next door, then returned to their place to get settled.

The next morning, Kandova and Hilton woke up and had breakfast together, then headed over to her family to spend the remaining moments left with them. After a morning of swimming in the pool, they enjoyed lunch on the rooftop terrace, and then the family got ready for the day. They cried as they said goodbye to M. O. Kandova and I. P. Hilton. The duo waved as they watched the vrodilop ascend above the canopy.

"I already miss them so much. They're so funny, and I really enjoy just spending time with them," Kandova said with an arm around Hilton's waist.

"Now I understand firsthand what you were saying about them before. Your parents are amazing."

The couple rented a vrodilop for the stay and went on local trips in between relaxing days at their rooftop pool. They fell in love more and more deeply as they enjoyed spending every second of the day with one another. They swam under the stars and kissed each other for hours at a time in the pool. She made the excuse that she was staying with her family, and he said that he was living with local friends. The rest of the crew was so busy that they did not question anything.

Toward the end of the two weeks, they felt very comfortable as a couple and were even more in love. On the last day of freedom, Hilton had a giant bundle of vibrant exotic flowers delivered to the house and presented them to his love. She smiled from ear to ear, kissed him, and held him tightly. For their last night at the rental property, Kandova cooked a traditional meal and they ate on the rooftop terrace by candlelight next to the pool. Hilton started talking carefully during the dessert.

"You are a very talented chef. I can see where you learned it from, too."

"Well, my mom always said that when you put love into the kitchen, people can taste it." She smiled and laughed.

"You know, I really liked meeting your family. More importantly, I have enjoyed getting to know you as my girlfriend. I need you to know that you are someone who has made a deep impact on me, and I want you to always be a part of my life." Hilton had a serious expression on his face, but he looked nervous.

"You are so sweet. I feel the exact same way. You are someone that I hope to be part of my life for a very, very long time. Being together over the past few weeks has made me feel even closer to you, and it has validated my feelings that you are my person." Kandova's eyes twinkled in the flickering light.

"I have something major that I need to share with you. During this vacation, I have been giving myself freedom to figure out when it would be right to tell you. I want you to know that you are free to feel however you like, and I respect your response if it is not good." He appeared even more nervous.

She looked deeply in his eyes and said, "You are freaking me out. Is everything okay? What is it?"

"I'll be right back."

I. P. Hilton got up and went downstairs. While he was gone, M. O. Kandova sat alone with her thoughts, imagining different worst-case scenarios. She was concerned, because this was the first time she had seen him look anxious since they had met. He walked out of the elevator toward her and sat down.

"You know that I love you, and no matter what comes of this, I hope that we can stay together, even just as girlfriend and boyfriend."

His brow was furrowed and his voice shook when he spoke.

CHAPTER
TWENTY-NINE

Kandova interrupted him with her assertive personality, "Just tell me, I can't *take* it any longer. Is everything okay?"

Hilton considered the fact that he could not back out at that point.

"Give me your hand, sweetie." He held it with both of his. "Will you marry me? I want to get engaged. I am head over heels in love, and want nothing more than to continue to grow in adoration with you. I had a ring delivered with the flowers earlier today."

He was prepared for ultimate rejection or a drastic change in their relationship. She gathered her thoughts while he reached into his pocket and revealed a sparkling ring that had to have cost around a year's wage.

Kandova had not been expecting what he said, imagining instead a negative announcement about something he had been hiding from his past. She had been preparing herself for news of children with another woman, that he had an incurable disease, or various other tragic situations. She looked at the ring for a while to process what was going on.

Then she gazed into his eyes and said, "Yes, I would love to marry you and be with you forever, my cutie. You are my person and the love of my entire life."

A look of relief washed over his face. Hilton had been afraid that coming on too strong would jeopardize what they had. He put the ring on her finger, and they held each other with both hands and stared into each other's eyes, recognizing that they were experiencing the moment of a lifetime.

"You know that this is a defining event in our lives. Right now, we are experiencing something that will change our futures forever." She looked at him as he pulled out another ring and put it on.

"Check out my band. Do you love it?" Hilton plastered a relaxed smile across his face.

"You really outdid yourself with this one. I had no idea," she whispered.

"I spoke with your parents yesterday when you went to get groceries. After they approved, I told my parents and they were really happy. I had filled them in on you after we became exclusive, so it wasn't a complete surprise. You can speak with them soon, since they will be your future family also. They are really excited to get to know you."

She kissed him on the lips and said, full of gusto, "That's my man—taking charge and making life happen! You have nothing to worry about here. I am so happy. Over the past few days, I actually have been picturing our future together, after the military service."

The couple spent their last night together, enjoying every second of freedom because they both knew that they would have to hide their true feelings soon. They attempted to avoid thinking about the inevitable reality and simply relish the occasion.

The next morning, they had a final breakfast on the rooftop and swam in the pool one last time. Then they returned the rental vrodilop and separately arrived at the barracks.

Over the break, Jaway and Krizzles had spent a lot of time together secretly as well, and grown madly in love, but had not progressed as far in their relationship as Hilton and Kandova.

As the crew boarded their newly refurbished glider, they met the black orchid in the central area outside of their living quarters. It had fared well, with new blossoms. Pama was excited to see that her pet plant was in good spirits. After the crew got settled, they gathered in the control rooms for an information briefing. On each level, a blobe appeared with introduction music and an animation.

"Wow, look at the production value in this one." Pama nudged Jaway with her elbow, and they laughed together.

The picture showed a vast rainforest and then zoomed into one area through the trees, stopping on an attractive man in a military uniform. He stood among lush green foliage in the depths of the forest.

"Welcome back from your repair docking. We hope that you are refreshed and ready for your next assignments. Before you learn about these, another information-gathering crew has discovered important, detailed intelligence about those residents choosing to live in the Wild Territory."

Both Kandova and Hilton had found it strange to turn off the relationship that had become second nature, but they quickly slipped back into their professional roles. The man in the blobe continued with a serious look on his face. His hands were touching in front of his body, and his intertwined fingers created an upside-down triangle between his bent elbows.

"We have information on the tribe that attacked your glider. We cannot reveal how this was obtained; however, it has been confirmed to be true. As you know, those residing in the Wild Territory have rejected offers to integrate into The Land and are therefore under the pressure of force to join. Although they use an ancient language of their people, many of their highest-ranking members have learned how to speak, read, and write our language too. It is speculated that this specific tribe learned it from people they have captured over the years."

The man disappeared, and the picture zoomed back and refocused on some of the people of the rainforest. A group of very tall, lean, sculpted men and women were covered in elaborate purple tattoos of different shades, with only small cloths covering their private parts. The tattoos even covered their faces, and many had intricate geometric designs that harkened to their ancestors, who were engineers and built ancient pyramids that still dotted the landscape, but were mostly covered by vegetation.

All of them had long hair in opulent braids, many of them platinum silver, a color that had developed as a byproduct of living under constant stress. Some were completely silver, while others just had streaks. Many were adorned with opulently braided patterns. They swiftly walked through the rainforest without being noticed, even by the wildlife, and without disturbing the flora.

"As you can see, these individuals know the terrain like the backs of their hands and can travel freely without leaving a trace. Not one branch snaps, and there is not a leaf out of place. Some of them have been known to live among the forty thousand ancient camouflaged pyramids. These were created for their dead to live in during the afterlife, so many were outfitted with complete functional living spaces that can be used today, if one is shrewd enough to outwit the sophisticated booby trap protection systems."

The blobe then showed one of the pyramids, which had been absorbed by the rainforest.

"As you can see here, this pyramid has become overgrown with natural camouflage. Let's take a tour inside and see what could be in one of these."

The camera abruptly switched to animation and showed an entrance path far beneath the ground. A dark tunnel filled with different booby traps that had been set off led to an illuminated great room in the center of the pyramid. Beams of light swirled with years of dust, leading to the outer world through vents that had managed to remain open. A brook of clear water ran through the middle of the large room and swirled around the center before washing through the space and exiting. A bedroom filled with every functional need was also lit by vents that had stood the test of time. A bed covered in dust sat across the room from an ever-flowing shower next to a bathroom with a toilet that revealed plumbing and sanitation. The inventive ancient minds had included solutions for maintenance-free, undetectable, biodegradable sewage systems. A functioning kitchen contained options for lighting coal. The smoke was funneled through a series of pipes and filtered before being released into the rainforest without a trace.

The host appeared again. "These people have an engineering foundation that goes back multiple generations. They know how to build innovative and advanced weaponry and mechanisms, such as the bombs that punctured your glider." The gentleman looked very focused.

Then the picture became another animation and showed how the people hunted and trapped. One of the residents of the Wild Territory dug a large pit for capturing animals. Another dispersed hooks with bait in a river to catch eels.

"As you can see, these people are expert hunters and gatherers. They also can find clean water quickly and easily, at a moment's notice. They have worked for centuries with the local wildlife by sending messages with birds. It simply takes a few months of feeding monkeys and training them to squeal in case they see a non-native person in the area. In conclusion for this informative section about developing data on the native residents of the Wild Territory, be on the lookout, and be very careful."

Closure music played, and the video ended with a sunset overlooking the rainforest.

The crew members broke the silence and began talking. Some of them had not seen each other for a long time, and they discussed their different experiences during the few weeks of freedom.

"Alright crew, let's wait, because they are going to explain our next assignment soon with another blobe." Jaway's voice was projected through both control rooms.

Shortly after, a woman appeared, addressing them on behalf of Central Command in Zander.

"Now that your glider has been repaired, we have a new mission for you. As you all know, any information that we learn about these people is like a puzzle piece, and we can put these together to gain an overall understanding. The next four weeks will be spent conducting general mapping of the rainforest floor to reveal any hidden pyramids. We installed a modern, laser-based technology in the glider to read the ground and below. Your glider will be slowly scanning and recording huge sections to reveal hidden structures, even if they are deep under the surface."

With this news, many from the troop looked at each other with an obvious expression of surprise because of the boredom that they would have to endure, levitating and slowly scanning every small plot of land as far as the eye could see. They had just received an incentive break at the waterfall, followed by two weeks of freedom in an eco-tourism hub, so most of the crew members felt settled about the monotonous mission.

They spent the next month slowly floating above the canopy as the laser technology scanned the forest floor and created a map of different parts of the endless rainforest. Every so often, an ancient pyramid would show up on a device, covered by the naked eye, and Jaway would examine it for any signs of current use. The culinary experts worked hard each day to provide perfect, individualized nutrition plans for the battalion. Pama watered her black orchid weekly, and it grew more and more blossoms. Jaway secretly continued to build a relationship with A. P. Krizzles, while doing everything it took to run daily operations as usual.

I. P. Hilton and M. O. Kandova functioned as a secretly engaged couple who were very much in love. They purposely volunteered for overnight watches together and would sneak up to the top level of the glider, above the upper control room, to view the stars and whisper about their love for each other and talk about anything on their minds. They had a lot of time to plan their exit from the military, a smooth transition to living together as an engaged couple, and a wedding.

The crew members worked out regularly according to individual exercise plans in the gym on the bottom story next to the engine room, and returned to being the finest specimens of the human species, ready for any physical challenge they might be presented with.

P. G. Churchill continued to offer career advice, and many individuals took the opportunity to study in order to pass exams for certifications. Lieutenant Commander Pama spent extra time in the gym, and played cards with the others in the central area, just outside the living quarters on the bottom floor. She also got a few more tattoos as she became inspired to record life events or symbolize an important person. Captain Serra remained a devoted father, sending messages to his children and wife as much as possible. He resumed revealing secret stashes of chocolate parrots—his favorite cheat snack.

Krizzles grew more and more in love with Jaway as they steadily built their relationship. She read books about her role as agricultural personnel and honed her skills to be more aware of different signs in the rainforest. With the additional information about the people, she knew it was important to read signals from nature, because they could move almost completely undetected. She often played her drogger in her living quarters upon request, and provided motivation to the crew. She also showed blobes of her precious udringa back home.

T. A. Curtis and T. A. Roberts were very busy, as this assignment was based on analyzing the terrain. They were researching data constantly, looking for any signs that pointed toward human activity.

Kandova continued as the troop jokester. She had ample time to experiment on new material with an always-captive audience. Now that she was in a fully realized relationship, she became more comfortable with herself, and felt as though she had transitioned to being a young woman, with the help of her loved ones. She imagined herself in the future as a caring mother with a family, and she brainstormed where the two, from opposite coasts, would ultimately settle down. In her work as a mechanical operator, she fixed different components of the glider and amazed the crew with her knowledge of machinery and any sort of appliance.

M. O. Dario also worked with mechanics on the glider, and remained a close friend with Roberts, because they were both from the city of Ezlay on the east coast. He continued to explore possible career choices for a tentative return to civilian life during the next year. His mother applied constant pressure to move home and work at a nearby stone quarry; his military training made him qualified for many jobs there. After nearly losing the race running down the pyramid at base camp, he'd pushed himself in the gym to be as fit as possible.

Hilton also worked extensively on the new mission as the information processor. He was an integral part of mapping the surrounding areas, and he evaluated the data before it was passed off to Central Command. He stayed madly in love with Kandova and understood the importance of secrecy for their relationship. Jeffers often did small favors for him out of gratitude for saving her life from the pit.

E. M. Price planned details for future excursions in case they had the chance to create a base camp again. Unfortunately, the large scope of the latest mapping mission made it seem far away. In case they had the opportunity, he developed many different itineraries, complete with food options and local information about the topography of the land. At thirty-three years old, he continued to mentor the other younger crew members informally with his experience in the military and life. His muscles grew even bigger and more ripped as he focused on nutrition and fitness so he would be ready for any climbing opportunities that arose. He learned more about nature by memorizing unique plant and animal species and characteristics.

M. A. Sickles grew into adulthood at age eighteen. She practiced the hobby of enjoying life, as was characteristic of people from the Highlands Region. As the medical attendant, she participated in training activities to be more prepared for different scenarios.

Her happy dance brought joy to the crew, although she rejected casual and fun requests for more black orchid elixir with the reply, "Until we get the go-ahead, you can make some yourself, because we have a plant downstairs now!"

She laughed, because it obviously was not possible to get enough elixir from such a small amount of blossoms. Sickles felt increased confidence after succeeding at the most challenging experience of her life during the trek through the rainforest at the last base camp.

Jeffers, as a technology officer, was also highly necessary for the latest mission. She continued to explore what her visions at the base camp meant and spent a lot of time with her fydonmates, Kandova and Krizzles. She purposely avoided the topic of possible relationships to support whatever they might have going on. She began meditating daily, trying to calm her mind as much as possible, and explored ideas for her career after the military, if she were to get out within the next year.

Churchill was a steady source of stability as the oldest crew member, at forty-one years old. He helped the other members with emotional wellness, led trainings, and monitored the psychological health of the squad. Because he got to spend some time in his home region, he was relaxed and felt more grounded afterward. He worked to improve his cardiovascular health, because he'd lost the race and was reminded of it every so often. After the experience at base camp, he realized the importance of being current in knowledge and ability to aid in any health emergencies. So he took courses for first aid and advanced health practices. He still snuck snacks often, but stayed incredibly fit.

Upon completing the four weeks of gathering information for Central Command, Jaway received instructions about the next mission.

That morning, he played a blobe for the crew members who congregated in the upper and lower control rooms. An attractive woman with a structured outfit appeared. She spoke with a standard accent and seemed welcoming.

"Congratulations on completing a mission to uncover and record the rainforest floor. It will be helpful in completing puzzle pieces for larger end goals for The Land. Today will be your last day of wrapping up loose ends, and the next three days will be spent in recovery at a local waterfall."

Jaway paused the blobe and interjected, "She means the same one we went to last time."

They quietly rejoiced, and then the woman in the blobe continued, "Many typical foods from each region will be delivered for your enjoyment, and we have increased compensation for a job well done. Central Command is watching, and they are very happy with your work. We hope that each of you feels motivated and appreciated. Have a great time in paradise!"

The woman disappeared, and Jaway took over. "Alright crew, I also hope that you all feel energized and excited. Think about what the next few days may look like for you, and we will come up with options and an overall plan soon. Send any requests my way, and we will see what we can do. I encourage you to take advantage of the time off to get some rest and recover from the past month."

After the announcement, Jaway met with different crew members to plan everything from food to any other logistics of the stay. E. M. Price organized all of the information and made an overall plan. That night before dinner, he briefed the entire team as they gathered back in both control rooms.

"Alright, we were just here not too long ago, so you should have an idea of the area already. The glider will be docked, as usual, under camouflage, and all of the normal procedures will be in place. We have double-checked the fydons and they are all in working order, but remember to fill each water tank when you land. Your culinary experts just got a list of ingredients, and they will prepare special, home-cooked meals that should be reminiscent of all regions.

"We should arrive tomorrow around noon, so we can get set up by dinnertime. It looks like the weather is going to be scorching hot, so keep that in mind. We have taken all of your input and have planned many different options for you. Back by popular demand, we will start the second day by waking up to another sunrise on the side of a pyramid. Then the rest of that day will be reserved for hanging out by the waterfall. Believe me, you will thank us that we are only planning time by the water because of the expected heat.

"That day, Churchill will also be available to meet if you want to get input about anything he provides. For those of you who want to brush up on studying for certifications, or make future career plans, this will be perfect.

"For the final day, I will offer a trek, again, for the entire crew. It appeared that everyone loved the first one, so we may be going on the same cave swim, mountain climb, and parachute fall with a trek through the rainforest. This will be very interesting for those of you not from the Rainforest Region who didn't get a chance to go the first time. We want to do this as a team-building exercise because of the lessons for increasing trust and working together. So make sure you bring every conceivable gadget with you from the glider. We will also have a huge dinner on the last night, with the special foods flown in from all of the regions. Does anyone have any questions?"

Price paused, but no one did.

"Alright, I assume that we are quite aware of the options, since we were here before. This looks like it will be a chance to recharge and relax, and we hope you take advantage of this time. Okay, Barbour, on to you."

"I just wanted to say thanks to all of you for taking charge and being willing to coordinate and lead different aspects of this incentive time. If you have any questions or aren't sure about anything we mentioned, feel free to come to E. M. Price or myself, and we can clarify anything for you. Our wonderful culinary experts have prepared a delicious meal for tonight as well, so we hope you enjoy. In conclusion, you'll have tonight and tomorrow morning to get ready for the time off of the glider," Jaway said, relaxed but serious.

The group ate and then got ready for the evening. Hilton and Kandova planned to be placed on night-watch together under the protection of darkness.

CHAPTER THIRTY

Most of the crew would be asleep, so Kandova and Hilton could spend some time together and nobody would notice. They both took the elevator at different times, all the way to the top, and met on the roof of the glider. Permanent, secured cubes for sitting rested there, and Kandova was relaxing on one of them as Hilton arrived. He walked over, and it seemed like her hair flew through the air in slow motion as she turned to see who was approaching.

"Hey babe, having a raging party without me?"

"Yeah, I couldn't help myself. I'm having a *solo* rager!"

She jumped into his arms and bent one knee to kick out a pointed toe while kissing him closely, like someone eating after a long starvation. After setting Kandova down, Hilton situated his jacket on the rooftop and then lay on it, next to the cube. He bent his arm behind his head as a pillow, and she stretched out beside him, laying her head on his chest as they both peered into the heavens. The moon was bright, and faint clouds passed by quickly, as if in a hurry. The mostly clear sky revealed twinkling stars and well-known constellations.

"Alright, look at the brightest star over there. That is a planet, for sure. And follow it over to that major star. That is a crab. Did you learn that in school?" Kandova asked, interested to learn about her mate.

"Yeah, we memorized all of them in school. Sometimes it is more difficult to make out the picture because there are just a few points of reference, but I remember the crab has two bright stars that kind of look like the eyes, and then two on the sides of them for the claws. I can see it too," he whispered.

He adored everything about the woman who was committed only to him.

They continued talking about the evening sky and how beautiful the stars looked as they flickered. I. P. Hilton grabbed his engagement band out of a compartment within a pocket in his jacket and put it on. "Do you have your ring with you, baby?" He hoped for an affirmative response.

"Of course I do, my love."

M. O. Kandova reached in a pocket and slipped on the ring, which sparkled just as much as the stars. He placed his hand on his stomach with his palm up, and she put hers inside. Then he flipped them over so they could see the rings next to each other.

"I love the way our hands look. Yours is about twice the size of mine." They laughed, and she continued, "But it feels so real that sometime in the future we can be together forever."

"I'm so lucky that we met, and I'm really glad that we got to get to know each other initially in our work environment, just being ourselves. We witnessed how we react to a lot of different situations."

She whispered, "I wouldn't have had it any other way. I believe that we were brought together by fate. You know, looking at the night sky, I'm reminded about what my parents were saying—that love is the only thing that is real. It makes sense. Because in many years, everything will change, but the love that we have and our union will still be. It's like it stands the test of time, when everything else wears down or gets replaced."

She looked at their hands and rings while listening to his heart beat. His rock-hard, six-pack abs rose and fell with every breath.

"That was really deep, and it made me realize that if your parents were so supportive after seeing us in each other's company, especially your dad, that this was definitely my fate also. Well, actually, I would have believed you were my fate either way, but it helped." His soft laugh made her head bob up and down as his chest shook.

She turned her head to look at his face and placed her ring-yielding hand on his jaw. His smile revealed bright-white teeth, and his eyes seemed to grin independently as his love surfaced to his face. She rubbed his beard gently and then gave him a peck. He rolled over and they kissed each other while lying on their sides. They stopped and looked into each other's eyes in the tranquil night until she rubbed the red cosmetics off of his lips.

"We have to double-check that all of this is gone before you go back on board." They chuckled.

"You Owantay girls, always made up!"

They laughed more. He was joking about her region and what was common there, not expecting to highlight the fact that they were from opposite points in The Land.

"So while we are on the topic, do you know where we want to settle down? I mean, we have some time before we get to that, but it couldn't hurt to talk about it ahead of time." Kandova spoke freely because of the trust they had built.

"I'm fine as long as we are together, baby. We could live in a box in the Southern Plains and I would be happy. I doubt that would ever happen because neither of us is from there, but as long as I'm with you, I'm good." His eyes looked kind but serious, and the ends of his mouth curled up as he took a deep breath.

"Aw, that is so sweet. See, this is why I'm in love with you." She tickled his obliques, making him squirm.

They talked about future kids and the fact that she still had a few years left of compulsory service. He offered to stay in so that they could be together, and then they could get out at the same time to start their lives as one, as civilians. They trusted each other completely, and both were equally in love with the other as young, bright, and kind individuals.

"If we ever part for any reason, I want you to look into the night sky and search for the crab, and you will know that we are always with each other, under the same stars. And our love, the only thing that lasts, will bring us back together soon!"

Her chest burned with passion, and she often felt herself being pulled to him during the long days. She woke up thinking about him, and laid her head on her pillow each evening doing the same. His heart melted inside just like hers, and when he was around her, he felt like everything was going to be okay. No matter what happened in life, Hilton was always going to have his person.

He had spent so many years deeply desiring a strong connection and something that was real, and he felt as though he'd finally found what he wanted. It was like being in a desert and searching for water, and he had a map of where it might be located, and then one day he stumbled on an oasis, where he was taken in and fed luscious food and drinks, and was invited to stay forever. Most of all, he was comforted that he saw a bright future with the woman he loved. They were both the finest specimens of human beings in peak condition, and were pleased with each other's physical attributes.

"Well, I hope that we can always stay together, my sexy, sweet nobter. But I definitely will have this burned in my mind forever if we part. I will stay awake at night, just to find the crab in the sky, and I'll send you good energy from my heart, baby," he said.

"See, this is another reason why I love you so much. You are so romantic."

She laid her head on his chest again and held his hand while they cuddled in silence, enjoying the moments that they could be as one, while dreaming of a tomorrow when they did not have to hide. Every once in a while, they glanced around to officially watch the surroundings. They were on watch in case the technology failed, which seemed highly unlikely.

They fell asleep for a few minutes, and then he got up and lifted her in the air while they kissed.

"I love you forever, baby," he whispered in a deep voice.

"I love *you* forever, my sweet, sexy man." She looked deep into his eyes.

"I want nothing more than to stay up here until the end of time, but that would definitely blow our cover for good." He offered a slight smirk.

"Yeah, I suppose we should call it a night. How about you head down first?"

"Sure, no problem."

They kissed, Kandova wiped off the lipstick, and Hilton took the elevator to the upper control room to complete his lookout obligation through the floor-to-ceiling transparent walls. Kandova left an hour later and went directly to her living quarters on the bottom floor.

They both felt as though they were carefully fighting for love by covering up a relationship that was completely against regulations. For them, the risk was worth it, and Dlamp and Yordup's story of devotion had encouraged them to continue. They each went to sleep that evening content, and dreamed of each other and the future that they both wanted, more than life itself.

The next day was a scorcher as predicted, and the crew arrived back at the base camp they'd visited before stopping in Kritziddle for repairs and completing a month-long mission. The zornpa scanned the area so that it could remove any traces of their presence in a few days. By noon, it was already so hot that the group was drenched in sweat when they stepped out of their fydons to assemble tents for the night. Everyone was excited to enjoy the next few days of fun, a feeling amplified by having spent four weeks of monotonous, slow gliding above the rainforest.

It smelled like vanilla and fresh foliage as each of the fydon teams filled up with water. The culinary experts planned meals for the duration of the stay and set up the campfire near the pool with the same outdoor kitchen. Two circular benches were constructed around the campfire with a pargle, in order to convert the smoke to colorless gas and make the heat untraceable. M. O. Kandova set the expadier to operation mode, and Jaway double-checked that it was scanning the radius of a two-hour walk for human activity. They were even more careful to remain safe because of the most recent information. Each crew member set up their personal tent, and then everyone was ready to cool off.

Jaway called for a meeting in the shade when the fydons were ready to operate, "Thanks again for all of you who are preparing to make this a fantastic experience. Right now, you all have free time until dinner. I want to make sure that our culinary experts get loads of relaxation as well, so a few of us are here to help with anything you might need. Feel free to take a dip to keep your body temperature low. Be careful of the area with the trap, and remember that the eels won't harm you. They just look spooky if you run into them under the water when diving or playing trudles. Does anyone have any questions?"

T. A. Roberts said, "I don't have a question, but know that we have been concerned for your safety. We double-checked under the ground for huge pits, and there is just the old one. We found a different vine that returns to a firm plot of ground, so we can still swing into the water. Just be careful, because the zornpa recreated the old pit back into its original state. We did, however, cover it, and we marked off that space. It's a good idea just to avoid that altogether."

"A huge thank you to our terrain analysts. I'm glad you mentioned that. Yeah, just be on the lookout for that, everyone," Jaway said.

Every member of the troop immediately put any tasks on hold and changed to swim gear for the water, in order to maintain healthy body temperatures. A few brave souls dove directly into the pool without acclimating first. It felt like needles compared to the sweat-inducing warmth that seemed to continually increase. A small group played trudles while others took advantage of the gigantic, inflatable toys that morphed from tiny, coin-shaped multicolored diamonds. Some intricately dove from the top of the waterfall into the turquoise water below. Alternating crew members grabbed onto the new vine and carefully swung into the refreshing liquid, escaping the heat of the day.

The culinary experts started preparing the meals because they wanted to participate in all of the team-building exercises as well. Didier particularly wished to go on the trek on the third day—she'd heard so many wonderful stories about the adrenaline-inducing activities.

Hilton and Kandova dove at the same time and, within all of the bubbles created from entry, managed to inconspicuously kiss while under the water, surrounded by a wall of white bubbles. After getting out, Hilton took orders and made drinks with fancy ornamental fruit arrangements on the top, mirroring his mom's juice shop. He delivered Kandova's order first, giving her the most elaborate garnish. It looked like plumage from a magnificent bird, with bright colors and unique shapes. As the battalion cooled off, many youthful and incredibly fit bodies lay on the banks of the beautiful, bluish water to enjoy the soothing sounds and take in the sun.

Jaway checked again that everything was in place and that they were safe. He confirmed that the glider was in the clear, and that they could relax and enjoy the time. He finished a data report while sitting in his swimsuit, then sent it to Central Command so that he could also enjoy the entire incentive time. A luscious dinner was served that night with unique ingredients from around The Land. After the meal, Krizzles played songs with her drogger, by request. She and Jaway, Hilton and Kandova, and other crew members stayed up late to bask in the cooler weather and chat. They all slept soundly that night in their tents after a long day of physical activity and an evening void of any nutrition plans.

The whole crew woke up the next morning, ready to watch the sunrise as a team, and were met by the dormant campfire with yawns, stretches, and soft voices. Because this had been done before, it required less planning and explaining. They wore shirts with flashlights that illuminated the paths. Each member brought along their wongers and any sort of gear that might prove handy at any point, partially to avoid humiliation from Pama. She was sure to jovially reinforce the importance if anyone forgot simple gadgets like the last time at base camp. Price coordinated with the culinary experts for breakfast, so the hikers stopped by the kitchen area and grabbed a compact, wrapped package.

Jaway addressed the group as they were standing in the pitch-black with only a few illuminated flashlights. "Before we begin, I wanted to thank our talented culinary artists for preparing a meal that we can take on the morning journey." He waved in their direction, and they smiled while the crew rubbed their hands together in a soft applause. "And thanks to E. M. Price for giving us an overall plan and gathering all of the requests. I can already feel how sweltering it will be today, so I'm looking forward to a lot of time later on next to our resident waterfall. Double-check that you have anything you may need now. I'll give you a minute, and then I'm going to hand it over to our wonderful terrain analysts, as I'm sure they have a fantastic plan as well."

"Yes, we will be leading you all through a different route than the one we took the first time. Just be mindful that we are chopping with our laser machetes, so watch out for the beam of light and steer clear. It can be a little difficult in the dark." Curtis spoke on behalf of both terrain analysts.

"And try to be as quiet as possible to not disturb the sleeping rainforest," Roberts added before they both unleashed their laser machetes and the crew followed them into the lush foliage.

The group aimed the flashlights built into their shirts toward the darkness, so the terrain analysts could prepare a path. In forty-five minutes, they arrived in a wide, open area with a stone floor, where they could see parts of the ancient, abandoned, towering pyramid. Roberts extended his jipty so they could climb up the side of the structure above the canopy. They quietly filled a new space that was farther down than the last time they'd been there. A cool, fresh breeze delivered relief, and it was clear that the daytime would not be as gracious. They all sat perfectly silent in the dark, looking out over the equally mute rainforest as their eyes adjusted.

When the light began to create grays, the rainforest gradually woke up. High and low calls from mysterious creatures echoed as insects joined in the fugue until the blazing orange sun revealed a sliver above the farthest curve of the earth. Then even more sounds bathed the listeners as the sky became a spectacle of morphing pastels with elegant flocks of brightly colored birds. Each crew member felt reborn that morning. After reliving the event of a lifetime, they climbed more and ran to the top, without a race this time. Upon reaching the ground after descending from the pyramid, they sat and ate carefully prepared breakfast wraps and discussed anything and everything, like a family. Then they walked back through the previously slashed path and were shocked by seeing the actual terrain, which had been covered in a blanket of darkness that morning.

After returning, the gang changed into bathing suits and swam in the fresh water. Churchill took a few appointments in his fydon to provide career advice and answer questions about specific career paths. The culinary artists used local ingredients to create a lunch feast, focusing on cold dishes due to the high temperature. The afternoon was simply a waterfall of fifteen perfect bodies diving from above, playing in the water, and relaxing on the banks. They laughed, joked, and rested until a more elaborate feast was served in the evening, filled with dishes that reminded them of home. The youthful troop finished eating, then changed into loungewear in the fydons to enjoy some time around the fire. Adding to the heat seemed impossible at that point, because it had been unbearable all day long, but they wanted a fire for ambiance.

Krizzles sat across from her fydonmate, Jeffers, and said, "I feel really off right now—do you feel okay? I don't know if it has been a long day in the heat." Her eyes held a worried expression.

"I'm fine, but I'm not the one with an extra sense. Do you think there will be a huge storm, earthquake, or stampede?" T. O. Jeffers was always fascinated by Krizzles's ability to perceive the most minute details as a highly sensitive person.

"I don't know what it could be. I went through every scenario and can't figure it out. I just sense that something is not right. Maybe it's the temperature and I should cool off."

A. P. Krizzles was frustrated by not being able to pinpoint the cause of her feelings. She dipped her feet in the fresh water and sat on the edge of the deep pond.

CHAPTER THIRTY-ONE

"Barbour, Roberts, and I are going to head out and get some firewood because we are running low for tonight," I. P. Hilton said.

"Alright, sounds good. I'll be here relaxing. How far away is it?"

"About twenty minutes."

"Alright, try to be back in before it's completely dark."

"I think we will be fine. Roberts found a patch of trees that are super dense and burn slowly, but they fell long ago and are all dried out now." Hilton was eager to have a reason to stay up late and spend quality time with the love of his life.

"Alright, that sounds great. You guys be safe, and I'll see you soon." Jaway shook the hands of his good friends and fydonmates.

Hilton and T. A. Roberts arrived at the site, where there were many solid, dry fallen trees ready to be converted to firewood. They started by quickly chopping the smaller trees, as they would transport and cut easily. Then Hilton split some larger pieces while Roberts loaded a carefully stacked, levitating wagon.

"Man, I have to admit, I am so dehydrated that I'm getting light-headed. I really need some water now. Do you want to head back with me or finish those pieces?" Roberts asked.

Hilton took a break as his bulging arms pressed his pecs together under a sweaty shirt.

"I'll be fine. Go ahead. This way you can bring back even more and I can finish."

"Okay, good idea. I'll take the full wagon, then return to get you. We should be fine for daylight. Can you load me up?"

Roberts was carrying three logs, and placed both arms under them so that I. P. Hilton could add more, up to his chin.

"Alright, I'll be back."

Roberts walked swiftly to camp, feeling like the desert inside. Upon returning, he stacked the firewood and then went to his fydon to cool off and drink fluids.

As darkness started to set in, many of the crew members were still near the water. Krizzles asked, "Did you see that? Was there something over there behind the tree?"

She'd seen what looked like a moving shadow out of the corner of her eye.

Lieutenant Commander Pama, who had amazing eyesight, was sitting next to her. "I thought it was just the heat of the day that was getting to me. What was that?"

She peered deeply into the colors, which had shifted from greens to grays. Pama lifted her feet out of the water and walked to retrieve her backpack, which was nearby, just in case there was a large animal around.

"Something is not right. Get ready," Pama whispered, and the others in the vicinity stood up.

A trudle was drying off near the edge of the deep foliage and vanished into thin air. The lieutenant commander only noticed it because of the sparkles.

"Did you see that?" She looked at Krizzles.

"Yeah, what in the world is going on? Earlier, I knew something was off about tonight, but I couldn't figure out what it was."

They whispered in order to not scare whatever it might be. Everyone near the campsite was on edge, and Krizzles finally figured it out.

"*Emergency*! We are being *invaded*!" she screamed to the other members as she saw a hand pop out from behind a large frond and take another trudle.

She concluded that it must be citizens of the Wild Territory, and that they were aiming to stealthily take anything possible. The crew assembled near the campfire and stood their ground, expecting the worst.

Jaway grabbed a horn and spoke into it at a booming volume, "Attention, code eighty-four! Attention, code eighty-four!"

The crew knew that this meant that they should immediately drop everything, abort mission, and get back into the glider as soon as possible. Pama quickly lifted her glowing, neon-pink laser machete from the case and held it in front of her body.

"Retreat to the fydons! I'll keep them at bay," she shouted an order to the troops, who were filled with adrenaline and partial confusion.

When the rainforest people saw her machete, four of them walked out of the foliage; their cover was fully blown. They surrounded the lieutenant commander, the only one left. They each had metal weapons that were the height of a man, usually used for chopping through the rainforest or harvesting food. A huge, flat blade perched on the end of each metal pole. The shiny, freshly sharpened blades were in the shape of a crescent moon and were used to pull on huge leaves, branches, or food, then slice them off with a yank.

The four tall, lean, muscular men were covered in tattoos and wore only a cloth around their waists. They each had long hair, some in braids, containing different amounts of silver within a dark black base. Deep- and light-purple tattoos covered their entire bodies. Pama took a second to assess the situation and get into her zone.

She thought to herself in a nanosecond that seemed to last a lifetime, *This is the exact scenario you have been preparing for. Make it count! Rise to the occasion!*

In strange synchronization, the four rainforest people moved in on Pama, each dropping their weapons halfway and leaning them diagonally, creating a wall around her. Her pixie haircut encouraged peripheral vision, and her large eyes felt the surrounding space. Her dripping feet showed a vine tattoo with hot-pink flowers, the same color as her blazing machete. Her toned arms were ready for the fight as she took a deep breath.

One of the people of the Wild Territory made a heavy swipe at her from above, and she deflected with her machete by swinging her arm up. The metal blades bounced off of each other, creating huge sparks in the low, dusky light. She understood that her life was on the line and that she had to deliver. The next swipe came from below. She found a low center of gravity by crouching, and then touched his blade with hers.

Lieutenant Commander Pama used the force to flip back, landing on her feet with the machete in front of her body. She twisted around, surprising the men, then aimed at one of the curved weapon tops, splitting it in two with the hot-pink protector. After the fighter's blade fell to the ground, she lifted her leg quickly to go into perfect diagonal splits and kicked his head on the side, using the force to regain her balance. This felt like an automatic reflex after all of the Kurjintel training she'd received growing up. The man dropped to the soil, passed out. But that only provided more motivation for the others to fight harder, like punching a beehive.

As the next blade swooped from above to slice her in two, she pulled her machete up with all of her might, cutting the weapon at the pole. The blade fell forward, and she moved out of the way just in time. It grazed her, then planted deep into the earth. Next, she jumped high in the air to avoid a razor-sharp crescent swinging for her ankles, ready to cut her down like a tree.

The fighter, now wielding just a pole, whipped it around so fast it whistled. He made windmills above his shoulders and twirled it in front of him before dropping it sideways toward her abdomen at lighting speed. She clenched her core muscles and waited for the hit. When she still stood there after, looking at him with the pole in *her* hand, the attacker could not believe his eyes. She used the millisecond of surprise to pull the pole from his hands, leaving him unarmed, and plunged it at the fighter behind her. Sparks rained down on his silver locks and put him on the defense.

Pama's Aldroot training kicked in, and she realized that they were moving strategically, and she might be able to predict combinations or next moves. She did a backflip and split her legs while her head was upside down, kicking the weaponless man in the chest. He fell to the ground and lost consciousness when his head bounced off of a rock. As her arms flew through the air, she lifted the machete and pole toward the two men who remained, without making contact, but reminding them that she was in control. When the lieutenant commander returned with both feet on the ground, she crouched and held the two weapons in front of her body. She began swinging them in horizontal figure eights, nearly meeting in the middle.

The two fighters were on opposite ends and wanted to work together to defeat Pama. They both grunted loudly, communicating their next move. Then one swung the huge blade low, and the other swung his blade high from the opposite direction. As Pama had predicted, this move was a coordinated attempt to cut her in the torso and at the shins, and she performed a side flip to evade the weapons completely.

After regaining her footing, she went after one of the threats that was resting on the soil with the blade in the air. Using the bar as an extension of her arm, she thrust it at the pole end near the earth. As the blade end fell sideways, she used her laser machete in her other hand to slice the crescent from the bar, and it fell into the ground as she kicked the remaining rod out of the man's hand, leaving yet another fighter weaponless.

Spectating Wild Territory citizens saw her ability and did not dare to join. They forgot about the retreating crew and focused on the outcome of this epic battle of precision and strength. They were entertained and impressed by Pama's flexibility, power, endurance, conditioning, reaction time, and awareness. When the last two adrenaline-filled fighters realized they had no chance, they made more grunting noises and both retreated abruptly, leaving Lieutenant Commander Pama alone near the abandoned campsite. She looked around quickly and saw that the crew was gone, then noticed a fydon flying up to the glider. She began walking backward swiftly, carrying her machete and the recently earned metal pole.

Crumpler and Price had followed protocol and were waiting in the fydon for their last fydonmate. Pama released the door that slid down and converted to stairs before running inside as they prepared to travel back to the glider. Once onboard, she turned off the pink laser and instinctually placed it in a safe space.

"Phew, those guys were tough, but I am *tougher*!"

Pama high-fived Crumpler, and he gave her a hug. Price immediately started operating the fydon up to the glider.

"I just wanted to hold them off so everyone could get back," the lieutenant commander said, still in fight mode.

"That was insane—you are my hero!" E. M. Price shouted while concentrating on the task of safely retreating.

Suddenly, Pama realized that she had a new weapon in her hand. Everything had happened so quickly; she was operating off of reflex and did not realize she had taken the pole from her opponent up to the glider. Their vehicle entered the fydon room in the bottom floor of the glider, and they started looking around to see which others had already arrived.

"Barbour's fydon is not here." Price noticed it right away, and whispered to keep crew members from panicking in case they could hear. His eyes were wide and alert.

"I'm second in command, so let me get to the upper control room!" Pama whispered, wiping sweat from her brow and the back of her neck.

She left the pole in their vehicle and calmly walked, with no shoes, over to the elevator, which she took to the upper control room. Others disembarked from the fydons, some still dripping, and manned their stations in lounge clothes and whatever they were wearing near the aqua pool.

On the ground, Jaway and T. A. Roberts had been waiting for Hilton, according to protocol, when the group of roughly fifty people of the Wild Territory noticed that the fydon was still there. One of them threw a thick metal spear and broke off a corner leg, making it fall to the earth on that side while the other three legs held. Immediately after, another citizen of the Wild Territory ran up to the fydon and smashed the side with one of the crescent-moon-shaped weapons. Then the large group enclosed around the two. At that point, Jaway realized that if their fydon was boarded, the entire glider would also be invaded, and he needed to leave immediately. They ascended successfully and flew toward the glider with heavy hearts. A tear fell from Jaway's eye and stone-cold expression as he left Hilton behind.

"I thought you two were together. What happened, Roberts?" Jaway asked while wiping his face.

"I came to get some water and return a load of firewood, so he was still out chopping. I was going to go right back."

Roberts felt terrible, and looked down.

When they arrived at the glider, Kandova was sitting in the central area outside the fydon room, anxious and concerned. She was relieved when the fydon finally pulled in, and she ran up to greet the fydonmates. When she saw that Hilton was missing, she delayed the inevitable reality and asked.

"I. P. Hilton is in the bathroom, right?" She tried to not accept that he was the only crew member left at the camp.

"We had to leave him—they were just about to take the fydon," Jaway said in response to her terrified face, pointing to the damaged leg and outer wall.

For a second, she didn't believe it. It seemed unfathomable, like an out-of-body experience. But when reality set in, her knees gave out and she fell to the floor. Krizzles and Jeffers were walking in just as she collapsed, and they rushed over to help her. Her chest pulsed up and down, but no sound came out. She could not breathe, and her long, straight, flowing hair covered her face, which emoted the deepest look of devastation.

The fydonmates lifted her on each side, but M. O. Kandova still could not walk. They carried her, her legs dragging on the floor, to their living quarters that were next to the fydon room, on the same level. The women placed her in the bed on her side, then lifted her legs so that she could lie on her back. They flopped back over the edge as the others sealed the door tightly.

Kandova finally took a huge gulp of air when her abdomen stopped pulsing in and out. Her first exhale was a shrieking groan that would have traveled over mountains if not held captive by the soundproof room. She continued to moan and wail as her pain grew more and more. She lay in child's pose with her face in the pillow and began punching the mattress as hard as she could. Her fydonmates stood back, allowing her to feel the pain. Kandova stopped crying and punching when she ran out of energy. Her face was covered in endless tears. The loyal friends helped her to sit next to them, and they held her close, hugging her tightly from each side as she stoically looked into a nonexistent abyss.

A calmness covered her, although she was still in immense pain. So she reached in a pocket and pulled out her engagement ring and put it on. Before boarding her fydon, she'd run to her tent, and it was the only thing she took. Now the mechanical operator held it in front of herself, and the three women all looked at it, two of them very surprised.

Kandova slipped it on her finger. "That man is the love of my life, and I will fight for him, to my grave."

By this time, small veins were visible on her skin, and her face was covered in deep red dots from the crying and pressure. Krizzles and Jeffers were certain that this would have to be kept a secret forever.

They looked at one another and, without saying a word, understood that they would have to help their friend, who could not reason at that time. They knew that Dario would take over any tasks necessary for the mechanical operators to complete. They simply hugged her more, now that they realized she had devoted her entire life to I. P. Hilton, and waited to listen to their close friend in mourning. Kandova's body had gushed as many tears as possible, and her soul ached to the core. She knew there was a high chance that Hilton was in serious danger. Still, she tried to reason that there was a possibility that he would be found.

"As you can both see, we were engaged. I had to hide it from everyone because I didn't want to get anyone else in trouble, in case we were found out and reprimanded." M. O. Kandova's voice was scratchy and deep from wailing.

"We totally understand, and we support you. We are here with you, and we are going to make sure you are taken care of," Jeffers said as she released her hug and they all sat on the bed.

Krizzles got up and handed Kandova a cloth to wipe her face with, then took a seat next to her.

"You know, there is a significant chance that we will get Hilton back, because he has a traceable kleck. They can find him anywhere. I mean, we may not go in, but a combat crew could find him. Let's try to stay optimistic," Krizzles said.

"Yeah, you're right—there is a high possibility that he will be recovered. I'm going to try to believe that," Kandova said.

"First of all, we need to keep your relationship under wraps, and you must keep *that* out of sight." Krizzles pointed at the obviously very expensive ring on her hand.

"Yeah, that's very true." Kandova took it off and placed it inside her pillow through a tiny, inconspicuous hole in the fabric.

"And you need to appear more casually upset, like everyone else. So let's take care of your face. Don't worry, but you don't have to look at it right now," said Krizzles.

She got up and fetched a pradimptor, setting it on heavy coverage. Then she gently wiped the sweat and dried tears off of her friend's cheeks and eyes. Kandova wiped her own nose, then placed the pradimptor on her face, and a few seconds later, she appeared rested and completely covered with natural tones. No trace of the small marks or tiny veins remained.

"They are going to be wondering where we are, so we are going to cover for you. Take as long as you need alone, and we will come check on you every once in a while. And let us know if you want anything. On second thought, let me run across to the kitchen to get you some juices and a snack," Krizzles said.

They all hugged, and then Jeffers and Kandova left the room. Everyone else was conveniently consumed with completing tasks. Jeffers went to her post, and Kandova returned to hers after delivering some refreshments.

A. P. Krizzles headed to the upper control room, as the fourth in command. She sat at a station and noticed that the crew was compiling information to be sent to Central Command, while flying the glider carefully to safety. Protocol noted that if any members were left behind, the glider should retreat to an area of safety and contact Central Command for further instructions. They were careful to not get distracted while traversing the uncertain terrain—any wrong move or delayed response could be the end of the entire glider and troop.

Jaway had taken a moment to process his feelings earlier, and then gone to a happy place in his mind. He took a few breaths and tried to focus on what he had to deliver in the moment.

"Thanks, Lieutenant Commander Pama and Serra, for taking care of everything as the second and third in command. Let's get this report sent quickly," he said.

Shortly after, they submitted a detailed report to Zander, as was customary in any situation like this. A high-ranking female member of Central Command appeared as a blobe and requested to speak in real time with Jaway and the most senior crew members.

"It appears that citizens of the Wild Territory tried to steal as many items as possible under the cover of the receding light, and when their camouflage was blown, we were attacked. Pama held a group off through the use of combat, and then I and my fydonmate waited according to procedures, but we were forced to retreat after around fifty armed members of the Wild Territory began attacking our fydon. One member was getting firewood, and he is still behind, but everyone else made it back to the glider." Jaway remained composed only because of the visualization he'd practiced earlier.

"Alright, we are not casting blame on anything that happened. Not assigning fault is our main priority after the safety of the crew. We have received your compiled report, and we will run a diagnostic check and come up with a plan to collect your lost compatriot. We should be able to track him by his kleck, and we can send in a combat crew on a retrieval mission. Do you think your troop and glider can travel all the way to Kritziddle tonight?" the Central Command representative asked.

"Affirmative. We should be fine to make it to Kritziddle tonight," Jaway responded without emotion.

"Alright, you are definitely resilient. So let's say, focus on the well-being of your people and get to Kritziddle, and we will take care of the diagnostic and retrieval mission from here."

"Affirmative. Thanks for your support."

They concluded the discussion and went back to work.

Krizzles took the elevator to the bottom floor to deliver the information to Kandova, who was still quietly dealing with the recent trauma and could not bear to eat or drink anything.

"You really have to try to at least drink something, girl. You cried out your body weight in tears." Krizzles passed some water to her close friend. "I just heard that Central Command is sending a combat team on a retrieval mission for Hilton. They'll track his kleck, and they'll get him back."

They both sat quietly, just looking at the wall. M. O. Kandova could not even speak; she felt as though if she did, she would begin wailing. And she knew that her body had no more liquid left for tears.

A. P. Krizzles broke the silence. "They wanted everyone to know that it was a priority that nobody in the crew felt blame. And we are heading to Kritziddle right now."

Kandova worked through the urge to cry. She breathed in and out. "Thanks for being here for me. I really appreciate it. I can't help but imagine the worst situations. I mean, The Land stole their virgins for thousands of years and threw them into *volcanoes*, not to mention the other atrocities that are ignored and covered up by the history makers."

"You are exactly right. I probably would feel similar if I were in your shoes. Just know that we are here for you, and tell us if you need anything. Don't feel pressure to even leave the room tonight. We are heading to Kritziddle, and M. O. Dario is fully on board and probably quietly covering anything under your responsibilities. We are *all* here for you."

Krizzles hugged her, then returned back to her post as they traveled through the uncertain rainforest in the Wild Territory, remaining ready for unexpected attacks.

After Roberts had left on the journey for water, I. P. Hilton had put on his engagement ring and continued chopping wood loudly. The cracking and splitting sounds covered up any signs of what was happening back at base camp. The information processor imagined spending quality time with the love of his life that night after the sun set. He cut an enormous dried tree down and began chopping it into round chunks, then split these to make many smaller, burnable pieces. He filled a levitating wagon with the heaviest burden of the wood, took off his ring, and filled his arms with as much as he could manage.

The excuse to stay up later was stacked up to his chin, and he placed both arms under the wood so he could hold them for the journey. The wagon followed him into an unknown fate. Because of the lush foliage around base camp, he did not see signs of the invasion until he was already surrounded by at least twenty men with large, bladed weapons. He quickly realized that one man with an ax had no chance against them. They created a circle around him, then gradually approached, making it smaller and smaller.

CHAPTER THIRTY-TWO

One of the enemies spoke many languages and told Hilton, "You have no chance. If you fight back, you will immediately die."

The soldier dropped the load of wood, wiped sweat off of his brow and the back of his neck, and then placed his hands in the air. One of the Wild Territory citizens confiscated the axe through a fence of weapons, and then they bound Hilton's hands behind his back.

They made him sit, guarded by three men, near the roaring waterfall. It seemed like such a strange juxtaposition—that the same place that brought so much happiness and joy could also deliver quite possibly the most frightening and threatening experience of his life. While the Wild Territory people gathered items left behind by the crew, the aqua-colored water in the dim light still sparkled and the gushing waterfall continued to flow.

One of the men watching him came up with an idea. He removed all of the wood from the levitating wagons, then filled them with the heaviest articles they planned to pillage. All of the tents contained personal items as well as devices, and most of them were visible because the crew had been planning to go to bed soon. After the fifty men collected everything they wanted, they untied Hilton and forced him to carry many heavy items and operate the floating wagons. They began walking through the rainforest, with a band of ten scouting in front, using the blades on the ends of the poles to slash any foliage. Although they all could navigate the rainforest easily without a trace, they needed to chop it down in order to get the loot through.

They entered a piece of the rainforest where the ground was covered in large, violet mushrooms. I. P. Hilton had not seen these, because he'd stayed back to enjoy the waterfall when part of the crew went on the adventure trek.

"This is what we actually came for, my friend; the famous quickly regrowing purple mushrooms. And you just happened to be an added bonus for our trip," a Wild Territory citizen said.

Around a dozen of the captors began slashing the fungi out of the ground with the crescent-shaped blades, careful to leave the patch of dirt underneath. Hilton realized that this was not a common group of hunters; they were mushroom gatherers, wielding weapons that were perfect for navigating the rainforest as well as harvesting the coveted food. It finally made sense why they had no real armor or weapons.

When they'd stumbled upon the crew, the original plan had been to steal some of the technologically advanced items, but when they were found out, they had no choice but to fight to the end. After the men harvested enough mushrooms, they walked another fifteen minutes to a pond of clean, fresh water, where they set up camp for the night.

When they arrived, one of them made an intricate fowl call, and five minutes later a bird with elaborate plumage flew through the canopy and found the man who'd made the sounds. It was light pink in color, so although the light was low, it was easy to see. It had many feathers on its head, creating a peak at the top. Its tail feathers were twice the length of the body, elaborate and with huge flat ovals on the ends. The feathers were full of thousands of plush pink barbs that looked almost like the tail of a fluffy cat. The man fed the bird some of the fungi, and it tore through them with its massive beak, seeming satisfied with the offering.

One of the gatherers slashed his weapon into the ground nearby, revealing bamboo placed side by side, covered in layers of soil. They directed Hilton to remove the bamboo poles, exposing a deep, dark hole that was used to entrap large game. It was similar to the pit next to the waterfall that he'd climbed into in order to save T. O. Jeffers. They also made him chop into a tree stump until it was converted into an expansive, flat table, close to the ground. After Hilton completed the labor, they bound his hands and had him sit next to it. Nobody spoke to him during the time he waited.

A man came through who seemed eccentric compared to all of the others. He was the only one who wore necklaces with clear crystals. His hair was completely silver, and braided in noticeably more intricate patterns than any of the others'; it also contained different-colored crystals. The man held a clay pot with a lid. When he removed the cap, steam rose, revealing that the contents were very hot. After mixing it for a while, he set it on the tree stump.

Then four men with the huge weapons arrived, and Hilton was instructed to place his head next to the ceramic pot. The crystal-covered man dipped a tool into the warm mixture and Hilton closed his eyes, expecting the worst.

He breathed in and out many times, imagining that he was in his mom's juice shop, where he loved to spend time with her. Images of the two-week holiday with the love of his life flashed vividly.

I. P. Hilton was confused when he only felt a light tugging on his ear. When he realized they didn't plan to behead him, he opened his eyes and saw a gem-showered, braided masterpiece strolling away. The four imposing men also left with their weapons, and Hilton was alone, not sure if he should stay down.

He kept his head on the table for the next ten minute, watching the massive pink bird clutch a bundle with its large talons. Then another man came over.

"Stand up, my friend. The pit will be your bed for the night. I hope you like to be cozy."

The man threw in some enormous leaves and slid a huge ladder made of bamboo to the bottom of the pit.

"Walk down. Be careful, because if you fall, you may be pierced and left for dead."

Hilton carefully stepped backward down the ladder, with his hands bound behind his back. When he reached the bottom, the ladder ascended quickly and disappeared. Then the hole was resealed with bamboo, as dirt and debris fell from above.

Now that he was alone, he spit out the ring that he hid under his tongue, and put it on his finger behind his back. When the men had captured him, the first thing he'd done was place the ring in his mouth for safekeeping. Soon after making this move to preserve his only reminder of the love of his life, every single item of interest was removed from Hilton's possession and placed with the rest of the booty.

He felt around in the dark and used his feet to move many of the leaves into a bunch for a pillow, covering the ground, carefully avoiding the sharp poles that still might deliver a gruesome fate. Thankful to be alive, he finally had time to deal with the reality of the situation.

That night was the lowest point of I. P. Hilton's life. Not only was he deep in the ground, but once he realized he was safe for the evening, he allowed himself to emotionally descend, as he understood that there was a significant chance that his dreams with M. O. Kandova might never come true.

Up to this moment in captivity, he'd focused on being alert and watched every single detail that might aid in survival or escape. Now, he could finally focus on the feelings of loss, deep within his soul. He wept and ruminated about the fact that he may never see the woman he loved so deeply again. He mourned that he might not be able to spend every day with her forever, as they had planned. The family they'd dreamed of might remain a fantasy, the debate on where to settle down irrelevant. Hilton fought images of being absent from her life, and tried to imagine a possibility of still being with her.

He could not even look at the night sky like they had planned. The information processor yearned to be out of the ground and look for the crab constellation they'd viewed not long before. He found motivation to do anything necessary to make it through this ordeal alive, and to return to his beloved. In that moment, he caressed the ring on his finger.

Tears ran down his face while he blubbered, "I will make it back to you, if it is the last thing on earth I ever do. I will fight for you, my baby."

With that he fell into a deep sleep. He imagined being with his love at the rental house in Kritziddle, sleeping next to her and smelling her lovely scent as they both felt fulfilled inside—simply lying next to the love of his life. He woke during the night and tried to manage the anxiety that terrorized him intermittently. He reminded himself that he was safe, and tried to imagine the best outcome.

The next day, he woke by being prodded with the ladder.

"Get up here, we are having breakfast," a voice called. It had an interesting accent.

Hilton realized that the nightmare he'd thought was a dream was in fact reality. He removed the ring and placed it in his underwear; hopefully his captors wouldn't search him again. Carefully stepping up the ladder, he rose out of the hunting pit safely. When he got to the top, a man cut his hands free and motioned for him to follow. Hilton walked over to the water and rinsed his face and drank a lot. He didn't know what the day would bring, and wanted to be as hydrated as possible in the immense heat. After a very interesting and surprisingly tasty breakfast, the entire group set on a hike through the rainforest, with all of the spoils from the day before, but without the help of the levitating wagons.

They passed fascinating wildlife during the long day of hiking inside thick brush, until they arrived at a massive cobblestone area, covered by a canopy. There, they marched through a square to a massive ancient pyramid that had been cleared and repaired. Trees in gigantic planters were placed all around the pyramid, to provide camouflage from above and make it appear as one of the thousands of other pyramids that were engulfed in centuries of dirt and plant life. They set the items on the cobblestone square and bound Hilton's hands again.

Two of their largest men held his arms as they walked toward an entrance to the majestic, ancient pyramid. Two massive doors swung open to reveal a hallway lined with fire sconces. The three entered and wandered into the unknown. By that time, a combat mission had been released to find Hilton, and the crew had made it back to Kritziddle. Churchill had submitted psychological reports for each member, and as a result Sickles delivered two doses of elixir per person, in the barracks. Instead of singing together by a campfire, they all went to bed out of respect for the loss of a crew member, hopeful for a timely and successful retrieval.

Central Command assigned a full crew and glider from Bingdole to the mission. After a complete report and plan was devised, they left the morning after the attack and successfully arrived that evening, within a half hour of the kleck signal. Thirty trained combat troops took smaller fighter fydons down to the rainforest floor. The vehicles landed on the open cobblestone area, and the fighters disembarked with laser weapons that could have annihilated five pyramids. The highest-ranking member was in communication with colleagues in the glider, who guided him to the kleck signal. The group walked to the entrance of one pyramid—two massive doors that swung open in the middle. The highest-ranking fighter shot a laser and blew a hole through the gates. A huge, dark hallway led into the depths of the pyramid.

They lit the way, and the other fighters moved into a strategic configuration, for the most advantageous position, in case they were approached by opponents. After evading multiple booby traps, the smaller battalion that had entered the pyramid saw a room that appeared to have a huge access window near the ceiling, leading to the rainforest outside. Luxurious, light-pink feathers lined the floor, seemingly fallen from a large nest in the corner.

"Sarge, look over there. What is that?" one of the soldiers asked.

An unidentifiable manmade item lay in the corner. Cream-colored burlap fabric had been wrapped around a circular article and tied at the top with twine. The sergeant walked over to it and scanned the package to see if it was explosive. After receiving an all-clear notification, he got down on one knee and proceeded to untie the rope that held the bundle together.

The fabric opened to reveal a coconut that had been sliced in two and then sealed shut again. He used the back of his laser machete to crack it. Inside was a message written in the characters of the official language of The Land.

He read it slowly. "We have your man. You will never get him back. He is partial replacement for thousands of years of stealing our virgins and murdering them in your volcanoes. We will never surrender to The Land. We will always live as our own people. We are our own independent nation, and this will not change anytime soon."

When he set the coconut down, he heard a small jingle, so he shook it from side to side again. When he illuminated the inside, it revealed a tiny object.

"They must have cut out his kleck, and placed it in here for us to find. This just made retrieval nearly impossible. What a disappointment," the sergeant said.

He was right. The inhabitants of the Wild Territory had carefully removed it from I. P. Hilton's ear when it was numb. Then they'd placed it in the coconut, wrapped it, and instructed the spectacular bird to deliver it to the pyramid deep inside the rainforest.

The combat crew successfully navigated out, and after relaying the conclusions to Central Command, returned back to Bingdole that night.

When Jaway received the report that evening, he called a somber meeting with the sleepy crew, which had disembarked from the glider for the day, in one of the rooms inside the barracks. Everyone came except Kandova. She could not bear to take any more news, and even more importantly, she could not risk revealing her relationship to the other members.

"Alright, so we realize that you all have a lot of questions, and they may not be answered tonight. Before we begin, we understand that this was probably a traumatic experience for all of you. I have been discussing information from Churchill, and we have been granted two doses more of elixir per person tonight."

Normally, this would have provoked jokes and cheers for late-night festivities. Because one of their own was in the hands of the enemy, however, nobody reacted, out of respect for Hilton. Although Central Command had made it clear that none of the crew members should take personal blame, most of them were devastated and wondering if it was their fault.

"Sickles will be around, and she will administer the vials," Jaway continued slowly and carefully. "I realize that most of us had high hopes that the retrieval team would be able to trace Hilton, and at one point they were quite certain that they'd located him, but unfortunately they only found his kleck. It had been removed and placed inside a coconut, then somehow was transported, most likely flown by a bird, into one of the ancient pyramids. They got through the booby traps to find it with a message of resistance from citizens of the Wild Territory and confirmation that they had Hilton. I realize this may be difficult to process, and we are here in case you need to talk. P. G. Churchill is really good at walking us through challenges, so utilize him as a resource."

Jaway paused and bit his lip, staying strong for the crew. "The following information just came in from Central Command, and you may find it comforting. We all were wondering what in the world happened, because the expadier should have been protecting us, and we definitely turned it to operation mode. We are also all aware of the immense heatwave that has spread over the Wild Territory. According to the diagnostic that Central Command ran, they show the expadier successfully working in operation mode. After we ran our own examination, it is clear that nobody switched it into standby mode.

"Four hours before the attack, the expadier stopped working. We know this because of Central Command's extensive evaluation. Their findings suggest that a device next to the expadier created a temporary fire, due to the high temperatures, and an explosion left it inoperable. Because it was not scanning the area, we were not notified about the enemies. You might be asking about the backup plans that are in place. Well, cables were destroyed on other devices as well, so we received no notification of the explosion. Unfortunately, the automatic window vents were open to let in fresh air, and the small amount of smoke must have exited immediately, so the secondary warning system did not pick that up either.

"With all of these factors, the monitors believed the expadier was turned off manually, and were not able to sense the damage. That is why we didn't receive notice that the expadier was out of order. No matter how advanced our technology gets, we still have room for improvement. And hopefully this will serve as an example of how we can revamp the entire system in all gliders.

"The devices are still not in working order. So, although this has been a very trying experience, it is good to know that none of us, specifically anyone working with mechanics, was at fault."

Jaway had seen M. O. Kandova fall to the ground, and he wanted to make it clear that the mechanical operators had done their job and were not negligent.

"In the end, the culprit was the heat, and there is nothing that we could have done."

Jaway checked a device for a new message that came through from Central Command.

"And I have some more information, just in, about the weapons that the Wild Territory citizens wielded against us. Central Command intelligence believes that the long metal poles with crescent-moon-shaped blades on the end were not weapons at all. They were for harvesting or navigating through the rainforest. It is most likely that this group of citizens were simply foraging or on a mission through the rainforest and that they randomly stumbled on our crew, and our expadier provided no cover. It appears that originally, these people may have just wanted to take our devices and items, and then they chose to attack."

Jaway stopped to check the messages in more depth.

"Those are some highly trained farmers, Barbour." Pama's eyes were wide, and she raised a brow.

"Agreed, Pama, but they are no match for your stamina and training. Now, I'm not certain how you want to take this, but I am going to relay a message from Central Command. The emperor heard of your heroic fight against many foes, and he wants to present you with a medal of recognition for holding off the fighters for so long. Just some advice—although it is fresh and we are grieving a crew member, it is wise to follow through with a request from the emperor, even as a formality. If you went, then I would accompany you as the commander. Just think it over, and if any of you want to give input, feel free. You are not required; however, this is a serious request from the emperor himself. He is big into Aldroot and Kurjintel training, so I'm certain he will take this as an opportunity to publicly promote them as combat sports that have practical applications."

Jaway paused to go through more of the data. None of the crew said a word. It was completely silent now that most of them had been put at ease that the fault would not come down to one of them. Kandova's fydonmates, Krizzles and Jeffers, were the most relieved, because Kandova had been in charge of engaging the expadier, and she was probably already beating herself up because it had resulted in the love of her life being taken by the enemy.

"Alright, so it looks like that is all the info I have from Central Command. We are in the perfect place for the glider to be repaired, but just be ready for more orders over the next few days. We will stay put in the barracks for now and just wait it out. Are there any questions?" It was eerily silent. "Alright, so our competent medical attendant will be around with the orchid elixir tonight, and just try to get some sleep. Remember to reach out to me or Churchill if you need support."

Jaway stood up, which was an indication that the meeting was adjourned. A. P. Krizzles and T. O. Jeffers immediately went to see Kandova, making sure nobody could hear and that the door was locked. They entered the room to find her under the blankets in her bed. The two girls slowly went over and sat, then hugged her tightly to wake her up.

"We have some information for you that you are going to want to know. Are you in a headspace to talk?" Krizzles asked.

"Yeah, at this point nothing can get worse." Kandova yawned.

"We have bad news and good news—what do you want first?"

"Hit me with the good news first."

"Alright, well Central Command found out what happened. The expadier burned up, and that was why we did not receive protection. There was nothing anyone could have done."

"Wow, that is such a relief. I have been fighting the voices in my head that said I was responsible."

"Secondly, and this is just intelligence from Central Command—the members of the Wild Territory were probably just walking through as harvesters and stumbled upon us." She paused to give her a moment. "I'm glad you are sitting for this next piece of information, though. Brace yourself. A combat crew was sent to retrieve Hilton, and they only located his kleck. It had been surgically removed and left inside a pyramid. The Wild Territory people cut it out and placed it into a coconut, then had a bird fly it into an ancient structure, so the retrieval mission found only the kleck with a message of resistance."

M. O. Kandova stared blankly at the wall, grieving a future with the only man she'd ever loved.

T. O. Jeffers said, "I don't know if you want any, but they are offering elixir tonight. Make sure you talk with Sickles."

"Yeah I'm going to have to think about that. I'm not sure that I want to be out of it or forget anything about my experiences while the love of my life is missing."

"Yeah, I get that," said the technology officer.

That night Kandova gave her doses of black orchid elixir away to her comrades and fell asleep under the stars in a patch of open ground, staring at the crab constellation and hoping that her love had found it too.

CHAPTER THIRTY-THREE

I. P. Hilton walked down the firelit corridor with an attendant at each side. Then one of the men covered his eyes with a blindfold. For all he knew, they could have strolled laps in the same hallway and then up and down some stairs in between.

He was shocked by what he saw when the tied fabric was removed. They stood in an expansive space that had very high ceilings and windows opening to the rainforest. Fresh water from a nearby river ran through the center of the room. The stone floor sank from end to end in a cubic shape, the size of an arm, to house the internal stream. It created a soothing sound that echoed throughout the generous hall.

Three beautiful young women sat in one of the corners and chatted softly while smiling, lounging on plush couches with brightly colored fabric. One of them focused on creating a textile with needlework. The men held Hilton in the center of the room and waited quietly. After they stood still for an hour, another man entered. The women greeted him as Brundoon. He seemed important because the two other men bowed low when he stepped toward them.

"Get up, my friends. Let me see your wonderful smiles!" Brundoon greeted them by cupping the sides of their faces and then gave each one a hug.

Hilton was surprised to hear his language spoken fluently by citizens of the Wild Territory.

"You didn't think we could hold off the most powerful civilization in the history of the planet by being a group of dolts, did you?" Brundoon said to him.

The information processor realized that he had not been successful at covering up his thoughts; they must have shown on his face.

"I am Brundoon, and these are my wives. We welcome you to our home. We plan to make your stay as comfortable as possible. Unbind him. How was your trip?"

Hilton was even more shocked, and initially did not know what to say, but felt relieved that his hands were finally free. He realized that he had to pivot quickly to win over his captor as much as possible.

"To be honest, being a prisoner was a lot better than I ever imagined it would be."

"So you are not only physically fit, but you have a sense of humor too? We are going to get along very well, I tell you."

Brundoon looked I. P. Hilton directly in the face, then turned his head and clapped twice.

"Let's get some refreshments for the gentleman."

Many servants swiftly entered the space from a door and set platters of fruits, vegetables, dried meats, mysterious recipes, and drinks on a long table that could seat thirty.

"Thanks, my friends."

Brundoon immediately started eating some of the tasty food, to show Hilton that it was not poisoned. Because he did not know when he would next have a chance to eat again, Hilton also ate some of the carefully prepared spread. He was surprised that a lot of it had been chilled.

Brundoon was the first person from the Wild Territory that Hilton had seen who had completely black hair, without any trace of silver. His tattoos were intricate geometric patterns in many shades of purple. He was nearly as tall as Hilton, with huge pecs and arms, but with a tiny waist and defined leg muscles.

"This pyramid was designed long, long ago by master engineers. I just had to find it and get through all of the booby traps. I cannot tell you how many I had to go through before I found this one. I am a booby-trap master at this point." He laughed, and it echoed through the large space. "Don't worry, we have running water and sanitation. You don't think they would let their ancestors live in the afterlife without them, do you?"

He chuckled again before wolfing down another plate of food and drinking some wine. They sat at the grand table and ate together; the two chaperones had left the room. I. P. Hilton was surprised that Brundoon was calm and collected with a newly captive citizen from The Land, but after looking at the man's arms a second time, he realized that Brundoon had nothing to be afraid of, and he respected his confidence.

"You know, other men who find a functional pyramid usually have scars all over, but I have none. Can you imagine why? Because I'm *fast* as lightning and *wittier* than a hundred-year-old grandpa."

Hilton laughed with Brundoon, realizing that the man he was dining with probably had ultimate power over his fate.

"Shakradia, come on over and meet the new member of our household."

An additional woman had entered the hall, where the other women were chatting, but Hilton had not noticed because he was trying to be as alert as possible with Brundoon. Shakradia was one of the most beautiful women he had ever seen. Her completely platinum hair went to the floor, flowing in big spiral curls. She wore a revealing, bright-blue dress that appeared to be made of silk. The other women wore the same dress, but her curves made it look like a work of art. She elegantly strutted over to the two tall men eating at the oversized table. Many locks of her hair were interwoven to create a net-like texture over what looked like millions of curls that stopped just before hitting the ground while she walked. Small crystals dripped from the net structure and sparkled as she turned to greet them.

"Brundoon, my good cousin, who do I have the pleasure of meeting? A citizen of The Land, I presume?" Shakradia's voice commanded attention, and she seemed smart and relaxed.

"You are correct, cousin. This is Tramrul. He just arrived a while ago. He is the newest member of the household."

"Pleasure to meet you, Tramrul. Don't worry about Brundoon. He looks intimidating but he is a tiny, squishy udringa inside."

"Pleased to meet you as well, Shakradia," Hilton said.

He tried to process the fact that he had just been renamed in an instant, but was also aware that he needed to appear civil to his captors.

"Alright, I'm turning in. I'll make sure your room is set up for tonight, Tramrul. Don't want to leave it to just *anyone*. You never know what could end up in there!"

She laughed, and Hilton did the same, trying to be charming. After saying something he couldn't understand, Shakradia spun around and her curves shuffled toward the exit, revealing even more sparkling gems in her twinkling silver hair. She was arguably the most attractive woman alive on the earth at that time, and was the same age as I. P. Hilton.

As soon as she left, Brundoon's eyes became very large, and he tilted his head back slightly.

"Gotta watch out for that one. She's particular about hospitality. It doesn't matter who it is—if we have a guest, she won't let anything slide. Everything has to be the best. I think it was from her parents. They just did that with all of their guests." The man spoke about her as a close family member.

Hilton was shocked that someone who was, most likely, high in the leadership of the Wild Territory would reveal so much information about himself. What if Hilton were to escape? Then he would be able to report everything about Brundoon, including the details of his home and family members. It made Hilton even more suspicious of what Brundoon had planned for him. But he also knew that he had to appear calm, relaxed, and respectful in order to win over his captor as much as possible.

"I'll be on the lookout for any signs of hospitality gone rogue!" Hilton comfortably jested, and Brundoon laughed loudly.

"You've got jokes. I like that, my friend. You know, you remind me of a cousin." He paused. "Alright, well I'm going to turn in for the night. Feel free to eat whatever you like. We'll have a servant show you to your room."

When he said that, one of the hefty men who'd escorted I. P. Hilton earlier walked up and stood next to the table. It was a way to seem friendly, but also let him know that his new home was heavily packed with guards who would never let him flee.

Brundoon got up and grabbed Hilton by both sides of his face, pressing gently. Then he rubbed his ear and said, "Make sure you keep this very clean, even though they did some great stitches," revealing to Hilton that they had removed his kleck.

He had felt very different that day, but he'd been distracted along the path. Now, he thought back and took note that the devices had been deactivated since that morning.

Hilton nodded his head. Brundoon exited, and the three women left shortly after.

The soldier was still hungry and did not know when he would get another meal, so he continued eating the mysterious dishes until he felt satiated. He followed the guide through different corridors and up many winding stairs to his bedroom, which was lit by candlelight. His room had an attached bathroom with running water, a shower, a bath, and a hole in the floor that he assumed was indoor plumbing. The windows near the top of the ceiling were covered in bars, and when the large attendant left, Hilton heard some sort of lock or barricade block the door. A plush bed with bright linens and pillows was pushed against the wall across from the windows. The first thing he did was put on his ring. Then he took a warm shower, where he used the cleansing products that rested in alabaster jars throughout the bathroom.

While he was scrubbing off layers of caked dirt, Shakradia entered the room with many different clothing options, as well as more candles and writing materials. She popped her head in the bathroom and surprised him over the sound of the rushing water.

"I've come with some extra necessities for you. Enjoy!"

He wiped his eyes, careful to only use his ringless hand, and leaned out of the stream of water. Shakradia looked him up and down, making it obvious that she was interested in what she saw.

She flirtatiously flipped her hair and batted her eyes at him before turning around and leaving without saying a word. I. P. Hilton was still processing the entire idea that he was being transported to a prison, but being treated as a brother and cousin. It was incredibly peculiar, and he also recognized that playing by their rules would be his only hope of escape. He constantly thought about Kandova, how he loved every inch of her and every nuance of her personality. He admired how loyal she was to him, and how she loved him unconditionally. He saw a future with her exclusively. She was the only person he had ever met who made him feel that way. Looking back at his life, he was astonished that he had met thousands of people over the years, but only this specific person provided such fulfillment.

When he got out of the shower, he put on one of the cozy, stretchy articles of clothing that Shakradia had just delivered. He stacked a few pieces of furniture, then climbed up them in order to peek from the windows between the bars. The night sky was full of stars. Hilton found the crab, hoping that the love of his life was doing the same. He watched the constellation in silence for a few hours, caressing his ring the whole time, standing on the tips of his toes upon the stacked furniture.

That night, he slept comfortably and tried to remember details from the two weeks back in Kritziddle. He attempted to envision a future with the single love of his entire life, Kandova.

The next day, the crew waited for orders from Central Command. Because the glider needed to be upgraded and repaired, it would be in Kritziddle for the next month. The crew was granted leave, due to the traumatic situation they had experienced with the loss of a colleague. They each went to their hometowns.

When Kandova returned to Owantay with Yordup, Dlamp, and Jussol, she broke down and told them everything. They were supportive to her during the time she needed to heal. Every night, she looked at the stars and imagined the love of her life watching them under the same sky, but far away. She was no longer a silly jokester, but she made it a priority to heal without forgetting. Kandova fought to believe that the love of her life would be found alive. She could not bring herself to reach out to Hilton's family, because she knew she would only wail loudly, without the ability to speak.

Jaway went back to Zander and stayed with his parents and two younger sisters. He studied for the next certifications and remained fit, enjoying his family and friends. He took extra doses of elixir, as well as other forms of therapy, to deal with losing his close fydonmate, whom he thought of daily.

Pama continued training in aldroot and kurjintel in Wratshide, on the border of the Rainforest Region and the Highlands Region. She had her own home as one of the older members of the crew, and her father took her on many adventures through the rainforest with her two brothers and two sisters.

Serra traveled to Nodgedrowde in the Plains Region in the south. At twenty-five, he already had three kids, but they wanted more, so they made efforts to expand with the unexpected time together. He was happy to witness how their large extended families helped raise the kids, as though they had two full-time parents. His five brothers and four sisters stopped over frequently to help out and deliver items from their gardens. He snacked on chocolate parrots without the need to hide them, and he remained physically fit by working out often. He helped his relatives to produce and sell beer and sophisticated spirits in many different forms.

A. P. Krizzles went to Grinzol, the inland town among the rolling hills of the Highlands Region. She jumped into farming activities with her five brothers and two sisters, who all resided in the area still. At nineteen, she was enthusiastic to meet often with Sickles, who also lived in Grinzol. She practiced her instrument frequently, and met with Jaway once when she visited Zander for a drogger competition, which she won. From there, their relationship grew, and they became closer and closer as the days passed.

Curtis returned to her mother and father in Pragadol on the west coast. Because she was an only child, she went on many adventures that were inspired by the trek they'd taken in the rainforest and the trip to the power plant near Kritziddle.

Roberts went back to his folks in Ezlay, a beach town on the east coast. He met with Dario often, who lived in the same city, and they mingled at the beach with their friends. He seriously explored career paths while studying for different certifications. He focused on fitness, so that he would be prepared for life in the glider.

Crumpler traveled to Inablay on the east coast and spent time with his mom, dad, and brother. They enjoyed going to the beach, and he studied techniques in culinary artistry. His father, who was also a cook, continued to provide endless advice that made him an even better chef. His friends love hearing the story about losing consciousness after parachuting into a tree in the rainforest on a hike.

Didier quickly traveled nearby to Kritziddle. Srondi, Blute, Nrode, and Cruld were surprised but elated to see her. She relished living in her home next to her loved ones. They all cooked dinners and alternated pool-top terraces under the canopy of the rainforest. She remained focused on fitness, and practiced new grilling techniques for dinners.

Dario returned to Ezlay and was equally excited to socialize with his dear friend from the crew. His mom continued to apply pressure to find a job close by, and the family went to the beach often with his brother. He worked out daily to stay in shape.

Hilton's parents and siblings mourned every day. His mother closed the drink shop and advocated in their home city of Bingdole for her son's recovery to be the highest priority. His two brothers and two sisters also halted daily life, but his father never stopped teaching.

Price went to Fowdlek in the southernmost part of the Plains Region. At thirty-three years old, he had grown more independent from the rest of his family over the years; however, he still spent a lot of time with his three brothers, two sisters, mother, and father. As an avid nature lover, he took advantage of any chance to be outside and identify plant life. He studied the latest trends and most current practices for excursion managers.

Sickles was thrilled to return to Grinzol, because it meant she could see Krizzles whenever she wanted to. At only eighteen years old, she had not been gone long, so she quickly slipped back into familiar routines. She helped around the farm with her six brothers and two sisters. She invented more happy dances and searched for opportunities to experience an adrenaline rush. Because of the multiple brushes with dangers on the trek, Sickles investigated rainforest hiking skills as well as climbing techniques. She overcame her fear of skydiving during the incentive days, and then went many times with a few of her more adventurous siblings.

Jeffers went to her folks in Najeeram on the west coast in the south. She explored ideas about a future career and focused on jobs where she could peacefully serve others. She enjoyed being with her sister and parents and went with them on a pilgrimage up the fourth-largest volcano in The Land, which was located near her hometown. The technology officer continued creating original blobes in her pictogrammer, justifying the activity as being potentially helpful in her job with the crew. After her brush with death, she took the loss of Hilton particularly hard. She remained thankful for his generosity, and intensely wanted him to return safely.

Churchill traveled back to Albronder in the eastern part of the Rainforest Region. At forty-one, as the oldest member of the crew, he spent time with his two brothers and parents, although he was more involved with devoted friends. He learned strategies to help others in need because he liked being able to support people through difficulties. Any research-based methods would come in handy, so he added them to his tool belt of skills. He could use them without preparation, for any of the crew members. Churchill enjoyed working out, and stayed true to his individually assigned fitness and meal plans. He learned more hands-on knowledge about different emergency situations.

Each member mourned for I. P. Hilton to be found, and thought of him every day. It was like a constant, dull pain—present even during the most euphoric times. No amount of black orchid elixir could erase the loss that each of them felt about their stolen colleague, who was more like a blood relative.

Hilton, meanwhile, learned how to live a new existence in the strange family-style prison, with the new name Tramrul. Shakradia made it her mission to wed him, and took every chance to tempt him with her beauty, but Hilton was madly in love with Kandova still, and found the crab in the starry sky each night before sleep. From the depths of his soul, he mourned losing the love of his life, and was not ready to move on. Although outwardly he appeared jovial and relieved to become Tramrul with the new forced family, he was certain that his future would be in The Land with Kandova, and he would escape when the perfect opportunity arose.

GLOSSARY

Aldroot – A sword combat conditioning sport that requires protective clothing and shoes, in which athletes learn strategy. Matches last thirty minutes, and points are recorded.

Andoofers – A set of glasses that cast an invisible shield over the wearer in order to repel the rain.

Bicktrude – A bracelet that protects passengers by casting a transparent suit around the body.

Black orchid elixir – A thick, glowing liquid that clears the lymphatic system and heals the brain during a euphoric session.

Blobe – Moving images with accompanying sounds, which can be played from a pyramid-shaped device called a pictogrammer.

Central Command – Located in the capital city of Zander, an office that receives information and makes all decisions for military operations.

Chilnor – An invention that creates tattoos quickly, yet painfully. Human creativity is required as the chilnor does not apply the design automatically.

Dopridam – A contraption that evaluates wounds, then uses lasers for healing. When not activated, it looks like a thick, flat, red triangle, and then transforms into a small box upon activation.

Drogger – A three-sided string instrument, easily transportable, that always stays in tune.

Elitser – A device that looks like a small pyramid and projects words into the air. It is used for writing essays or other documents, with the user speaking words inside their mind. It can also send messages to other elitsers.

Expadier – A machine that monitors human activity within a two-hour walking radius. It also keeps sound from leaving a designated area.

Fairybird – A medium-sized bird with ornate, light-pink plumage that constructs a unique nest.

Fydon – A small, four-sided transport vehicle that seats four people and has a bathroom and shower. The door slides down and converts into stairs. Legs on each corner keep it off of the ground when at rest.

Fydonmates – People who are assigned to the same fydon.

Glawtor – A portable, thin, foil-like fabric that wraps around a person to scan for serious bodily harm. It is attached to another device that indicates the results.

Glider – A massive, levitating, octagonal, multi-level military vehicle that houses troops and fydons. It contains a central elevator, a fydon storage room, bathrooms, a kitchen, a dining room, a gym, an engine room, living quarters, lounge spaces, and more.

Harvestium – A holiday that celebrates the harvest with intimate family time and is characterized by large meals.

Hildent – Metal ovals used for climbing and securing to hard surfaces. They have a suction cup on one side, while the other end opens and closes. They distribute climbing ledges for easy, medium, or difficult ascents.

Infogrammer – A small pyramid that projects words into the air and is used to retrieve information through the use of a kleck.

Jipty – A cylinder that becomes a ladder.

Jurprodian – A morphing item of clothing that is controlled by a kleck. Multiple settings create different outfits and features, such as a shorts-and-T-shirt combo, yet the lightweight material is incredibly durable.

Kleck – A chip in the ear cartilage that connects the subconscious mind to external devices.

Kurjintel – A mixed martial arts sport practiced with no shoes. It develops precise muscle movements. Ribbons hang from practitioners' tight uniforms, and only body movements are utilized to make contact with the ribbons. Participants must stay on their feet or else lose. Jumps and flips are incorporated to respond to an opponent's moves.

Laser machete – A large knife that contains a neon-colored laser.

Lensicator – Glasses that improve sight.

Mokdon – A self-driving vehicle, used primarily to quickly transport goods.

Nobter – An irresistible dessert, generally enjoyed over an open campfire.

Objerner – A large freshwater fish.

Pargle – A round disk with three extendable legs that is placed above a fire to camouflage the heat and smoke.

Pictogrammer – A small pyramid that projects realistic pictures, moving images, and sounds.

Pradimptor – A round, head-sized device that applies makeup.

Ruduhkom – A slow, lyrical ballad that tells a life story with a sad or reassuring message. Typical in the Highlands Region, where it is considered folk music.

Saturn fruit – A delicious fruit with internal rings like the planet Saturn. It carries high vitamin and nutritional content, and is difficult to find.

Smidalia – A black device that maps out a vertical climb with a bright beam of light. It connects to hildents and has a three-dimensional diamond shape.

Summer End Celebration of Crawldsay – Festivities that are celebrated with wine and produce from the harvest and include fireworks.

Tabot spiderweb – A lightweight, impenetrable, and durable fiber that is used for many different applications.

Tikompay – A plant-derived medication that blocks pain receptors and induces visions.

Trongole – A tall green and black animal that lives in the rainforest and has small, furry horns. All four of its hooves are black, and it was traditionally hunted as game.

Trudles – An underwater sport with robotic fish and nets.

Twarpen – A majestic animal with the body of a horse and spiral horns. It produces rich milk and is a beast of burden. A male is called a stud, and a female is referred to as a mare.

Udringa – A tiny lap animal known for its loyal personality.

Vrimp – A device for breathing oxygen underwater. It covers the mouth and nose, with goggles attached.

Vrodilop – A vehicle typically used by a family.

Wonger – A coin that acts as insect repellant.

Xyloblut – A team sport involving a bouncy rubber ball filled with air. It must be played on a special court. The uniform includes laced shoes with rubber bottoms.

Yobstrang – A calm and sweet, long-haired, four-legged animal that is used for making textiles. It has a flat face and no horns, and produces milk.

Zornpa – A device on the bottom of a glider that scans an area of land to later erase manmade disturbances.

ABOUT THE AUTHOR

Jacob Lightman lives in the Twin Cities area of Minnesota and is the author of the science fiction adventure novel *A Buzz*. He is passionate about creating new worlds with exciting, dynamic, and fun characters. Jacob has completed multiple adrenaline-filled adventures through Latin America, Europe, and Asia. These international experiences have helped him, as a cultural outsider, to channel science fiction themes and develop different societal norms in his stories. Jacob has wanted to be an author since childhood, when he would invent elaborate tales for his mom as a captive audience. He earned a writing-related master's degree, and speaks a little Spanish, German, and French. When he isn't writing, Jacob enjoys lifting weights, cooking, and collecting old books.

Visit jacoblightman.com for free supplementary material and more information.

Facebook- https://www.facebook.com/JacobLightmanAuthor

Instagram- https://www.instagram.com/JacobLightmanAuthor/

Twitter- https://twitter.com/JacobLightman